UNTANGLING CLAIRE

A NOVEL

JAMES RANDALL MILLER

Inquiries should be addressed to the author at:
JamesMillerBooks@gmail.com

Printed in the United States of America

ISBN-13: 978-0-9834150-7-7 (paperback)
ISBN-13: 978-0-9834150-8-4 (eBook)

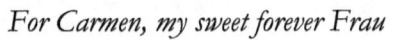

For Carmen, my sweet forever Frau

When I let go of what I am, I become what I might be.
— LAO TZU

They slipped briskly into an intimacy from which they never recovered.
— F. SCOTT FITZGERALD

1

THE INSPECTOR SIGNED the paperwork and handed it to the homeowner. "The electrical work is good to go." He glanced at the man who had his arm around a young boy and smiled. "Jake, you did a fine job wiring this home."

"Thanks. It was fun spending the summer here with my son. He got a lot of on-the-job training."

The homeowner looked relieved. "I still smile about negotiating the wiring cost with Jake. He said the price would double if I watched and triple if I helped. I'm glad I left him alone. Now we might finish the house in time to beat the first snow."

The negotiation remark drew a chuckle from the inspector. "I hope you're shooting for mid-October—anything past that is iffy."

"That's the plan. I'm looking forward to retirement and the mild winters here. Compared to Alaska, this will seem tropical."

"Congrats on retiring. I'm ten years away from the good life. Twenty-two is our average temperature in January, so I hope you haven't thrown away your long johns. We can get a foot of snow here in December and January. How long were you in Alaska?"

"Thirty-one years."

"Geez. Guess you liked living there. I see what you're saying about our winters being more agreeable to you." He turned to the electrician and shook his hand. "I wish they were all like you, Jake. It was a pleasure working with you. Maybe your friend here can talk you out of heading back to Alaska."

"It's God's country, and we love living there. Say goodbye, Keenan."

"Goodbye, sir."

"Goodbye, young man. I hope you two enjoy the trip back. I always wanted to drive the Alaska Highway."

"My dad says we'll have to hurry to make it in time for my school's first day."

"Well, if I were a kid, I'd be praying for the car to break down a few times along the way so I'd miss a few days of school."

"Dad's a teacher, so they'll be mad if he shows up late."

"Yeah, I suppose you're right. Well, I'm off to the next site. I can assure you it won't be this pleasant. They're a bunch of bozos, and I'm going to issue a stop-work order." He shook hands with everyone and left.

"Jake," the homeowner said, "I can't thank you enough for coming down here and doing such a fine job. We loved having you. The welcome mat is always out for you and Keenan."

"Thanks, Mark. I hope you and Anna enjoy retirement. I'll miss you, and the school won't be the same without you. I'm grateful you hired me. Being a teacher is the perfect job for me."

"Hiring you made me look like a genius. I hope you'll take my place in the principal's chair one day."

"I'm having too much fun to consider it. But in the future, you never know." He turned to his son. "It's time to head home."

In their Honda Pilot, Jake looked at Keenan. "Here's the plan. Let's pick some apples at that U-pick place called Roediger Orchard on Highway 2, so we'll have some healthy snacks to eat on the trip home and then have lunch in Leavenworth at the Andreas Keller German restaurant. I'm dying to try their schnitzel sandwich and potato salad. How's that sound?"

"Das hört sich toll an, Papa." [It sounds great, Papa.]

"Also, los geht's." [Good. Let's head out.]

Their car's nav system guided them to the U-pick apple place without difficulty. A modest sign marked the entrance to the orchard.

Welcome to Roediger Orchard, Est. 1953

Current Fruits in Season:

Gala Apples and Bartlett Pears: 50¢ a pound

Parking in Rear

Good Manners Expected

Jake smiled. "I haven't seen the cents symbol used in ages, and it's not often someone says they expect good manners. This should be interesting."

There were five cars in the lot, which had a ten-car capacity. "With so little parking, this place doesn't cater to the masses, which is a good sign." They parked and admired a well-kept mid-century house on the property, probably the orchard owner's home. Jake glanced at the cloudless sky. Yesterday's thunderstorms cleansed the air and cooled the previous mid-90s heat to an agreeable eighty. He put an arm around Keenan. "This is a good day to pick apples. I'll bet they'll taste a lot better than store-bought ones."

"I know, Papa. I've never eaten an apple that I picked."

They walked to a pergola where several people had gathered. An older woman greeted them. "Hello. My name is Maddy Roediger. I'm the owner of this orchard. My granddaughter is about to lead a tour for the kids. Little fella, you're welcome to join them."

"May I go, Papa?" Keenan excitedly asked.

"Sure. I'll wait here with the other adults." He smiled at the woman. "My name is Jake, Mrs. Roediger. I promise we'll be well-behaved."

She chuckled. "I see you read my sign. Call me Maddy."

"Yes, ma'am."

Keenan hurried over to be with a dozen children who were with a pretty, twenty-something woman and her dog. The gangly creature looked like a dust mop with long legs, a peculiarity of nature likely conceived with little thought of the consequences. She began. "Hello, everyone. My name is Claire, and this is Bluebell. She's a Labradoodle, which is a cross between a Labrador retriever and a poodle. She's friendly, so you're welcome to pet her."

The kids swarmed around the dog, who loved the attention. Claire let them love on the animal for a few moments before resuming. "I want to welcome each of you to Roediger Orchard, which my grandparents established over sixty years ago. I'm proud to say we grow certified organic apples, which means they're good for both you and the environment. How many of you are from Washington?"

Most of the kids raised their hands.

"Okay, for the rest of you, shout out what state you're from."

"Oregon!" "Montana!" "Alaska!"

She pointed to the kid from Alaska and smiled. "You live the farthest away. What's your name?"

"Keenan. My dad and I live in Anchorage."

"I'll bet it's exciting to live there. Okay, do any of you know how many types of apples there are worldwide?"

They all shrugged their shoulders.

"Would you believe there are more than 7500 varieties? In Washington, we mainly grow nine varieties for commercial sale and harvest about 130 million bushels a year. Can anyone name the nine main varieties we grow here? What are some of your favorites?"

"Red Delicious!" one boy yelled.

"Granny Smith!"

"Cripps Pink!" an adult yelled from the pergola.

Jake appeared mesmerized by the beautiful lady. Someone touched his arm, startling him.

"Sorry to scare you, young man. You must've been off in your own world." It was Maddy.

"You're right. I tend to spend a lot of time in 'Jake's World,' as my father used to say."

She gestured at the adult who shouted out the apple's name. "It's funny, isn't it, how some people never grow up? So, you're from Anchorage?"

"Yes, ma'am. I'm originally from Spokane, but work brought me to Alaska."

"What do you do?"

"I'm a high school teacher."

"I was a teacher, too. I taught right down the road from here for thirty years. Elementary school. Claire's a third-grade teacher, walking in my footsteps, I suppose you'd say."

"I enjoy teaching teens, but third grade is a good age. They're still so innocent."

She nodded. "How true. So, where's your wife?"

"There's no wife, ma'am. It's just Keenan and me, and has been for most of his life."

"I don't envy you, being a single parent in this day and age."

"It's not so bad. When you have a routine, things go pretty smoothly."

"Back in my day, fathers never got the children. Times have changed, and here I am, looking like a fossil."

He looked at the trim, gray-haired woman whose stern features were offset by a charming smile. "You're quite lovely, Maddy. You have a wonderful place here."

"Thanks. We sell most of our apples to commercial growers nowadays and open our place to the public only on Saturdays. I guess this is your lucky day."

"It is. After picking some apples here, we plan on having lunch at the Andreas Keller restaurant, and then we'll drive back to Anchorage. Is there a German community here? The town looks like it's right out of Bavaria. I notice your last name is German."

"My husband's roots and mine are German, but Germans are scarce around here. Leavenworth was founded in 1906 as a timber community, but things got tough when the railroad moved to Wenatchee. Times got even worse in the early sixties, so a committee got together and decided to transform the city into a mock Bavarian village. The hope was to revitalize the economy with tourism. It worked. We have a population of about two thousand, but crowds from the big cities often pack the place and congest our roads. I liked it better back in the fifties when it was a sleepy little town, but I suppose you can't fight progress."

"It's still a beautiful place. I envy you for living here."

"Well, Claire's single, and you appear to be enamored with her. A fine young man such as yourself might find her to be an enticing reason to move here."

Jake chuckled. "I see you don't mince words."

"Well, at my age, I've earned the right to be blunt."

"Tempting as your offer is, Keenan and I are doing well in Anchorage." He looked at her granddaughter again. She was helping one of the kids up a stepladder to pluck a few apples and looked radiant with short, blonde hair and delicate, fawnlike features. "It's hard to believe she's single," Jake absently said while studying her. "How many years has it been since somebody broke her heart?"

Maddy looked at him, shocked. "You're very perceptive. A guy in college badly hurt her, and her heart has yet to heal."

Jake sighed. "Whoever hurt her was a fool."

It was Keenan's turn to climb the ladder, and Claire helped him up. He paused when he spotted his father. "Papa, look, these are called Gala apples!"

Jake acknowledged him with a smile and nod. Just then, another kid, excited about bringing his apples to his parents, bumped the ladder. It wobbled and down went Keenan. His face hit a low-lying branch. A trickle of blood fell from his nose. He touched his nose, saw blood on his fingers, and panicked. "Papa!" Jake rushed to him as the trickle of blood turned into a stream.

"Sit down, son, and lean your head forward." He looked at Claire, alarmed. "Can you get me a towel or something to help stop the bleeding?"

Claire waved at Maddy. "We need a towel here!"

Seeing the flow of blood increase, Jake didn't wait for the towel. He tore off his shirt and pinched Keenan's nose with it. Blood now covered the child's white shirt. "Spit out the blood. If you swallow it, you'll throw up." He looked at Claire. "Is there a hospital nearby?"

Shocked by his overreaction, she nodded. "Yes. It's a few miles from here. I don't think he—"

He cut her off. "I need to take him there immediately." He picked Keenan up. "How do I get there?"

"I can go with you if you'd like and show you how to get there," said Claire as Maddy arrived with a towel.

"You two go ahead," said Maddy. "Claire, I'll pick you up after we close."

Claire nodded and followed Jake and Keenan to their car. She sat with Keenan in the back seat and held the towel to his nose. The bleeding showed no signs of abating. In the driver's seat, Jake glanced back at her. "Which way?"

"Turn right at the end of our driveway and then go a few miles to 9th Street. Turn left there."

He stomped on the gas, and the car's tires spit out a shower of gravel. On the road, he floored it and quickly reached sixty miles per hour. Up ahead, a farm tractor moving at a snail's pace slowed the traffic. Jake pulled behind the other cars, which had now stopped, and worriedly glanced over his shoulder to see how Keenan was doing. Claire was soothing Keenan by running her fingers through his hair. She lovingly kissed his cheek. Her kindness brought tears to Jake's eyes.

Claire saw his tears. "Sir, it's probably nothing. I'm a third-grade teacher, and I see bloody noses frequently. Most kids are fine within an hour."

"He won't be fine. Keenan has a bleeding disorder." He unleashed a long horn blast and yelled. "Come on! Get moving!" His sense of urgency frightened her.

"Mach Dir keine Sorgen, Papa, es wird schon alles gut warden," said Keenan, while resting his forehead on the back of the front seat.

"Ich weiß, mein Sohn. Wir warden bald im Krankenhaus sein," Jake replied.

Their speaking a foreign language surprised Claire. "What language are you speaking?" she asked Keenan.

"German. I told Papa not to worry, and he said we'll be at the hospital soon."

The tractor turned on a side road, and it took another agonizing mile to reach the speed limit. "Right up ahead," said Claire. "Turn left on this road. He did as she said. "Okay, go a few hundred feet and turn right on Commercial Street." A few moments later, she pointed to a building. "That's the hospital."

Jake pulled in front of the entrance and ran to the rear door. He was shirtless and had Keenan's blood spattered on his chest. "Sir, I'll park the car if you leave me your keys. I see you have luggage, so I can bring you both fresh shirts."

"Thanks. Here are the keys. Our shirts are in the green duffle bag." He hurried away with Keenan in his arms.

Claire parked their car and opened the duffle bag. After retrieving a couple of shirts, she went to the admissions desk. "Excuse me. A man just came in with a little boy with a bad nosebleed."

"Yes. The doctor is seeing him. Are you his mother?"

"No. I came with them. I have clean shirts for them and their car keys."

"You can leave them here. I'll make sure they get them."

"Thank you."

"You can wait over there if you want. From what his father said, I think it might be a while."

"Okay. Thanks."

A half-hour later, Maddy walked in. Claire stood to greet her. "They took them right in. His father said he has a bleeding disorder. What should we do?"

"Let me find out," said Maddy. She went to the front desk, spoke to the lady, and came back. "I left our business card with a note to call us if they need anything. That's all we can do. Claire, we need to go. I left with a bunch of people still in the orchard."

Claire frowned. "Yeah, I suppose you're right. I hope the little boy will be okay. His dad was frightened."

"He's a good man. You can tell how much he loves his son."

2

"MR. HOLLAND, KEENAN was lucky because it was an anterior nosebleed, so we were able to cauterize the errant blood vessel," said the doctor the following morning. "I think he'll be fine. Needless to say, come back to the ER if it bleeds again."

Jake sighed. "We're from Alaska, and I'm facing a tight deadline to get back for my work. Is it okay for us to travel?"

The physician frowned. "I'm concerned about him flying with all the air pressure changes."

"We aren't flying; we're driving up the Alaska Highway."

That drew another frown. "You realize, if something happens, you'll be far from any medical facility other than maybe a clinic, and they won't be equipped to handle his bleeding disorder."

Jake nodded. "I plan on driving all out, getting back in four days. Doc, I'm a teacher, and being there for the opening day of school is important."

The doctor glanced at Keenan again. "Well, my best guess is he'll be okay, but I can't guarantee it. Let's keep him on desmopressin to help his body release more of the von Willebrand clotting factor into his blood, and go easy on physical activity, such as hiking, running, or—" He paused and smiled. "I'm sure you know the drill with his condition."

"I do. Thanks for all you've done." He shook the man's hand, and Keenan offered him a shy thanks. After completing the discharge paperwork, they left and found their car in the parking lot. Gratitude filled him as he thought about the pretty lady named Claire. He hoped she made it home okay. He pulled out the business card they had left for him and debated whether to call or thank them in person. He glanced at his watch and frowned. It was too early to show up at their door, and soon, they'd be out of cell phone coverage in the Cascades. After a moment of deliberation, he opted to write a thank you letter when they returned to Anchorage. Writing for him was always easier than expressing feelings face-to-face.

"Hey, son," he said in German, as they always did when they were alone, "since we just had breakfast here, let's hit the road. We won't be able to see Grandma and Grandpa in Spokane since we lost a day."

"Ich verstehe, Papa" [I understand, Papa.]

Jake opened the tailgate. "I have a gift for you to enjoy on the way back." He reached into a bag and pulled out a box. "Mark and Anna bought this to thank us for wiring their house."

Keenan opened the box and let out a whoop. "All seven Harry Potter books on audio, Papa!"

"Yep. Mark said the collection contains over a hundred hours of audio, so we can listen to Harry's trials and tribulations all the way back to Anchorage."

"What are tribulations, Papa?"

A tribulation is something that tests your endurance, patience, or faith. It's like how you had to overcome your nosebleed yesterday. Hey, let's get in the car and figure out the easiest way to Canada."

Four days and 2400 miles later, familiar territory came into view—the town of Eagle River, then Fort Richardson, and then ... Anchorage! Jake smiled as he drove past the Tikahtnu Mall on the city's east side. "Hey, Keenan, wake up—we're almost home."

The little boy woke and rubbed his eyes. "Welcome home, Papa," he said with a yawn. "What time is it?"

His yawn caused Jake to yawn as well. "It's two in the morning. I'm beyond tired, so when we get home, let's leave everything in the car and go to bed."

The house smelled stuffy when they walked in, and Jake made a mental note to air the place out the next day. He tucked Keenan in and kissed him goodnight.

As he lifted the comforter to get in his bed, he paused. There was one last thing to do that couldn't wait.

He went to his desk and began writing …

Dear Miss Roediger (forgive me if this isn't your last name),

We made it back to Anchorage, and I'm writing to let you know Keenan is fine. Fortunately, the doctor was able to cauterize the blood vessel, which stopped the bleeding. They kept him overnight, and we left in the morning. We both wanted to stop by and thank you and your grandmother, but due to the early hour and that we were facing a tight deadline to make it back in time for opening day at school, we had to leave right away.

It touched me seeing how kind and attentive you were to my son, and I am grateful to you for getting us to the hospital so quickly. I apologize for my poor behavior when I yelled at the stopped traffic on the way; Keenan nearly died as an infant from a nosebleed, so that's the reason behind my outburst.

I've thought about you a lot while driving up the Alaska Highway, and I'd like to share some things with you. Before I do, I promise that I seek nothing from you, and I'm a quite sane person. So please humor me and read on.

Since I was a child, I've had the ability to "see" others, to sense a person's feelings, and I can readily determine their motives, intentions, or their sense of well-being often before the person is even aware of it themselves. I dislike calling it "mind-reading" because I don't think it is. Rather, it's more like I'm quite perceptive. With you, the feelings I felt were enormously powerful. I'd like to share my thoughts of you, and you're welcome to tell me if I am right or merely foolish. This is what I "see" in you:

You're a quiet, modest person, spiritually wise, agreeable in nature, kind and giving, but hard to get to know, and "not fitting in" has been an issue you've grappled with for most of your life.

Although introverted, you relish deep, meaningful interactions with others, but sadly, such authentic exchanges are rare because most people are incapable of speaking the same "language" as you. You have a rich inner life, and daydreaming has always been a cherished way for you to escape and recharge, but others in your life view it as an affliction. You savor solitude, love communing with nature, and covet the serenity of your orchard. You can be hurt easily (not just by former loves) and tend to withdraw when it happens, protecting yourself, if necessary, by building elaborate emotional walls to keep people at arm's length.

You are prone to imagining the worst possible outcomes in any situation, so change, for you, is often unsettling. Other stressors for you are socializing, noisy or disorganized environments, not being appreciated, ambiguous/indecisive people, and lack of follow-through from others.

You abhor conflict and therefore tend to withdraw or "go chameleon" to appear to fit in. Because you're reluctant to engage with others, you are perceived to be a complex or aloof person and are often dismissed by many as a puzzle not worth their time to solve.

As a teacher, you are quite adept at reading your students' emotions and can easily sense if something is wrong at home or with their social interactions at school. You often use this skill to help them find their peace. A curious paradox is while you have an uncanny ability to read others, you have difficulty doing the same with yourself. You favor idealism and, despite your efforts to tame it, perfectionism. If you're not careful, you become obsessed with and mired in details. Although you loathe the limelight, you will tirelessly work behind the scenes for something dear to you, quietly and lovingly exerting your influence on others. A school play comes to mind when I say this.

You have a legendary love of words and learned at an early age how they can magically transport you to a rich, abstract world known only to you. You also love words because it is far easier to express how you feel in writing rather than verbalizing. Someone once said this, which will make perfect sense to you: "My words sound better coming from my hands than from my mouth."

You relish a good metaphor and often use them to condense your complex ideas into something easy for others to understand. If you had children, you would love reading stories to them, and no doubt would picture yourself being in the story, right there among the characters, fighting evil, comforting the downtrodden, and cheering for the vanquished as they ultimately triumph over their adversaries. By the way, Keenan and I listened to the Harry Potter series of audiobooks all the way from Leavenworth to Anchorage. Had you been with us, I'm sure you would've been captivated by Harry's trials and tribulations.

You have been confounded your whole life with thoughts of why you don't fit in, why it is so hard for you to be understood, and why you're the proverbial "square peg" trying to fit into a round hole. Aspects of your life don't seem right and never have, despite spending years trying to comprehend why. Because of this, you rarely are at peace with yourself. You've suffered bouts of depression your whole life due to an assortment of troubles such as feeling isolated, misunderstood, and, most recently, from your heart being broken.

Miss Roediger, as I watched you at your orchard that day, I saw the enormous pain in your heart. It nearly took my breath away. I mentioned this to your grandmother, and she confirmed my suspicions. You hide it well behind your shy, easy smile, but I see it. Your eyes so convey your inner sadness. You no doubt propped up the relationship until your rich imagination could no longer dilute reality, and that's when your heart was devastated. My heart, too, was once afflicted in such a way.

Above all else, I see your extraordinary inner beauty—how kind, caring, and compassionate you are. I was captivated by your goodness and decency. Your beauty, both inner and outer, is stunning. I see you, Miss Roediger, so clearly; you are quite unlike any other person I have met, and I was drawn to you.

I have something enormously important to share with you that could help answer many of your lifelong questions about being a "misfit." When I was in college, while attending a psychology class, I learned of a method for classifying human personalities called the Myers-Briggs Type Indicator. It's essentially a simple questionnaire (available online) developed by Isabel Myers and Katharine Briggs as a way to assess psychological preferences in an individual. Their work was based on the pioneering research of the Swiss psychiatrist Carl Jung. Today, the Myers-Briggs Type Indicator has become one of the world's foremost psychological assessment instruments and has helped millions of people gain insights about themselves.

With Myers-Briggs, there are sixteen distinct personality types (each identified with four letters). I discovered I was an INFJ, which is rare, making up about one percent of the population. I think you are an INFJ, too. Although rare, many with this personality type leave their mark on the world. Famous INFJs include Mother Teresa, Nelson Mandela, Johann Wolfgang von Goethe, Mahatma Gandhi, Eleanor Roosevelt, and the Dalai Lama. I invite you to take the assessment and think it could answer the many deeply rooted questions you have always had. In my case, knowing why I am "different" proved to be a godsend.

Well, there you have it. Miss Roediger, you have affected me deeply. The characteristics I "see" in you are also a good description of me. Eerily so. I think we are kindred spirits, part of the perplexing personality type I call "the one-percenters." For 2400 miles, these thoughts have played in my head. If you are open to it, I would like to enter into a correspondence with you. Said Emily Dickinson: "I felt it shelter to speak to you." My hope is one day we will use those words to describe our friendship.

   Kind regards, Jake Holland

He addressed the envelope with the info on the business card they had left for him at the hospital, turned off the light, and got into bed. A few seconds later, he got up, returned to his desk, and pulled out a blank piece of paper. He began writing ...

Note to self: I don't know why I feel this so strongly, but I cannot shake this overwhelming notion. A woman named Claire sent shivers through my body, and her soul touched mine. I cannot explain this, and as insane as it sounds, I'm hopelessly in love with her. I know she is God's perfect choice for me. One day, Claire, whose last name I do not know for sure, I'm going to marry you. Jake Holland

He dated the letter and stared at the words. With a sigh, he grabbed another envelope and wrote "Claire" on it. Then he placed the letter in it and put the envelope in the desk drawer. He returned to bed and quickly fell asleep.

3

THE FIRST WEEK at Osborn Elementary went by in a flash. Claire shook her head at how much her seventeen students had forgotten over the summer. They had a lot to cover this year. Third grade is when many new subjects are introduced: multiplication and division, basic physical sciences and chemistry, health and nutrition, social studies, history, and reading involving a variety of genres such as fiction, fantasy, and folklore. Since this was a farming community, weather and climate were also important topics for discussion. All this would make for a busy year.

Typical of eight-year-olds, her kids had high energy and were becoming more physically agile and daring. Also, they were beginning to be aware of the concept of self-consciousness, as in: *I wear glasses,* or *My clothes don't look like what the other kids are wearing.* The ability to establish friendships also blossoms at this age. Claire sighed. For her, this age was when being different became painfully evident. Her being quiet and socially inept ushered in the start of many lonely years. She sighed again and sat for a while longer in her empty classroom, marveling at how quiet it got without students.

The trip home took less than five minutes—such were the perks of living in a small town. A light rain began to fall, which was forecast to intensify later in the evening. The hot summer days had waned, and deciduous trees were ablaze in fall colors. Claire loved this time of year, with wisps of fall being carried on the day's breezes and crisp nights. This was the prime apple-picking season— the Honeycrisp and Golden Delicious were ready to be harvested in mid-September, followed by the Red Delicious in late-September, and by mid-October, the Braeburns. Their orchard consisted of Gala-producing trees, and most of their apples had been harvested. She was grateful they were now closed for tourists, and the few apples left on the trees were reserved for students coming there on class field trips. Maddy loved hosting the events, and for a brief time, she could be a teacher again.

Claire parked her car in the garage and walked into their house. Bluebell greeted her, barking and wagging her tail. "Hey girl, where's Maddy?"

"I'm upstairs! Come up; I have something for you."

Claire placed her keys and purse on the credenza and bounded up the stairs. Bluebell barked excitedly and raced after her. In her bedroom, Maddy was changing the bed linens. She hugged Claire. "How was your first week at school?"

"Busy. I feel as if I need to start all over. Kids forget so much during the summer."

"They don't forget as much as you think. In a month, you'll marvel at how well they're doing."

"I suppose you're right. So, what do you have for me?"

Maddy reached into her apron pocket. "This letter came today, addressed to Roediger Orchard, attention Claire Roediger. It's from Alaska. The return address says Jake Holland. I remember him. He was here with his boy, the one you helped take to the hospital."

Claire raised an eyebrow. "I wonder why he's sending me a letter."

"Maybe he's suing us."

"Leave it to you, Grandmother, to think of something like that."

"Hey, we live in a litigious world. I'm glad we didn't serve hot coffee, or he'd have a twofer lawsuit against us."

Claire rolled her eyes. "I'll read it later and let you know if we need a lawyer. I'm starved. What's for dinner?"

"You're in for a treat tonight. I got fried chicken from Dan's Deli to celebrate you surviving your first week at school."

"Potato salad, too?" Her eyes conveyed hope.

"Of course. And I made an apple pie for dessert."

"Should I kiss you now or later?"

"Now's fine."

After a pleasant dinner, they did the dishes. "Well, I'm going to head upstairs and work on next week's lesson plan. It'll be a great thing to do on this rainy night."

Maddy laughed. "Yeah, right. You're going up to read the letter. I see through your ruse."

"I'm sure he's writing to say how his son is doing. I felt bad about not returning to the hospital to check on them."

"Hey, if you're not family, they won't tell you a thing, so going back would've been pointless."

Claire nodded. "Where's Mrs. Kerfuffle?"

"The last I saw, your cantankerous cat was under my bed, waiting to pounce on me."

"She reminds me a lot of you," Claire said with a mischievous smile.

"Well, I prefer the word feisty to cantankerous, but I get your point. Go on upstairs, but let Bluebell stay so I can discuss the presidential candidates with her."

"Bluebell the liberal versus Maddy the conservative. It'll be a debate for the ages."

Maddy laughed. "Go read your letter. Tell Mrs. Kerfuffle her dinner is ready."

Claire turned the light on in her room and plopped down on the bed. She opened the envelope and pulled out the letter. It was written in longhand, in blue ink. She liked the thought of an old-fashioned letter.

The first two paragraphs were nice, she thought, although somewhat perfunctory, with him stating Keenan was fine. Her smile disappeared in the third paragraph, which said, *"I'd like to share some things with you."* Maybe Maddy was right, she thought—he *is* going to sue us. She read on.

The next paragraph made her mouth fall open—who *was* this guy, saying he could "see" her? She zipped through the rest of the paragraphs, stunned. It was as if he were looking right into her soul, precisely describing *everything* about her. Her heart pounded. She folded the letter with trembling hands, put it back in the envelope, and placed it on her nightstand. *"My God,"* she whispered. *"My dear God ..."*

Maddy walked upstairs under the guise of being on a Mrs. Kerfuffle hunt. She poked her head into Claire's room. "Well, do we need to hire a lawyer?" Claire's ashen face shocked her.

"What's wrong?"

"Nothing. He said his son is fine, and they're back in Anchorage. I don't think they're going to sue us."

"Well, then, why are you looking as if you're about to pass out? What happened? What did he say?"

Claire pursed her lips, struggling for something to say. After a few moments, she responded, her voice soft and shaky. "He just thanked me for being kind to his son on the way to the hospital. He said his son nearly died as an infant from a nosebleed, and that's why he panicked." Not wanting to talk any more about what he had written, Claire ended the conversation. "I think I'm going to take a bath."

Maddy took the hint. "Mrs. Kerfuffle, if you're in my skeins of yarn, you *will* be homeless again!"

Claire eased into the hot bathtub water, careful not to let the letter get wet. With her hands still shaking, she reread it. Twice. *"My God ..."*

She put the letter aside and closed her eyes, her mind racing. *How could he know I love words? How could he know so much about me ...?* She thought back to that day ... *he and his son were the last to arrive for the tour ... she didn't even meet him until his son fell ... on the way to the hospital, how panicked he was when the traffic backed up, him honking the horn and yelling for the other drivers to hurry up ... the tears rolling down his cheeks when he said his son had a blood disorder ... his little boy telling him in German that he'd be okay ... him replying, also in German, in a tender way ... he loved his little boy, that was for sure ... getting out of the car, him picking up his son; he was shirtless with blood on his bare chest ... his chest, muscular, but not overly so ... he was a tall, handsome man; his boy looked like a miniature version of him ... the total of their time together being no more than twenty minutes ...* She shook her head—no one could know things like that about someone in twenty minutes. *My God.*

She added more hot water, her thoughts ablaze. *He wants to start writing to me. He wants me to take some kind of test.*

When the bathwater turned cool again, she decided what to do about the letter. *There's only one thing to do. Ignore it. Pretend the letter never came. I mean, he's in Alaska, so you'll never see him again. Yes, ignore it. That's the thing to do.*

After draining the bathwater and toweling off, she scooped up the letter and returned to her bedroom. She put the letter in her dresser drawer, slipped into a nightgown, and went downstairs. "Hey, Maddy, would you mind letting Bluebell out later? I'm tired and think I'll turn in early."

Maddy looked perplexed. "Claire, it's seven-thirty."

"I know, but I've had a rough week."

Maddy looked at the dog, who was dozing in front of the fireplace. "Bluebell, it's just you, Mrs. Kerfuffle, and me tonight. I'll make some popcorn, and we can watch *The African Queen* again. Kate Hepburn reminds me of me." The dog cocked her head, heaved a sigh, and rested her head on her paws again.

"Thanks, Maddy. Goodnight, Bluebell. We'll play tomorrow." She got a few tail wags in reply.

Upstairs, Claire switched the light off in her room and went to bed. Her down comforter became a makeshift cocoon, sealing her off from the world, and she hugged her body pillow. The letter had left her emotionally exhausted.

She woke with a start at two in the morning. A bad dream had visited her. *Keenan had fallen again, and she raced to help him. Blood was everywhere ... he looked at her and said something in German that she couldn't understand ... he was so scared.* Her breaths came and went in explosive gasps. The dream seemed so real, so vivid.

She went to the bathroom and rinsed her face. After toweling off, she ran her trembling fingers through her sweat-soaked hair and forced herself to slow the rate of her breathing to calm down.

Back in her room, further sleep was hopeless, so she turned on her laptop. The glow from the screen bathed the room with an eerie light. She googled "Myers-Briggs" and began reading an article about it. With her curiosity aroused, she decided to take the personality assessment and answered a series of questions as they appeared on the screen, such as: *Are you easily affected by strong emotions? After prolonged socializing, do you feel the need to get away and be alone? Do you easily understand new theoretical principles? Are your decisions based more on the feeling of a moment rather than thorough planning?* It didn't take long to answer the fifty-or-so questions, and she clicked on the button to indicate she was finished. Her personality type flashed on the screen: INFJ. "Oh my God, he was right!"

She opened the "INFJ" information page, read about this personality type, and was stunned all over again. Everything about her, all the things she spent her whole life trying to figure out, was laid out before her. No wonder she always felt like she didn't fit in. Only one percent of the population was like her … *and Jake.* It was just as he said. *Everything.* She closed the lid on the laptop and went back to bed, lost in thought. It was as if someone had handed her a Rosetta stone, a key to understanding herself. *God.*

She tossed and turned the rest of the night, unable to sleep. When morning came, Claire knew what to do. Her prime directive to herself after the awful breakup with her boyfriend was to protect her heart at all costs. Getting involved with someone who could read her like a book had trouble written all over it. *This man is dangerous. Do not respond to his letter.* She put his letter in her nightstand drawer, and that was that regarding Mr. Holland. The following day, despite her best efforts to suppress it, thoughts of him danced in her head.

It was mid-October now, and Claire looked forward to having the next week off for Fall Break. After six weeks of "whipping her students into shape," she was happy with how well they were doing. And she was happy with the progress she was making in learning more about her personality type. During lunch breaks, she visited INFJ sites on the net. She had something to celebrate now—she wasn't a misfit after all, but rather one of a select group of people, like a rare fine wine. It sounded much better than misfit.

When she arrived home that night, Bluebell bounded up to her from behind the house, excitedly barking. Her being out meant

Maddy must be outside as well. With Bluebell jumping up for attention, she walked to the backyard. Maddy was there, bundled up in a sweater, removing freshly washed bedlinens from the clothesline. Even though they had a dryer, Maddy always insisted that air-dried laundry felt and smelled so much better than clothes coming out of an appliance, and Claire had to admit she was right. She smiled as she walked up to her. "Hey, Maddy, look at me. This big smile isn't from my dog being so delighted to see me. I have the next seven days off!"

"I know you've been looking forward to it. Maybe we could drive to the coast for a change of pace. Or, we could go to Port Townsend. I love all the shops, galleries, and restaurants on Water Street. We could spend a few days there."

Claire's smile vanished, and an awkward silence ensued.

"Okay, okay, I'll drop it, but Claire, it's been over three years since your relationship ended. How long are you going to keep up your hermit existence? Trust me, withdrawing from humanity is not the way to a rich, fulfilling life."

"I'm sorry, Maddy." Her voice was whisper soft. "I ... I'm just not ready yet ..."

Maddy draped a sheet over the line and hugged her. "Hey, don't do guilt over my request. You're doing quite well since having the debilitating depression. I'm so proud of you."

Claire kissed her grandmother's cheek. "I love you so much. Thanks for understanding."

"Enough of this affection. If someone sees us, I'll be branded as a softy. When you go inside, there's another letter from Alaska for you on the kitchen table."

Claire's heart flopped. Her cheeks flushed. "Really? I thought I'd never hear from him again."

"Well, since you've been so tight-lipped about his last letter, I couldn't hazard a guess as to what he wants. Maybe he's smitten with you."

Claire rolled her eyes and ignored Maddy's comment. "Unless you want help out here, I'm going in to change."

"No, I'm finishing up. Let's go to Andreas Keller to eat. Dinner's on me."

"Great idea! I can be ready in a half-hour."

"Take your time. You have a letter to read."

Claire scrunched her nose in mock exasperation and walked to the house. Bluebell looked disappointed that she didn't stay to play. Maddy saw Bluebell's frustration and tossed a stick for her to fetch. For the goofy dog, life turned sweet again.

Inside, Claire reached for the letter on the dining room table and hesitated. *Should I even open it?* She debated the thought for a few moments and snatched it up. The return address confirmed it was from him.

With a frown, she sat at the table, opened the envelope, and began reading. It was handwritten again, in a manly way.

Dear Miss Roediger,

The reason for this letter is that I can't get you off my mind. I have to be honest and say I'm disappointed by not hearing from you and hope I haven't offended you by what I said in my previous letter. If I did, I offer this, by Carl Jung: "Everything that irritates us about others can lead us to an understanding of ourselves."

Since perhaps I've already upset you, I might as well swing for the fences even though I well know it's the fastest way to strike out. I keep dwelling on the melancholy inside of you that nearly took my breath away. I'd like to talk to you about it. I love these words by Kamenashi Kazuya: "There's something beautiful about keeping certain aspects of your life hidden. Maybe people and clouds are beautiful because you can't see everything." I think his words are a perfect metaphor for you. Outwardly, you are a beautiful woman with an unassuming and agreeable quiet, but inside, a dark storm swirls, raining on all aspects of your life. I, too, have known such a storm within me, and that's why I feel I can talk to you about your hurt inside. To help get past the pain, I found wisdom in the words of Ijeoma Umebinyuo in what he called the three routes to healing: "1. You must let the pain visit. 2. You must allow it [to] teach you. 3. You must not allow it [to] overstay."

I don't know how long you've had your pain, but from the enormity of sadness I felt in you, it seems, to me, as if you've had this pain for quite some time. I think what you must be feeling inside is best described by Charles Baudelaire: "Do not look for my heart any more, the beasts have eaten it." Claire, I know you are heartbroken and believe your heart is beyond repair. I feel this deeply. But I am here to tell you that there is a blessing hidden within your pain. When you have plumbed the depths of misery's soul, and the sun finally reappears, and your darkness fades, your days will be sweeter, and your happiness far more appreciated. Someone once said, "I'm stronger because of the hard times, wiser because of my mistakes, and happier because I have known sadness."

You have much to offer this world. At your orchard, I saw how you captivated those children, how drawn they were to you, and it was wonderful to see. You also captivated me. I just stood there, watching you, utterly mesmerized by your kindness and goodness. But I also saw how you hide who you are, showing nothing but a mere shell of yourself, which is a testament to the epic sadness within you. Don't give up, Claire. Life has many blessings to bestow upon you. I feel this, too, deeply.

Regarding you and me, I so wish you would reply. As I said in my previous letter, I feel a strong affinity to you. I'll close with the words of Rachel Macy Stafford: "We are all just waiting for someone to notice—notice our pain, notice our scars, notice our fear, notice our joy, notice our triumphs, notice our courage. And the one who notices is a rare and beautiful gift." This could be how we feel about each other, Claire. Please give our friendship a chance.

Yours sincerely, Jake Holland

She put the letter down and had to remind herself to breathe. "My God, who *is* this guy?" she said aloud, dumbfounded. His words echoed within her. A few tears rolled down her cheek, which threatened to turn into a river of them.

Maddy walked in and saw her anguish. "What on earth is wrong?"

Claire wiped her tears away and looked at her, unable to speak.

"May I read the letter?"

She nodded. Maddy took the letter, put on her glasses, and began reading.

A few minutes later, she looked at Claire, stunned. "My, oh my. Was the other letter like this?"

Claire nodded. "I'll get it for you."

Maddy read it and sighed. "Good Lord. I've never seen anything like this. The way he described you with such clarity, it's as if he's known you all your life. Claire, that day at the orchard, he was studying you so intently that he nearly jumped out of his skin when I touched him to get his attention. He looked at me and said, *'How many years has it been since somebody broke her heart?'* His certainty shocked me." She dabbed Claire's eyes with a tissue. "So, what are you going to do about it?"

Claire shrugged her shoulders, her way since childhood of saying she didn't know.

Maddy mercifully changed the subject. "Let's not allow these letters to ruin our evening. How soon can you be ready to go?"

She smiled as if putting distance between her and the letters would dilute their potency. "All I need to do is change."

At the restaurant, Maddy scanned the menu. "The smoked pork chop with fried potatoes and sauerkraut sounds enticing, don't you think?" With a sly smile, she winked at Claire.

"I see how you're trying to sway me into ordering it, but I'll have my usual schnitzel salad platter with a pretzel appetizer."

A half-hour later, they enjoyed their meal at the quaint eatery on Front Street, which looked like a Straße, or street, in Germany. The dining room, fashioned like a Bavarian-style barn, featured a rich assortment of hand-painted murals on its wooden walls. Maddy took a bite of her chop and swooned. "Claire, try this, and you'll be ordering it from now on."

"Mmm, it's delicious. Maybe, just maybe, I'll order it next time. It never hurts to try something new."

Her grandmother jumped on the innocent remark. "Speaking of something new, I like Jake Holland. We talked while you were giving the kiddie tour. Did you know he's a teacher, too?"

Claire reached for her Schöfferhofer grapefruit beer, took a sip, and shook her head. "No. What grade does he teach?"

"High school. We didn't discuss it, but I'd bet he teaches English from the eloquence of his letters. That or maybe extrasensory perception."

Her remark drew a feeble smile from Claire.

"So, did you take the Myers-Briggs assessment?"

"Yes."

"Well? Come on, Claire, stop being so aloof."

She sighed. "He was right. We have the same personality type." She absently poked her fork at her salad before looking up. "Maddy, you'll be amazed by my personality description. It's eerie how closely it describes me, and now I know why I never fit in. Only one percent of the population has this type."

"As the old proverb goes, 'Birds of a feather flock together.' I think that's why he was so taken by you."

"He wasn't taken by me. We barely spoke to each other."

"Claire, the man is smitten with you. The two of you will make a fine-looking couple, and your children will be gorgeous."

"You're both in for a disappointment because I want nothing to do with him or any other man ever again."

"For God's sake, Claire. He's a good man. His relationship with his son says a lot about him. Don't dismiss him out of hand. What harm could come from being pen pals? He's probably the last guy on earth who sends handwritten letters. He's gainfully employed, intellectually gifted, and has feelings for you. I saw it with my own eyes. He'd be a good husband and father. Grandpa would've liked him."

A look of sadness passed over Claire's features. "Maddy, I'm done with relationships. I have you, Bluebell, and Mrs. Kerfuffle. That's enough for me."

Maddy sighed. "Claire, I'm an old woman, and you're acting as if I'll live forever. I'm in the twilight of my life and worry that I've done you a disservice by allowing you to have a sheltered existence. While a respite from your pain was needed, you've dug in for the long haul."

"I like my life, Maddy. I love living with you."

"Claire, you're my best friend, and I adore you, but it's not healthy for you to be a hermit."

She shook her head, a silent plea to end the topic.

"Writing him a letter is not a marriage contract. Just think about it."

Claire forced a smile. "Okay. I'll think about what you've said."

Maddy knew she'd pushed too hard and wisely steered the conversation to something cheerier. "For dessert, let's share a slice of cinnamon apple cheesecake."

Claire relished having the week off and stayed busy working around the house. At night, she read Jake's letters. On Sunday, after saying goodnight to Maddy, she began writing a letter to the bothersome Mr. Holland. After a week of pondering what to do, she decided that protecting her heart was the only viable option.

You intuit deftly, Mr. Holland. Amazingly so.

I care not to dwell in the specifics of your conjectures, other than to say, indeed, as you surmised, after taking the assessment, I'm also a "one-percenter." For giving me this Rosetta stone, I thank you. Answers to my many questions, questions mainly centered on my perceived shortcomings regarding "fitting" into this world, came leaping forth. For untold years, I have yearned to be understood and to be accepted and indistinguishable from others and have failed miserably. Now, after reading about our personality type, my soul feels somehow sated, knowing I am a rare breed, a swan apart from the rest of the swans, although just as beautiful, just as vital to the whole of the flock.

Sir, I appreciate the kindness of your words, the gift of your insights, and certainly your doggedness to elicit my response, but my wounded heart, I fear, has not recovered, and tears still fill an abundance of my days. Given your apparent fondness for quotes, I offer this from Adam Zucconi: "I am guilty, just like every human is of romanticizing their pain by using pretty and cleverly worded metaphors to somehow make the heartache seem remarkable. The words wrap our wounds in silk ribbons; beautifully dressed, but it's not gonna stop the bleeding."

Embracing those words, this time, for you, I'll forego the use of intriguing metaphors for the hurt still vivid, painful, and alive within me, and simply say I hope you'll understand why I choose not to invite you into my troubled sphere or vex you with wretched, poor-little-Claire anecdotes.

Despite what you may have fancied, mine is a quite ordinary life, devoid of whimsical notions. I'm a small-town girl who cherishes the quiet of days and the beauty of small moments, where trusted companions are few, and mainly come with a coat of fur. A goofy dog and persnickety cat, along with my cherished, though feisty grandmother (who has a penchant for barking in her own way), are more than sufficient to occupy my days. "Quiet Claire," as I have been known from the earliest reaches of my memory, tried once at love and then has retreated to the safe and predictable ways of a solitary existence. You may think I want to change what I have, and in this regard, your impressive intuition has failed you.

I cannot force my heart to open or my words to flow, not for you, not for anyone. The definition of my life requires the word fragile, and I have lost all desire to venture back to the uncharted waters of relationships. These words from Nikos Kazantzakis describe how I feel: "Once, I saw a bee drown in honey, and I understood."

For these reasons, I request the termination of correspondence between us. I simply have nothing to offer you, and doubly so if any hope of romance crowds your thinking. From what I can divine, you appear to be a decent man and a loving father. I wish the best for you and Keenan, Mr. Holland. I hope, one day, what you seek will find you.

Goodbye. Claire Lofton

She reread her letter to make sure it conveyed her intent. After addressing the envelope, she tiptoed past Maddy's room and walked with Bluebell to the mailbox. "Goodbye, Mr. Holland," she whispered as she pushed the letter through the mailbox slot. "C'mon, Bluebell, let's go to bed. Tomorrow's a school day."

4

AS JAKE HEADED home with Keenan after school, the car radio blared out a warning: *"The National Weather Forecast office is predicting tonight's storm will produce strong and potentially damaging wind gusts in Anchorage and along Turnagain Arm. Gusts could reach 85 to 100 miles per hour."* He glanced back at Keenan. "They're going to cancel school tomorrow because of this storm. It's going to blow all the leaves from the trees, so take one last look at the fall colors."

"Yay! No school. What are we going to do, Papa?"

"Well, we'll stay home and batten down the hatches. I hope we won't lose any more trees or shingles like we did two years ago."

"Can Tommy come over and play?"

"Sure. They're predicting power outages, so let's stop by the store and buy some things that don't require cooking."

"Like what?"

"Nuts, trail mix, dried fruit, beef jerky, peanut butter and jelly, stuff like that. Plus, I'll buy more batteries for our flashlights."

"Can we get Cheetos? You don't have to cook them."

Jake laughed. "Sure. With enough Cheetos, we could survive any apocalypse. Hey, if we go to Costco, we can eat there and get our supplies."

Keenan nodded eagerly. "Their pepperoni pizza is my favorite."

"Let's order a whole pizza, and we can munch on the leftovers tomorrow for lunch."

After the Costco run, Jake pulled into their subdivision and stopped at a cluster of mailboxes at the end of their street. As he walked around the car to his box, he noted the nippiness in the air and the wind gusts rising. He grabbed the mail and hurried back to the car.

Inside their house, Jake turned his attention to the mail, which was mostly bills. One item stood out, smaller than the rest and beige in color. He read the postmark: Leavenworth, Washington. He excitedly scanned the return address. "Claire Lofton," he said aloud. "Her last name isn't Roediger; it's Lofton!"

"Who's she?" Keenan asked.

"She's the lady who went with us to the hospital the day we picked apples in Leavenworth. Remember?"

"Oh, yeah. She was nice. Can Tommy come over and play?"

"Check with his mom. Tell her we'll bring him back before the storm fully arrives."

A few minutes later, Tommy knocked on the door. After waiting until they were deep in play in the family room, Jake sat at the kitchen table and opened the envelope. His joy soon vanished. A second read didn't make her words sound any better. He tossed the letter on the table and sat quietly, lost in sadness.

By nine o'clock, gusts of wind buffeted the house. Jake decided to take Tommy home before it got worse. He forced a smile when saying hello to Tommy's parents and kept a firm grip on Keenan when they walked home to prevent the wind from knocking him over. Back inside, they got creative and made a respectable bachelor snack of Cheetos mixed with vanilla ice cream.

Later that night, after saying goodnight to Keenan, Jake went to his room and looked out the window. Shingles were flapping on his neighbor's home, which meant the same thing was happening on his roof. He frowned, hoping they'd still be there by morning. He touched the windowpane and felt it flexing with each gust. If it got worse, he'd sleep in the guest bedroom, which didn't face the wind.

Unable to sleep with the storm raging, he read Claire's letter repeatedly. After much thought, he went to his desk, picked up the Mont Blanc pen his grandfather had given him as a college graduation gift, and began writing.

Dear Miss Lofton,

Forgive my trespass upon your beautifully articulated no-correspondence dictate, but I beg from you one last indulgence, and that is to read these words. Afterward, if your heart finds no resonance with what I propose, I will take your non-response as a silent farewell and tender no further letters to you.

All my life, words have affected me deeply, be they singular or in combinations strung together by skilled artisans like pearls on a necklace. They sparkle and shine and dance within me. The words of your letter affected me in such a way.

With you, I feel a powerful kinship, even more so after reading the way you state your thoughts so eloquently. However, there is more to you than your sublime descriptive passages. My thoughts repeatedly circle around the day when you soothed my son when he was hurt. Such tenderness is beyond the capability of a woman with a heart of stone. Should you doubt its existence, I am here to tell you that your heart is alive, Claire. I saw it that day. Your kindness and goodness are reasons for the kinship to you of which I speak.

I understand as fully as anyone—perhaps even more than you—the pain of a broken heart. I know only too well the territory of sadness. Fortunately, I found my way out of the darkness, and now I see much light and beauty in the world. I hope you, too, will find your way back to that which is tender and beautiful. These words, by an unknown author, helped me get through my dark times, and I offer them to you: "Bless this pain, for it will reveal its perfect gift to me at the proper moment."

I seek not your romantic affections and have no intent to lay claim to your heart. Rather, I ask that we write to each other as lovers of words, as survivors of unspeakable wrongs, as friends who feel and think deeply. My hope, with you, is for an allegiance that transcends the superficial acquaintances I've spent a lifetime enduring. A one-percenter once wrote, "I feel as if I'm made to understand but not to be understood." That's you and me, Claire. You'll be one of the few people who understands me, and I'll be one of the few who understands you. That's why I've been so persistent in writing to you.

With a goofy dog and a persnickety cat being your closest companions, your message is clear: access tightens the closer one gets to your heart. Yet here I am, writing to you with my heart exposed, asking for your friendship, asking for the opportunity to become one of your trusted few. I will not let you down should you open the door, be it ever so slightly. André Breton eloquently expresses how I feel: "All my life, my heart has yearned for a thing I cannot name." Claire, I invite you to help me find what I cannot name, and I will likewise do the same for you.

Kind regards, Jake Holland

Without proofing what he had written, he folded the letter, placed it in an envelope, and sealed it. After transcribing her address to the envelope, he licked a stamp, put it on the corner, and called it good. As he went to bed, the sad look on his face conveyed little hope of a response.

The next day, in winds still gusting to forty miles per hour, Jake dashed to the mailbox to send off his letter, shielding his eyes from blowing dust and debris. On the way back, he looked at his roof. Half of the shingles were gone. "Damn!" he shouted into the wind with an anger not entirely due to the damage from the storm.

Back inside, while Keenan set up the Monopoly board game, Jake pulled a crockpot from the cupboard. Dinner tonight would be a pot roast. For a single father, the crockpot was a godsend: In the morning, dump in some root vegetables, a frozen chunk of meat, and beef broth out of a can. After it cooked all day, you'd have a heavenly-smelling, delicious meal. Even the most inept cooks, such as he, could master that. Before they started playing the game, he called their insurance company to report his woes. Five hundred dollars, his deductible, would soon vanish from his bank account. He sighed. "Hey, Keenan, I feel like having some Cheetos."

5

THE DAY BEFORE Halloween, a new round of snow fell on Anchorage. Wet and slushy, it blanketed every nook and cranny, resulting in highway medians being littered with stuck vehicles. The only redeeming grace of this kind of snow was that it was perfect for making snowmen. Jake glanced at Keenan in the rearview mirror. "Days like today make me appreciate our four-wheel-drive Honda. When we get home, I think a snowman would look good in our front yard. What do you think?"

"Yeah, let's build a big one!"

At their mailbox, Jake grimaced as the cold, wet slush filled his shoes. He opened the mailbox and spotted a beige-colored envelope—a letter from Claire!

Inside the house, they took off their shoes and hung their coats on hooks in the hallway. Jake peeled off his wet socks and wrung them out in the bathroom sink. "Hey, Keenan," he said as he draped the socks over the shower curtain rod, "let's have pizza before we build the snowman."

"Okay! Do you want me to get it out of the freezer and preheat the oven?"

"Yeah. I'll be up in a few minutes." He closed the bathroom door and pulled out the letter.

Dear Mr. Holland,

Persuasive, your words are, so much so that I will, as you say, open the door ever so slightly, but only if my terms are agreeable to you. To even write this letter has required immense courage on my part. I pray, sir, that you handle my heart with extreme care, for it is exceedingly close to being damaged beyond repair.

I propose addressing each other by our surnames; you calling me Claire is much too personal for me to bear. I cannot bring myself to call you Jake, as it implies a familiarity that is not there. "Mr. Holland" echoes favorably in my head, as if you are grandfatherly, and somehow, I find the notion appealing. As for our correspondence, you must agree that our words will never descend into a misery-loves-company litany, where we feed off the carrion of our past. I request posing a quote or question to each other and limit our response to what the quote or question means to us. Yes, doing this is a form of constraint, but it's a necessity for me.

I'll begin with a quote from Samuel Langhorne Clemens that resonates within me. I wonder what these words will summon in you. "It is a time when one's spirit is subdued and sad, one knows not why; when the past seems a storm-swept desolation, life a vanity and a burden, and the future but a way to death."

Good day to you, Mr. Holland

He read and reread her letter and looked in the mirror. "You did it, Jake! Now don't blow it by saying something stupid when you reply."

All through dinner and making the snowman, the smile that came to Jake after reading Claire's letter never left his face. Later that night, as he played Monopoly with Keenan, he pondered how to respond to her letter.

After saying goodnight to Keenan, he went to his desk and began writing.

Dear Miss Lofton,

I accept your terms of correspondence, though daunting is the task of crafting my words in such a way as they appear grandfatherly. The best I can do is perhaps include a few words that are either outright defunct or leaning toward anachronistic in the current English vernacular. However, you, as an educator, can certainly understand the challenge of waxing anachronistically without appearing ostentatiously lofty. A tightrope you make me walk, fair lady. As you can see, I'm stalling.

On to the business of responding to your quote …

I see the multiple facets of it and will begin by addressing the obvious: toss a verbal mortar shell his way such that, when it explodes in his awareness, he will think you to be so troubled as to run away in terror, never to annoy you again.

Sorry, Miss Lofton, but this verbal artillery is simply too weak to elicit panic in me. Nice try, though.

On to the next facet: Clemens is one of my favorite authors. Beyond his playful wit, his skill at crafting sentences that communicate with my heart leaves me, at times, in awe. He went through several periods of deep depression after his daughter's death in 1896, his wife in 1904, and another daughter in 1909. I cannot imagine the depth of despair I would descend into if something happened to my son. To this day, the epitaph he wrote for his daughter remains, for me, one of the most moving passages I have ever read: "Warm summer sun, / Shine kindly here, / Warm southern wind, / Blow softly here. / Green sod above, / Lie light, lie light. / Good night, dear heart, / Good night, good night."

I have learned a lot about depression, which was a constant and unwelcome companion in my young adult years. Two quotes regarding depression are indelibly seared into my memory. The first, by Miriam Toews, will surely resonate in many one-percenters: "Perhaps depression is caused by asking oneself too many unanswerable questions." The second quote, by Martha Manning, perfectly captures how I felt in my darkest of days: "Depression is such a cruel punishment. There are no fevers, no rashes, no blood tests to send people scurrying in concern. Just the slow erosion of the self, as insidious as any cancer. And, like cancer, it is essentially a solitary experience. A room in hell with only your name on the door."

It was in my freshman year of college, during an introductory psychology class, where my professor, a gray-haired lady a year away from retirement, gave me what you called "a Rosetta stone." With her help and insights, and with much effort, I was able to evict the unwelcome darkness from my existence. I'd like to share with you what I learned.

Her first assignment for everyone in the class was to write a one-paragraph description of your life. Try as I might, I could muster only a single sentence: "To my family, I am an enigma; to myself, I am an enigma within an enigma." I turned it in, feeling forlorn and wondering if there were still time to drop the class and take some other elective, like basket weaving. The next day, she called my name, and I sheepishly raised my hand. "Come to my office after your last class," she said. I nodded, imagining I was in for a brutal scolding, beginning with "Mr. Holland, you sanctimonious twit ..."

Instead, when I slinked into her office looking like a sad little puppy, she hugged me warmly and said, "I know you, Mr. Holland. I see in you a reflection of a younger me, and I know what you're going through. You are not an enigma, Jake. You are a treasure, and my intent is to show you why." When I saw in her eyes such a certainty of conviction and an unmistakable kindness, somehow, I knew she knew me. I burst into tears, unable to contain myself. Imagine a lifetime filled with people listing all your shortcomings and their incessant "what is wrong with you" diatribes, until their voices become your own inner, critical voice, and then, along comes someone who says, "Jake, they were all wrong." She shared with me the words of Carl Jung, which I've never forgotten: "Individualism is a natural necessity ... its prevention by leveling down to collective standards is injurious to the vital activity of the individual. The privilege of a lifetime is to become who you truly are." I cannot begin to tell you how these few words put my life into perspective. I became good friends with her and her husband, and sadly, she passed away two years ago. But a part of her will never die, the part that still lives in my heart.

She was the one who introduced me to the Myers-Briggs Type Indicator, and that's when I learned I was an INFJ, the rarest of personality types. When I read about my personality, it set off a seismic shift within me. Everything suddenly began to make sense; everything fuzzy came into crystal-clear focus. I learned how the characteristics and idiosyncrasies of my personality type were, in fact, not something to be scorned or ridiculed (chiefly by me), and I was able to go on and celebrate my uniqueness. To quote Popeye, "I yam what I yam," and I no longer fear whether or not others will accept me, nor do I put much emphasis on trying to explain myself. I came to love the words of Barbara Marciniak: "Everything changes when you start to emit your own frequency rather than absorbing the frequencies around you, when you start imprinting your intent on the universe rather than receiving an imprint from existence."

When I shared Myers-Briggs personality profiling with my parents, they read about the characteristics of INFJs and kept saying, yep, he's that, and that, and, oh yes, that too! My dad, especially, was finally able to understand why I was like I was. Incidentally, they both took the assessment, and, not surprisingly, he is the diametric opposite of my personality type. We laugh about it now. It brought us closer.

I also learned about my form of depression and its vicious circle, where hopelessness, anxiety, apathy, anger, helplessness, criticalness, and mental exhaustion triggered chemical imbalances within my body, which in turn fueled and heightened the negative emotions, and round and round it went. For me, the key out of darkness was taking control of my emotions by evicting the negative voice within me. I found my own voice, a kinder voice, which was not an amalgam of others.

I don't mean to trivialize depression, and I know that many forms of depression are much more difficult to treat and control than the type besetting me. In your case, I rather suspect yours is quite similar to what I experienced. I invite you to learn more about our wonderful, unique personality type and to closely examine the voice in your head to see if it is yours and not a mere melding of others.

The last facet I see in your quote to me can succinctly be described in four words: "Help me, Mr. Holland." In the spirit of my wonderful professor, I'm hugging you now, saying, "I know you, Miss Lofton. I see in you a reflection of me, and I know what you're going through. You are not an enigma, Claire (oops … Miss Lofton). You are a treasure, and my intent is to show you why."

And let me address the voice in your head that's probably speaking now: "Why is he doing this, wasting his time with me? What's in it for him? What's his angle? What does he want? I'm not worth anyone's time and attention."

My response is easy. I see you. I see your inner beauty. I see your kind heart. I read your beautiful words, written in a way that leaves me breathless. What's in it for me? Something that makes me want to camp out by my mailbox each day, eager to get your letter as soon as possible, so I can read your words, which take an express route to my heart.

My quote for your response is written by yours truly: "My gift is myself." Please describe the gift that is you.

Fair winds, sweet days, Miss Lofton

He put his pen down and read his words. Satisfied with what he had written, he folded the letter and put it in an envelope. He looked at the clock and frowned. It was two in the morning, and tomorrow was a school day. *"Give me strength,"* he muttered as he went to bed.

6

FOUR DAYS LATER, Claire and Maddy entered Dan's Food Market, Leavenworth's family-run grocery store, to stock up. "Hello, ladies," said Wes, the owner. "I could set my watch by the way you show up every Saturday at ten o'clock."

"There's nothing wrong with consistency," said Maddy. "Besides, if we came late, you might sell out of your freshly baked bread."

"You're in luck today, Maddy. Our bakery crew made your favorite German brown bread."

"Now, you have my attention." Her love for the tangy bread made with rye meal, rolled oats, sourdough, and molasses was legendary.

Wes turned to Claire. "Today's mixed-berry scones are sublime."

"I'll bet they are. We'll give them a look. How's Eric? School going okay?"

"He's fine. Thanks for asking. It's hard to believe he's only a year away from middle school. You're still his favorite teacher."

"Please tell him I said hello."

"Claire, let's get a couple of meaty pork chops," said Maddy.

After shopping and having lunch at the in-store deli, they headed home. Claire stopped at their mailbox, and Maddy got out to collect the mail. She returned with a big smile. "Guess who got a letter from Alaska?"

The lightheartedness of Claire's day ended. "I … I'm still not sure writing to him was a good idea."

"You wrote to him? As usual, tight-lipped Claire failed to inform me of this."

"I told him I'd consider writing, but only with tight constraints on what we discuss. I also said having a romantic relationship is out of the question."

Maddy frowned and shook her head. "You're trying a different tactic to run him off, aren't you? What else did you say to scare him away?"

Claire rolled her eyes. "See, that's why I didn't say anything to you about him. I knew you'd hound me for details, and I was right."

"Uh-huh."

Claire parked the car in the garage and faced her grandmother. "Can we please drop all talk of him? I wish I'd never written him back."

Maddy handed her the letter. "I like him, Claire, a lot. He's perfect for you."

"Don't start planning my wedding because it's not going to happen. I'd rather be a nun than be married."

"It's too bad you can't be a monk because you have the silent, solitary existence thing down pat."

Tears came to her eyes. "I'm not going to be hurt again."

Maddy touched her cheek. "Oh, sweet girl, I so hope one day you'll start living again. I'm sorry I've upset you. I'll let it go."

Claire wiped away her tears. "Thanks." She glanced at the letter. "No matter what he says, I'm going to end it. Writing back to him was an enormous mistake."

Maddy sighed. "C'mon, let's put the groceries away."

Later that afternoon, Claire came in looking happy. Playing outdoors with Bluebell elevated her spirits. Maddy smiled as she hung up the phone. "I called Helen and invited her to dinner. I'm thinking about making spaghetti."

"I'd like that. Do you need any help?"

"No. I'll be fine."

"If you don't mind, I think I'll take a bath and do some reading afterward. Bluebell, girl, please stay with Maddy so I can have some peace."

"Get me a couple of treats from the cupboard, and she'll be happy to be with me. And tell Mrs. Kerfuffle she's welcome to come down after she destroys my yarn."

"Sorry about her always getting into your things. I think she does it to let you know who's boss around here."

"I'll be darned if I surrender alpha status to that ill-tempered alley cat."

"Despite all her antics, I know you adore her."

Maddy smiled. "She reminds me of me."

Claire went upstairs and drew the bath. Before getting in, she thought about Jake's letter and returned to her room to retrieve it. With his letter in her hand, she eased into the tub. "Ahhh, perfect."

She took a few moments to enjoy the hot water and then turned her attention to the letter. *Well, let's hope he gave me an easy way to end further correspondence ...*

She started reading and, despite herself, cracked a smile about his *"waxing anachronistically."*

Her smile soon ended. He deftly perceived how she tried to scare him off with her quote. *"A verbal mortar shell,"* he called it. *God, how does he know me so well ...*

She read on, intrigued.

Tears poured down her cheeks after reading how his professor had helped him. She knew what he experienced as a child; the *"what is wrong with you"* voice of her mother still echoed within her.

She smiled at his Popeye quote and delighted in how he beat his depression. It made her wonder if she could do the same to defeat the depression plaguing her off and on since she was a teenager. She pondered this for a while before reading on.

More tears came when he applied his professor's words to her: *"You are a treasure, and my intent is to show you why."*

"My God," she said aloud. It then occurred to her how every letter from him elicited those words.

She sat in silence, her mind racing. His letter didn't end the way she had hoped. There was no benign quote, requiring nothing but a few fluffy words from her in reply. His quote was troubling: *"My gift is myself."* These were nonsensical words. *Me, a gift?* The idea seemed abstract and unworthy of frivolous conjecture.

She retrieved the letter and read it again, oblivious to the bathwater turning cold.

During dinner, she found it difficult to converse with Maddy and Helen, whose friendship with her grandmother dated back to long before Claire was born. Jake's words played in her head.

Later in the evening, she googled "Jake Holland" and found his homepage on the Anchorage School District's website. She and Maddy had guessed wrong: he wasn't an English teacher; he taught construction electricity at the King Career Center. That was a blue-collar profession, and he sure didn't fit the mold for that line of work, not with his eloquent letters. She clicked on his bio and was shocked. He had a Ph.D. in geology. *Why would a person with an earth-related doctoral degree be teaching electricity classes?* She read on and gasped. He won a Milken Educator Award for "exceptional educational talent as evidenced by effective instructional practices and student learning results in the classroom and school." This was a prestigious national award honoring top educators around the country. *He's a nationally recognized teacher,* she thought, utterly astonished.

She turned off the computer and went to bed, unable to make sense of his being interested in some small-town girl thousands of miles away. *God, he knew I'd be thinking this.* The words of his letter sprang forth: *"And let me address the voice in your head that's probably speaking now: 'Why is he doing this, wasting his time with me? What's in it for him? What's his angle? What does he want? I'm not worth anyone's time and attention.' My response is easy. I see you. I see your inner beauty. I see your kind heart. I read your beautiful words, written in a way that leaves me breathless. What's in it for me? Something that makes me want to camp out by my mailbox each day, eager to get your letter as soon as possible, so I can read your words, which take an express route to my heart."*

"My God," she said aloud. It was the last thing she said before drifting off to sleep.

In the morning, she got up early, reread his letter, and went to her desk. She began writing to the mysterious man from Alaska.

Dear Mr. Holland,

I read and reread your letter, feeling your young adult pain, reveling in your self-discoveries, rejoicing in your subduing of darkness, and I cried shamelessly for the gift of hope you conveyed to me. Every word in your letter resonated in me. I thank you so for sharing your life with me.

In your letters, I marvel at your innate ability to rummage so effortlessly through my soul, laying my thoughts and fears bare, casually mentioning secrets I've protected for years with formidable defenses; I find it in equal parts terrifying and exhilarating, like a roller-coaster ride on a pitch-black night. You scare me, Mr. Holland. I am terrified of yours being a siren call, seductive and alluring, enticing me to my doom on your rocky shores. I beg of you, sir, be of me ever so careful. My tendency to always assume the best in people makes me gullible and open to their malicious mischief. Just know my heart is too fragile to endure anything but good intentions on your part. If your words are indeed genuine, Mr. Holland, I can truthfully say you are quite unlike anyone I have ever known, leaving me to wonder if we were brought together by the silent song of an unseen piper. For what purpose, I cannot say, other than perhaps the appeal of friendship. As I already told you, I have nothing to offer in matters related to the heart, and I hope you will not stray into these dangerous waters, for you will founder.

To your "my gift is myself" quote, I tentatively tread. Had this exercise also been given to me as an assignment in college, my reply would have been as concise as what you first tendered to your professor and equally troubling. No. That's not true. My response would have been something sweet and charming, parroting what they wanted to hear, wrapped with a pretty bow, and bereft of truth. The sum of my life, as I'm sure you know, has been a failed attempt at conforming, with normalcy being merely a pose, while on the inside, I have felt so lost, so desperate to be understood. Acceptance takes an exacting toll on your psyche. So, Mr. Holland, my reply to your quote will be constructed on my new-found "one-percenter" foundation, where my thoughts will not have to be marginalized or disguised to meet someone's expectations. Such a notion I find refreshing.

My gift is myself.

I am Claire. I am different from others, and that's okay. I am a quiet, private, even-tempered woman, sensitive to the needs of others, competent and trustworthy, with an uncommon range and depth of talents. Though hard to get to know, I am very loving to those I hold dear, and I treat everyone with respect, understanding, and kindness. I have deep, inherent wisdom, a talent for listening, and a rich inner life. I favor idealism, am intuitive, and identify with the words creative, curious, and introspective. I feel intensely connected to nature and forever marvel at soft, billowy clouds painted on a vivid-blue canvas. True love, for me, requires physicality, spirituality, and emotionality. My dream is to one day have a house filled with love and laughter and an abundance of children. I have much to offer this world, much to offer a husband. As Gandhi said, "In a gentle way, you can shake the world." For my students, I do my best to shake their world every day and awaken them to their potential. This is the gift I bring; these are the hopes I have.

There you have it, Mr. Holland. Although I have nowhere near your uncanny ability to intuit others, I have empathic abilities as well. My guess is you are fixating on the apparent paradox of my words "I have ... much to offer a husband," so let me explain this, ever so briefly, to assuage this inconsistency. In your first letter, you correctly surmised I had been hurt deeply. I loved him totally and completely, and in the end, I was played for a fool. His talent was for offering empty words, and the allure of other women proved to be far more enticing than the burdens of monogamous love. One day, when I am able to collect the pieces that once formed my heart and meticulously glue and wire all the pieces back together, my hope is for this patched-up part of me to be able to function again. The repair of my heart has been exceedingly slow and, sadly, could take several more years of restorative efforts, with no guarantee of ever reaching full viability. Given this, it would be unfair to ask someone to wait for my recovery, so the words "much to offer my husband" are more of a future hope rather than a current possibility.

Since the subject of inconsistencies is now on the table, you, sir, appear rife with them. You teach electricity classes, which implies a respectable, blue-collar existence, yet your letters portray a person with a nimble, refined intellect. Curious as I always am, I visited your school's website and viewed your homepage. A Ph.D. in geology, it states. And you failed to mention how you won a prestigious Milken Award for being an outstanding teacher. What else about you have you not mentioned, and why? Most people are compulsive self-promoters, but you gloss over epic accomplishments in your life as if they were meaningless. You are a handsome and talented man, Mr. Holland, and no doubt are doggedly pursued by a host of damsels. Yet you toy with me, a thousand miles distant when you could be enjoying the fruits of local ladies. Is there a dark reason for this, sir? Your college assertion of being an enigma remains an apt description of you. These questions I find troubling; these questions make you so very alluring. Such are the pendulum swings of my musings.

If you are unable to dispel my concerns, I ask that you end our correspondence. If your character is, indeed, credible, then my quote for your response is by Gillian Flynn: "There's a difference between really loving someone and loving the idea of them."

Good day to you, Mr. Holland

Claire didn't emerge from her room until late morning. She looked out the kitchen window and saw Bluebell with Maddy, who was hanging laundry on the clothesline, despite it being only thirty-nine degrees with a breeze. She put on a jacket and joined them.

Bluebell went into convulsions of joy on seeing her and barked excitedly. "Hey, girl! Good morning, Maddy." She hugged her grandmother and grabbed a sheet from the basket without being asked.

"You must've been tired since you slept in so late."

"I didn't sleep in. I was in my room, writing to Mr. Holland."

"So, what did you say to end it?"

"I didn't end it." She reached for another sheet and secured it to the line. "I think we're the only people in Washington who still dry their clothes the old-fashioned way."

"Claire Lofton, for once, tell me what you're thinking."

"Okay. I'm thinking I'll have a blueberry bagel when we go back inside."

Maddy started to say something, and the scowl on her face indicated her words would've been harsh. She bit her tongue, which didn't come easy to her.

They hung more clothes without speaking.

"He has a Ph.D. in geology and teaches electricity classes."

"That's an odd subject for a geologist to teach."

"I thought so, too." She hung up a pair of socks and looked at Maddy. "He recently won a Milken Award; it's a national award given to a select few for teaching excellence."

"Wow. Mr. Holland has talents."

More silence.

"He had a tough childhood, like me."

"His parents abandoned him?"

"No. He was different. Just like me."

"I see."

"He met a professor when he was a freshman in college. She changed his life."

"How so?"

"Her first assignment to the students in her psychology class was to write a one-paragraph description of their life. Jake wrote, 'To my family, I am an enigma; to myself, I am an enigma within an enigma.' He thought he'd incur her wrath by writing something so glib."

"What happened?"

"He said she called him to her office, hugged him, and said, 'I know you, Mr. Holland. I see in you a reflection of a younger me, and I know what you're going through. You are not an enigma, you're a treasure, and my intent is to show you why.' He spoke eloquently of all she did to help him and how they remained close friends until she died."

"It sounds like he's paying her kindness forward by being a good teacher to his students like she was to him."

Claire nodded and handed her the empty clothes basket. "I think I'll play a bit with Bluebell and then come in."

Maddy knew not to press her for more; that Claire had shared this much was extraordinary. Whatever Jake Holland had said in his letter, it was clear his words affected her deeply.

7

A FEW DAYS later, Jake delighted in receiving a letter from Claire. He let her words stew in his awareness before replying.

Dear Miss Lofton,

Your letter touched me. It was so beautiful and genuine. Thank you for sharing your heart with me.

I'll begin by addressing my "inconsistencies." Regarding a host of ladies beating a path to my door, I am the pet project of several colleagues, who never tire of trying to "fix me up." I even ventured a few times into the jumbled world of singles, but it's not for me. In truth, I love being a father, and the waking hours of my days are eagerly spent with my son. I find it much more rewarding lying in bed with him on a lazy Saturday, having a spirited conversation in German, than sitting in some bar responding to "what's your sign" and other tedious exchanges.

You mentioned my Ph.D. in geology; the reality is I spent less than one year in the profession before becoming a teacher, so I think it would be disingenuous for me to toot my horn, acting as if I'm a bona fide working geologist when I'm not. I take far more pride in saying I'm a Cub Scout leader for Keenan than I do bragging about my schooling. I also play the guitar, a vintage six-string Gibson owned by my grandfather, and I love strumming out folk songs. But don't expect me to sing because my voice is worse than a crooning, hormone-infused alley cat with a hernia. Friends tell me I'm an adequate watercolorist, and I'm striving to perfect a technique called "splashing." Perhaps my most glaring deficiency is not being the tidiest of people, which I mask by saying our house has a comfortable, lived-in look. It seems there are not enough hours in the day to touch every domestic chore, but we do manage to rise above the level of a pigsty. Besides, life's too short to learn how to fold fitted sheets. I've heard it can be done, but it would require someone with brainpower far superior to my humble intellect to accomplish.

As a cook, well, were it not for store-bought rotisserie chicken and meals made in my crockpot, I would be in trouble. With this handy device, I manage to outshine the disagreeable cuisine that comes from the freezer, such as chicken nuggets and tater tots. Oh! In our house, there is no such thing as separating clothes for the laundry. Everything we own goes into our large-capacity washer for one load on Saturday. If an item of clothing can't swim with the sharks, it has no business being in our home.

There you have it, Miss Lofton. All my secrets are out. I'm not sure if this satisfies your concerns regarding my accomplishments and other non-disclosures, but the simple truth is I'm an ordinary person, striving to be a good father and now, your friend.

After two hours of writing and pondering, he put his pen down and went to bed. In the morning, before Keenan arose, he continued …

A night has passed, and here I am, resuming this letter. Mine was a restless night, with thoughts centered on your concern of my genuineness. I awoke, knowing what to say. I offer you these three words: "time and deeds." Do not assume me to be an honorable person, and do not fall prey to your tendency to assume the best in people. Rather, judge my genuineness by my deeds as the days pass between us. And, I say with confidence, with those three words as your touchstone for judging me, I will not come up short. I am a man of honor and integrity. This, you will come to see.

Now, on to more important matters: your heart.

Getting through heartache is a daunting task, and there are no easy ways to subdue the hurting. Just know you have in me someone who cares, someone who will listen, and someone with admirable patience, who is willing to take a chance with you despite long odds. Regarding the person who damaged you so, what a fool he was. Try as I might, I cannot imagine how he found you wanting because when I look at you, I see your kind heart, and when I read the rich words emanating from you, I see nothing but beauty and how wonderful you are in every way, like the most beautiful flower in the world, aglow with every color imaginable, whose roots are anchored in goodness and decency. I look at you and marvel at how anyone could not see such beauty.

Of your quote about the difference between really loving someone and loving the idea of them, I will let my heart be my voice. I want you to feel my heart's words, for they are genuine: When I first saw you at the apple orchard, seeing how loving you were with those children, seeing your shy smile and effortless grace, hearing your soft voice and the way you put everyone at ease, my heart said, "Oh my, she's something special." Then, when you held Keenan on the way to the hospital when he was hurt, and you loved him so tenderly, my heart knew, right then, that yours was the heart "we" have been seeking. I don't care if your heart is damaged because my heart was once damaged too, and from that, I learned how damaged hearts, when they find new love, know how special it is, and know how to "be ever so careful" as you have said. In your letters, cautiously, your heart has been speaking to mine. I suggest that your heart is not broken but merely dormant, and here I am, gently shaking you, saying it's time to wake up, it's time to explore more deeply "the pendulum swings of your musings."

To your quote, I also offer this, a proverb: "A beautiful thing is never perfect." But it nevertheless is beautiful, Miss Lofton, and that's more than good enough for me.

Of broken hearts, to this day, I cannot fathom how my former wife could not love her son and me. Peace came to me when I realized it was not our inadequacies but rather hers, and I found solace knowing I have enough love for both me and my son. I love this quote by Rune Lazuli: "Be the love you never received."

I hope, one day, you, too, will find a way to love yourself; I guarantee when this happens, you will see enormous strides being made in the mending of your heart. These words, written by a wise person, appeal to me: "Pain can change you, but that doesn't mean it has to be a bad change. Take that pain and turn it into wisdom."

What I'm about to say will be disconcerting: Your heart will never know peace until you forgive the man who broke it. I can almost see you wincing as you read this, but hear me out, and then decide if what I'm saying is right for you. Think about this: kind, loving people do not wantonly hurt others; it's not in them. Rather, hurt people hurt others. They may appear unblemished on the outside, but inside, their emotional wounds drive them to be the way they are. For those who have hurt you, your task is not to figure out what happened to them or try to fix them, but to bless them, forgive them, and move on. Regarding forgiveness, T. D. Jakes wrote: "I think the first step is to understand that forgiveness does not exonerate the perpetrator. Forgiveness liberates the victim. It's a gift you give yourself."

Also, tell your critical inner voice—the one saying what a fool you were for falling in love with him—that life comes with no guarantees, and anything good requires some sort of risk. Your wounded heart is a testament to your having the courage to try. One day, should love find you again, the hurt you experienced will allow you to appreciate and savor your new love all the more. I believe this deeply.

Here's something more to ponder. You have a pulse, which means you have survived the worst that life has thrown at you, the bleakest of days, the darkest of nights, and the most crushing of pain. None of it ended you. Do you realize how strong you are to have endured these hardships? Accept what happened to you, but don't be diminished by it; the next time darkness invades your thoughts, touch your fingers to your wrist and feel your pulse. That's your heart, telling you it's still alive, still beating. It's time to give your heart new experiences—there's so much good out there, waiting to be allowed in—me, for instance.

I offer these words for your consideration by Louise Erdrich; I believe she could have written them for you: "Life will break you. Nobody can protect you from that, and living alone won't either, for solitude will also break you with its yearning. You have to love. You have to feel. It is the reason you are here on earth. You are here to risk your heart. You are here to be swallowed up. And when it happens that you are broken, or betrayed, or left, or hurt, or death brushes near, let yourself sit by an apple tree and listen to the apples falling all around you in heaps, wasting their sweetness. Tell yourself you tasted as many as you could."

Only after forgiving my former wife was I able to open again to the good that life offers. It took me a while to realize that my darkness gave me gifts, which I now treasure—a beautiful boy and the ability to discern what true love is, for example. I appreciate kindnesses so much more now, and the beauty of innocent moments, such as enjoying the heavenly aroma of freshly baked chocolate chip cookies I make with my son, or when he and I cross-country ski through the forest at night on one of the city's lighted trails. Although life offers no guarantees, my darkness taught me the power of having faith and how there's an unimaginable strength within me capable of defeating any despair. Might I stumble again? Yes, but oh how exciting it is to try. Miss Lofton, you are stronger than you could ever imagine; you've already proven it. Pretending you are broken chains you to the past and robs the present and future of joy.

Instead of a quote for you to respond to, I'll give you a question, a hard question to answer, but you can do it. Ready? Okay, here it comes ...

What gifts did my failed relationship bring to me?

Saying "none" is not an option. They are there. What are they? Also, no cynicism is allowed in your reply, such as, "I received the gift of wisdom to never trust men again."

Oh! A general comment: One-percenters tend to overthink everything. Don't, in this case. Just write what comes from your heart.

Here's some inspiration for your reply by Mary Oliver: "Someone I loved once gave me a box full of darkness. It took me years to understand that this, too, was a gift." And this, by an unknown person: "Everyone is a lesson."

Good day to you, Miss Lofton

He reread his letter and realized he had pushed way past "friendship" with some of his words. Debate raged within him on whether to wad it up and start over or go for broke and risk everything by sending the letter to her. With a sigh, he folded the paper and put it in an envelope. His heart demanded no changes be made.

8

Dear Mr. Holland,

Lost in your words I've been, unaware of time, my heart racing as I read and reread your letter. Your every word resonated in me. "... the most beautiful flower in the world, aglow with every color imaginable ..." Sir, those words touched me. I thank you so. As other writers have done to you, so too have you done to me, leaving me in awe. I will cherish your letter, always.

It stunned me when you said that darkness brings gifts; your assertion initially seemed absurd and untrue. Yet, with Keenan as your chief exhibit, your case for there being gifts is undeniable. This was a revelation to me; I now admit that I have been mono-dimensional in my thinking about my heartache. Though the idea of it being a teacher of beneficial life lessons remains disconcerting, I will do my best to answer your question, free of cynicism. Forgive me if my words are not polished; I feel like I'm entering a new territory with no map to guide me.

What gifts did my failed relationship bring to me?

The gift of courage: I am far stronger than I ever imagined.

The gift of knowledge: sad endings can promote fresh beginnings.

The gift of choice: I can choose how something will affect me and can view disappointments as learning opportunities.

The gift of forgiveness: how forgiving others can free my spirit.

The gift of appreciation: how my grandparents loved me in my darkest of times.

The gift of wisdom: how infatuation is so very different than love.

The gift of awareness: how emotional pain cannot be diminished by withdrawing from life.

The gift to discern: the man I wanted desperately had no hope of making me happy.

The gift of mindfulness: self-love is a prerequisite for truly being able to love another person.

The gift of truth: relationships can't supplant a self-love deficit.

The gift of deeds: true love is measured in countless kindnesses to each other and not in empty words.

The gift of gratefulness: there is much beauty in the world if I am open to receiving it.

The gift of heartbreak: my ability to feel deeply lets me know how alive I am.

The gift of realization: sometimes, it's better to let go and move on.

The gift of discovery: learning I am more powerful than all the darkness I've faced.

There you have it, Mr. Holland. Seeing the other facets of heartache is, for me, a revelation. Thank you for the gift of your vision. I will do my best to absorb your words and put them to good use to repair my heart.

On another note, though grateful for our correspondence and how you have enriched my thinking, I note, with dismay, you apparently wanting more than friendship. Your kind words touched me, more than you will ever know, yet also set off alarms within me sounding danger. Please, sir, do not take lightly my resolve to lead an unencumbered life. Rest assured you will not sway my heart toward any form of courtship; if that is your aim, disappointment is sure to visit you. If no possibility of a romantic relationship troubles you, then ending our correspondence is the proper thing to do. I will understand and wish you well. Should you wish to continue our writing endeavors, I would be willing to drop the quotes and questions for us to respond to in favor of a more free-flowing format. However, regarding the specifics of what happened to my heart, sir, it is a very private matter and not subject to disclosure.

A day has passed since I wrote the above words. The callousness of the last paragraph troubles me, for I am so very grateful for your letters. Mr. Holland, I say this with tears in my eyes—had we met earlier, in the age of my innocence, I would have loved you with an extraordinary fierceness. But as you said in a quote to me in one of your previous letters, do not look for my heart any more, the beasts have eaten it. More than you could ever know, I so wish I had met you earlier. Now, there are only the tattered remains of the person I once was. You deserve much more than what I could offer you. I hope you understand.

Blessings to you, Mr. Holland

9

IT TOOK THREE days for Jake to respond to Claire's letter. In his head, he constructed several responses and scrapped them all. The right words weren't coming. On the third night, he dreamed of making love to her. The taste of her lips, the scent of her skin … it seemed so real, as if she were right there, next to him. He awoke, breathless, and lay in his bed for a while. His heart was still pounding when a wave of anger swept through him. The words he needed to say came to him, and they weren't tender. He went to his desk and began writing.

Dear Miss Lofton,

Do you really think, after all I have been through, that I would want an innocent babe, naïve to the ways of the world, someone who put a guy in charge of her self-esteem because she was incapable of loving herself, someone unable to fathom the difference between true love and infatuation? Is that what you think I'd find attractive? If so, forgive me, but you are lost, utterly lost.

I want, I desire, a woman whose mettle has been tested; the naïve innocent waif you regard as desirable, to me, would be boring, have no sense of self, and surely would bolt when even the smallest of storm clouds appeared on the horizon. The truth is, in your "age of innocence," you had no idea what love was. Now, you do. If the present-day you gave me your heart and told me you genuinely loved me, I would know you would covet what we have, and our love would be given to each other with a mutual "extraordinary fierceness." We both need this kind of love.

It astonishes me how you cannot see your own inner beauty and your huge capacity to love—astonishes me. Your statement of being undesirable is nonsense. Wake up, Claire! Spirits, in the form of pain, often come to us with guiding lights that burn. Your hermit existence cannot dim these lights, and when you accept the lessons illuminated by them, you, the "tattered" you, will be able to love someone so much more than you ever could have before. Eartha Kitt said, "It's all about falling in love with yourself and sharing that love with someone who appreciates you, rather than looking for love to compensate for a self-love deficit."

Until you figure this out and accept it wholeheartedly as truth, then count me out in regard to wanting your heart. If the day comes when you are ready to say, "Jake, I stand before you as a confident, life-tested woman, who, having walked through fire, has learned my lessons and am now capable of loving you," then I will say in reply, "Claire, welcome home, welcome to my heart." Until then, only friendship is agreeable to me.

Forgive the harshness of my words, but true friendship at times demands bluntness, even if it means losing everything. You are an extraordinary woman, someone I could love with all my heart, someone I could thank God for every day. I see you, Claire. I see you. But until you open your eyes and see yourself, I will revert to calling you "Miss Lofton" and cultivate nothing more than a simple friendship with you. I love the wisdom of Pema Chödrön: "Nothing ever goes away until it has taught us what we need to know." You will never find peace until you learn the lessons taught by the teacher called Pain. When you do, oh, my, you will be something. I will wait for you, Miss Lofton; such is my confidence about what we could one day have.

I wish I could explain how powerful my feelings are for you, how I see so clearly who you are, and how appealing I find you, but you hardly know me, and you rightly are guarded about letting me in. How I wish you could see the purity of my soul. I am a good person. Stay with me. Stay in this friendship. You will see my goodness one day. Of that, I am sure.

Regarding you awakening and blossoming, I am less confident. Ask yourself this: What is the payoff for being "poor little Claire" and living like a hermit? Saving your heart from potential hurt? Okay, fine, I get it. But I ask you to ponder this: Imagine us having a beautiful life together—our hearts, bodies, and spirits blissfully entwined. Imagine me touching your cheek each morning when we wake, kissing you softly, looking into your eyes, and you saying, "I love you, Jake" with such tenderness that there is no doubt, for me, that yours is the most beautiful voice in the world. Imagine years of happiness and joy together, our amazing connection radiating pure love, our home filled with children, and, one day, grandchildren. How does remaining a hermit compare to this?

The sad truth is that you've reduced your life to a numb and dull existence, free of risk and devoid of feeling. If indeed "Birds born in a cage think flying is an illness," as Alejandro Jodorowsky said, then I have to think of you in a cage of your own making, looking out at a relationship with me as an illness. It's not, Claire. It's not. I can only hope that the bird will discover the joy of flying one day, and you will discover the joy of an authentic love. Someone scribbled this on a wall at a homeless shelter where Keenan and I volunteer serving meals. I see it in my mind and can't help but think of you: "Broken crayons still color." The kind soul within you during your "age of innocence" is still there. I see it, and it is beautiful.

The curious paradox of pain is that it often is a bridge to good. The person who "dumped" you did you a great service. The lesson from him is you have to change; you have to love and celebrate yourself. It's time to become who you are. You are not a hermit. You are a remarkable woman, beautiful, inside and out, and most worthy of love. Within your grasp is a poetic love with me, but, as Jack Canfield said: "Everything you want is on the other side of fear."

I care for you, Miss Lofton. Quite deeply. Jake

10

MADDY WAVED A letter as Claire entered the house. "Guess what came in today's mail?" Claire's eyes lit up, and a smile came to her face. She forgot about being exhausted from the tough week at school, which included parent-teacher conferences.

"Do you mind if I read it in my room?"

"Go be with your man," she said with a mischievous wink.

Maddy's playful banter didn't draw the usual denial from Claire. "I'll be down in a few minutes to help with dinner." She bounded upstairs with Bluebell barking at her heels and opened the letter, her heart pounding in anticipation of his praise for rising to the challenge of his *"What gifts did my failed relationship bring to me?"* question.

The kind words didn't materialize. She gasped multiple times while reading, and by the last paragraph, she found it hard to breathe. Dumbfounded by his bluntness, she put the letter down and stared into space. *"My God. Oh my God ..."*

A half-hour later, Maddy came up. "How long does it take to read a—" She saw Claire's tears. "What happened?"

Silence.

"Claire?"

She didn't answer and just stared at Maddy with troubled eyes.

"Did he say something to hurt you?"

More silence.

"Please say something. Did he say something to hurt you?"

Claire shook her head.

"May I read what he wrote?"

"No." Her voice trembled. "He said personal things I needed to hear."

"Are you okay?"

"Could you leave me alone? I need to be alone."

Maddy looked worried. "Are you sure it's wise?"

"Please, Maddy, let me be for a while."

Her grandmother hesitantly nodded and left, leaving the bedroom door partly open.

Bluebell put her head on Claire's leg and gazed into her eyes. She patted her. "Oh, Bluebell, Mr. Holland is a force to be reckoned with."

She moved to her bed and hugged her furry companion, who joined her. Bluebell licked her cheek, offering empathy and love. An hour later, still reeling from his words, Claire whispered to her confidant. "He's right about everything, girl." She fell asleep holding Bluebell and didn't notice Maddy checking on her several times.

In the morning, Claire woke with the sun, went to her desk, and reread his letter. It took two hours for her to write a reply.

Dear Mr. Holland,

With each of your letters, I find the need to read them repeatedly, for they are rich in content and must be savored and pondered. At times, I see your playful side, your dry wit and humor, and I love it. Whenever I now do my wash, I look at my unmentionables and picture them "swimming with the sharks" and smile, thinking, no way would they survive at Jake's house. At other times, you erupt in bluntness, and I wince at the pointedness of your words. Such was your last letter to me. You pulled no punches, yet the dismal truth is everything you said was merited. You shake my soul, Mr. Holland, through and through. Please be patient with me. Not a minute goes by without your words echoing in my thoughts. You were right, entirely, about how clueless I was in my innocent age. After reading your letter, it seems almost laughable how I thought I would be more desirable as a naïve girl. Your insights and your idea of love between us leave me breathless.

Sir, I've been on the precipice for so long, staring downward, without hope, ready to leap, and you have pulled me back from the edge. You were right when you said I've reduced my life to a numb and dull existence, free of risk and devoid of feeling. I want so much to live again, to feel, to take those crayons and begin coloring again. I could easily picture you and Keenan in what I draw. To do so will require much work on my part, beginning with learning to love myself.

The roots of my self-love deficiency go back to my childhood when I was discarded as unlovable by my parents. Not even the love of my grandparents could heal those wounds. Being socially inept growing up seemed to validate my parents' rejection of me. In college, the men I met continued this cycle of rejection. I have no doubt that once you get to know me, you too will tire of me. This is what I have to overcome. I now see the most important relationship I will ever have is the one with me. Until I am able to look in the mirror and say, "Claire Lofton, I love you," then you are right to seek only a friendship with me. But, I want to assure you I finally "get it," and you were right about nothing to be gained by being "poor little Claire." The turbulent times of my past don't have to cloud my future.

It's hard for me to say this, but I've been lazy, which is so unlike me, in regard to dealing with my past. It was easier to hide rather than to learn the lessons the "guiding lights" have been trying to teach me. Your letter unambiguously spelled out what I need to do to claim my place in life, and now, because of you, I am ready to embrace the wisdom that lives in my pain.

Mr. Holland, your letter was stunning, utterly stunning, in so many ways. I have never received anything so beautiful in my life, and I thank you. In an earlier letter, you said, "You are a treasure, and my intent is to show you why." Sir, you are, with superb skill, accomplishing this lofty objective.

Please be patient with me, dear friend. Claire Lofton

P.S. Thanksgiving is soon upon us. Grandpa never favored turkey, so we always had prime rib. Even after his passing, the tradition continues as our way of honoring him. As a child, I loved this holiday more than all the others, and I still do, I think, because in our family, we focused on being grateful for having each other, and for me, my grandparents' love meant everything. In my thoughts, I've imagined you and Keenan at our table, and the idea of us all being together is lovely. Please don't construe my musing as an invitation, though perhaps, one day, it will be. For Christmas, would you be open to exchanging a few modest gifts? If it's too personal, I will understand.

P.P.S. You remind me of my grandmother when you are blunt. It has a familiar ring to it. In many ways, you two are like peas in a pod.

A sense of peace filled her as she wrote the letter. After showering, she went downstairs, looking happy. With a big smile, she kissed Maddy's cheek, saying she was starved and would be back in a minute after mailing a letter to Jake. As Claire ran out of the house playing with Bluebell, Maddy was baffled. She was expecting a distraught granddaughter in desperate need of comforting, yet Claire looked more radiant and full of joy than she had in years. Whatever Jake Holland said had profoundly affected her. It brought a smile to Maddy's face.

11

A FLURRY OF letters passed between Jake and Claire in the days leading up to Christmas. Although they still addressed each other by their surnames, this formality did little to mask the closeness developing between them. Their words to each other came in the form of beautifully crafted sentences, rich in content, teeming with metaphors and subtle humor. To others, their words would appear innocent and unassuming, but Jake and Claire had an uncanny ability to use words to sound out the other's depths; it was like an exquisite dance whose steps only they knew.

On Christmas day, Keenan woke his father. "Let's open gifts now, Papa!"

Jake looked at the clock. "Keenan, it's six in the morning. You're torturing me; you know that, right?"

"Papa, you'll like what I got you! C'mon, you can take a nap later."

"Argh. If I get up now, I'll hold you to letting me nap later. Deal?"

"Deal!" He grabbed his father's bathrobe. "You can wear this."

"Okay, okay," he laughed. "At least let me brush my teeth."

When Jake got to the living room, Keenan had already turned on the Christmas tree lights. The spruce tree they had cut the week before looked handsome, with an abundance of homemade decorations and popcorn garlands they had spent two days making. Only half the popcorn went to the tree—they smothered the rest with butter and wolfed it down. A few small gifts lay at the base of the tree. Jake was determined the meaning of Christmas wouldn't be hijacked by extravagant gifts, and to emphasize this, he and Keenan volunteered to serve meals to indigent people at the local food shelter.

"Here are the two gifts I got for you," said Keenan, beaming. One was cylindrically shaped, and the other had a rectangular shape. Both were haphazardly wrapped with newspaper comic-strip paper.

"Don't you want to open your gifts first, Keenan?"

"I can wait."

"Okay." Jake took the cylinder and shook it. "Hmm. I wonder what this could be?"

Keenan hopped up and down, looking as if he were about to explode. "Open it!"

With a smile, Jake peeled off the wrap. "Pringles! Memphis BBQ is my favorite flavor. How did you know?"

"Because you always buy them," Keenan said with a big grin.

"This gift deserves a huge hug. Come here."

After the hug, Keenan gave him his next gift. "I know you'll like this one, too."

Jake opened it and let out a whoop. "Junior Mints! May I have a few before breakfast?"

"Sure. You can have some Pringles, too!"

Jake laughed. "I'll save those for lunch. You got two of my favorites. Thank you." He shook a few mints out of the box for Keenan and downed several himself. "Are you ready to open my gift to you?"

Keenan nodded eagerly and grabbed the box. He tore off the comic-strip paper and looked in. Nothing but a tiny note was inside. He grabbed it and read the message aloud: *"Go to the garage to see your gift."* His eyes went wide, and he dashed off. Jake followed with a big grin.

"Skis and boots! You got me new skis, Papa!"

"You've outgrown your old gear. I found the skis on Craigslist, and they're practically new. You'll love them; they're waxless and have hands-free bindings. I bought the boots at REI, so we can take them back if they don't fit."

"Can we go skiing today?"

Jake shook his head. "Remember, we're volunteering at Bean's Café. We can go tomorrow."

"Okay. Thanks for these cool gifts, Papa."

"You're welcome. Let's see what Claire got us. They're the fancy-wrapped gifts."

"Okay!" He raced back to the tree.

"Here, Papa, this one's for you."

Jake took the small package from him and opened it. She got him a book. He gasped when he read the title, which was in German: *Briefe an einen jungen Dichter.*

"Letters to a Young Poet," said Keenan, translating the title. "You already have that book."

Jake ignored him for a moment and read a note from her on the title page:

Dear Mr. Holland,
I first read this book as a teenager, and it remains, for me, magical.
Merry Christmas,
Claire Lofton

He closed the book and looked at Keenan. "I know, but I don't have it in German." His voice choked up as he spoke. "The author, Rainer Maria Rilke, originally wrote it in German."

"What's it about?"

"Rilke was a famous German poet when a young, aspiring poet wrote to him, asking for advice on poems he had written. They became friends and wrote to each other for several years. This book is a collection of Rilke's letters to him, and they offer wonderful insights about life." He struggled to get the words past the lump in his throat.

"What's wrong, Papa? Don't you like her gift?"

"I like it very much. Claire found the perfect gift for me." He gestured to the other gifts from her. "Go ahead and open her gift to you."

Shaking it didn't reveal any clues. Keenan unwrapped it. "Look, she got me a book in German, too! *Die Schatzinsel.'* What's it about?"

"Treasure Island, as it's called in English, is about a young boy who finds a treasure map, and when he sets sail in search of the fortune, he discovers he boarded a pirate ship captained by Long

John Silver, and the pirates also want to get the treasure. I know you'll love it."

"We can read it at night when I go to bed, okay?"

"That's a good idea. Let's open Claire's last gift, the one for both of us."

Keenan tore off the wrap and found a tin box. He opened it and read the note on top. *"Dear Holland boys: These are our famous iced apple cookies made with apples from our orchard. Maddy and I hope you like them. Merry Christmas! Claire"* Keenan looked at his father with sparkling eyes. "Can we try them?"

"Oh, yeah!" Jake took a bite. "Mmm, these are delicious. What do you think?"

"They're good!"

"After breakfast, let's write them a 'thank you' letter." He hugged his son again. "Merry Christmas."

"Merry Christmas, Papa."

For the rest of the day, they speculated about how Claire found books written in German.

In Leavenworth, Claire and Maddy had a Christmas-day breakfast of French toast topped with strawberries and blueberries. After taking Bluebell out, Claire returned, happy and red-cheeked from the mid-20s cold. "Maddy, do you want to open our gifts?"

"Sure. Let's start with the ones from Jake."

Claire picked up a box and handed it to her. "Here's his gift to you. It's heavy."

Maddy opened it and smiled. "It's a package of ground coffee." She read the label. *"Red Goat, an organic coffee made by Kaladi Brothers Coffee, Alaska's premier coffee roaster.* Interesting. Do you mind if we try some now?"

"Not at all. It'll help me warm up."

Maddy filled a couple of mugs with the steaming brew and took a tentative sip. "I love this. Way to go, Jake Holland! By the way, tell your man I caught his subliminal inference of giving me something called Red Goat."

"With his dry sense of humor, you might be right." She took a sip. "Mmm … this *is* good."

"I like his playfulness," said Maddy. "Let's open his other gifts."

"Here's the one for both of us," Claire said with a smile. She handed it to Maddy, who eagerly opened it.

"A gift box of jellies and jams made from Alaska wild berries," said Maddy with a smile. "I'm sure we'll love them."

The last of his gifts was for Claire. She looked at Maddy. "Well, here goes."

It was a book. Claire gasped when she saw it.

"What's wrong?"

She showed it to Maddy. "I sent him the same book: *Letters to a Young Poet.*" She opened the cover and read what Jake had written.

> *Dear Miss Lofton,*
> *I first read this book at the tender age of twelve.*
> *It remains one of the most profound books I have ever read.*
> *Merry Christmas*
> *I love you, Claire*
> *Jake Holland*

In tears, she closed the book, her heart pounding.

"Well, what did he say?"

"He wished me a merry Christmas." Claire didn't mention the bombshell words *"I love you,"* which caused the tears.

"You two are wired the same, no doubt about it."

"Maddy, don't even start. He's just a friend." She hoped her pounding heart wouldn't betray her words.

"Okay, okay. Let's open the rest of the gifts. Here's what I got for you."

Claire removed the wrap and opened the small box. "Maddy, this is beautiful."

"I thought you could use a fine pen with all the writing you've been doing lately. Cross pens are the best."

She put the gold-colored pen in her hand as if she were writing. "I like the weight and feel of it in my hand." She hugged Maddy. "It's perfect."

Maddy nodded. "I'm glad you like it. Here's my other gift to you, something I think you'll make good use of."

"Wow, it's heavy." Claire opened it and smiled. "Thanks, Maddy."

"I figured a fine pen needs fine stationery."

Claire smiled. "Now, something from you will be in all my letters. I'll try my new pen tonight." She kissed Maddy's cheek. "I love you."

"Yeah, yeah. I'm dying to see what you got me."

Claire smiled. "I think you'll be pleased."

"It better not say 'Red Goat' or anything else inferring something disparaging about my radiant personality."

"Fear not, Maddy. I got you something to wear."

That evening, after saying goodnight to Maddy, who was proudly wearing her new sweater, Claire went to her room with Bluebell. She sat at her desk and began writing to Jake using her new pen and stationery.

Dear Mr. Holland,

I wonder who gasped the loudest when we opened our gifts to each other. I am at a loss for words, sir, on many fronts. And troubled, too.

I continually marvel at your ability to see my soul. It seems inconceivable how you could know me so well after our brief encounter at the orchard. I don't know what to make of you, yet, somehow, my feelings for you are palpable, just as you say yours are for me. Beyond the issues of my heart being able to love again, let's temper any thoughts of romance with reality. For example, you described your house as having "a comfortable, lived-in look." In contrast, I take pride in having a clean home. By the way, Bluebell and I maintain an unsteady truce between us regarding standards of cleanliness. And, for your information, you tossing one of my dainty items into the sea of sharks would be more egregious than Bluebell eating one of my purses. I wonder how many unsteady truces we would have in the reality of living together. I say this not because I'm thinking of a romance with you; rather, it points to my previous letter to you with the quote: *"There's a difference between really loving someone and loving the idea of them."*

Sir, regarding what you wrote in the book, it drew a second gasp from me. While I bow to your impressive empathic abilities and was momentarily swayed by what you wrote, I am convinced your fertile imagination has concocted an idea of who I am, and reality is likely far, far different, and not in an agreeable way. Keep it real, Mr. Holland, is all I ask. Please don't say you love me when you barely know me. It's reckless, and I am far less lovable than you think. Your words brought joy to me, but then a surge of fear. As friends, our relationship could go on indefinitely; as lovers, I see you quickly tiring of me and moving on. I doubt you've given a single thought to our even being compatible. Though I am trying to imagine the idea of being lovable, it remains an elusive concept. I am capable only of friendship, nothing more, and ask that you honor this.

Many thoughts are swirling within me regarding you. I can sum it up best with the quote in your first letter to me by Emily Dickinson: *"I felt it shelter to speak to you."* I find your words to be shelter. The true gift you have given me is your letters. I will always treasure them. This quote, from Susan Colasanti, captures how I feel about you: *"One of the most amazing things that can happen is finding someone who sees everything you are and won't let you be anything less. They see the potential of you. They see endless possibilities. And through their eyes, you start to see yourself the same way as someone who matters."*

Mr. Holland, you give me hope for a brighter tomorrow, and I am beginning to see possibilities that would've been inconceivable before knowing you. For these reasons, you have made this Christmas and the months preceding it very special to me. I thank you. Please be patient with me.

Your friend, Claire Lofton

P.S. Yesterday, I finished rereading one of your letters, the *"blunt"* letter. I cannot get through it without my heart pounding. Mr. Holland, I wonder what you would expect in a relationship, what qualities you would hope your ideal partner would have. Again, I ask this not for any interest in us as a couple, but rather as a general question which I'm sure you have pondered. I thank you for accepting nothing more than a friendship between us. I highly value what we have.

P.S.S. It's my turn to say something reckless: Yours is not the only fertile imagination.

The next morning, a storm swept in from the Pacific. Though Leavenworth is on the lee (dry) side of the Cascades, not even these mighty mountains could ring the moisture out of this storm. The aroma of coffee and bacon frying in the skillet woke Claire. She went downstairs in her bathrobe.

"Good morning, Maddy. Waking to the smell of bacon and coffee sure beats being jarred awake by an alarm clock."

"Look outside, and you might retract your 'good morning' statement."

Claire went to the kitchen window. "Wow, it sure is coming down. Looks like eight inches already."

"More's on the way. I guess we'll have to cancel our Saturday trip to town."

"I suppose. After breakfast, I'll start shoveling."

"How do you want your eggs?"

"With a day like today, I'll take mine sunny side up."

After breakfast, Claire went to work shoveling the snow off the front porch. Maddy let Bluebell out, and the frisky hound went nuts frolicking in the snow. Claire laughed at her antics as she labored away on the fluffy powder. A half-hour later, she came in, her cheeks beet-red. "Whew, it's cold out. I sure burned off a few calories. I'll warm up and go back out a bit later."

Maddy handed her a cup of coffee and frowned. "The weatherman just said we could get another foot overnight."

Claire's eyes widened. "We could be housebound for a couple of days. On the bright side, it'll be fun spending the day around a nice fire."

Maddy nodded. "I'll call Ed and tell him to wait on plowing the driveway. If he plows today, the old coot will charge us again for doing it tomorrow." Bluebell barked to be let in. She was coated with snow from head to toe.

"Bluebell, don't even think of shak—"

Maddy's plea was too late—the abominable snow-dog shook her body back and forth briskly, sending white debris flying. She looked so happy to be inside and free of snow that both of them couldn't help but laugh.

"I'll go get some towels to wipe her off if you hold her," said Claire. Maddy grabbed the furry tornado, an effort that proved to be futile. Mrs. Kerfuffle noted the mayhem with indifference from her perch on the mantle. The cat's expression could be summed up in one word: *Dogs*.

Once things calmed down and they mopped up the melted snow, Maddy looked mischievously at her granddaughter. "Since we're housebound, this would be a good time to talk about him."

Claire rolled her eyes.

"I know you like him. Is it becoming something more?"

Claire hesitated. "He … he wrote in his Christmas gift book that he loves me." Her face flushed at the disclosure.

"And you, how do you feel about him?"

She shrugged her shoulders.

"Claire, it's okay to say you have feelings for him."

"I don't want to get hurt again, Maddy. I feel myself falling for him, and it terrifies me."

Maddy nodded but didn't say anything. Her silence drew more out of Claire.

"I mean, we get along fine as pen pals, but I know that once he gets to know me in person, he'll be disappointed …" A tear rolled down her cheek. "Every guy I've ever been with moves on."

"Is Jake like those other guys?" Maddy asked softly, already knowing the answer.

Claire shook her head. "No. None of them are even half of what I think he is. Maddy, besides you and Grandpa, no one else ever really loved me."

Maddy sighed. "You have ancient wounds, Claire. How my daughter and that man of hers treated you as a child is something I'll never forgive them for. You look at me now." She waited for Claire's eyes to meet hers. "You're the most wonderful human being I have ever known. Jake sees that plain as day. He knows what Grandpa and I know. He will never tire of you." She got up and hugged her granddaughter. "You're precious to me, and you'll be precious to him. I know it."

"You and Grandpa always made me feel special. I hope I tell you enough about how dear you are to me and how grateful I am for you and Grandpa raising me."

"You do. He and I were the lucky ones to have you in our lives. Grandpa often told me you were God's gift to us."

They spent the day enjoying each other's company, oblivious to the storm swirling outside.

12

THE FIRST DAY after Christmas vacation was taxing for both Claire and her students. Compared to how quickly the two-week recess passed, this day seemed to drag on forever. They all let out a sigh of relief when the last bell sounded. When Claire pulled into her driveway that afternoon, she honked for Maddy to let Bluebell out to play. No matter how tired she was, frolicking with Bluebell was rejuvenating. When they went inside, Maddy was putting the final touches on dinner. "Hey, pretty lady, you look happy. How was school?"

"The kids weren't very enthused about being back in class, and the same could be said of me. My thoughts have been elsewhere."

Maddy chuckled. "I'll bet your thoughts are spelled J-A-K-E."

"Well, you're wrong. I've been thinking about Keenan reading the *Treasure Island* book I gave him for Christmas."

"Wasn't it in German? He can read the language as well as speak it?"

Claire nodded. "He's a bright boy. Jake said reading and speaking German comes easily to him. He says several studies have shown how learning a second language at an early age increases a child's critical thinking skills, concept formation, creativity, and general reasoning. If I ever have children, I'd like them to learn another language, too."

"Interesting. So, am I right to think your children will be fluent in German?"

Claire smiled. "Maybe."

"Speaking of the father of your German-speaking children, another letter arrived from him. They seem to be coming rather frequently as of late." She winked to emphasize the point.

Claire rolled her eyes. "I see you've moved past planning my wedding to having me with a flock of bilingual children. He's just a friend, Maddy. I've made it quite clear to him."

"Uh-huh. Whatever you say. But don't think for a moment I don't see the expectant look in your eyes each day, wondering if there's a letter from him. And after you read one of his letters, the glow on your face speaks volumes. Back in my day, we called it love."

"It's not love. That's wishful thinking on your part."

Maddy smirked and was going to say something more but decided to let it go. Nothing would be gained from pushing the subject. "Can you contain yourself long enough to have dinner before reading the letter?"

Claire sighed. "I suppose. What are you making?"

"Lasagna with Italian sausage. After your first day back at school, I figured you could use a treat."

"It sounds yummy. I'll set the table."

After a delicious meal and doing the dishes, Claire excused herself. Upstairs, she plopped on her bed, and with a smile, opened the letter.

Dear Miss Lofton,

"Yours is not the only fertile imagination." These words from you infused me with hope, and I congratulate you on your "recklessness." Thank you for opening the door just a bit more to the concept of us. I am so very happy for the trust (and maybe something else) forming between us. As for being patient with you, my answer is yes, an easy yes. As to my concocting the idea of what I want you to be, not so much. How can I explain this ... hmmm ... this will be tough to articulate. It will probably make no sense to you, my saying I just know we're compatible, but I feel it, and this feeling is powerful. We belong together, and you will be the one I will love for the rest of my life, so my heart informs me. You're like a tender song that only I can sing. A vibrant confidence swirls within me as I say this. Claire, I just know.

All my life, I've been searching for you, and that day at your orchard, when I stood watching you, utterly mesmerized, I felt—this is the part that's so hard to describe—a certain familiarity, as if we'd known each other forever. I knew, in that moment, my search was over. I found you. Search your heart, Claire. I think you feel it, too. I think there are many things you want to say to me, tender things. I feel this. Intensely. But I know you cannot yet say these words. I know you're feeling them, though, and it's enough for me. I will leave it at that and move on.

Me, pondering a relationship and what my ideal partner would be like? Truly, I haven't given the notion a single thought. Okay, I see you rolling your eyes. You know me so well.

Last night, I wrote you a letter describing an ideal relationship, which, coincidentally, happened to be between you and me. My writing took me well into the wee hours of the morning. When I woke the next day and read what I had written, I crumpled the letter and threw it away. Had you read it, well, it would've scared you away, especially the part of you tearing off my clothes with your teeth and ravaging me mercilessly. Um ... I'm kidding. It was a tender love story. I threw it away because my heart knew the words in this letter could only be said when I'm looking into your eyes. I hope, one day, to speak the words to you. Let me just say that in this letter, our souls were so entwined that it would be a hopeless endeavor to ever get us apart. Saying anything more about what I had written would require me to step far beyond the bounds of friendship. I hope, one day, you will say, "Jake, look into my eyes, and tell me what you said in your letter." Afterward, my confidence abounds that you would say "Yes" to something requiring me to take a knee.

Yikes! I need to shift to other subjects, and fast.

Keenan and I went cross-country skiing today, trying out the new skis I got him for Christmas, and we had a blast. I packed sandwiches and a thermos of hot chocolate, and we skied at Kincaid Park, a 1500-acre forested oasis in Anchorage that borders Cook Inlet. The morning sun brilliantly lit the Alaska Range, and it was spectacular. We nearly ran into a moose when we went barreling down a hill with a blind curve, but fortunately, she took no exception to our trespass. There's something about being outdoors on a crisp winter day that elevates my spirits. I wish you could've been with us.

I think about you often, Miss Lofton. I think, "Oh, I'll bet Claire would like this," or I wonder if you'd like my crockpot-made blueberry chipotle barbeque ribs (yes, there is a recipe for it). Now when Keenan and I cram our washer with a week's worth of clothes, I again smile, imagining you being nearly apoplectic should a delicate item of yours find its way into our manly mix. I imagine you in bed with Keenan and me on Saturday mornings, being part of our lively conversations, the three of us laughing at one of his jokes or tall tales. The jokes he tells are really funny; he's quite good at delivering the punch line. Sometimes my sides ache from laughing.

On Sundays, Keenan reads me the newspaper comics and acts out each of the characters. It's hilarious. Then there are the quiet times at home, at night, when I'm alone with my thoughts. I imagine us together, making love, sweet love. Sigh. I'm sorry … here I go again, straying into forbidden territory. Forgive me. Just know you're in my thoughts, and you bring comfort to my days. For that, I am most grateful.

In my effort to know you better, I've thought of some questions for you. You're welcome to do the same with me.

— How do you express love to those whom you hold dear? (mental image: ancient Rome, you feeding me grapes while fanning me)
— What is the most/least important thing in your life?
— What is your biggest fear? (aside from further damage to your heart)
— Compose a six-word story about your life (example: Shortly after my divorce, I read this from an unknown author, and it touches me to this day: "I felt too much, he didn't.")
— What would you do without electricity for three days?
— Do you believe long-distance relationships can work?
— Do you believe in God? (I do, although I'm not enamored with organized religion)
— Are you able to forgive and forget? (example: my accidentally washing your delicates)
— Name three of the most beautiful places you've been (I hope you won't say Disneyland)
— How many children do you want to have? (caution: a two-digit number will cause me to gasp)
— Whom do you admire? (Ah, shucks, I mean, besides me)
— What are your hobbies or things you love doing? (I hope writing to me is at the top of your list)
— What is your favorite cuisine/restaurant? (Dear God, please don't let her say anything featuring a chicken nugget)

— What is your favorite book/movie? (My all-time favorite movie is "Leaving Normal." It's a one-percenter flick. I hope one day we'll watch it together)
— What is your favorite song? (Mine is "Hallelujah" by Jeff Buckley; hear it on YouTube)
— What are some important things you desire in a relationship? (I'm winking at one possible answer)
— Are you a morning or a night person? (I mean, when you're not on caffeine)
— What is your favorite day, and why? (Hint for mine: TGIF)
— What are your pet peeves? (Excluding, of course, my desire for wanting more than a friendship with you)

There are so many things I want to learn about you. It's exciting! I'll close by saying you warm my heart, Miss Lofton. Oh! Keenan says hello and wants you to know that Gala apples originated in New Zealand. Your saying there are more than 7500 apple varieties in the world aroused his curiosity, and he's been surfing the net, looking up all things apple. He wants to plant an apple tree in our backyard and says adding a little antifreeze to the irrigation water will allow it to survive our cold winters. Yes, he's right up there with Isaac Newton.

Good day to you, Miss Lofton

Claire put the letter down with a smile. A few moments later, she picked it up and reread his first paragraph. *You're like a tender song that only I can sing.* A warm feeling flowed through her body. Without realizing it, her heart was pounding. "I love you, too, Jake Holland," she whispered.

She practically floated downstairs and found Maddy on the couch, knitting, with Bluebell dozing at her feet. Maddy took in her obvious glow and smiled. "I take it you liked what he had to say."

"I did. I like him a lot, Maddy."

She rolled her eyes. "I think you moved way past liking him. If you ask me, it's full-blown love."

"I love his words, but they don't guarantee we'll love each other in person." She changed the subject. "How about watching a movie? I'd be happy to make buttered popcorn."

Maddy smiled and nodded. "Do you have any movie in mind?"

"How about *Singin' in the Rain?*" she asked with sparkling eyes.

"Good choice. I love Gene Kelly and Donald O'Connor."

After spending the evening with Maddy, Claire crawled into bed and read Jake's letter over and over until her eyes were too heavy to continue. Snug under her down comforter, she fell asleep, fondly thinking of the man she loved.

The good feelings did not survive the night.

In the morning, in tears, she wrote her last letter to him.

Mr. Holland,

What you said in your letter was riveting. After I read it, I imagined you gazing into my eyes, speaking the words in the letter you crumpled. Contemplating what those words might be triggered pulse-pounding excitement within me. Under my covers, I hugged my body pillow, pretending it was you. Had you been here, I would've said yes to anything you asked of me. Such was my euphoria. I fell asleep with thoughts of you dancing in my head ...

I wrote the above paragraph for reasons I will state later. Sadly, the jubilation I felt did not last long. I woke from my sleep gasping, with fear ripping through me so intensely that I could hardly breathe. I dreamed you told me it was all a joke, that everything you had written was just an exercise in wordplay to see how quickly you could sway an innocent lady's heart. With a revolting laugh, you boasted of how you delighted in toying with me. I wanted to die right then and there. It's morning now, and I am still trembling. All I can think about is a quote from John Banville: "The past beats inside me like a second heart," and I feel so foolish for falling for your charms.

I warned you, sir, multiple times, about having nothing to offer in matters related to the heart, yet you have continually disregarded my requests, and with your last letter, glaringly so. I have no other choice than to end whatever it was we had. You are lost either in evilness or in the fantasy of what you want me to be rather than who I am. If it is the latter, the words of Mahmoud Darwish so describe the folly of your thinking: "Maybe the moon is beautiful only because it is far."

With my dream, I have come to my senses regarding you. I'm sorry, but no sane person could feel the way you do after meeting someone for less than twenty minutes. It isn't possible. Someone once wrote this, which accurately describes me: *"My problem is that I fall in love with words, rather than actions. I fall in love with ideas and thoughts, instead of reality. And it will be the death of me."*

I don't know why you would toy with me. I am a simple country girl; I have no agenda, no desire whatsoever to hurt people, so I cannot fathom why you want to hurt me. Tears are pouring from me now, Mr. Holland. If you intended to hurt me, you are quite skilled at your sordid craft. Consider the first paragraph of this letter to be your "trophy" for a successful hunt. Show it proudly to those who might be involved in your evil play.

Should your intentions be honorable, you simply cannot understand how damaged I am and how terrified I am of injuring my heart further. You are much stronger than I, much more willing to take chances. I live in a sheltered world, and it is all I want. You drastically overestimated my ability to mend my heart and love again, and all your words, though wonderful, are just words. I know only too well how words, spoken with apparent sincerity, often come to nothing.

Mr. Holland, I do not ever want to hear from you again. I know there is something wrong with you, be it evil or mental illness. I "see" you, as you're so fond of saying, and Charles Baudelaire captures well how I feel about you: "The devil's finest trick is to persuade you that he does not exist."

Please do not write to me anymore. I state with conviction that any letter from you will be summarily torn into pieces. Shame on you for your evilness, if that is what your play has been; if you are, indeed, legitimate, which I highly doubt, then your quest for my affections has failed. There is no room in my heart for you. Goodbye forever, Mr. Holland.

Claire Lofton

In tears, she ran past Maddy, who was in the living room, and raced out the front door to mail her letter to Jake. She returned a minute later and charged back upstairs, locking her bedroom door behind her.

Twenty minutes later, Maddy knocked on her door. "Claire, you're going to be late for school." There was no response. "Claire, are you okay?"

"Tell them I'm not coming in today."

"Okay. Why?"

"Just tell them, Maddy!" she cried. "Make up something."

Maddy went downstairs, called the school, and told them Claire had a nasty stomach bug, probably from eating leftovers, and wouldn't be in today."

She went back upstairs and listened at Claire's door. Claire was crying. "Claire, open the door." Maddy rattled the doorknob. "I mean it. Open the door."

Claire opened the door, her eyes puffy and bloodshot. "Please leave me alone."

"I will not. You're going to tell me what happened."

"I ended it with Jake, Maddy. He's not who we thought he was."

"What happened?"

Silence.

"Claire, what happened?"

More silence.

"You've got to talk to me, sweet girl. What happened?"

Claire spoke, her voice shaky and wobbling. "He told me it was all a joke, and everything he had written was a sham. He said he was toying with me for his amusement. He laughed as he said it, enjoying his evil game."

"I didn't hear the phone ring. Did you call him on your cell phone?"

"No."

"Did you email him?"

"No."

"Claire, I'm an old woman, so you're going to have to spell things out. If you didn't call or email him, how could he have said those things to you?"

Silence.

"Claire, talk to me."

"He said it to me in a dream."

Maddy's eyes went wide. *"He said it to you in a dream?"*

"Yes."

"Claire, for God's sake, you can't condemn him over a dream."

She gripped Maddy's hand. "It was so real, so vivid. Jake Holland is not a nice man. He played me for a fool. I know it."

"I'm sorry, but you're wrong. Jake is an honorable man."

"How do you know that? He was here for less than an hour. He was with me for less than twenty minutes. No one could feel that way about another person after such a short time. He's been playing me. Maybe he wants our land."

"That's nonsense. Claire, it's nonsense. It was just a bad dream."

"No, Maddy, it was real. He laughed at me, mocking me. Jake Holland is a detestable man. He used his intellect to seduce me. How sick is that?" She started crying again. "I wish I were dead."

"Don't say that. Oh God, Claire, don't say that."

"It's my fault. I trust men and then get my heart broken. I knew this would happen. See what pushing me into a relationship caused—I'm in agony again."

"It'll be okay."

"No, it won't. Not this time. Just leave me alone, Maddy. Leave me alone."

Two days passed with Claire holed up in her room. Maddy brought food to her, but she didn't eat. Her depression was back. Pacing outside the closed door, Maddy debated about taking her to the hospital, thinking professional help might be needed to prevent her from descending into a full-blown depression. She fought the urge to call Jake and tell him what had happened.

On the morning of the third day, Claire got up early, dressed, and went downstairs. "I'm going to school today," she said to Maddy, who was reading the newspaper at the kitchen table.

Maddy's eyebrows shot up in surprise. "Are you sure that's a good idea?"

"Something occurred to me when I woke this morning. I've survived the worst that life has thrown at me, the bleakest of days and the darkest of nights, and it didn't end me. Colin didn't end me, and Jake Holland won't end me either. I'm stronger than both of them, and I don't need a man to give me the love I need. I can love myself now. Jake Holland will not get the pleasure of seeing me crumble as Colin did. That is *never* going to happen again." It dawned on her that she was parroting many of Jake's words, which momentarily stunned her. She smiled with a realization: The words he used to toy with her only strengthened her.

"Claire, I don't think Jake is a bad person. He seemed so nice."

Claire raced upstairs and returned with her hands full of papers. "Okay, Maddy, here are all his letters, plus copies of what I sent to him. Read them, read every one, and you'll see I'm not losing my mind. You'll see all his lies and manipulations."

"Are you sure you want me to read them?"

"Yes." She got a blueberry muffin from the fridge. "I'm going to school. See you this afternoon." She left without waiting for Maddy's goodbye or acknowledging Bluebell.

Later that day, Claire came home looking sad and haggard. Bluebell did her best to welcome her home, but her affection was ignored.

Maddy was sitting at the kitchen table, looking frustrated as she tried to untangle a jumbled ball of twine. On the other side of the table were the letters. She looked at Claire and offered a sympathetic smile. "Did your day go okay?"

Claire shrugged a shoulder. "I'm glad it's Friday. Maddy, I'm going to skip dinner and take a bath instead."

"Okay. If you get hungry later, there's a chicken salad wrap for you in the fridge."

"Thanks." She glanced at the letters. "Well, did you read them?"

Maddy nodded. "When you want to talk about them, let me know."

Claire took a seat across from her. "Now's fine. So, did you see what a con man he is?"

Maddy reached over and took her hand. "Claire, I've never seen anything as beautiful as these letters. There's so much love between you two. My God, you need to reread them. He's done nothing but pour his heart out to you. He desperately wants to be your husband and the father of your children. He'll adore you for the rest of your days. If you can't trust yourself on that, trust me."

"You're wrong, Maddy. You're blind to his evilness because you want me married off before you're gone." Looking at her grandmother shaking her head, disagreeing, caused her to erupt. "We don't *know* him!" the usually soft-spoken woman railed. "You spoke to him for what, five minutes, and now you're saying I should marry him and have his babies? God, am I the only one around here who has any sanity?" Bluebell whined, unaccustomed to the harsh tone of her words. "I expected more from you."

Maddy scooped up the letters and handed them to her. "Your dream was just a dream, nothing more. The problem isn't Jake Holland; it's you."

"Me!" She bristled with anger. "You're taking his side over that of your granddaughter?" Her face flushed to a vivid scarlet. She tossed the letters back on the table. "I've never been angry with you, ever, until now," she spat. "I guess there's a first for everything."

"Be mad at me if you want. You're scared, and you needed a reason to run back to your sheltered existence, the one I made the mistake of giving you. You've let your fears rob you of life's goodness for far too long, and I'm *not* going to play along with you any longer."

"Fine. Maybe I'll find my own place, so you won't have to deal with 'poor little Claire' anymore."

In tears, Maddy didn't ease up. "Jake was right. Being poor little Claire is all you want in your life." She held up the jumbled mass of twine. "Mrs. Kerfuffle got into this today. Claire, this tangled ball of twine is a metaphor for you."

Steaming mad, Claire jumped out of her chair with enough force to send it flying backward. "I'm taking a bath!"

Two hours later, she came downstairs looking humble and tenderly hugged her grandmother. "Please forgive me."

Maddy touched her cheek. "Tomorrow, you need to go to Claire Hill and do some serious thinking. It's time you pray for guidance."

Claire nodded. "I'm sorry for being so awful; directing my anger at the person I love most in this world makes it even more dreadful."

"I know you're hurting. Claire, read the letters again. There's a quote in one of his letters that's so true: 'Everything you want is on the other side of fear.' He's the one for you. I feel it in my bones."

Claire frowned. The look in her eyes did not reflect her grandmother's certainty.

13

ON SUNDAY, THE phone rang. Maddy picked it up in the kitchen. "Hello, Roediger residence, Maddy speaking. How may I help you?"

"Hi, Maddy, this is Jake Holland. Do you remember me?"

"Jake! Of course, I remember you. How are you, and how's Keenan?"

"Keenan's fine, ma'am. Me, well, I've been better. Maddy, I need to talk to Claire."

"I'm surprised you didn't jump on a plane, fly down here, and come banging on my door to try to talk some sense into her."

"If it weren't for my son, I would have. Maddy, I really need to speak to her."

"Jake, she's somewhere in the orchard. Whenever she's sad, she finds solace there."

"Do you know when she'll return? I'll call back every hour on the hour if you don't mind."

"It wouldn't do any good. She won't talk to you. And if you showed up at our door, she'd barricade herself in her room. Claire has a stubborn streak. Frankly, I don't see where she gets it." Her attempt at humor was lost on Jake.

"Maddy, she thinks I'm either evil or mentally ill. I assure you I'm quite sane, and my intentions are honorable." His voice trailed off. "I love her."

"I know you do, Jake. You're not evil or mentally ill. You're the most genuine man I've ever met. Several days ago, in tears, Claire brought me every letter you had written, along with copies of what she sent to you. She said, 'Read them, Maddy, read every one, and tell me if I'm losing my mind.'"

"Well, I'm glad at least one of you doesn't think I'm evil incarnate or just plain nuts."

"Jake, in almost eighty years of living, I've never seen anything so beautiful as what you two have written to each other. I've spent years trying to tell her what you said in a few well-crafted paragraphs. I marvel at your insights on life and your gift for putting your thoughts to paper. Hell, if I were six months younger, I'd fly up there and make a pass at you myself."

He couldn't help but laugh, but the levity quickly vanished.

"Maddy, I'm not the idiot who hurt her. Her heart will always be safe with me."

"I know, Jake. I know. I saw it that day at the orchard. The way you were looking at her, I knew. If there is such a thing as love at first sight, I witnessed it. That's why I told you Claire was single and how you might find it to be an enticing reason to move here."

"I remember. Maddy, I thought about her all the way back to Alaska. As soon as I got home, I wrote my first letter to her. I also wrote another letter afterward and put it in my desk drawer. I said I was going to marry her. I just knew."

"After reading your first letter, I knew it, too."

"So, tell me what to do. Are you sure flying down is a bad idea? Maybe, in person, I could sway her. I could try to get friends to watch Keenan and be there by tomorrow afternoon."

"No, don't do that. It would end in disaster. She needs time to digest things. Leave her to her thoughts. Give her the time and space she needs."

"What happened to her, Maddy? Her heart is so hurt."

She sighed. "It was ugly, Jake. He left her for another woman and callously told her that she never meant anything to him. Until you came along, I thought her spirit was beyond repair. I wish you could've known the carefree girl we sent off to college; she was something. It's been heartbreaking to see a once-vibrant young lady become numb to the world and just go through the motions of life. Your letters invigorated her. But she's scared—petrified, actually—of being hurt again. Your last letter was the excuse she needed to bolt. If you push her now, I guarantee you'll lose her forever."

"I hear what you're saying. Pushing too hard is what got me into this mess. I'm sure you saw it in my letters."

"Yes, I saw it, but I also saw the thoughtful love emanating from your words. You have much wisdom in you, sir. I suspect it was hard-won."

"Yes." His voice turned soft and low. "Very hard-won."

"You two deserve each other, and you have my blessing regarding pursuing my granddaughter's affections. Claire holds a special place in my heart, Jake, and for me to tell you this is the greatest honor I can bestow on you. I love my sweet girl so much. Believe me—she's everything you've imagined her to be and more. The way you two write to each other, it's eerie how your minds and hearts meld. I've never seen anything like it. And Jake, that Myers-Briggs personality thing you told her about, well, it brought tears to my eyes. Claire has always been different from most people, and now, she and I know why. I'm glad you learned to celebrate your rare personality type, and I hope Claire will too."

"We're odd ducks in society's eyes, that's for sure. I've learned how being different can be a wonderful thing."

"Jake, she loves you. Trust me on this. You need to calm down and let her find her way. Let her make the first move. You won't regret it."

"Okay. Maddy, after reading her farewell letter, it crushed me. I want you to know if she does approach me again, I'm going to tell her it'll be over between us if she sends another such letter. I can't endure a yo-yo relationship where I get farewell letters for no coherent reason. My heart can't take it, and my sadness affects my son. In any relationship, there must be boundaries."

"You're right to insist on conditions. I'm sorry you've had to go through this—and Keenan, too. But, if you can be patient, you'll have a lady who'll love you forever. Jake, I need to tell you something …"

There was silence on the line for a few moments.

"Maddy, how long have you been ill? How bad is it?"

She sighed. "Well, you've just proven your empathic abilities. I'll tell you, but only if you keep it in the utmost confidence. Are you able to keep what I say between us?"

"You have my word."

"I'm not well, Jake. I've been having abdominal and back pain. While Claire was at school, I had a friend take me to see my doctor, who felt a pulsating bulge in my abdomen and immediately had me get an ultrasound, and after that, a CT scan ..."

"Go on. I'm listening."

"I have something called an abdominal aortic aneurysm. The doc says it has developed slowly over the years."

"Oh, Maddy, I'm so sorry. Can they repair the blood vessel?"

"The aneurysm is in a bad location, so my doc favors a conservative management approach because surgery carries a high mortality risk for me. She's got me on a bunch of meds that I hide in my room. Jake, if Claire finds out about this, she'll be devastated. Her dealing with both you and me at the same time will be too much. She had an awful episode of depression after her breakup, and I'll do anything to keep her from going down that dark hole again. I'm all she's got, and it scares me to think about how she'll do when I'm gone."

"She won't be alone, Maddy; she'll have me and my son."

"It warms my heart to hear you say that. Jake, the best thing you can do for her is to find your calm and wait for her to come to her senses."

"I understand, and I will. Thanks for giving me hope. By the way, I'm going to call you every day during my lunch hour for a health report. It's not negotiable. You can't tell me such news and expect me to ignore it. I also want to talk to your doctor because I'm now your health advocate. That's not negotiable, either. I care about you. One day, we may be related."

"It's not necessary. The doc is keeping a close eye on me. I'll be fine."

"Maddy, I'm a doctor, so I'm qualified to be your health advocate."

"Nice try, but I know your doctoral degree is in geology."

"You're quite right, madam, and if you think you can get by without a health advocate, you have rocks in your head. So, enter me, the rock doctor."

She laughed. "Beaten into submission by an idiom. You crack me up, sir. Okay, you're my guy until you get tired of it."

"Good. My first act as your health advocate will be to request a second opinion."

"Thank you for your concern, Dr. Rocks. We'd better end this conversation before she returns. I'll continue to give her my assurances about your being a good man. Jake, she's beautiful, inside and out. From your letters to each other, I have no doubt you'll have a happy life together. She'll adore you and will love Keenan like her own. If you take anything away from our conversation, let it be this: My granddaughter loves you and needs to come to terms with it. For her, it's an overwhelming idea. She reads your letters every day. She often takes them to a treeless knoll on our property we call Claire Hill. Ever since she was a little girl, she would go there to find her peace. Just know you're in her thoughts."

"I understand. Thank you for raising her and loving her so tenderly. When you're no longer able to love her, I will, if she'll have me, and I won't let her or you down. That's a promise."

"I believe you. I hope I'll live long enough to see great-grandchildren."

Jake laughed, his mood noticeably uplifted. "I think a bunch of Jakelets and Clairelets running amok through your apple orchard would cause you to reconsider such a fanciful notion."

She chuckled. "You appear to have forgotten I was once an elementary school teacher. I used to eat little brats and bullies for lunch. No child would ever consider messing with the iron lady called Mrs. Roediger."

"I love your feistiness and how you say what's on your mind. Thank you for talking to me."

"Jake, your letters melted the heart of this old battle-ax. Now, get on with your day. Act as though Claire loves you because she does."

"Okay. I wish you could see the big smile on my face. Tomorrow, I'm calling you at noon my time for a health report and to get your doctor's number. Oh, and please tell your doc I'm now on the team. I'm serious about this, Maddy."

"Yes, sir."

"That's the spirit. Goodbye."

"Goodbye to you, too. I'll give you an update on Claire when you call tomorrow. You stay incommunicado with her, hear?"

"Yes, ma'am. I hear you loud and clear. Bye, Maddy."

14

TWO WEEKS PASSED with Claire's opinion of Jake Holland remaining unchanged. She fell asleep each night reading his letters, looking for the slightest inconsistency to bring to Maddy's attention to say, "See, look at this, I told you so." But her sleuthing bore no fruit; in fact, it brought only tears. His words were so beautiful. Each day when she got home from school, she'd check the counter when Maddy wasn't looking to see what mail had come. Each day without a letter from him brought sadness, despite her best effort to quash it. If his intentions were honorable, he would've written to make a case for his genuineness. But no letters affirmed her suspicions. Still, she so looked forward to his letters.

Saturday, after shopping, they stopped at their mailbox before pulling into the driveway. Maddy retrieved the mail and got back in the car. "There's a letter for you." Claire's stomach did a flip-flop. "It's from Spokane, Washington. There's no name on the return address, just a street and house number. The writing looks feminine. Should I open it?"

"Sure."

Maddy opened it, and her eyes went wide. "Claire, it's from Jake's mother. Her name is Nancy." She folded the letter and put it back in the envelope. "This is for you to read, not me."

"I don't want to read it. I mean, it's pretty sad when you enlist your mother to do your bidding."

"You were raised to have good manners, Claire Lofton. She took the time to write to you and deserves the courtesy of you reading it."

Claire frowned but didn't argue.

After helping to put the groceries away, Claire went upstairs with Bluebell. On her bed with her furry friend, she reluctantly took the letter out of the envelope and began reading.

Dear Miss Lofton,

My name is Nancy Holland. I'm Jake's mother. Forgive me for being so forward by writing to you, but as his mother, I have some things to share with you about him that I feel you should know.

He called me shortly after you broke up with him, utterly devastated. It took a while for me to pry loose what was troubling him. He told me about you, how he felt about you, and what you said in your last letter to him. Miss Lofton, Jake has been through a lot in his life, and he has always handled hardships with courage and dignity. Yet regarding you, he was inconsolable. Aside from Keenan's hospitalizations, I've never seen my son so distraught. As his mother, it troubles me greatly.

Claire, Jake is a special person. I knew it from the moment I held him in my arms. As a boy, he was quite unlike his "normal" older brother; with his deep thoughts and feelings, it was as if Jake were an old soul coming back to earth. He was different than other children too, often in his special world, and his quietness and, at times, seeming aloofness, confounded us, especially my husband. Imagine a three-year-old boy wanting you to read him a book of adult poetry at bedtime instead of a children's story, or a six-year-old telling you he didn't have time to talk because he was too busy flying a spacecraft in his head, about to land on a distant planet. Little Jake could also look at people and know when they needed comfort; he would often say, "Momma, this person needs our love today."

When Keenan was born, I wish you could have seen the smile on my son's face. I will never forget his pure elation that day. And I will never forget his heartache when he watched his little boy fighting for his life because of a blood disorder. The tender way he loves his son is heartwarming to witness. He loved his wife, too, despite her many imperfections, and he took the loss of their marriage quite hard. The years since their breakup have been difficult for him; I see his loneliness and yet his determination to avoid frivolous relationships. He has been very cautious about dating, and quite honestly, I was stunned to learn of his feelings for you.

I want you to know that my boy is the most kind and loving person I have ever met. I'm not saying this because I am his mother; rather, I say this from many years of observing his actions. It is a privilege to be his mother. Claire, Jake does not toy with people. If you knew him, you would see the inconceivability of such a notion. Also, when he told me about you, what he saw in you, how he felt about you, I thought, goodness, you must be very, very special. If anyone else told me a story like his, I would say, you couldn't possibly know that about someone after knowing them so briefly. But, with Jake, it's not the case. He "sees" people, always has, always will. If you note an apparent inconsistency in his empathic abilities regarding his former wife, let me just say his proposal of marriage averted an abortion and quite literally saved his son's life. I say this not on conjecture; he told me before marrying her that longevity in their union was quite unlikely. It speaks well of his character that he knew before Keenan was born that he would one day be a single father.

He spoke briefly about your heartache. Claire, I understand your cautiousness and perhaps outright disbelief of his intentions toward you, and all I can say is, give him a chance. He has the capacity within him to love in ways that most of us will never know. I pray you are everything he "sees," and if you are, then you both are very fortunate to have found each other.

I found your address online and ask that you keep this correspondence confidential. Jake would be mortified if he knew I wrote to you. But as his mother, he will always be my little boy, and I love him dearly. I assure you he is quite a capable man, and I never meddle in his life. Yet, in this one instance, I feel compelled to write to you.

I hope, if you and Jake find a common path, we will one day meet. I have no doubt you must be a very special lady.

Sincerely,
Nancy Holland

In tears, Claire put the letter aside, lost in the words of Mrs. Holland. She imagined little Jake asking his momma to read poetry to him at bedtime and smiled at the thought of him telling her he didn't have time to talk because he was too busy flying a spacecraft in his head. *Yes, that's so like my Jake.* When those words entered her awareness, she wept.

When there were no tears left, she wiped her eyes and knew what she had to do. She went to her desk and began writing.

Dear Mrs. Holland,
I read your letter and just cried and cried. It was beautiful, so pure and honest, with the love for your son so clearly evident. Your eloquence explains

where Jake acquired his love of words. If you were here, I would wrap my arms around you and say, from the bottom of my heart, thank you for your insights about Jake and for your reassurances. I needed them more than you will ever know.

My life also has not been easy. I was abandoned by my parents at an early age and raised by my maternal grandparents. Their love for me is so like yours for Jake. I still live with Maddy, my grandmother, and my love for her is beyond measure. Sadly, Grandpa passed away a few years ago, and not a day goes by that I don't think about him. Mrs. Holland, I want you to know that I, too, am a good and decent person. I am a third-grade teacher and lead a quiet, ordinary life. We own an apple orchard in Leavenworth, and between that and teaching, my days are fully occupied.

I have never been married, but as Jake told you, I have known heartache. It happened in college; I thought we would marry, but he announced a fondness for another woman. It devastated me, and I have never dated again. I moved back home, where I've been ever since, wanting only to live a solitary existence, which I've managed to do for the last three years. Then Jake entered my life, seeking a place in my heart. Quite honestly, given what I have been through, the possibility of being hurt again terrified me.

He and Keenan came to our orchard last summer to pick a few apples for their return to Alaska. Keenan fell, bumping his nose, and it began to bleed severely. I went with them to the local hospital. My entire time with your son amounted to no more than twenty minutes. After Jake returned to Alaska, he wrote me a letter, an amazing letter, where he described me with an accuracy that left me dumbfounded. He then mentioned Myers-Briggs personality profiling and said he thought I was an INFJ, a "one-percenter" as he calls it, like him. I took the test as well and was stunned yet again when he correctly guessed my personality type. Like Jake, when I was growing up, I felt different from everyone else, and after reading about my rare personality, the reason I never "fit in" finally made sense. I am profoundly grateful to him for sharing his knowledge with me.

Jake asked in his first letter that we correspond to each other for the simple reason of being "one-percenters." Guarding my heart, I chose not to reply, and he sent me another letter, such was his persistence. Mrs. Holland, the richness and depth of his writing astonished me; I simply could not ignore him, and we started writing to each other. His subsequent letters have left me in awe; there is simply no other word to describe it. His last letter, which was deeply personal regarding his feelings about me, was overwhelming. I told him no one could feel the way he did after meeting someone for less than twenty minutes. It just wasn't possible. The only thing that seemed to make sense was the possibility he was toying with me for some perverse pleasure. I ended our correspondence quite bluntly, I'm sad to say. And then you sent me your letter. I hope this explains my tears when reading your words.

I'll close by saying that a mother's genuineness has calmed my heart, and I now know I must, in the days ahead, find the courage to make amends to your son, for I love him deeply. This quote from Emily Brontë describes how I feel: "Whatever our souls are made of, his and mine are the same." I cannot fathom what the future holds for us, but I want to assure you, should we ever walk a "common path," I will love him tenderly and with a fire in my heart that will burn forever.

Goodbye, Mrs. Holland, and thank you. I hope these are the first of many letters to each other, for you now hold a special place in my heart.

Warm regards, Claire

She addressed an envelope and went downstairs. Maddy, who was with Mrs. Kerfuffle on the couch, looked at her expectantly. Claire offered a feeble smile. "Here, Maddy. Please read her letter. I wrote a reply and am taking it to the mailbox. After that, I'm going with Bluebell to Claire Hill."

Maddy looked at her, noting her puffy eyes. "Well, what did she say?"

Claire shook her head. "Just read it, Maddy." Her voice cracked as she said it. She hugged her and left.

Maddy opened the letter and began reading. By the second paragraph, she brought her hand to her open mouth and kept it there. After finishing it, Maddy carefully folded the letter and put it back in the envelope. She stroked the purring cat who had nestled on her lap. "God bless Jake's mother, Mrs. Kerfuffle. You did good, Nancy Holland."

Claire returned a couple of hours later, looking troubled. Maddy hugged her. "Do you want to talk?"

She nodded. Maddy gestured for her to take a seat on the overstuffed chair. Claire tried, without success, to swallow the lump lingering in her throat. She couldn't utter a word.

Maddy took the initiative. "With Nancy Holland's letter, I think we can now dismiss the validity of your dream. I suggest your dream wasn't about Jake; it was about Colin. He still haunts you."

She nodded again.

"You love Jake, don't you? Drop all your damn fears and give me an honest answer."

"Yes."

"So, what are you going to do about it?"

A look of sadness passed over her features. She shrugged her shoulders, looking like a lost little girl.

"Claire Lofton, you're at a crossroads in your life, right here, right now. One direction leads to Jake and a lifetime of potential happiness. The other is more of the same joyless existence you've had for the last three years. Only you can decide which way to go, but now it's decision time." She stared intently at her. "I want you to close your eyes and listen to me, and I want you to feel this deep in your heart, okay?" Claire nodded. "Close your eyes, and don't open them until I say so." She dutifully did as asked.

Maddy waited a few moments before speaking. "Imagine you have a beautiful baby girl. You love her with all your heart. She means everything to you. Imagine her growing up, her first day at school, then middle school, and high school. You watch with pride as she blossoms into a wonderful young woman. Imagine her leaving for college and coming home one day, saying, 'Momma, I've met the man I'm going to marry.' Now, imagine her telling you that man is Jake. Would you be happy for her?" Claire gasped. "Okay, open your eyes." Maddy's eyes met hers. "Would you be happy for that precious child of yours?"

Tears fell down her cheeks. "Yes. I'd tell her she found the most wonderful man in the world."

"What if I said it was Colin, your college love? Would you be equally as happy for her?"

Claire turned ashen. "I would say, *'You'll marry him over my dead body.'*"

Maddy smiled. "I think the road you need to take is clear."

Claire nodded. "I love you so much, Maddy. Thank you."

"Come give this old lady a hug."

Claire held her tightly and whispered in her ear. "Tell me what to do, Maddy. I've blown it with him; I know it."

She cupped her granddaughter's face in her hands. "You haven't blown it. Write to him and let your heart speak to his. Your two hearts speak to each other like nothing I've ever witnessed. Don't try to get too fancy or over-eloquent with your words because that'll mean your head is trying to write the response, not your heart."

"Okay. Do you mind if I do it now?"

"Go ahead. I'm so happy for you. When I spoke to you when you closed your eyes, just know you're that little girl for me, and I couldn't be happier with Jake Holland being the one for my precious girl."

"Maddy, I'm so lucky to have you. You're just as precious to me as I am to you." She kissed her cheek and went upstairs.

15

IN HER ROOM, at her desk, Claire closed her eyes. *"Please, God, help me find the right words. I love him."* She picked up her pen, thought for a few moments, and began writing.

Dear Mr. Holland,

Forgive this shaky handwriting, for my hand is trembling as I write these words.

A few days ago, my cat got into mischief with my grandmother Maddy's ball of twine. When Maddy picked up the tangled mess, she looked at me and said, "Claire, this tangled ball of twine is a metaphor for you." She was right.

Mr. Holland, I have read every letter of yours countless times in the past few weeks, and try as I might, I could find nothing in your many heartfelt musings to support my dream-prompted ill feelings toward you. Beyond your letters, something happened today, of which I cannot speak, that proved your genuineness. I know this sounds cryptic, but I ask that you not pursue any further explanation. Just know I was wrong about you, sir, and I'm deeply sorry for hurting you so unjustly.

I cannot begin to describe how elated I would feel when a letter arrived from you, and how I would breathlessly read your words. I still wake each morning, wondering if I'll receive a letter from you, and then a wave of sadness rolls through me, knowing I ended the very thing I so desire. My heart aches for you.

If you are willing, I am ready to move forward in this relationship, but you must understand that my heart cannot match the swift cadence you have set. Please allow my heart to advance slowly, for the territory is unknown, and I am not a seasoned traveler. Get to know me, Mr. Holland; ask questions, as you did in your last letter. Be playful with me. Allow me also to ask questions of you. If we spend the rest of our lives together, ten years of letter writing, in the grand scheme of things, isn't too long to get to know each other (I'm kidding; I meant to say no more than seven years).

You correctly assumed there are many tender things I want to say to you in your last letter. In the days ahead, I will work on mustering the courage needed to say them.

I wouldn't blame you for ending what we have after my last letter, which was hurtful. Just know I, too, have come to see the possibility of a life with you. I hope my words are enough to hear from you again.

A wise person once said, "I am homesick for a place I am not sure even exists, one where my heart is full and my soul is understood ..." Mr. Holland, I now believe this place, for me, is with you. I wonder, sir, if I knocked on your door, would you open it and invite me in? Would you be willing to help untangle Claire?

Sincerely, Claire Lofton

A week later, when Claire returned from school, Maddy greeted her with a letter in her hand and nodded, indicating it was from Jake. Claire tentatively reached for it, her eyes conveying fright. "I'm going to Claire Hill," she said, her voice shaky.

"I've been praying for you two."

"I've been praying, too." A tear rolled down her cheek. "C'mon, Bluebell, let's go for a walk."

On the trail, an uncharacteristically subdued Bluebell stayed close to her, sensing her distress.

It was cold on Claire Hill, with dark, threatening clouds dominating the sky. With trembling hands, Claire opened the envelope and began reading. She took in every word, imagining his voice, stern in some paragraphs, soft in others ...

Dear Miss Lofton,

For two hours, I have stared at this blank piece of paper, my mind on fire regarding how to respond to your letter.

One voice in my head says to offer soothing, comforting words of reassurance, all fluffy and benign, as I'm sure you want to hear.

Another voice demands I vent my anger for the way you skewered me so mercilessly in your farewell letter.

And I can't discount the voice within me saying, "Tell her how you cried through the night after receiving her letter, so aching for her. Tell her how the dark, lonely night swallowed you whole, gripping you with a sadness so overwhelming that you could feel your heart breaking into a million little pieces.

"Tell her how very real is the danger of her destroying your wellbeing, and how you might not recover from another farewell letter.

"Tell her the folly of betting all your hard-won peace on an emotionally stunted, closed-off woman who often professes no hope for a life together and shows stubborn resistance to accepting any form of change.

"Tell her the very thought of her leaves you breathless, and you'd walk willingly through the gates of hell if that's what it took to rescue her."

It's two in the morning, and finally, my heart and head have reached a tenuous accord that allows me to fill this page. For me to stay in this relationship, you must agree to certain conditions. Untangling Claire and a life together depend on it. Pointed words are about to follow that will insist on courage and hard work from you. If you are unwilling to fight and change for your happiness and our union, then stop reading, crumple this letter, and that will be the end of it. Otherwise, read on.

If you think all you have to do is say, "Jake, oh baby, I love you," and then your world will go instantly fairytale, and we'll live happily ever after, well, no offense, but get real. Sorry. In life, there are no wizards behind the curtains, able to make everything better with some magical words and a few animated pulls on some behind-the-scenes levers. It doesn't work that way. I had to work my butt off and face some nasty demons to find my peace. Try looking at your little boy fighting for his life and learning how your bad genes are what put him in intensive care if you want an example of what I've had to deal with. Life hasn't been easy for either of us. But, Claire, believe me, being happy is a choice. I chose happiness, and you can, too. I'll now tell you how I did it. The words of Nikita Gill went off like a lightbulb in my head: "Let it hurt. Let it bleed. Let it heal. And let it go." That's it; that's all you have to do. You've already let it hurt and bleed, and now you have to let it heal and let it go.

To heal and let it go, you have to forgive, not only that guy from college, but, I suspect, your mother and father, and anyone else, including yourself, who has harmed you along the way. I can't force you to forgive; that choice will have to be made by you. It will be the hardest thing you've ever done.

If you can't forgive, you will remain stuck in the past, and you will have doomed us because peace will never come to you, and you cannot love in a pure way with all that darkness inside you. I will commit to helping you with abundant love and support, and all I need from you now is for you to say you're on the path to forgiving others. But if you have no intention to heal and let it all go, untangling Claire is impossible, and we're wasting each other's time. Thich Nhat Hanh said, "Letting go gives us freedom, and freedom is the only condition for happiness. If, in our heart, we still cling to anything—anger, anxiety, or possessions—we cannot be free."

Until you release Mr. Heartbreaker and the others through forgiveness, they will always have power over you and will keep hurting you. Let him go, Claire, let them all go, and choose happiness. Doing so will liberate your life.

I abhor being called "Mr. Holland" by you. It sounds so cold, as if I am a stranger, unworthy of even scraps of your affection. From this day forward, "Mr. Holland" will be what you say when you're talking to my father, and even he will likely insist that you call him Ethan; Jake will be how you will refer to me. In this relationship, Mr. Holland is history.

Regarding subsequent correspondence between us, there will be no more conversation constraints: everything will be on the table, with the understanding that questions we pose to each other will just be questions, with no "What did he or she mean by that?" and all questions deserve an honest answer.

Moving on, I want to say something, and I want you to hear me, loud and clear. Regarding your dream of "me" that resulted in your farewell letter, I am NOT your former lover. I dwell in decency and integrity, and I despise the man for doing what he did to you. I fear he may have poisoned you forever, and I can envision a series of farewell letters each time you try to imprint his sordid characteristics on me. You said in your last letter that any doubts about my genuineness are behind you. They had better be because another farewell letter from you will be the end of our relationship, period. I am not a man to be trifled with, and on this, I mean what I say. Claire, you must understand that when I am sad, it affects my son, and a yo-yo relationship is, for that reason alone, unacceptable.

It is unlike me to stomp my foot and say all these harsh words. It makes me uncomfortable and sad. Mine is a tender heart, and I prefer using gentle words with everyone, especially with you. But these harsh words are required for a lifetime of tender words to come.

I applaud the courage it took for you to write your letter to me. Isaac Marion demonstrated wisdom when he said, "What wonderful thing didn't start out scary?" Just know the scariness is mutual; as you said to me, I will now say to you: Please be careful of my heart. Regarding my last letter to you, I admit to behaving foolishly and recklessly, pushing too hard, wanting too much, too soon. Forgive me. I am the poster child for putting the proverbial cart before the horse. I understand how your heart could not keep up with the pace of my desires, and common sense dictates we be more playful and keep it light. I promise to behave myself and contain my feelings, but you know they are there, as I know yours are there for me, and that is enough to sustain me for the next seven years of letter writing.

I so hope what I've outlined is agreeable. We can do this, Claire, you and me. We can love and support each other in ways that will help us both grow and blossom. We both "see" each other; we see the abundant goodness that's in us. Olivia Pope offers some wonderful words for us to consider: "If you want me, earn me." So here we are, alone, staring into each other's eyes at a crossroads. You can go your way, and I can go mine. Or we can earn each other's love by joining hands and exploring the rich, new territory of a life together. I want a life with you. I love you, Claire Lofton, and cannot defer saying this to a subsequent day. Here is my heart. Whatever shall you do with it? Jake

Claire finished the letter and brought it to her chest. "Thank you, God," she said, looking upward. His words danced in her awareness. He was right about her wanting fluffy words. What he said was far from that, she thought with a cringe. *He flat lowered the boom on me.* She considered his conditions, wondering if she could meet his demands. Calling him Jake would be easy; she'd already been calling him that in her head. *Could she let her past go? Could she forgive Colin? Her parents? Herself?*

His stern words rolled through her, booming like thunder, impossible to mute. Yet in those harsh words, his love for her was so pure, so undeniable. She looked at Bluebell. "He's right, girl. Until I let 'Mr. Heartbreaker' go, let everything go, I will never know peace. Remaining in my sheltered world, chained to the past, now seems repugnant." She hugged her companion. "I'm choosing happiness."

Back home, she went upstairs and wrote her shortest letter ever to Jake.

Dearest Jake,

I accept your terms. With tears in my eyes, I welcome your love. Your heart will be safe with me. What does this mean for us now? I am so scared.

I love you. Claire

16

Sweet Claire,

Now the fun begins. Two "one-percenters" taking off the gloves, going at it with a host of questions that would leave the other personality types blushing, weak-kneed, and trembling. How exciting!

Regarding your "What does this mean for us now?" question, allow me to state the obvious: you could jump on a plane, fly to Anchorage, look into my eyes and proclaim your everlasting love for me, and then savage me unmercifully, followed by calling me "Stallion" around all my friends and colleagues. Or ... we could continue with our letters, learning more about each other, taking our time, asking pertinent questions until we both know our love is indisputable, and only then agree to meet in person. I vote for the latter, but you're welcome to make a case for savaging me.

Should you opt for continued letter-writing over immediate insane sex, you probably have the time to continue reading rather than booking a flight, so I will press on and speak of something you said in your "untangling Claire" letter.

"... something happened today, of which I cannot speak, that proved your genuineness." I am smiling here. It took only a couple of minutes for me to solve this mystery. If I were a hunter tracking game, the ground would have been littered with mother tracks. On that hunch, I called her and said, "Mom, whatever you did with Claire, I thank you." The silence on the other end of the line confirmed my suspicions. I don't know what she did, but I told her I was grateful. This is a first for her, meddling in my affairs, but I suppose you now know why I love her so dearly. Although she said nary a word about what happened between you, I could sense she likes you immensely. Perhaps I should bow out of my conquest of your heart and turn the job over to my mother. After you two have concluded negotiations, please inform me of what church I should show up at, where I will promptly say, "I do." I say this with a smile and a wink and with a heart full of good cheer.

Kidding aside, I want you to know I take seriously your desire to go slowly and keep it light until you say, "Let's kick it up a notch." If I had my last letter to you, I would grab a big marker and black out all the intimate lines, as if I were the most zealous of censors, and then say, "Please answer the questions I posed to you in what remains."

Thank you, Claire, for having the courage to stay in this relationship. Your heart is safe with me. I promise to earn your love every day. This relationship is going to be a beautiful, lifelong love. Gone are my doubts. I now know my home is where I can put my arms around you. I love you. Jake

P.S. Enclosed is a picture of Keenan and me. He likes you, and I'm sure one day he'll love you as well.

17

Dear Stallion,

Your playful side delights me. I love you so much.

Jake, as tempting as the idea of hopping on a plane and "savaging you" is, we both know how reckless that would be. I so want this to work between us, and for this reason, I'll opt for slow and steady. By the way, just for the record, I am not a very good "savager," but oh, how I could make sweet love to you.

I know you were kidding about "insane sex," but I want to share something with you by the poet E. E. Cummings, who so beautifully describes the love I hope to have with you: "we are so both and oneful / night cannot be so sky / sky cannot be so sunful / i am through you so i."

I crave intimacy, and I hope you do, too. The man who broke my heart favored crude intercourse, devoid of tenderness and love. I accepted it because it was all I had known. But afterward, I'd always feel an intense emptiness, which I would try to rationalize away, thinking, it's just me being me. In college, my girlfriends would rave about wild sex, and I remember thinking, "What is wrong with me—yet another example of Claire being different from everyone else." What I yearn for is "I am through you so I," where making love is a tender physical, emotional, and spiritual union, something beautiful, something so much more than sex. I have never experienced this, but I have the hope of it being possible. Do "one-percenters" make love in this way, Jake, or do they too just have sex?

Regarding "the ground being littered with mother tracks," sir, your wit and sleuthing are both superb. I can almost hear you saying, "Solving this mystery was elementary, my dear Ms. Lofton." Jake, your mother wrote me a wonderful letter, telling me about you and including a few tidbits about "Little Jake." It was endearing, and I was touched, truly touched, by how ardently she loves and admires you. After finishing her letter, all doubts of your genuineness vanished, and an enormous sense of peace filled me. In that moment, I knew I was in love with you. I love your mother, too, for what she did to calm my heart.

I'll shift to answering your questions. By the way, your side notes are hilarious.

— How do you express love to those whom you hold dear? (mental image: ancient Rome, you feeding me grapes while fanning me)

Smiling here. Mental image: ancient Rome, you in a toga, being my boy-toy after you're done cleaning our villa. With you, I would learn the territory of Jake, meaning I'd observe what is meaningful to you and listen as you share with me your wants and needs. I would love you in simple ways, such as playing with you/being your friend, bantering with you in the kitchen as we prepare our favorite meals, and always being a safe harbor for you when there is a storm. With Keenan, I'd give him a mother's kind of love, offering kindness, tenderness, and plenty of one-on-one attention. Lastly, with Maddy, my love shows in my respect for her and in how much fun we have when we do things together.

— What is the most/least important thing in your life?

Family (to include Bluebell and Mrs. Kerfuffle) is the most important thing in my life. And please know that I consider my students my extended family. Least important: materialism. I believe happiness and well-being diminish as you become more materialistic. One day, I'll explain why.

— What is your biggest fear? (aside from further damage to your heart)

My biggest fear is Maddy going to heaven. She is nearly eighty and has had high blood pressure for years, which fosters a host of health disorders. I can see the years catching up to her; she is no longer the bundle of energy she once was, and arthritis has slowed her fingers. She loves to knit, but often her joints say, "No, not today." I see the sadness in her eyes when it happens. Her less-acute hearing and eyesight are a measure of her years, but she remains feisty in spirit. I love her and cannot imagine my life without her. The fear of being alone one day is very real. Sigh ...

Speaking of fears, there's something about me you should know. I have a form of agoraphobia, which I'll explain. After my breakup, I moved back home. Now the thought of going anywhere besides Leavenworth causes me to have a panic attack. I do fine in and around my little hamlet, but force me beyond my safe, secure world, and I'll have a meltdown. Maybe, subconsciously, I'm afraid I'll see my former lover, but he now lives on the East Coast, so the odds of it are small-to-none. As you can see, rational thought cannot appease my anxiety. By the way, this disclosure fuels my fear that you'll leave me once you get to know me.

— Compose a six-word story about your life (example: Shortly after my divorce, I read this from an unknown author, and it touches me to this day: "I felt too much, he didn't.")

Oh, Jake, how poignant, that story. Okay, here's my six-word story, which reflects how I feel today: "He awakened the phoenix within me."

— What would you do without electricity for three days?

How fun! Power outages are common here in winter, so Maddy and I are always prepared. We have a wood-burning fireplace to provide warmth, lots of candles for lighting, and an outdoor gas grill for cooking. We spend our time conversing, reading, and playing board games. I once remember we were having so much fun that we both groaned in unison when the power came back on after being out for two days.

— Do you believe long-distance relationships can work?

In general, no; with you and me, an enthusiastic yes! When I read your letters, I feel like you are right next to me, speaking with such tenderness and sincerity that I am often left breathless, with my heart pounding. When I write to you, I feel an intense, intimate union. Jake, I've been in the arms of other men, but I feel much closer to you, a thousand miles away, than I ever did with them. Perhaps only "one-percenters" can feel this way.

— Do you believe in God? (I do, although I'm not enamored with organized religion)

When I am walking through our orchard on a calm day, I feel a presence, and I know Spirit is with me. In nature, I feel like I am in a church; the feeling is powerful and soothing. Should we ever get together, I would, as a couple, like to explore and deepen our relationship with God. I would be most open to hearing more of your thoughts on this subject.

— Are you able to forgive and forget? (example: my accidentally washing your delicates)

Warning: The ill-treatment of my unmentionables may significantly shorten your life span! Kidding aside, this innocent question is difficult to answer. I am quite forgiving when Bluebell chews on one of my purses or runs through our house with muddy paws. People are fallible, so I have no problem letting petty things go. Regarding our potential relationship, I would hope we'd resolve issues as they arose to avoid a backlog of resentment and anger. Resolving our differences in an atmosphere filled with mutual respect and love would be vital to our well-being as a couple. Oh … and just so you know, I am not a person who nags or rehashes old stuff, nor do I gloat when I'm right. Such behaviors are toxic to a relationship. I suspect you feel the same way.

Now, on to egregious behavior. Forgiving and forgetting? My response is both yes and no. Yes: With your insights, I understand how my forgiving "Mr. Heartbreaker" is vital to healing my heart; No: Even if I forgive him (which I'm working up the courage to do), I could never forget or condone what he did.

Jake, here's where answering this question gets hard. Suppose we were married, and you cheated on me. Even if I could forgive you, it would never be the same between us, for the purity of what we had would be lost. And how could I forget what happened? Reverse it: Could you forgive and forget my having an affair? Sigh … on to more pleasant questions.

— Name three of the most beautiful places you've been (I hope you won't say Disneyland)

Hey, I love Disneyland! Okay, here are my three: There is a treeless knoll in our orchard that offers sweeping views of the mountains and valleys. Grandpa and Maddy named it Claire Hill in my honor. As a child, I would go there, lie on the ground and watch clouds floating by, imagining shapes and animals in the fluffy white masses. I would spend hours there, lost in my thoughts, blissfully alone in Claire's World. It remains my favorite place on earth.

For my second most beautiful place, I climbed Mount Rainier with my grandpa when I was sixteen. We trained for six months before attempting the feat, and I will always treasure that time together. We took the Ingraham Glacier route up the mountain in early May, and fortunately, the weather cooperated. The view from the summit was exhilarating, and that I did it with Grandpa will make me savor the experience forever.

The third beautiful place for me is Puget Sound. The family of the man who broke my heart had a sailboat, and I adored sailing with them through the San Juan Islands. Being aboard a sailboat as it swiftly skips across the sea is soul-stirring. I became a capable sailor, and if I ever subdue my agoraphobia, I'd love for us to rent a sailboat and explore the San Juans. I'll bet you and Keenan would love sailing too.

— How many children do you want to have? (caution: a two-digit number will cause me to gasp)

Smiling here. A few, Jake. Certainly less than a dozen, but I would be open to negotiation on any number that appeals to you.

— Whom do you admire? (Ah, shucks, I mean, besides me)

Maddy and Grandpa top my list. That they could love me so much amazes me to this day. I don't keep up with world events because the news focuses too much on negativity and not enough on positive kindnesses, which are everywhere. So you will rarely hear me saying I admire some political figure, a celebrity, or an athlete. Yesterday, I saw a boy helping his elderly grandmother into their car. For me, those small kindnesses far outweigh the lofty, grand intentions of politicians, which often come to nothing. I admire tender moments, such as a mother kissing her newborn child. When children display good manners, I admire their parents for instilling in them a set of values.

I do admire you in many ways. I admire how devoted you are to Keenan, how purposeful you are regarding his character development, and how you interact with him in a way that celebrates his unique personality. I admire how you can touch a person's heart with your words—my heart, for example. I admire how you are quiet and gentle by nature, but when your values are threatened, oh my, you become a force to be reckoned with. I can say this now from direct experience. Winking here.

— What are your hobbies or things you love doing? (I hope writing to me is at the top of your list)

If daydreaming were a sport, I'd qualify handily in the Daydreamer Olympics. I love reading, especially stories that warm my heart, and I love hiking in our local mountains, enjoying and finding renewal in the solitude. I think you would call my love of solitude a one-percenter thing, as is daydreaming. I love sitting with Maddy by the fireplace, with no television, radio, or other distractions. While I read, I steal glances at her as she knits, and I find it comforting. I love playing with Bluebell and telling her how my day went. She is an excellent listener.

I also enjoy the company of Mrs. Kerfuffle, my persnickety stray cat. One day while jogging, I found her by the side of the road, emaciated and near death. Now she is the picture of health, but as a formerly feral cat, she has, um, issues, hence her persnickety-ness. She's learning to tolerate humans; Bluebell, however, remains her chief nemesis, despite my goofy dog's untiring efforts to win her affections.

Speaking of jogging, a fudge shop in town is my nirvana, so I try to run every day as a penance for having a sweet tooth. I wonder if you have a sweet tooth, too. Yes, dear man, writing to you is now my chief hobby, as is pondering your eloquent letters.

— What is your favorite cuisine/restaurant? (Dear God, please don't let her say anything featuring a chicken nugget)

Laughing here. Chicken nuggets—the bane of parenthood. I have a fondness for Thai food. Fresh rolls, Pad Thai noodles, and spicy lemongrass chicken make my taste buds swoon. Authentic Punjabi (Indian) curries also evoke a Pavlovian response in me. For dessert, odd as it sounds, I favor apple pie; Maddy and I have perfected a pie recipe that will bring tears to your eyes. I don't care for heavy, greasy, or fried foods, but I can usually find something that appeals to me in any restaurant. Chipotle Mexican Grill is my favorite for fast food, but sadly, the closest one is over fifty miles away.

I love cooking, as does Maddy, so we are content staying home, having fun as amateur gourmets. We've become fond of anything involving wraps. We like the lightness of such meals, and a wrap is an excellent way to use leftovers. Last night, for example, we made Mediterranean wraps stuffed with leftover rotisserie chicken, feta cheese, and couscous, with a hint of lime and a sprinkling of fresh herbs. Yum!

— What is your favorite book/movie? (My all-time favorite movie is "Leaving Normal." It's a one-percenter flick. I hope one day we'll watch it together)

I just finished a book titled "Howling Across Bridges," about a troubled, war-weary veteran and his ugly-but-loveable dog. They traveled across North America by motorcycle on a quest to find his noble purpose in life. I went through a box of tissues reading it. As for movies, my all-time favorite is "It's a Wonderful Life." Maddy and I watch it every year at Christmas. I have never heard of "Leaving Normal," but the idea of watching it together sounds wonderful. I hope you like popcorn made with real butter, as it's at the top of my list of favorite snack foods.

— What is your favorite song? (mine is "Hallelujah" by Jeff Buckley; hear it on YouTube)

I listened to it, and oh my, it's hauntingly beautiful. Thank you for sharing it with me. Sissel Kyrkjebø, a Norwegian soprano, is my favorite singer. She has the most beautiful voice I have ever heard. Listen to her sing "Pie Jesu" on

YouTube, and you'll see what I mean. I could easily picture us—after we've put our twelve children to bed—lying in front of a fire on a cold winter night, cuddled up and listening to these songs. It would be heavenly. Forgive me for stating these thoughts, which are well beyond friendship. I am violating the prime directive of keeping it light.

— What are some important things you desire in a relationship? (I'm winking at one possible answer)

The multilayered man of my dreams will touch my mind, body, and soul with a quiet confidence and make me desperately love him for his simple decency, his strength, his unapologetic softness. A lover of words and banter, my man will engage me in lively discussions or play with me with his wit. And when we are alone, he will effortlessly shift to soft words conveying genuine emotions, delivered in a way that touches my soul. We would read to each other, sharing our love of words, and I would delight in listening to poems he writes just for me. Always respectful of my heart, he will have earned unhindered access to the tender, hidden parts of me, and I will know I am completely safe in his all-encompassing embrace. I will tremble in his arms when he kisses me with such conviction that it makes my imperfections pale, my fears wane, and my deeply entrenched wounds heal.

I will love this man always, and he will see this with my simple gestures, my tender touch, and my frequent words, which will leave no doubt he is the one— the only one—for me.

And yes, oh mischievous one, that for which you winked in your question is what I wish for as well, along with everything it entails. Should your life one day merge with mine, I offer you this from Nicholas Sparks: "Making love, she'd always believed, was more than simply a pleasurable act between two people. It encompassed all that a couple was supposed to share: trust and commitment, hopes and dreams, a promise to make it through whatever the future might bring."

— Are you a morning or a night person? (I mean, when you're not on caffeine)

A family that owns an apple orchard follows Ben Franklin's maxim: "Early to bed, early to rise ..."

— What is your favorite day, and why? (hint for mine: TGIF)

Again, as a member of an orchard-owning family, I am predisposed to love the day of rest: Sunday.

— What are your pet peeves? (Excluding, of course, my desire for wanting more than a friendship with you)

Goodness, I have more than a few. I'll limit my answer to ten: 1. Child, spouse, or animal cruelty; 2. Unflushed and/or messy public toilets; 3. Rude/disingenuous people; 4. People who don't cover their cough or sneeze; 5. People who argue in public; 6. People who dwell on the negative; 7. In restaurants, vulgar talk at the dinner table, especially when children are near; 8. Dirty dishes in the sink; 9. Student tardiness; and 10. People who talk down to someone else.

I hope these insights about me are compatible with your wants and needs. I am not a complicated woman, Jake. I'm a working girl and don't expect to be catered to, nor do I feel in any way entitled. I wish I could give you a list of questions like those you sent to me, but it's late, and I have so many things I want to ask you that my mind is a blur.

I'm looking at you and Keenan now. It's a beautiful picture of you two. Thank you for sending it to me. Please tell Keenan I like him, too. I hesitate to mention this, but since our new agreement puts everything on the table, here goes: Will your subsequent children have the same disease that afflicts Keenan? Can you tell me more about what he has? Let me assure you that anything you say will not be a deal-breaker; it's just important for me to know.

Enclosed is a picture of me with Bluebell taken a few months ago in our orchard. If you look closely, you will see she has my shredded purse in her mouth. Oh, the stories I could tell you about this dog. But she is so very lovable, and I adore her.

My dear man, I'm struggling to keep my eyes open. This has been a long letter, and it feels good writing to you again. It's comforting when you occupy my thoughts. Just so you know, I've taken to calling my body pillow "Jake," and I hug "you" lovingly as I fall asleep. Good night, dear Jake. I'll see you in my dreams. Love, Claire

18

Dear Claire,

Your letter confirmed, in every way, why I love you, and it was my turn to be left breathless, with my heart pounding. Your description of what you want in a relationship is beautiful. Claire, I have no doubt that, for us, sex will be an expression of our love, a communion of our souls. When I saw you that day at the orchard, I saw us having an "I am through you so I" love. For 2400 miles back to Anchorage, it was all I could think about. When I got home, I immediately wrote my first letter to you. I had to be with you; it was as if the universe demanded it. Your words captured everything I envisioned our love could be. I love you so much. I hope you feel it.

Just so you know, for me as well, sex has rarely risen above the physical realm, and I am more than acquainted with the emptiness of which you speak. It's the reason I'm reluctant to date. With the women my colleagues introduced me to, I'd look into their eyes and instantly know there was nothing there; no coy smile, flirtation, or suggestive look can disguise a woman's inability to love in the way you described. But with you, when I first saw you, I felt an immediate, soul-stirring connection. No other woman has affected me in such a way. I thought you should know.

I'll shift to your responses to my questions.

I've been online, shopping for a nice toga; the challenge is finding a fabric that's boy-toy sheer yet rugged enough to withstand the rigors of cleaning our villa. I've read how grapes grow well in your part of the world, so I hope you're considering planting an acre or two of them. I favor seedless red grapes. Claire, I will learn your territory as well, and I will always make your happiness a priority in my life.

Of Maddy one day leaving you, it's a valid fear. I hope you two will have many more years together. Should something ever happen to her, you won't be alone, for you now have me. If our lives "merge," as you say, you will be warmly welcomed into the Holland clan; we're a lively, barbarous bunch of ill-tempered, grog-loving pirates who delight in telling tall tales of plundering villages and squeezing the treasures of tawdry bar wenches. You'll fit right in.

Regarding your agoraphobia, here's something to consider: Since Keenan entered my life, his blood disorder has created restrictions on where I can go. So you having limitations on where you can go is nothing new for me. I'll be patient with you on this. As a tease for you to see the world again, I'd love to cruise among the San Juans with you as the captain of a swift sailboat. It sounds wonderful, the ideal thing for solitude-loving us. Oh, and tell your subconscious there's a new sheriff in town who doesn't take kindly to ruffians hurting his fair lady. I've already kicked Mr. Heartbreaker's butt in my dreams and stuck a few pins into a voodoo doll of him in a place that never sees the sun. It was dark in my bedroom when I stuck him, so he either has impotence or hemorrhoids, but either one is suitable justice for him having hurt your heart.

One more thing about your fears. In your response to what you wanted in a relationship, you said, "I will tremble in his arms when he kisses me with such conviction that it makes my imperfections pale, my fears wane, and my deeply entrenched wounds heal." That will be me, Claire, loving you, singing you lullabies to calm your soul when you are frightened.

I read your six-word story and marveled at how far you've come since my first letter to you. I'm honored to be included in your new story. Here's my story: "I saw her and instantly knew."

I laughed at you and Maddy groaning when the power came back on. That you turn a hardship into something fun says a lot about you.

Claire, regarding long-distance relationships working, I feel the same. I read your words and feel so close to you. For one-percenters, words are nearly as powerful as physical touch. Imagine the day when our words and bodies meet. Yikes!

I'm back from taking a cold shower, so on to another question. As for me having a sweet tooth, not so much. I crave salty things like chips, peanut-butter-filled pretzels, and any orange cheesy thing that leaves your fingers stained for a week. The idea of having buttered popcorn with you sounds heavenly.

If Keenan knew of your culinary skills, he'd demand, with a great sense of urgency, that I marry you. Maybe someday you can teach us how to cook without employing a crockpot. What a fanciful concept. I like Thai food, too. I've never tried Chipotle, as there aren't any in Alaska, but I do like Mexican food.

I listened to your Sissel recommendation and agree she's one of the best at her craft. I also listened to her version of "Shenandoah," and it's beautiful. If you're ever bored, look up Eva Cassidy on YouTube and listen to her sing "Over the Rainbow" or "Fields of Gold." I know you'll love her.

I like the thought of us as a couple exploring and deepening our relationship with God. I envision us having this discussion while lying on Claire Hill, watching clouds go by. Your description of walking through your orchard and feeling Spirit resonates in me. I have the same feeling when hiking in the mountains here.

The way you covered your ability to forgive and forget was perfect. Thanks for sharing such genuine feelings with me and for giving the notion of forgiving that impotent, hemorrhoid-plagued idiot some consideration. Claire, regarding your mention of infidelity, cheating on you would come at a terrific cost. I would have to surrender my character, my honor, and my integrity, along with knowing it would break your heart. For these reasons, having an affair is unthinkable. Even flirting is a form of cheating because it would be disrespectful of our love. Should I ever place a ring on your finger, it will come with my promise to you and to God of my faithfulness. I think you already know this about me.

I'd love to recite poetry to you on Claire Hill or would delight in having you read me a story while I'm lying there with my eyes closed, absorbing your words. Either of those intimate, peaceful scenarios sounds wonderfully comforting.

To your quite valid pet peeves, I'll add a few that drive me nuts: litterbugs; unimportant emails/spam; grocery carts with bad wheels; telemarketers; and uh, um, people who insist on doing ten loads of laundry when one large load will do. Smiling and winking here.

Thank you for sending me your picture. You are so beautiful. I look at it and can easily imagine a life together. Yep, that purse of yours looks mighty mangled. I have to tell you that Bluebell appears to have been designed by a committee. As my mom would say, "God love her."

On to Keenan. Suddenly, the levity in writing this letter leaves me ...

He has von Willebrand disease, which, although akin to hemophilia, is different in that it involves another blood clotting factor. In 1926, Dr. Erik von Willebrand, a Finnish physician, published the first description of the affliction. Briefly, it's a bleeding disorder caused by a deficiency of von Willebrand factor (VWF), a protein in blood necessary for proper clotting. When a blood vessel is injured, and bleeding ensues, VWF helps platelets mesh to form a clot. People with this affliction do not have enough VWF, or it does not work the way it should, resulting in prolonged blood loss. The disease is rare, afflicting one percent of the population. So I suppose you could say Keenan is also a one-percenter, though not in a way to be envied. Like hemophiliacs, he's vulnerable to severe bleeding episodes such as what happened that day in your orchard. There is no cure for VWD, and for Keenan, it will be a lifelong condition. But there are effective treatments that make it a manageable disease.

Both VMD and hemophilia are usually inherited. In Keenan's case, he has Type 2N VWD (there are several types), where the "N" stands for Normandy, France, where this particular subtype was first identified. For a child to get Type 2N, both parents must pass on the abnormal gene. It was just blind luck that his mother and I both carry this defective gene. The chances of you having it are highly unlikely. Should we have children and they get a normal gene from you and a gene for Type 2N VWD from me, the child will not have VWD, but he or she will be a carrier. Genetic testing for both of us should help ease your concerns. I hope this adequately answers your question.

I have a few questions for you. Tell me about your family. Do you have brothers and sisters? Do you get along with your parents, grandparents, and siblings?

We've covered a lot of ground with these two letters, Claire. It feels good. Cheers! Jake

19

Dear Jake,

Thank you for describing Keenan's condition so well. It isn't as scary as I had imagined. I have to be truthful and say I'm relieved to know that if we have children, they will not have to endure his challenge. Jake, I felt your pain as you described his blood disorder and hope you know you have nothing to feel guilty about. With advances in the medical arena, there may be a cure in his lifetime.

I had tears from laughing so hard about your description of the grog-loving Holland clan. If your mother knew what you wrote, she'd be aghast. Maddy came in while I was laughing and asked what was so funny. I read aloud your description of your grog-loving family, your voodoo efforts regarding "that impotent, hemorrhoid-plagued idiot," and your observations of Bluebell. Jake, we haven't laughed so hard in ages. She said to tell you she agrees with your assessment of Bluebell being designed by a committee.

Maddy likes you. I hope one day you'll get to know the lady I love. Regarding my agoraphobia, your offer to be my protector touched me. I love you so much. Sailing with you might be just what I need to break the grip of this fear. Maybe we could give it a go this summer. I hope you'll consider visiting us. We can shop for red seedless grapes to plant in our orchard at the local farmer's market. This invitation, of course, includes Keenan. I already love him, and Bluebell would be in heaven having a boy to play with.

I want to turn serious for a moment. Maddy and I never talk about "Mr. Heartbreaker" because any mention of him would send my spirits plummeting for days on end. Yet with a little humor, you have reduced this despicable man to irrelevancy. In all my laughter of his voodoo-induced afflictions, I suddenly felt my heart mending. I have tears in my eyes as I write this. Thank you, my dear man. Thank you so. This evening, I'm going to Claire Hill, where I will forgive him. You were right. He did me a service. He caused me to change, so I'd be able to love and epically appreciate you. I'm also going to forgive my mother, my father (for reasons I'll discuss in this letter), and me. Yes, I need to forgive myself for my lack of self-love.

Speaking of Claire Hill, you reciting poetry or me reading stories to you there would be my version of heaven. I loved listening to Eva Cassidy! Oh, and regarding cooking, it would be fun having Keenan as an apprentice. You in the kitchen with me—gasp! That's a scary thought. Winking here.

Jake, about what you said about being faithful to me, I want you to know you could have the same confidence in my faithfulness to you. We feel the same about this issue. Being able to trust each other will be the cornerstone of our love.

I'm going to Claire Hill now to say my words of forgiving and thank God for you. I'll resume this letter tomorrow ...

Good morning! I woke this morning feeling so light, as if I could float away. Yesterday at Claire Hill, I had my last talk with Mr. Heartbreaker. I forgave him and told him he no longer has power over me. I told him the pain he inflicted on me forced me to change, and the gift from this pain was me learning what true love is. I also spoke to my parents, wished them well, and forgave them. I forgave myself for all of my self-belittling for not being "normal," and I told myself it's time to become the hero of my life's story rather than the victim. A great weight has been lifted from me, Jake. The darkness in my soul is gone. I feel so joyful; such is the power of forgiveness. I wish you were here so I could wrap my arms around you and tell you I love you.

Jake, I've been saving the best part of your letter to respond to. When you described how you felt when you saw me at the orchard and how the universe demanded we be together, all I can say is thank you for your patience, persistence, and insights. I know you must've felt like I was a Rubik's Cube, with all my colors hopelessly jumbled. Yet with abundant patience, you took me in your hands, did all kinds of gentle-but-intentional twisting and turning, and now look at me, close to being solved! You saved me, sir, in more ways than I can ever explain, and I love you for it.

Maddy hasn't stirred yet, so I have time to respond to your new questions. I'll begin by telling you about my family. Okay, here goes ...

I am an only child, so there is nothing to discuss regarding brothers and sisters. Sadly, I am estranged from my parents and have been for years. They divorced when I was six years old, and I haven't seen or heard from them since. Maddy and my grandfather (his name was Max) raised me. They're my maternal grandparents. Grandpa passed away three years ago. He was a towering presence in my life, and I loved him dearly.

My time with my parents would almost be laughable if it weren't so sad. My mother was born here in Leavenworth. She always had itchy feet, and her ticket out of this "dreadful little town," as she liked to call it, was through academic achievement. She excelled in high school and won a scholarship to Yale. The educational opportunity afforded to her there was secondary to her real reason for going to an Ivy League college; she was man-shopping, intent on landing a gentleman of means, and she found just that with my father. He was from old money, an aristocratic family whose fortune was made in West Virginia coal.

The little country girl erased her humble small-town origins and remade herself into a dazzling socialite, one of the beautiful, privileged people, adorned in jewelry, flitting from party to party, rubbing elbows with the elite at the finest country clubs. My parents' wealth was such that you could easily get lost in our house, a Gilded Age mansion in Newport, Rhode Island. She knew her talons would sink ever deeper into the aristocracy by having my father's child. I can't tell you how depressed she was when I turned out to be a girl. She quickly tired of the new "encumbrance" and turned me over to a series of nannies so she could resume her life hobnobbing with "the beautiful people."

Not only was I a disappointment to her for being the wrong gender, but I was a quiet, awkward little girl, so unlike all the other refined, charming, poster-child-pretty daughters of her peers. While the other little girls would play at tea party get-togethers in one of the countless mansions, I would sit by myself, daydreaming, which was my favorite pastime. This infuriated my mother; her job and, by extension, mine, was to fit in, to be one of the crowd. She became convinced that something was wrong with me and paraded me from doctor to doctor. One of them mentioned I might have Asperger's syndrome, a form of autism. The symptoms seemed to fit: I was quiet, exhibited poor social interactions, disliked changes in routines, and I had what my mother called "peculiar mannerisms."

The doctor wanted to get me tested, but she would have none of it. She had the perfect "disease" for me and didn't want the initial diagnosis to be refuted by testing. Having an Asperger's child was ideal for her: It could be invoked to explain my odd behavior in any social setting, plus it carried the bonus of her receiving sympathy points for being a long-suffering mother. I grew up convinced I had Asperger's, which was why I was so different. Like my mother, I could blame all my troubled feelings and behaviors on that convenient disorder.

She tolerated my father's womanizing (which explains why I had so many nannies) right up to the day he announced he had found his true love and wanted out of their "fairytale marriage," as she used to call their troubled union. Parting ways amicably was possible, my mother told him, as long as the compensation was adequate. A few lost millions here and there was nothing to my father, so that was that. Except … neither of them wanted me.

So, I was shipped to that "dreadful little town" under the proviso of allowing a few months for them to adjust to their new lives. For me, Leavenworth was Eden. I loved everything about life in an apple orchard, especially the quiet and the reverie of communing with nature. I loved this small town and soon came to love my wonderful grandparents, whom I'd never met before coming here.

Maddy (she insisted I call her Maddy because, she said, being called Grandma made her feel old) was an elementary school teacher, so she knew a thing or two about childhood behavior. After two weeks with them, she scoffed at my "Asperger's disorder" and had me tested. Turns out not only was I "normal," but my IQ was far higher than most. Gone was the convenient excuse to explain all my problems and troubles. Now all I had was the sad truth of being just plain different, which garnered no sympathy points from anyone.

After a month with them, Maddy called my mother and said they weren't sending me back. My mother went through the motions of shedding a few crocodile tears, but it took less than a minute for her to say okay. My father, I think, probably said, "Claire who?" when he was told I was staying in Leavenworth. And that was that, in terms of me and my parents. Oh, that's not quite true. When I turned eighteen, Maddy sent a succinct letter to my father, stating that if he didn't pay for my college education, she would sue him for over a decade's worth of child support. I'm sure after he calculated the cost involved in the latter, he agreed to fund my education. Neither he nor my mother came to my graduation, but that didn't surprise me since they never communicated with me in any way, ever—no telephone calls, letters, birthday cards, Christmas gifts, child support—nothing. But I am grateful for him paying for my college tuition.

The last I heard, my mother found another gentleman of means when her settlement money began running low, and my father is now on his fourth or fifth wife. Truly, if I now walked through one of their mansions, their crude displays of opulence would make me nauseous.

In contrast to my birth mother, I love the words of Eartha Kitt, which describe me perfectly: "I'm a dirt person. I trust the dirt. I don't trust diamonds and gold." Jake, I'm a country girl through and through, dreadfully underprivileged if you ask my parents or their affluent friends, but I'm richly loved by Maddy and my pets.

As for getting along with my grandparents, oh, how I love and treasure them. Grandpa died of cancer; we think the use of pesticides in our orchard could've caused it. I can honestly tell you there was never a cross word between Grandpa and me. I always get teary when thinking about him. He was such a kind and loving man. After he passed, we subleased all but ten acres of our 160-acre orchard, and I am proud to say we now sell only certified organic apples as our way of honoring him. My relationship with Maddy is based on mutual respect and love. She has never been one to hold in her thoughts, but she says what's on her mind in a loving way. As far as I'm concerned, to my parents, I was an inconvenience; for my grandparents, I was a treasure. They filled my days with unconditional love, and words could never describe how I feel about them.

From your questions about my relations with my family, I think you might be trolling for how easy I am to get along with, so I'll address it. Like my grandparents, I am kind and loving. I have never yelled at anyone; it's just not in me. I am not a pushover, however. Being a schoolteacher, I find that you can get your point across without being loud or nasty. When you treat someone with respect, they tend to act in kind.

As for you, your "conditions" letter spelled out how you, too, are not a pushover, which makes me wonder what you are like in terms of temperament. I do not function well when being yelled at or belittled. I pray that these deficiencies do not dwell in you when you're annoyed. I don't remember where I heard this, but I hold the words dear: "I will not let you choose which days to love me." Should you ever be upset with me, I hope you will never let your anger rise above your love. With you and Keenan, my love will always outshine my anger—and that's a promise.

Oh, one more thing. I love this from R.D. Blackmore: "… because I rant not, neither rave of what I feel, can you be so shallow as to dream that I feel nothing?" Jake, I've experienced much shallowness in my life, be it in relationships or friendships. I'm sure you understand what I'm saying. With you, how you look into my soul is unlike anything I've ever experienced. Your depth astonishes me. It's important to me that you know. Likewise, I will never mistake your quietness as meaning you feel or need nothing.

I've covered a lot of territory today. The questions you asked me about my family relationships, I now ask you.

I love you. Claire

20

Dear Claire,

You are right: your story regarding your parents is almost laughable—that is, if it weren't so sad. God. I'm so glad you were raised by loving grandparents. It makes me love Maddy all the more. I wish I could've met your grandfather; I'm sure I would've liked him.

I felt like dancing a jig when you told me about going to Claire Hill and doing what had to be done. I can't even begin to describe the joy in my heart. I am so proud of you. Claire, don't expect everything to be completely better now, as if you uttered some magic words and all traces of him are gone. When he pops into your awareness—which he will—just say, "I forgive you, and I choose happiness." Say it enough times, with firm conviction, and he will eventually go away. There are days when I forget what my former wife looked like, and I assure you I'm not descending into dementia. It's just that her presence in my mind is ever fading, which is a good thing.

As for me, be careful not to let your feelings for me become infatuation, where you elevate me to near-mythical proportions. Just remember that being madly in love cannot carry a relationship. You need other things: trust, communication, support, caring, respect, commitment. Hey, wait a minute—I think we have those boxes checked! Claire, I'm an average guy, with strengths and weaknesses, trying my best to find my way. I'm afraid that you may love the abstract version of me, the writer of letters, more than the in-person me, who occasionally farts in bed and forgets to shave on weekends. Also, when you first kiss me, you might think, argh, there's no chemistry here. Okay, I know that's not possible, but you get what I'm saying.

I'm glad you and Maddy had a laugh at Mr. Heartbreaker's expense. Laughter can be a catalyst for healing.

The thought of spending time with you this summer sounds wonderful. Let's give it more thought and discussion in the days ahead. Forgive the practical me, but I have to ask this question: Does Mrs. Kerfuffle, with her feral "issues," ever bite or scratch you or Maddy? I ask this because of Keenan. If she bit or clawed him, it could cause significant bleeding. With him, there is no such thing as a minor scrape, and any skin abrasion or puncture requires immediate attention. Welcome to my reality. Sigh …

Okay, on to your questions. I have to tell you, after asking the question about Mrs. Kerfuffle, some of my exuberance has waned. Injecting a little reality into the calculus of our relationship has its risks.

Regarding my temperament, you've seen it in my letters. I am kind and gentle by nature, but if someone tramps on my values, watch out. I don't mean to imply that I become a cartoonish Tasmanian devil when I'm angry; when I disagree with someone, I'm a gentleman and always would be so with you.

I tend to internalize feelings more than I should, so please dole out any criticism of me in a kind and constructive way. I've gotten better at letting petty things go; I think when you have children, it's one of the lessons they teach you. After all the dark nights of the soul we've experienced before meeting each other, I have no doubt we'd be very careful to safeguard our love. Rest easy on my temperament, Claire, and know that mutual respect, civility, and love will be our strengths as a couple.

Okay, on to my relationships with my family. I have a brother, Eddie, who is two years older than I. We are reasonably close, but my intense introversion has always clashed with his equally robust extroversion. He loves entertaining and crowds; I am much more content hiking in the mountains, away from everyone. But we are brothers, and we've learned to accept our differences. He took over my father's business and has done quite well; he remains a diehard bachelor and loves partying and the thrill of new women. As I said, we're different, but I love him.

My father—yikes, that has been a wild ride! He's blue-collar all the way, and I drove him to near-distraction in my youth. Some of my earliest memories are of him yelling, "Earth to Jake! Earth to Jake, come in!" To him, daydreaming was an abominable waste of time because there was always something to be done; to me, being lost in Jake's World, as he called it, was a vital necessity (I smiled when you said "Claire's World" in your letter). I remember how he appeared apoplectic when, at six years old, I proudly showed him a poetry book I bought, boasting that it cost only a month's worth of allowances. "You could've bought a good hammer with that much money," he blurted out, aghast at the absurdity of my purchase.

He was a master electrician and founded his own business. When my brother and I were teenagers, he insisted that we learn the electrical trade so we'd have a way to make a living. Under his demanding tutelage, I became a certified journeyman electrician at eighteen. It proved to be a fortunate undertaking. With what I saved working for him during summers and later through college, I made enough to pay for my education. Being an electrician is how I met you. Keenan and I spent a few weeks helping my retired friend wire his new house at Lake Chelan, and a side trip while we were there is how we ended up at your orchard.

Dad took hard my wanting to become a geologist. He hoped Eddie and I would take over the family business. In fact, he was so sore about it that he hardly spoke to me during my freshman year. By the way, one day, I'll impress you. "Look," I'll say with a confident air of smugness, "see that thing, right there on the ground? It's a rock. I know that because I've had college." I wanted to be a geologist because I liked being outdoors, and you have to be able to visualize what's going on with strata several miles below your feet. I was quite good at visualizing; I spent my entire youth doing it.

Anyway, Dad is proud of me now that I'm working in the trade again, and he's equally proud of having a son with a doctoral degree. As with my brother, Dad and I learned to accept our differences, and now we have an easy, respectful relationship filled with love. He still doesn't understand what makes me tick, but he's gratified by how I turned out and often says he wishes he had raised Eddie and me the way I'm raising Keenan. Praise gets no finer than hearing that from your father.

My mom and I have always gotten along. She accepted me being me, and I still smile at how she patiently listened to me recite poetry to her every day, or how I'd excitedly tell her how I was exploring—in my head—the moon and other planets. "That's impressive, Jake. Go tell Sparky. I'm sure he'll want to hear your story." Sparky was our dog. I think if he could, he would've stuck a paw in an electrical outlet to end the suffering of listening to me.

Lastly, my relationship with Keenan: We just seem to be wired the same way, and we love being together. We've spoken to each other in German since he was a baby, and he felt like we had our own special "code" that nobody else knew. He was shocked when he went to German immersion school and discovered others who also spoke the "code." Now he loves having a group of friends who are also "code talkers." I'm sure having our own language brought us closer. He knows it's challenging for me to be a single parent, and he does all he can to help out. He's such a special child.

At some point, I know one of us will ask about the partners we've had in our lives and what went wrong. I guess I'll leave it to you to ask first.

I'm enclosing a card with my work, home, and cell phone numbers. I'm not saying it's time to talk to each other; I just want you to have them. I struggle with the notion of speaking to you on the phone. Doing so would likely spell the end of our letters, which I treasure. I know, it's a one-percenter thing.

Toodles, my sweet. Jake

21

Dear Jake,

Your letter made me laugh. I could easily picture Sparky and Bluebell getting together, comparing notes, saying, "Oy, those one-percenters ..." Surely there's a place in heaven for animals.

Sadly, Mrs. Kerfuffle does have a habit of using her teeth and claws to express her frustrations. If you and Keenan visit us, I'll ask a friend to watch her. Thank you for giving me a glimpse into your life with Keenan and how you need to do risk considerations for everything you do. I know it's second nature to you now, and I'll also learn to consider risks with him. Please don't feel bad about mentioning these issues; I understand and will fully support you. We'll be in it together.

I have to tell you that you weren't very convincing in cautioning me about becoming infatuated with you. I laughed as your caution quickly morphed into full speed ahead. But I hear you, and your point is well-taken. As for chemistry, Jake, we've already met, even though it was for just twenty minutes. I've seen you half-naked from the waist up. Remember? You used your shirt to stop Keenan's nosebleed. You, sir, are a handsome man. Trust me; there's chemistry.

Okay, I'll take your hint and be the first to bring up past loves. Gulp. Here goes.

His name was Colin. I met him in my last year of graduate school at the University of Washington. He was a premed student, handsome, and quite sure of himself. A child of privilege he was, which I should've known spelled trouble. He was friends with my roommate's boyfriend and one day came with him to our place. I was shocked when he took an interest in me, and I nearly fainted when he asked me out. I was wined and dined and then taken to his place, a swank condo rented and furnished by his parents. I fell completely for his charms and followed him around like a wide-eyed puppy. He was a partier, but I didn't mind going with him since he did all the talking. I was just the quiet babe by his side, hanging on his every word, laughing when others laughed, fitting right in with the "in" crowd. And so started my life as Claire the Chameleon, who deftly changed her colors to appear like everyone else. After a few months, the parties became far less exciting, and by then, I had heard all his "amusing" anecdotes a hundred times. Desperate for love and approval, I convinced myself that he was the man of my dreams, my express ticket to "normalcy." I hardly noticed losing myself in the process of loving him; having my needs and wants go unattended seemed, at that time, trivial.

I imagined being the wife of a surgeon who was a great healer of people, with a house full of kids and feeling blissfully happy. My "fairytale romance" (God, how like my mother's delusions this now seems) came crashing down two days before my graduation ceremony. After dinner and going to his place for the obligatory sex, he said he got accepted into med school at Johns Hopkins. I was so excited for him—and us—and mentioned how we had a lot of work to do to get ready for the move. "Oh," he replied, casually, "I'm sorry to tell you this, but you're not coming with me. Lisa is. She's one of my other girlfriends, and she is a far better lover and prettier than you." He then proceeded to tell me that he never loved me and that I was in his life simply for his amusement. "Besides," he said as if relishing twisting the dagger in my heart even more, "you are much too boring and quiet to be wanted by any man for a long-term relationship."

I staggered out of his condo and made my way to the hotel where my grandparents were staying. They had come for my graduation. I fell apart and had a nervous breakdown. Graduation day, for me, was spent under sedation at a local hospital. If Grandpa had known where Colin lived, he would've ended his life right then and there. By the way, he never liked Colin, and he repeatedly warned me about him, saying he was much too smooth, too vain and arrogant; and, for Grandpa, the greatest sin of all: superficial. How I wished I'd listened to him, but "love" had blinded me to the truth.

I went back to Leavenworth with them, lost in a deep depression that lasted for over a year. This passage, by an unknown author, eloquently describes my despair: "I wanted to write down exactly what I felt, but somehow the paper stayed empty, and I could not have described it any better." Cancer claimed my grandpa that year, which heightened my misery. Truly, those were dark days for my soul.

Gradually, with the help of counseling, I was able to resume some semblance of functionality. Then, at Maddy's insistence, I applied for a local school teaching position and was hired. Being among those beautiful third-grade children was my tonic for fending off the blues. I swore to myself that I would never let a man hurt me so badly again, and that's when the walls started going up around me, isolating me from the world. It's been years since I've dated, and until you came along, I had planned on a solitary life, with my heart closely guarded.

I'm sure you must be thinking, "How could a breakup destroy her so? People break up all the time, and it's a normal occurrence when you're young." I think the roots of my devastation can be traced to when I was living with my parents and experiencing what it was like to be unloved. That feeling has never left me. The message then, and later with him, was that I was unlovable. This issue rages within me, even now, with you. A palpable fear is that you will do the same as him once you get to know me. That's why I'm frightened to move beyond the letter-writing stage with you. In our written words, you like me; face-to-face, maybe not. From your last letter, it seems we both have this issue. Sigh. Baggage can be so burdensome, don't you think?

Since past loves is the topic, I might as well cover it all. My first kiss was at nineteen, in college. My virginity was claimed a short while later by the same guy, who quickly tired of me and moved on. In this relationship, I sadly discovered that sex was so unlike what I imagined making love would be, and sex with Colin was more of the same. Now you come along saying it will be different. I so hope this will be true; in my dreams of you and me, it already is.

So, Jake, there you have it. It's embarrassing to tell you of my choices in men. I hope my foolishness doesn't diminish your thoughts of me. I wouldn't fault you if it did. Care to delve into your past loves?

Love, Claire

22

Dear Claire,

Regarding my having any diminished thoughts of you, I offer these words by Mark Jackson: "You cannot disrespect the caterpillar and rave about the butterfly." We both were in love with the idea of love, and, with our fertile imaginations, that was enough to sustain us until reality could no longer be imagined away. I don't fault you for the choices you made; I've been just as foolish. To illustrate this, I wrote this passage shortly after I received my divorce decree:

Once there was love. Once there was magic. Once diamonds glittered, and passion danced to an endless tune, and hours together seemed like minutes, like treasures, like heaven. Once our bodies craved to be one, and together forever was a certainty. Once upon a time, but that was an eternity ago, before the seasons, which came and went leaving no color in our fall, and before the tears, running like rivers, desperately seeking but finding no comfort. Now angry dragons run roughshod on forever, trampling dreams and hopes and passion. Gone forever the magic; gone forever, our love. And so we proceed on courses divergent, two ships in the night, an ocean between us, each, in our own way, looking into the vastness of the universe, seeking guidance and solace from the stars. The search begins for what was once.

I think this illustrates both my imaginary world, where what we had was perfect, and reality, which was far different. The simple truth is that my relationship with my former wife was built on infatuation and torrid sex. Erin and I met on our first day at graduate school at Washington State. We both had bachelor's degrees in geology and were accepted into the Ph.D. program without having a master's degree, which in academia is rare. She was a wild-child, beautiful, untamed, and addicted to adrenaline rushes, so unlike any girl I had ever known; plus, she liked rocks. I was a goner.

It was a demanding program at WSU, and both of us were frequently away from each other, being out in the field, collecting data for our dissertations. Still, we found time to do thrilling things such as skydiving, whitewater rafting, mountain climbing—anything that would give her an adrenaline rush— including sex in public places. I loved the highs as much as she did, and, at my tender age, I was agreeable to any of her thrill-seeking activities. Then, toward the end of our first year at school, she got pregnant. She was hell-bent on getting an abortion; I was just as adamant that we have our child, and she relented only after my proposal of marriage. We eloped, and Keenan entered the world during our second year of grad school.

The burdens of motherhood were immediately disagreeable to her. It's hard to go thrill-seeking when an infant is hindering your every move. She resented being reined in by family. I took on the primary duties of parenthood and can't ever remember her changing a diaper. Those were hard times for me, trying to raise a baby and struggling to keep my academic life afloat. Without the help of my parents, I wouldn't have made it through grad school. My dear mother volunteered to care for Keenan when I was doing fieldwork; fortunately, they lived not far away in Spokane, so I had that resource when I needed it. With a baby, as you can imagine, our scorching sex turned lukewarm, and the thrill times were exchanged for the mundane requirements of childrearing. To my surprise, I found that I loved being a father; it just seemed to come naturally to me. Erin came and went, and she even started calling Keenan "my child," as if I went out and bought him at a rummage sale.

I first noticed something wasn't right with Keenan when he started learning how to walk. He'd be covered in bruises from falling. I mentioned it to my mom, but she thought it was just a normal part of growing up. I was in the field when I got a desperate call from my father to come home. Keenan had fallen and hit his nose. After several minutes of relentless bleeding, they called the paramedics. He was rushed to the hospital and nearly died from losing so much blood. A nurse saw all his bruises and reported it to child protective services. I drove like a madman to the hospital and was stunned to see my son lying in bed with a bag of blood feeding into his tiny arm. My shock at seeing my son in the hospital fighting for his life was exponentially magnified by some idiot lady asking, "How often do you hit your son, Mr. Holland?"

They suspected he might have hemophilia, but a series of tests showed that he had von Willebrand disease. The diagnosis devastated me, and I felt incredibly guilty for passing it on to him. He made it through that ordeal with the help of a medicine called desmopressin, a synthetic form of a hormone that occurs naturally in the pituitary gland. The case against me for being an unfit father was dropped on news of the diagnosis.

I took him home and watched him like a hawk. I was half-tempted to wrap him in latex foam and outfit him with a tiny helmet, so when he fell, he wouldn't hurt himself. He had three more episodes requiring hospitalization while I was in grad school. We had no health-care insurance, which made his condition even more challenging. My parents paid the considerable medical bills, and I will never forget that kindness from them. "He's ours, too, and we'll do anything for him," my father said with tears in his eyes. That's when I realized how much I loved the man who could never understand me.

Keenan's affliction hit Erin especially hard. Before learning of his bleeding disorder, she often said she couldn't wait until the awful baby years were over so we could take him out and do "cool" things. She so wanted a junior thrill-seeker. With his disorder, the reality hit: We could never be far from a hospital. Things such as skydiving, whitewater rafting, and rock climbing were life-threatening activities. Her response was to withdraw from him even further. I don't think she could come to terms with producing a "defective" child.

After college, she wanted to move to Alaska, so we both landed jobs with an oil company in Anchorage. Life as a geologist proved to be far less exciting than she imagined. The field season is restricted to summers here, so she was chained to her desk most of the time, with a few visits to the North Slope to sit on an oil well. It was far too tame of an existence for her. I, however, liked my job and loved living in Alaska. Keenan, for the most part, did okay, except for teething, which caused episodes of bleeding, and a few nosebleeds, but nothing was as bad as the first hospitalization. Fortunately, we found a good doctor for him, and our local hospital can handle his special needs. Having medical insurance that came with the job was a godsend.

On the night of Keenan's third birthday, after he went to bed, Erin announced that she was going to become a fighter pilot and had joined the Navy earlier that day. She would soon be leaving for Officer Candidate School in Pensacola, Florida. After being commissioned as an ensign, she'd attend various flight training schools in Florida before moving on to specialized training in Mississippi. With any luck, she said she'd be flying jets within two years. Needless to say, I was stunned. I still remember looking at her, shocked, and stammering, "What about us?" She replied that she had, for a long time, been "preparing" me for her leaving by staying out of Keenan's life so we could better bond with each other. And, she said, her insistence on keeping our finances separate and renting a house instead of buying one would result in no "entanglements" for us to deal with in our parting. Yep, she was near saintly in her concern for Keenan and me.

It soon dawned on me that being out in the field for extended periods wouldn't work as a single father, not with Keenan's blood disorder. So in a panic, I thought about what else I could do to earn a living. I even considered moving back to Spokane to work in my father's electrical business. That's when I read a newspaper article about the shortage of teachers in Anchorage. It occurred to me that since I liked kids, maybe I could be a teacher. This profession seemed ideal; it didn't require fieldwork, plus I'd have summers off to be with Keenan. I applied, and because I had a Ph.D., I was able to become a teacher under the Alaska alternative teacher certification program. Plus, when the school district found out I was a certified electrician, they snapped me up, and I became a teacher at the King Career Center. Just as with being a dad, teaching came naturally to me.

Anyway, we got divorced, and I got full custody of Keenan. One good thing about her working for the federal government is that Uncle Sam ensures I get an allotment from her every month for child support. Since Keenan is still considered a dependent of hers, the Navy covers most of his medical costs. She hasn't contacted Keenan in any way since she left, and the last I heard, she was flying F/A-18 Super Hornet fighters aboard the aircraft carrier USS Ronald Reagan. She married another pilot, so I suppose you could say the wild child is still alive, surfing the skies at Mach 2. By the way, before I forgave her, I used to tell my colleagues my former wife was a test pilot at a broom factory. I suppose I was half-right.

What did I learn from my marriage? My greatest lesson was, while opposites attract, they later repel. And I learned that while I can do things outside my comfort zone, I have no desire to make it an everyday thing. Passion, too, is nice, but it has no endurance, and when the passion subsided with Erin and me, there was nothing left for us to build on. She loved crowds and pulse-pounding excitement; for me, it was unsettling. I craved intimacy, and to her, that meant having "yawner" sex, as she called it. For her, it was always a race for the orgasm, and then the next orgasm, and once that was achieved, it was time to go out and party. I once read an article saying it is best to keep strangers from "petting" your INFJ, and I came to despise all those inebriated partygoers fawning over me.

Keenan's arrival gave me the excuse I needed to stay home while she partied. For all I know, she could've had more than her share of hookups with other men. It would fit with her thrill-seeking ways. In short, everything I treasured was tedious and boring to her, and all that she held dear was never in harmony with my soul. Am I bitter regarding her? No. I got a terrific son as a result of what we had. After she left, I found that I didn't miss her as much as I thought I would; in fact, my life became far more peaceful, and I like it that way. But I still hope for a deep love with someone. Care to apply for the job?

I won't bore you with my past loves other than to say I've never been with anyone where I didn't feel the emptiness you talked about. As for the last time I've had sex, it's been so long that it's hard to remember. If you need to know more, just ask.

Oh! I almost forgot—your fear of my leaving once I get to know you. Before I comment on that, Claire, do you realize what a powerful thing you did with that statement? You put that fear of yours right out in the open, saying, "Here it is." Wow! How courageous of you to confide something so personal to me. If that isn't a heart-mending step, I don't know what is. Now, to comment on your fear: You have no idea of the sheer power of your presence; that first day I saw you, I just stood there, hopelessly captivated. With our correspondence, that feeling has grown within me, not lessened. Me leave you? I smile that you harbor such a thought; it is me who wonders if I'll measure up to you.

Let me suggest this: Instead of dwelling on our fears, expecting the worst, let's both focus on what might be possible. It makes more sense, and it certainly makes life much sweeter to believe that ours will be a wonderful love. Our relationship working is a distinct possibility, so let's hold on to that; everything else is just noise, sure to drown out our music if we let it. It costs nothing to be positive, and it certainly feels better than focusing on the negative. So, act as if what we have is special because it is. I hope this helps you confront your fear.

By the way, I fear that you won't like/love Keenan or mother him because he's not yours. You now know the roots of that in me.

I'll end with something from Jonathan Carroll: "The first great real intimacy between two people begins when secrets are told."

Imagine me wrapping my arms around you. Love, Jake

23

Dear Jake,

It's sad how my parents and your former wife were incapable of loving their children, and it's hard not to get angry when thinking about their shameful behavior. But forgiving them was the right thing to do. I'll take peace in my life over anger any day. I look at Keenan and can't imagine her not loving him.

I almost fell off my chair from laughing so hard at your test-pilot quip. Jake, I cried when you said you realized how much you loved your father. It was so beautiful, as was what you wrote after your divorce. I admire you so much for all you've overcome and for being the father you are. Thank you for sharing your story with me. It makes me love you all the more.

Thanks also for calming my fear about whether you might leave and for saying let's dwell in the positive. Fretting and worrying won't make tomorrow any better, but it will surely rob today of any joy.

I'm glad you shared your fear about my ability to love Keenan, so I'll make him the focus of this letter. Many thoughts are swirling inside of me, so please be patient with me as I ramble on …

If you only knew how many times a day I look at the picture of you two. I say this because when my gaze reaches it, my eyes don't automatically go to you, with Keenan being an afterthought. I see him. I've already fallen in love with him. When he was hurt, and I held him on the way to the hospital, something about him touched my heart. That's why I kissed his cheek. And when he acted so bravely, trying to comfort you in German, I thought, this is an exceptional little boy. The powerful affinity I felt toward him that day has only increased since I've learned more about him. If we ever get together, oh, how I will love him. Since the subject is Keenan, how did you come up with such an interesting name for him? It suits him quite well.

I've sat here for a while, working up the courage to continue …

Although I do not doubt being able to love Keenan, something troubles me. I wonder, in your close father-son relationship, if there will be room for me. As you've said many times, it's been just you and him, and you two have an unusually strong bond. Will I be the proverbial "odd man out?" Will he resent me for taking some of your time? Can you love me as much as you love Keenan, or will you find you have only enough love for one? Jake, as a woman, I would need intimate time with you; it would be vital for my wellbeing. These aren't the musings of a selfish diva; I'm not that way. But if all I were to get would be scraps of your attention, it would be injurious to our relationship.

Also, what would be your expectations regarding my role in raising Keenan? Guiding, directing, and disciplining him come to mind as I ask this, along with making decisions together in matters related to him. For me to love him, truly love him, I would have to be an equal parent, not the person who does the cooking and cleaning as if I were the hired help. Have you thought about this?

Jake, you cautioned me about infatuation, and I now do the same for you. Maybe you are so preoccupied with me that you have ignored all practical potential deal-breaking realities.

I'm struggling to articulate my thoughts, and I hope you get the essence of my concerns. I have an enormous capacity to love and will be a wonderful mother one day. I just know it. I can easily imagine being Keenan's mom, and having him as my son would be such an honor. But equally important is having an intimate relationship with you.

Since I'm running amok in reality, I might as well talk about my child. Her name is Bluebell. You would have to love her, too, for she comes with the package. I hope you will have said yes to taking her on before she eats your wallet or chews on one of your shoes. Regarding Mrs. Kerfuffle, Keenan's health comes first; I never would expose him to potential harm.

Sigh. As you said in a previous letter, injecting a little reality into our relationship's calculus has its risks. Let me know what you think. If there isn't enough room in your heart for both Keenan and me, I will understand. Claire

24

Dear Claire,

"Running amok in reality" is good because it shows progression in our relationship. I welcome your thoughts and concerns, and as we agreed to in my "conditions" letter, every question deserves an honest reply.

Regarding Keenan, I do not want, nor have I ever sought, hired help for cooking and cleaning. However, in your case, I'll consider your services if your rates are reasonable. On the job application I send to you, be sure to complete the self-assessment questionnaire to determine if you meet the minimum qualifications for the job.

Okay, back to reality.

Claire, you would be an equal parent, in every way, should our lives merge. He needs a mother, not a maid, and I need a wife, not an afterthought. I honestly feel it won't be difficult to achieve harmony in our new family, where all our needs are recognized and met. Communication is key to achieving this harmony, and our letters have proven we are quite capable of productive dialog.

When you initially asked about your role in the guiding, directing, and disciplining of Keenan, I thought, "What is she talking about? I don't do those things." I mean, I can't ever remember disciplining him, and it's not because I'm a lax parent. Keenan is always courteous and well-behaved. The same goes for guidance and direction. I had to think about this for a while, and then it occurred to me that with Keenan, parenting seems to come naturally. We like being around each other, so guiding and directing him comes from him seeing my behavior. For example, I treat him with respect and he, in turn, does the same with me and others. On Christmas, we volunteered to help serve the homeless at a local shelter, so he learned about having compassion for less-fortunate people. For me, parenting is a one-on-one tutorship where I do the right thing, and Keenan emulates my behavior. This quote by Gabriel Andreas serves as my touchstone for being a parent: "The best teachers are the ones who show you how to use your heart."

So, with you, rather than "guiding, directing, and disciplining" him, I would ask that you simply be yourself so that he can observe and emulate your kindness and goodness. To me, parenting is that easy. As a third-grade teacher, I suspect you're thinking, "No way, kids aren't like that," and for most children, I would agree. But Keenan is so sweet and kind. God truly blessed me with this child, and you were right when you said he was an exceptional little boy. Once you spend time with him, you'll understand what I'm saying. As for the possibility he might resent you for taking some of my time, he is a loving boy who feels the void of not having a mother. All you have to do is love him, and he'll welcome you into our family.

I don't mean to imply that everything will be milk and cookies if we merge because routines would have to change. As a single father, routines are what keeps the good ship Holland afloat. For example, Friday is always pizza and shopping day, and Saturdays are reserved for doing the wash and cleaning the house. On Sundays, Keenan reads the newspaper comics aloud to me, and we do fun things like cross-country skiing. Changing routines that have been in place for years can't happen overnight, and this applies to you as well.

Also, I've not talked much to Keenan about you. He knows I care about you, and your Christmas gifts gave me a chance to discuss, in general terms, the idea of us one day getting married and him having a mother. Eventually, though, I need to talk more to him about my feelings for you. Since we're so far apart, the only practical way for him to get to know you is speaking to each other on the phone. We need to consider this wildly audacious leap forward in our relationship. Gulp.

I'll move on to the subject of Keenan and I speaking German. My maternal grandmother took care of me from the day I was born so my parents could work. Oma (my grandmother) and Opa (my grandfather) immigrated to the U.S. from Germany in the 1950s as newlyweds and settled in Seattle, where he worked as an aeronautical engineer at Boeing. After he retired, they moved to Spokane to be near my mom and dad. Being with Oma all day long, sitting on her lap, listening to her, is where I learned German. My brother wanted nothing to do with that "funny talk," but I loved it. I think it's where my affinity for words began. I loved talking to Oma and Opa in German and felt as if we had our own special language. I took German in high school and college, and they were the easiest credits I ever earned because I was fluent in the language, both orally and in writing.

When Keenan was born, I continued this tradition to honor my grandparents and because knowing another language enriches your life in many ways. It saddens me that he never met his grandparents, who both passed before he was born. When he is older, we plan to visit our ancestral village, called Gondelsheim, in southwestern Germany, to learn more about our roots. If you become part of our family, we'd love to teach you the language as well.

I wish I could dazzle you with my genius regarding naming Keenan, but such is not the case. Erin and I flipped a coin, and whoever won got naming rights. She wanted him to be named after warriors and chose Gunther Ajax (I swear, it's true). Thank God I won, and all I did was switch my first and middle name around. I am Jacob Keenan, and he is Keenan Jacob. When I was born, my mom wanted to name me Keenan Jacob, but my dad wouldn't have it, so Jacob Keenan was their compromise. With her grandson, she got the name she originally wanted. My dad rolled his eyes when I told them what we were naming him, and my mother kissed me and jokingly said she forgave me for everything. But as time has passed, even my dad has come to agree that Keenan is a worthy name.

Regarding Bluebell, no problem having your child be part of the family. I'm sure she and Keenan would become best friends. I'm sorry about Mrs. Kerfuffle not fitting in. Maybe we could find a way to keep distance between her and Keenan, a respectful avoidance if you will. I'd be willing to discuss it, but his safety cannot be discounted.

I could go on all day talking about Keenan, but I need to finish before the mailman arrives. There is room in our hearts for you, Claire. Abundant room. We both need you. We both will adore you.

I've been thinking about calling you. I know—it's a scary thought.

Love, Jake

25

AFTER CLEANING AND putting away the dinner dishes, Claire and Maddy retreated to the living room. Sunday evenings at their home were spent with no television or radio on, a tradition that started long before Claire was born. For this hard-working apple-growing family, Sunday was a day of rest, a time to recharge and be with each other. The quiet of such days and the closeness it fostered always appealed to Claire.

Claire sat on the cozy, overstuffed chair and rested her legs on an ottoman. After putting her portable desk on her lap, she began writing a letter to Jake. Bluebell brought her rawhide dog bone in from the kitchen and began gnawing on it. Mrs. Kerfuffle perched on the back of Claire's chair and purred when Claire reached behind and scratched the feline's ear. Maddy went to the couch and was soon lost in her latest project, crafting a blanket of small, brightly colored squares made from leftover yarn.

The calm of the evening ended when the phone rang.

"Hello, this is Maddy. How may I help you?"

"Hey. It's Jake. How are you tonight?"

"Jake! It's good to hear your voice. I'm fine. How's Keenan?"

Claire's heart flopped when Maddy said aloud who it was. Her wide eyes conveyed panic. *Oh, God, what should I say to him?* Her mind raced—there was so much to say …

"Keenan's well. Thanks for asking. I waited for him to go to sleep, so please forgive the late hour of this call."

"It's no problem. Claire and I are having a quiet evening. In fact, she's writing a letter to you now. I'll pass the phone to her." She hit the mute button as she handed the phone to her. "Take a breath, Claire. You look as if you're going to faint."

Claire looked at her, frightened, and took the phone.

"H-h-hello …" The solitary word somehow managed to cover a couple of octaves.

"Hello, sweet Claire. Yep, it's me. I'll bet you were hoping I wouldn't carry out my threat to call you."

His cheerful greeting was met with silence.

"Claire, are you there?"

Tears rolled down her cheeks. Unable to speak with emotions clogging her throat, she was devastated.

Maddy saw her distress and took the phone back.

"It's me again, Jake. I'm putting you on speaker." She touched a button. "Can you hear me?"

"Yes, ma'am. Is Claire okay?"

"She's fine, just overwhelmed to hear your voice, so I'll talk for her. Not a minute goes by when you and Keenan aren't in her thoughts. She loves your words and spends many hours in the orchard being with you—well, being with you in your letters. You both are lucky to have each other."

"Can you hear me, Claire? If you can, stomp your foot on the floor once for yes and twice for no."

Maddy laughed at his humor. "She's not a horse, Jake. Horses don't turn beet-red as she is now."

Claire's mouth fell open in shock at Maddy's banter with him. Mortified, she felt her blood reddening her cheeks, just as Maddy had said.

Jake spoke again. "Maddy, will you take me off the speaker and hand the phone to Claire?"

"Sure. Here she is."

"Claire, I'll talk, and you just listen. I know how overwhelming the concept of 'us' is. My hands are shaking as I speak, so it's not just you being nervous. I love you so much. As scary as this is, not having a life with you is even scarier. That's why I'm calling to tell you that. When you feel you can talk to me, please call. I'll say goodbye for now, and I apologize for catching you off-guard. Goodbye, my love."

He ended the call before she could say a thing.

Claire handed the phone back as tears poured from her. Maddy got up and hugged her. "God, how you love him. He knows, Claire. He knows."

"I-I blew it, Maddy. I couldn't say a word."

"You didn't blow it. He knows how you feel. A blind man could see it."

Claire smiled meekly and then nestled in Maddy's warm embrace. After a few silent moments, she looked at her grandmother, her face reflecting her anguish. "I need to go to bed."

Maddy kissed Claire's forehead and tenderly touched her cheek. "Okay," she said softly. "Just don't beat up on yourself. Your words will come, Claire, and when they do, he'll be a lucky man to hear all that's in you. A mighty lucky man."

Claire shook her head, dismissing her grandmother's words of reassurance, and went upstairs. Bluebell followed her, her head down, knowing that comfort needed to be given.

In bed, Claire covered herself with her comforter and curled into a fetal position. Bluebell jumped onto the bed and rested her chin on Claire's shoulder. She wiped the tears from her eyes and looked at Bluebell. "Why couldn't my words come out, girl? I blew it. God, I blew it." With sad eyes, Bluebell tenderly licked her cheek. Claire hugged her. She fell asleep with those troubling thoughts dancing in her head.

The next morning, Claire got up early and turned on her laptop. She googled Jake's school, went to his homepage, and clicked on the button to send him an email.

Dear Jake, it's me, Claire. I'm sorry about last night. Hearing your voice felt so good. There were so many things I wanted to say to you that my mind went into overload (plus, I was terrified). Just know I love you enormously. I wanted you to know this right away, so that's the reason for this email. I hope yours is a good day. I'm thinking about you, always. Love, Claire

She closed her laptop with a sigh and got on with her day.

The teenagers were full of energy after a weekend of recharging as they strode into Jake's classroom. "Hey, everyone, take a seat because we have a lot to do. Today's discussion is on single and three-phase electrical power systems." While waiting for them to get settled, he glanced at his homepage. There was an item in his inbox from Claire. He read the message and swung his fist through the air in triumph. "She loves me enormously!" Suddenly, he realized where he was.

"Woo woo!" one of the students yelled as if he pulled a truck air horn.

"Are you blushing there, Mr. H?" another one quipped.

Everyone laughed and wolf-whistled. Jake couldn't help but laugh, too. "Okay, okay. Even teachers can be loved." He pulled up the picture of Claire with Bluebell he had on the computer and turned it around so the kids could see it. "Her name is Claire, and man, she's something." He and his students had developed a tight bond as the school year progressed, and they were happy for him. For the rest of the morning, Jake walked around the class with a smile and a puffed-up chest. A little swagger never hurt anyone.

At noon, after his daily call to Maddy, he replied to Claire's email ...

Dear Claire, thanks for the email. My students got a kick out of hearing me shout, "She loves me enormously!" after reading it during class. I'm sure I won't be living this down anytime soon. Thank you for the email—truly, it made my day.

It was good talking to you last night, I say with a wink. By the way, don't give being unable to talk a second thought. I understand. Besides, I heard you loud and clear, and I love you, too. Jake

P.S. There being a perfect moment is a myth, so please don't wait to call.

26

"WHAT'S WRONG, CLAIRE?" asked Maddy after the pizza arrived. "I thought going out on a Friday night would be fun, but you seem to be a million miles away."

"Sorry for not being good company. I'm calling Jake this evening ..." She sighed and looked at Maddy with anxious eyes.

"Well, I suggest asking him how his week went, light stuff like that." Maddy took a bite of pizza. "Who would've thought mustard, bratwurst, sauerkraut, and red and green peppers would taste so good together? I love coming to Rudloof's Pizza."

Claire ignored her food appraisal. "I'm afraid it won't be the same as it is in our letters. You know I express myself better in writing."

"We talk all the time, and you're a wonderful conversationalist. If you attempt to impress him by saying something dazzling, you're sure to get tongue-tied. Keep things simple."

Claire sighed again. "I just hope I'll be able to talk this time."

"Claire, for God's sake, he's scared too. Why not flip it around? Imagine he's a lot more afraid than you are, and it's your job to calm him down. You do it with your students, so pretend he's like one of them having to get up in front of the class."

"I never think of him being scared. He always seems so self-assured."

Her grandmother smiled. "He loves you. That makes him afraid because he has a lot to lose if you don't like him. He's scared. Trust me."

"I suppose."

That night, alone in her room, Claire kept looking at the clock. Alaska was an hour behind Washington, so if she called at ten, it would be nine there, and Keenan should be asleep. When the hour arrived, she picked up the phone with shaking hands and dialed his number.

"Hello."

It was Keenan. *Oh God,* she thought ...

"Hello?"

"Um, hello, Keenan. This is Claire Lofton. How are you?"

"I'm fine. I liked your Christmas book. I read it to Papa at night, and we finished it in a week."

"I'm glad you liked it."

"Where did you find books in German?"

"I ordered them from Amazon in Germany."

"Oh. Hold on, Tommy. Um, can I tell my dad you're calling? My friend Tommy wants me to keep playing our game. He's sleeping over."

"Sure. It was good talking to you, Keenan."

He didn't answer.

A long minute later, she heard him in the background. "Papa, it's Claire from the apple orchard, remember?" Claire smiled and hoped his father would remember.

"Hello?"

"Hello, Jake, it's Claire."

"Claire who?"

His response shocked her, and she started to answer. "Claire Lof—" She laughed. "You know who I am. I heard Keenan tell you." Laughing put her at ease.

"I'm so glad you called. Did you have a good day today?"

"I did, right up until noon when I decided to call you this evening. After that, I've been a nervous wreck. Maddy said you'd be scared, too, so my job is to calm you down."

"She's right. I've always been able to express myself better in writing than speaking."

Claire gasped. "I told Maddy the same thing over dinner tonight. It's a 'one-percenter' thing, right?"

"It is. That and liking Cheetos."

"For me, it's pecan fudge. Jake, do you have to go? I tried calling late, thinking Keenan would be asleep."

"He has a friend over, and they're downstairs playing a game on the Xbox, so we're fine. I'm up in my room writing a letter to my other girlfriend, the one in Wenatchee. There's an orchard there that we visited the day after meeting you. I have a weakness for pretty orchard girls."

She laughed. "You must be going through reams of paper, writing to all your women."

"Yep. All the writing has given me hand cramps. Claire, I love you. I'm so happy you called."

"I love you, too. You know, I'm not as scared as I thought I'd be."

"Me, either. Since we've met, I think it takes some of the mystery out of things."

"It does. Jake, your letters have meant so much to me. I—" Her voice cracked.

"I know, Claire. I feel the same way. Tonight, let's not get all heavy and mushy. At this moment, all I can handle is friendship."

"Not wanting anything but friendship? Why does that have a familiar ring to it?"

He chuckled. "You know, subtle humor becomes much harder to employ the more a person gets to know you ..."

The conversation breezed along. At midnight, Jake checked on the boys and found them asleep on the two family-room couches. He covered them with blankets and turned off the TV and Xbox while talking to her. In his bed again, they talked until dawn, and even then, it was hard to say goodbye.

27

A WEEK LATER, Saturday morning passed quickly at the Holland homestead. Their usual chat-fest in bed, which included talk of their Wednesday conversation with Claire, gave way to chores. They brought a week's worth of laundry to the washer and crammed it in. While it ran, Keenan vacuumed, and Jake pulled toilet-cleaning duty. Then they emptied the trash and tidied up the house. After the dryer timer dinged, they folded and put away the clean clothes. Jake plopped on his bed and looked at Keenan, who had joined him. "I'm glad that's over."

"What now, Papa?" he said in German. "Can we call Claire again? I like her."

"She and I talked last night after you went to bed, and I said we'd call her tomorrow. How about this: we make a run to Lucky Wishbone for burgers and fries and then go to Russian Jack to ski on the lighted trail. After that, we can go to Cold Stone Creamery for ice cream."

"Ja!" [Yes!]

"Good. I'm starved, so let's hit the road. Be sure to bundle up. The temperature will drop to single digits after the sun goes down."

The parking lot at the Wishbone, a local institution since 1955, was packed when they arrived; fortunately, someone vacated a spot, and Jake nabbed it. Walking in their cross-country boots was a bit awkward, but since it snowed heavily that day, their boots and ski leggings were perfect for trudging through the unplowed snow. As they walked to the entrance, their breathing formed clouds in the cold air. "Hey, son, I'm beginning to think an above-zero temperature might be an optimistic wish." Keenan laughed, oblivious to the cold.

After the meal, it was dark outside even though it was only five o'clock. In the car, Jake glanced back at Keenan. "I brought our camera. Maybe we can get someone to take a picture of us for Claire."

"She'd like that."

They soon arrived at Russian Jack Springs, one of the city's oldest parks. "I'll park at the chalet, and we can get on the trail from there."

"Okay. Can we ski down the big hill first and then catch the trail?"

"Sure."

The parking lot was nearly empty when they got out and put on their gloves, face-covering hoods, and waxless cross-country skis. Jake took the camera out of his pack and stuffed it into his internal coat pocket. In Alaska, an exposed camera can get so cold that its battery won't function. He put his hands through the ski pole straps and tapped the poles on the ground to get the straps seated on his wrists. "Do you want to lead?"

"Ja. Let's race down the hill."

"Okay, but don't get overzealous and crash. I hope other skiers have broken trail, or we'll be huffing and puffing through this new snow."

Keenan nodded and used his poles to push off. "C'mon, Papa!" The race was on. He beat his dad by a ski length. "I won!"

"I can't believe you beat me. Your new skis make you lightning-fast. Let's ski over to the trail. We can follow these tracks."

They reached the lighted trail and paused to adjust their equipment. "I'm glad the park maintenance people set new ski tracks," said Jake with a smile. He reflected for a moment as he pulled his mask over his face. There were benefits and tradeoffs to skiing on groomed, maintained trails as opposed to backcountry skiing. As a solitude lover, Jake found backcountry skiing gratifying; however, it required a lot more effort to break trail through heavy snow. Tonight was the best of both worlds—there were a few people on the trail, but not too many to disturb the evening's quiet.

Keenan finished fine-tuning his ski pole straps. "Are you ready, Papa?"

"I am. Since you won the race, you get the honor of leading."

They pushed off and soon found a rhythm that matched the snow conditions. It started snowing again, and the snowflakes glittered like diamonds under the lights. It was magical. The five-kilometer trail, carved through a forest of birch and spruce trees, looked a bit eerie in spots not illuminated by the overhead lights, but this added to the mystique of the outdoor experience. Three kilometers into the loop, Keenan paused after laboring up a hill. He yelled to his father, who was twenty feet behind. "Do you want to take a picture of me here?"

Jake pulled up, breathing hard. "Yeah, this is good. How about you move a little closer to the light while I get out the camera." As Keenan skied to the light, Jake unhooked his skis, took off his pack, and reached into his coat pocket to retrieve the camera. Just then, something bounded out of the woods, straight at his son. Keenan screamed as a gigantic mass of fur bowled him over. A moose, with its hackles up and hooves flying, began stomping him.

"*No!*" Jake screamed. He grabbed a ski and covered the distance between them in a second. He slammed the ski across the animal's back with such force that it snapped in two. The enraged creature turned its fury on him. As large as a horse, it rammed Jake, knocking him down. Its sharp-pointed hooves pummeled him; each blow landed like a sledgehammer. A hoof found his face, and he saw stars. The beast stopped and looked to see if the perceived threat was over. Jake used the pause to drape himself over a terrified Keenan. The movement brought another round of stomps. Just then, a couple of skiers came to the bottom of the hill. Seeing what was happening, they shouted and waved their arms. The moose snorted and bluffed a charge at them. With its ears laid back, it veered off the trail and into the forest. The unprovoked attack ended as quickly as it began.

Jake tried to speak to Keenan, but he could hardly breathe. Each attempt at taking a breath brought staggering pain as if white-hot pokers were sticking him. "Kee-Keenan ..." As he tried to raise his right arm to comfort his son, a searing pain came to his upper chest. Keenan moaned, in severe pain. When the skiers got to within twenty feet of them, one of them shouted. "Are you two hurt?" There was no response. When they got to Jake and Keenan and saw their agony, the question didn't need words. One of them pulled out a cell phone and dialed 911. "We're on the lighted ski trail at Russian Jack, and a moose just attacked a man and his boy. They're badly hurt. Send an ambulance!"

Jake motioned for the man with the phone to come to him. "Tell them my son has a bl-blood, a bl-bleeding d-disorder. T-tell them he has von Willebrand disease. The emergency room will know what to do. Von Willebrand disease." The man repeated what Jake said to the 911 dispatcher.

Jake and Keenan began shivering; the sub-zero cold appeared to compound their injuries. Twenty minutes later, they heard noises on the trail. "We're over here!" the man making the emergency call shouted.

An EMT leaned over Jake. "Where does it hurt, sir?"

"N-never mind, me." He grabbed the rescuer's hand. "My son has von Willebrand disease. He bleeds uncontrollably, like hemophilia."

The EMT nodded and shouted into his two-way radio, demanding a medivac helicopter. He touched Jake's arm. "We're bringing an air ambulance, sir. Hang on." He went to Keenan, who was listless and no longer moaning. "Damn it." He got on the radio again. "Tell them to land behind the ski chalet. We'll be there in ten minutes." The other rescuers arrived with stretchers to carry Jake and Keenan. It was rough going through the snow.

Riding in a helicopter was a first for the father and son, yet neither would remember the flight. In the emergency room, Jake struggled to tell them about Keenan's condition. He pulled out his wallet and handed them a card with the emergency number of Keenan's hematologist. The ER docs called him to learn more about Keenan's blood disorder, a condition so rare that most doctors are unaware of it. Both Jake and Keenan had emergency CT scans. An hour later, a doctor came to Jake's room.

"Mr. Holland, my name is Dr. Neal Barrow. I'm the attending physician. I'll begin with you."

"No. Begin with my son."

"Okay, sure. Mr. Holland, Keenan has hematuria, which is the presence of blood in his urine. This indicates one or both of his kidneys have been damaged. He has contusions on his back where his kidneys are located—you can see hoof imprints on his skin. It helped that he was wearing several layers of clothing, so he has no skin lacerations. His CT scan doesn't indicate his kidneys were fractured or torn, nor do we see nonexpanding subcapsular hematoma, which is swelling of clotted blood within the kidney tissues. However, blood in his urine means something's amiss, so we're keeping him in the ICU—the Intensive Care Unit. Dr. Singh, our resident nephrologist who specializes in kidney trauma, will meet with you later. Also, we reached Keenan's hematologist, and Dr. Cassidy will be here shortly. He had us start Keenan on desmopressin and plasma-derived VWF concentrates.

The doctor sighed. "Mr. Holland, the danger is very real that a kidney could start hemorrhaging at any moment, in which case we'd have to do emergency surgery. You know with his VWD the multiple risks we face with any form of surgery. We'd like to get your consent ahead of time to authorize it. Every minute counts in these cases—kidneys have a large blood supply, so if he starts hemorrhaging, he could die from massive blood loss ..."

In tears, Jake nodded. "When will we know if he'll be okay?" The breath he took in to say those words caused staggering pain.

"We'll monitor his urine closely. That's the best gauge of his progress. With his bleeding disorder, we just can't predict how it will turn out. Now it's time to discuss your injuries."

Jake's injuries seemed irrelevant. He nodded meekly for the doctor to continue.

"Your CT scan shows you have four broken ribs and a fractured collarbone. It'll hurt like hell for a few weeks, but your bones will heal on their own. We put your arm in a sling to immobilize it, and that will help stabilize your collarbone. With your ribs, there's not much we can do except give you painkillers. It'll take about six weeks for them to mend; unfortunately, these fractures are quite painful because your ribs move when you breathe, cough, or move your body. Ice packs will help reduce the swelling. I've written you a prescription for Percocet, which contains oxycodone and acetaminophen. In a week or so, once the severe pain subsides, you can shift to a nonsteroidal anti-inflammatory drug such as ibuprofen to relieve the pain and reduce swelling and inflammation.

"Mr. Holland, one of the potential complications from broken ribs is pneumonia. If you don't breathe deep enough, moisture and mucous can build up in your lungs, giving rise to infection. As much as it hurts, you need to take several deep breaths each hour. It'll become easier in the days ahead, but it's critical that you do it now. You're going to have a hell of a shiner from the hoof hitting your face, but we didn't see any facial fractures." He touched Jake's good shoulder. "I'll have them bring you the Percocet. It'll help."

"No. I need to be lucid in case decisions have to be made about my son. Don't worry about me."

"Are you sure? You're in obvious distress."

"I'll take anything that doesn't cloud my thinking, but nothing stronger until my son is out of danger."

"I understand. We'll get you some ibuprofen, but I'll still prescribe the Percocet in case your pain becomes unbearable. We'll take you to Keenan. He's on strong pain medication, so he'll be asleep. I'm sorry, Mr. Holland, but accidents such as this happen. He's in good hands here."

Soon after the doctor left, a nurse gave Jake some ibuprofen tablets, and an orderly wheeled him to Keenan's room in the ICU. When he saw his son hooked up to monitors with an IV drip, he flashed to memories of Keenan as an infant, fighting for his life in another ICU. A tsunami of fear rolled through him. The orderly moved a chair to Keenan's bedside and helped him sit in it. The pain from moving was so unbearable that Jake thought he'd pass out. When the orderly left, Jake wept; crying was physically painful because it moved his ribs. "Please, God, help my boy …"

An hour later, he called Tommy's parents and told them what happened. They had a key to his house and offered to pack some toiletries and a change of clothes. Talking to them hurt because it required deeper breathing. They also said they'd pick up his car at

Russian Jack and drive it to the hospital. Jake told them where the extra car key was.

After the call, Jake became transfixed on Keenan's clear-plastic urine bag; the fluid in it was yellow with a reddish tinge. Yellow meant life. The mental image of it turning beet-red was terrifying. "Please, God, don't let his kidneys hemorrhage ..."

Another hour passed. Any movement, even breathing, brought excruciating pain. He thought of Claire. She had to know. He labored to get his phone from his pocket and called her.

"Hello, Jake!" She knew it was him from caller ID.

He didn't say anything.

"Jake?"

Silence.

"Jake, are you there?"

"Yes."

"Jake, what's wrong?"

Tears filled his eyes. "Keenan's in the hospital. A moose attacked him while we were cross-country skiing."

"Oh my God! How bad is it?"

He didn't answer. Saying the words would make it real.

"Jake, please tell me."

"His kidneys are damaged, and he's in the ICU. They might have to operate. If a kidney hemorrhages, he'll ... he'll likely die ..."

Keenan's hematologist walked in.

"I have to go. Keenan's doctor is here." He hung up.

Maddy saw her granddaughter turn ashen.

"What's wrong, Claire?"

"Keenan got attacked by a moose. He's in the ICU. He has trauma to his kidneys, and if they hemorrhage, he likely won't survive." She looked into her grandmother's eyes. "I'm going there, Maddy. They need me."

"Claire, Anchorage is a long way from here. What about your agoraphobia?"

"I'm going. Nothing will stop me."

"Okay. See if you can book a flight. I'll call Helen and ask if she can stay with me while you're away." Claire nodded and ran upstairs.

As she packed a carry-on, Maddy walked in. "Any luck?"

"I got a flight leaving in two hours. It should get to Anchorage by ten tomorrow morning. My return flight is scheduled for next Sunday. Can Helen stay with you?"

"She said she'll be here in the morning and will stay as long as necessary, so I'll be fine while you're gone."

"Good. I don't want you driving back from Wenatchee in the dark, so I'll leave the car at the airport. Would you call my school and tell them I'll be out all next week due to a family emergency?"

"I'll call them in the morning. Claire, I'll be praying for Keenan."

"Me, too. I have to leave now to catch my flight. Are you sure you'll be okay?"

"Yes. Go be with them. They both need you."

28

CLAIRE STRUGGLED TO banish the dark thoughts of what could happen to Keenan on the four-hour flight to Anchorage. A knot formed in her throat, and she fought back the tears. Her thoughts drifted to Jake. Would their love be as strong in person as it was in their letters, where they shared an intimacy that came so effortlessly? She wondered how it would feel to have his arms around her, to feel his lips upon hers, and then she chastised herself for thinking those thoughts; his little boy was fighting for his life, and here she was, acting like a schoolgirl on her first date. She flashed on when her grandfather was admitted to the ER and remembered that only immediate family members were allowed to be with him. *Oh my God, I won't be able to be with them.* An idea came to her. To see Keenan, she would lie and say she was his mother.

When the plane landed, Claire ran down the concourse and followed the signs for taxis. Outside, the five-above temperature barely registered as she waved to a cabbie.

"Good morning. Where to, ma'am?"

"The hospital."

"Sure. Which one?"

"There's more than one?"

"Yes. There's Alaska Regional and Providence. Are you not feeling well?"

"My son is in the ICU. Does one of the hospitals specialize in emergencies involving children?"

"Sorry, ma'am, I wouldn't know. If you want, I can head to Providence, and on the way, you can call them to see if he's there. If not, I'll run you over to Alaska Regional."

"Okay. Please hurry."

She looked up Providence Hospital on her smartphone and called. A female answered.

"Hello. I'm calling about my son, Keenan Holland, who was in an accident. I'm not sure if he's at your hospital or the other one."

"One moment, please." There was a long pause. "Yes, he's in the ICU here."

"Thank you." She looked at the driver. "He's at Providence."

"We'll be there in a few minutes. I hope your son will be okay."

At the hospital, Claire hurried to the information kiosk and asked for directions to the ICU. She rushed to it, but a double door prevented access. She pushed an intercom button.

"How may I help you?" said a disembodied female voice.

"Hello. I'm the mother of Keenan Holland. I flew here from Washington to be with my son."

"One moment, please."

An electronic lock was deactivated, allowing her to enter.

"Where's my son?" she said anxiously to a nurse who walked up to her. Her sincerity and urgent tone left no doubt that she was his mother.

"I'll take you to him, Mrs. Holland."

"What's his status?"

"No change from last night. His kidneys are still under duress. His doctor will be here soon."

Claire nodded and gestured for her to take her to him.

"Oh," said the nurse. "Since you said you flew in from Washington, I have to ask. Are you and Mr. Holland still married? Sometimes, former spouses clash, and we have to call security. Is there anything I should know?"

Claire had to think on her feet. "Jake and I had Keenan while we were in college. He has full custody, and we get along fine. There won't be any issues."

"Okay." She stopped at the door and looked at Claire. "I've been praying for both of them." She opened the door. "Mr. Holland, Keenan's mother is here." She motioned for Claire to enter.

When Jake glanced up, his mouth fell open. His shock at seeing Claire was equal to her shock of seeing him with his discolored eye swelled shut and his arm in a sling. He had said nothing on the phone about his injuries.

He labored to get up. "You came … you … came."

She rushed to him and wrapped her arms around him. He moaned when she squeezed, nearly collapsing in pain.

The nurse assisted him back to the chair. "Mr. Holland has several broken bones, so you need to be very gentle with him."

"I'm so sorry, Jake." She glanced at Keenan and back to him. He looked worse than his little boy, who was asleep.

The nurse touched Jake's hand. "Use the call button if either of you needs me. The doctor will be by soon." She smiled at Claire and left the room.

Claire knelt and tenderly touched his face. "Dear God, Jake, you never said you were injured. How badly are you hurt?"

"Several broken ribs and a fractured collarbone. I'll be fine." He labored to get the words out. A tear rolled down his cheek. "You came. I can't believe you came. Your agoraphobia … and you shouldn't be leaving Maddy alone." Each inhale caused spasms of pain. His contorted face reflected his hurting.

"My agoraphobia isn't as powerful as my love for you and Keenan. Nothing would've kept me from him. And Maddy's friend Helen is staying with her, so she'll be fine. How is Keenan?"

"No … change," he said, taking time between each word. "The doctor will be here soon with the latest lab results."

"Jake, I need to tell you this before anyone comes in. Only immediate family members are allowed in the ICU, so I told them I'm Keenan's mother."

He nodded. Beads of sweat had formed on his brow, even though the room was cool. He panted, taking in shallow breaths that didn't hurt as much as deeper ones.

She looked at him with alarm. "Jake, you're in obvious pain. Can I ask the nurse to get you something?"

He shook his head. "If something happens with Keenan, I can't be in a drug-induced fog."

She kissed his forehead. "I understand. I'm here for a week. Anything you need, just ask. I love you two so much."

He tried to smile, but it looked more like a grimace. Claire moved a chair over to his. Before sitting down, she touched Keenan, who was asleep. She turned to Jake. "I'm so sorry this happened. I know you, and I hope you won't beat yourself up about it." He nodded but didn't appear to take her words to heart.

"Claire, could you call my parents? It hurts too much for me to talk. Tell them not to come just yet, or they'll be on the next plane here."

He got out his phone, dialed their number, and handed it to her.

"Hello, Jake." From her caller ID, his mother knew it was him.

"Nancy, this is Claire. I flew to Anchorage to be with Jake and Keenen. They've been in an accident."

"Oh my God! Are they okay?"

Claire paused before answering. "Nancy, a moose attacked them while they were skiing. Jake has broken ribs and a fractured collarbone. He's sitting next to me. He's in a lot of pain, but he'll be okay. It hurts him to breathe, so that's why I'm calling. Keenan's in the ICU."

She heard Nancy gasp.

"Is he bleeding uncontrollably?" Claire knew Nancy was flashing back to him as an infant, bleeding profusely at their home.

"His kidneys are injured, and there's blood in his urine. His doctors are worried one of them could hemorrhage ..."

"Ethan and I will get the next flight out."

"Nancy, Jake asked me to tell you not to fly up just yet. He may need you later. I'm here for the week, and I'll call you immediately should something happen."

She was silent for a long moment. "Okay, yes. Claire, please don't hesitate to call, day or night. Call me if you just need to talk."

"I will. Nancy, you know I love both of them. I'll care for them in your place and will keep you updated. I'm praying for Keenan."

"I'm so glad you're with them."

"I should go. Keenan's doctors will be here soon. I'll call after we talk to them."

She hung up and handed the phone back to Jake.

"I'll be the one to update them. That's one burden I can take off your hands." She touched his cheek and frowned. "Oh, my sweet man, I'm so sorry."

"Please make sure I don't fall asleep. If Keenan's urine bag turns red, it means he's hemorrhaging. He could die if they don't operate immediately." It took him a minute to get the words out since shallow breaths were all he could manage.

"I will. Jake, please consider taking a stronger pain pill. I'm here. I'll be the clear head." She kissed him, a short peck on the lips. It was their first kiss, though not altogether memorable.

"No. I might have to make a life-or-death decision. I can't have clouded thinking."

The nurse who let Claire in came in with a bag. "Mr. Holland, your neighbor dropped this off and said your car is parked on the B level, near the elevator. The doctors are reviewing the latest lab results. They'll be here in a few minutes."

Claire did his talking. "Thank you." She took Jake's hand in hers. "We both appreciate your kindness."

Ten minutes later, Keenan's hematologist strode into the room, along with another doctor whom Jake hadn't met. Claire stood. "Hello. I'm Keenan's mother. My name is Claire Lofton."

"Pleased to meet you. My name is Dr. Cassidy. I'm Keenan's hematologist, and this is Dr. Singh. He's a nephrologist, a kidney doctor who specializes in these types of injuries." The other man nodded a hello.

Dr. Cassidy looked at Jake and shook his head. "Damn, Jake, you look like hell. Are you okay?"

"Dan, never mind me. How's Keenan?" It surprised Claire to hear them addressing each other by their first names.

"His CT scan and ultrasound didn't reveal any obvious signs of kidney trauma. We think one or both of his kidneys are bruised, which we call a kidney contusion. So far, the latest lab tests show no additional deterioration. Jake, most cases such as this resolve on their own with rest, but Keenan's VMD ups our level of concern." He glanced at the other doctor, who took his cue to speak.

"Mr. Holland, kidney injuries are classified into five grades, based on the severity of the injury. An example of grade one is kidney bruising, and grade five represents severe trauma—a shattered kidney, for example. As Dr. Cassidy indicates, our initial diagnosis is kidney bruising, which is grade one. For this type of injury, I recommend a conservative management approach for healing: intravenous fluids, close monitoring, and bed rest until the blood in the urine clears. While bruising is a much better outcome than what could've happened in a moose encounter, it's still a serious injury. Normally, the kidney will heal on its own without further complications within a week or so. After being discharged from the hospital, patients need to be monitored for signs of bleeding recurrence; we can check for microscopic blood in the urine with a simple dipstick test."

He sighed and continued. "Now, let's talk about how Keenan's VWD might complicate matters with uncontrolled bleeding. It's a real possibility, and that's why Dr. Cassidy has him on desmopressin and plasma-derived VWF concentrates. I want to stress that a kidney contusion is a serious injury even in patients without bleeding disorders. He'll likely have moderate-to-severe flank and back pain, so we'll give him something for it. For the next few days, we'll monitor the blood level in his urine around the clock to see if it improves.

"Mr. Holland, we still need to discuss what to do if things don't go well. If there is severe hemorrhaging because of his blood disorder, we'll have to stop the bleeding rapidly through surgery, or Keenan could bleed to death. My inclination—and Dr. Cassidy agrees—is to perform a nephrectomy, or full kidney removal. Surgical exploration of the injured kidney might reveal something we can fix quickly, but speed in stopping the bleeding is paramount, and removing the kidney is the fastest way to stop it. I'm just preparing you."

"I understand."

"Jake, we're guardedly optimistic, but we're ready to go at a moment's notice if he takes a turn for the worse. You know you can count on me to help get Keenan through this, and Dr. Singh is a damn fine surgeon."

"Dan, I can't thank you enough for being here. Thank you both."

"You're welcome," said Dr. Cassidy. "I'll come by later this evening. Call me if you have any questions."

"I have a question," said Claire. "Jake's in obvious pain. He's panting instead of deeper breathing, and he's clammy. Can't you give him something stronger than what he's taking now that won't fog his thinking?"

Dr. Cassidy responded. "I talked to Jake's ER doc, who gave him a prescription for Percocet, but he said Jake refused to take it. Mrs. Lofton, if Jake doesn't take deeper breaths, he runs a real risk of developing pneumonia. The Percocet will make it easier for him to breathe. Since you're here, you could make the decisions if an emergency happens."

Jake started to say something, but Claire squeezed his hand, cutting him off. "For reasons I won't go into, I gave Jake full custody when Keenan was an infant, so life decisions aren't mine to make. Could Jake take one Percocet without it adversely affecting his thinking?"

The two doctors looked at each other and nodded. "It won't be as effective," said the nephrologist, "but the way he looks, I'd say give it a go."

"Take the damn pill, Jake," said Dr. Cassidy. "You can't make sound decisions if you're in acute pain, either. One pill is a good compromise."

Jake nodded an okay.

"Mrs. Lofton, after the pill kicks in, insist that he takes deeper breaths. We don't want him getting pneumonia."

"It's Miss Lofton, Dr. Cassidy, and you're both welcome to call me Claire. Yes, sir, I sure will." She looked at Jake as she said it to emphasize the point.

The doctor smiled. "I like your spunk."

When the two physicians left, Claire smiled, trying to be hopeful. "It's good news about Keenan, much better than it could've been. Do you have the Percocet with you?"

With effort, he reached into his pocket and handed her the plastic bottle of pills. She popped off the cap, took out a tablet, and poured a glass of water from the pitcher on the bedside table. "Please drink all the water after taking the pill so you won't get dehydrated."

She checked Keenan again and took a seat. "Jake, please give me your mom's number so I can enter it into my phone. I promised I'd call her as soon as we heard something." He gave her the number, and she called.

"Hello."

"Hi, Nancy, it's Claire. The doctors just left. They said Keenan has bruised kidneys, and on a scale of one through five, with five being really bad, they rated him at one, so that's good news. However, with his VWD, the potential is there for significant bleeding. If that happens, they'll likely have to remove a kidney. His last lab work showed no further deterioration since being admitted. Keenan's sleeping and likely will be for a while because of the strong pain medication he's on."

"Thank God it's the lowest grade. How's Jake?"

"He's in a lot of pain. The doctor just convinced him to take Percocet, which is a potent pain pill."

"Should I fly up?"

"They plan on keeping Keenan here for at least a week, and there's no way Jake can stay by his bedside that long in his condition. He should be at home in bed. If you fly up, one of us could be with each of them. Hold on—let me see what Jake thinks."

She put the phone down. "Jake, you can't stay here for days on end. Having your mom come is a good idea. One of us can be with each of you. Please say yes."

He nodded.

"Okay, if you don't mind flying up, Nancy, we could use your help."

"I'll call you back when I book a flight."

"Sounds good. I wish we could be meeting under better circumstances." She hung up and looked at Jake. "I need to call Maddy. She's worried about Keenan."

"Will she be okay by herself?"

"She's having her friend stay with her, so she'll be fine."

She called Maddy and filled her in about Keenan and how Jake, too, had been injured. After telling her that her agoraphobia wasn't an issue, she said goodbye. She stood and checked Keenan for any signs of distress. He was sound asleep.

After sitting back down, she touched Jake's hand. "We'll get through this." She leaned over and kissed his cheek. "The first time we met, we went to the hospital. Now, here we are again. Jake, we have to stop meeting like this."

He nodded and squeezed her hand, hurting too much to say anything.

The door opened, and a policeman walked in. "Mr. Holland?" He glanced at Keenan after saying it.

"Yes?"

"My name is Officer Hernandez, and I'm with the Anchorage Police Department. I'm here to get a statement from you about the accident. How are you and your son doing?"

"He has bruised kidneys, and I have some broken ribs." It hurt, physically and emotionally, to say the words.

"Okay. It's obvious it's hurting you to speak, so I'll talk to your wife. Are you Mrs. Holland?"

"No," said Claire, "but one day, I'd like to be. My name is Claire Lofton. I flew up from Washington to be with them."

"Well, Mr. Holland, let's get it done, and I'll be on my way."

Jake nodded and took a few breaths before beginning, which confirmed the Percocet had kicked in.

"My son and I were cross-country skiing at Russian Jack. We stopped so I could take a picture of him. I kicked off my skis and reached into my coat for the camera when a moose shot out of the woods and attacked him. I tried to fend it off with a ski, and that's when it turned on me. Some other skiers arrived and scared the moose off. The attack didn't last a minute. We never saw the moose until it charged us."

"The other skiers confirm what you said. You're a brave man for deflecting the moose's rage from your son to you. We collected your pack and what's left of your skis. You can pick them up at our Tudor Road station when you're better."

Jake wearily nodded.

"Why did the moose attack?" asked Claire.

"We've had a lot of snow this winter, ma'am. It's easier for a moose to walk on a trail than through deep snow in the woods, so they get territorial about it. Maybe it was angry with skiers who had already passed and decided enough was enough. If it harasses anyone else, we'll dispatch it."

She nodded her understanding.

He finished writing a few things in his notebook and closed it. "I'm sorry you both were injured. Such is life in a city with an abundant moose population. We've had several moose-vehicle encounters this week. The deep snowpack forces more of them to come down from the mountains and into the city. I'll be glad when breakup comes."

He looked again at Keenan. "I hope he'll recover quickly, Mr. Holland." He reached over and shook Jake's left hand, avoiding his right because of the sling. "My boy is in your class. David Hernandez. You've made a difference in his life. He wants to be an electrician, and he speaks of you often. My daughter, Melissa, wants to be in your class next year. If there's anything I can do for you, let me know."

"David … is … a … a … good … kid," Jake replied, laboring to get the words out. He struggled to keep his eyes open.

Seeing his weariness, the officer turned to Claire and spoke in a hushed tone. "Here's my card. If you need anything, call me. Mr. Holland is well-liked in our community."

"I will. Thanks." He quietly left the room.

Claire touched Jake. "It seems I'm not the only one who admires you."

He didn't hear her. His eyes had closed. The medicine was giving him respite from the pain.

Nancy called Claire, saying she'd arrive in Anchorage before noon the next day. Claire asked her to take a taxi to the hospital from the airport since Jake was in no shape to drive, and she didn't want to leave them in case something happened. Claire then looked up the King Career Center, where Jake worked, and sent an email to the principal, telling him of the accident and that he would be absent for at least a week and probably more.

29

AN HOUR AFTER Jake nodded off, Keenan began to stir. "Paaapaaa."

Claire touched his cheek. "Keenan, it's me, Claire. I've flown up to be with you guys. Your Papa is right here, sleeping."

"Are we in Washington?" he groggily said.

"No, sweetie, you're in a hospital here in Anchorage. A moose hurt you and your dad."

"It hurts. My back hurts."

"I know, baby. It's going to hurt for a while until your body heals. Your dad is hurting, too. I'll ask them to give you something for your pain."

He reached down and touched his privates. "It hurts down here."

"They put something into your bladder to collect your pee. I know it's uncomfortable, but the doctors need to see if your pee is okay."

"It hurts, Claire." He reached for her hand, and she took it. With her other hand, she pushed the nurse's call button. "The nurse will be here in a minute. After she gives you some medicine, the pain will go away."

When the nurse came in, Claire pointed to Jake and motioned for her to be quiet. For him, sleep was the best thing. She whispered to her that Keenan was in pain. The nurse nodded, injected pain medicine into his IV line, and leaned in close to Keenan. "You'll feel better soon." She looked at Claire and whispered. "Call me if you need anything else."

"Thank you," Claire mouthed.

Claire returned her focus to Keenan, who was in tears. "Would it help if I lie next to you?"

He nodded.

She snuggled next to him. "It'll be okay. Go back to sleep; I'll be right here." She stroked his sandy-colored hair and began softly singing a lullaby that Maddy used to sing to her as a child: *"Hush, little baby, don't say a word, Mama's going to buy you a mockingbird. And if that mockingbird won't sing, Mama's going to buy you a diamond ring ..."*

Within a few minutes, he drifted back to sleep ...

Jake woke an hour later when his medication started to wear off. Through the haze of his pain, he saw Claire curled around Keenan. Both were asleep, their cheeks touching, his little hand in hers. They looked so peaceful, like two angels. The tears in his eyes had nothing to do with his discomfort.

Dr. Cassidy returned and knelt to whisper to Jake. "I think being with his mother is just what Keenan needs. He's holding his own, so let's let him sleep through the night." He saw beads of sweat on Jake's brow and frowned. "I want you to take another Percocet. The nurses are keeping a close watch on Keenan." Jake nodded and pointed to the container on the nightstand. The doctor gave him a pill, wrote a note with the time he took it, and put it under the bottle. "Sleep tight. I'll stop by tomorrow morning at eight."

At three in the morning, Jake stirred. His bladder demanded immediate relief. He opened his eyes and saw Claire watching him. She smiled. "I love you," he mouthed. She nodded and gave him a "thumbs up" gesture, letting him know Keenan was okay.

He pointed to the bathroom, indicating he had to go. He tried to get up, gasped in pain, and collapsed on the chair. Claire got out of bed. "Let me help you." With her assistance, he was able to stand but felt unsteady and unsure of his footing. "Oh, Jake, I'm sorry you're hurting so much."

By the time he made it to the toilet, the pain was so intense that he felt as if he were going to faint. In his agony, he didn't notice Claire pulling down his ski pants. She averted her eyes not to see him and helped him sit. "Call me when you're done." Back in the room, she noticed the doctor's note under his pain medication and frowned after reading it; he had two hours to go for another pill.

Jake's trip back to the chair was a repeat of the agony. Sitting hurt; breathing hurt; the slightest movement hurt; and try as he might, he couldn't find a comfortable position. Short breaths, in the form of pants, were the only thing even remotely tolerable. Any breath deeper than that was torture. Despite the pain, he couldn't help but look at Keenan's urine bag, which seemed to be less red-tinged than earlier.

A nurse checked on Keenan, changed his urine bag, and said they were sending a sample to the lab. She gestured for Claire to follow her out of the room. "Mrs. Holland, your husband is doing his recovery no favors by sitting in a chair. He needs to be home, in bed. Sitting puts a lot more stress on his ribs, and it's plain to see he's in anguish. If it gets any worse, I'm going to ask his son's doctor to insist that he leave. His shallow breathing makes the danger of pneumonia very real."

"I know. Jake's mother will arrive today from Washington, so the two of us will lobby for him to go home." She decided not to correct the nurse about her being his wife.

"Okay. Is he current on his pain medication?"

"Yes. He's due for one in another hour."

She frowned and nodded. "Rib fractures are the worst for pain because every breath moves them. If you need me, just call."

"I will. Thanks for your concern."

Claire watched every second tick by until the time came to give him another pill. His absence of complaint about taking it let her know how badly he was hurting. When Drs. Cassidy and Singh arrived that morning, her concern was more for Jake than Keenan. She stood and brought her finger to her lips, making a "hush" gesture, and pointed to the door. They walked out to the hallway with her.

"Doctors, I know you're here for Keenan, but Jake has had an awful night. I gave him a Percocet an hour ago, but they barely dull his pain. His mother will be here by noon, so she can watch Keenan while I take him home to rest. If he refuses to leave, I want you two to order him out of the ICU." Her tone made clear that her intent was not a negotiation.

"I agree with you," said Dr. Cassidy. "We're here with some good news. Keenan's kidneys are improving. The tests show less blood in his urine. We can use this as the reason for him to go home."

"Is Keenan out of danger yet?"

"No," Dr. Singh replied, "but his improvement is encouraging. We'll keep him on desmopressin and VWF concentrates, which appear to be helping."

"Keenan woke briefly last night in pain. I think when he's fully awake, the pain will be a lot worse. Do you have a plan for that?"

"We do," said Dr. Singh. "Just use the call button, and the nurses will administer pain medication."

"We'll be back this afternoon, Claire," said Dr. Cassidy.

"Doctors, may I tell you something in confidence?" She looked scared when she said it. Dr. Cassidy nodded for both of them. "I'm not Keenan's birth mother. Jake and I are dating, so I hope to be Keenan's mother one day. I lied about being his mother to get admitted to the ICU. They both need me, and I love them."

"I came in last night when you were lying with Keenan, asleep," said Dr. Cassidy. "I whispered to Jake how I thought being with his mother is just what he needs. As far as I'm concerned, you're his mother, and I'll swear it to anyone." He gave the other doctor a look that demanded concurrence. A nod from him sealed the secret accord.

Claire looked relieved. "Thank you both so much."

Dr. Cassidy looked at his watch. "I'll stop by around one. That's when I'll tell Jake to go home in no uncertain terms."

They left, and she went back in. Keenan was sleeping peacefully, Jake quite restlessly. He looked awful with his face bruised and rough with stubble. She sighed. His mother would be shocked when she saw him.

Keenan woke around ten. He didn't say anything, but when Claire glanced his way, his eyes met hers. He smiled. She stood and kissed his cheek. "How are you feeling?"

"I'm hungry. How's my dad?"

"He's hurting. The moose cracked some of his ribs and broke his collarbone. It's very painful. We should let him sleep. The doctors were here this morning and said you're doing better."

He nodded. "Claire ..." He looked embarrassed.

"What is it, sweetie?"

"I have to go poop."

"Okay. They don't want you to get out of bed, so you have to poop in something called a bedpan. I'll find someone to bring one for you—and to bring you some food. What do you like to eat for breakfast?"

"Pancakes."

"Okay. Keenan, I told them I was your mom so they would let me be with you and your dad, so can you act like I'm your mom while we're here?"

He nodded. "Can I call you Mom?"

She smiled and kissed his cheek. "I'd like that. I'll go talk to the nurse and be back in a few minutes. Let's try to be quiet to let your dad sleep, okay?"

"Okay, Mom." He said it with a smile, enjoying their secret.

She winked and left the room.

A nurse's aide came in with a bedpan, and the commotion was enough to wake Jake. He said something to Keenan in German, but his words were weak. His pain was back. Claire quickly updated him on Keenan's condition, and she smiled when saying that Keenan was hungry and wanted pancakes. Jake was surprised at what had transpired without his awareness. He squeezed her hand in thanks.

She excused herself to lessen Keenan's embarrassment about using the bedpan. In the hallway, she called Maddy and updated her on Keenan and her concern for Jake. Things were fine in Leavenworth, except for Bluebell incurring the wrath of Mrs. Kerfuffle for getting too playful.

She returned to the room when the nurse's aide left. "Hey, Keenan, they're going to bring you pancakes and bacon soon, and your grandma will be here in an hour or so."

"Thanks, Mom," he said with a mischievous grin.

Jake looked at him, and then her, puzzled by what he had called her. Claire laughed. "I told him about my claim to being his mom so I could be with you two. He's playing along."

He nodded and looked at her forlornly. "Claire ... I need to use the restroom again." He looked as if he were going to cry.

"Okay, we'll do it just like last night." She put his arm around her. "Ready ... go."

He gasped in pain from the movement required to stand; the deep breath he inhaled to gasp brought tears to his eyes, a reflex response to the pain. It alarmed Keenan to see his dad in such pain. "Let's just stand here for a minute," said Claire. "Let your body get used to being upright." The trip to the toilet was another round of torture.

When she returned to the room to give him privacy, Claire noted Keenan's concern about his father. She touched her ribs to emphasize what she was about to say. "Sweetie, when your ribs get broken, it's very painful because each time you move or take a breath, it causes the broken bones to move. The doctor said it will take six weeks for your papa to heal, and the next few days will be really hard for him. They're giving him pain pills, but it still hurts a lot. When your grandma gets here, I'd like to take him home so he can rest. Will that be okay with you?"

"Yes," he said quietly. "Mom, he covered me to stop the moose from kicking me."

His calling her "Mom" melted her heart. "I know. He's a brave man. While your grandma is watching you, I promise I'll take good care of him. Keenan, I love your dad very much."

"I know. He loves you, too. He told me."

She smiled and hugged him. Jake weakly called for her help. On the way back, he stopped at Keenan's bed and touched his hand. Bending over to hug him was impossible. "Es tut mir leid, Papa," Keenan said, meaning he was sorry to see him hurting so badly. Jake nodded in reply.

Claire looked at her watch and frowned; it was still too early for his next pain pill.

Shortly after noon, Nancy called, saying she was in the taxi heading to the hospital. Claire said she'd meet her at the main entrance. She gave her a quick update on Keenan but said nothing of Jake.

As Claire waited for her, nervous flutters arose in her stomach, the first anxiety she'd felt since leaving Leavenworth. She and Nancy knew each other through their letters, but now they would be meeting in person. She hoped Nancy would like her.

A cab pulled up, and a woman appearing to be the right age got out. Even with a coat on, Claire could see she was tall and trim, with naturally wavy, shoulder-length salt-and-pepper hair, and just enough makeup to appear casual rather than stuffy.

When she walked through the automated doors, Claire waved tentatively. "Nancy?"

The woman nodded, wrapped her arms around Claire, and kissed her cheek. "I'm so glad you came to be with them."

Her warm hello instantly chased the butterflies away. Claire held her embrace longer than a polite hello required. With tears, she looked at her. "I feel we already know each other."

"I feel the same way. Claire, you're even prettier than I imagined." She hugged her again. "My son is a lucky man."

"We're both lucky. I love him so much." She hesitated a moment. "Nancy, I need to talk to you before you see them." Even with her shy, soft voice, Claire conveyed an alarming sense of urgency.

"Did Keenan take a turn for the worse?"

"No ... let's sit over there."

Claire took Nancy's hand after they sat. "Nancy, Jake's doing worse than Keenan. He has four fractured ribs, a broken collarbone, and he has a horrible-looking black eye from being kicked in the face. He's in terrible pain. I'm saying this now so you won't be shocked when you see him."

"I understand. And Keenan?"

"The doctors are optimistic that he'll recover. He woke up saying he was hungry." She squeezed Nancy's hand to emphasize what she was about to say. "Jake's condition scares me. He's in real danger of getting pneumonia from not being able to breathe deeply. Sitting in Keenan's room is agony for him. He needs to go home so he can lie in bed and rest. I already spoke with Keenan's doctors today, asking them to order him out of the ICU. They agreed and will convey that to him when they come by to check on Keenan. Jake's pain was so bad this morning that he couldn't stop tears from streaming down his face. Percocet, a strong pain medicine, is barely helping."

Nancy nodded. "He can be stubborn, but now we outnumber him. I'll be the one who suggests he goes home if you haven't already, and you can say it's a good idea."

"I was waiting to say something to him until I got your buy-in. Thanks. Nancy, there's something else. They only let immediate family in the ICU, so I told them I'm Keenan's mother. This morning, when Keenan woke, I told him about what I did, and he asked if he could call me 'Mom.' So please don't be shocked if you hear him calling me that, and if they ask, I'd appreciate your saying I'm his mom, too."

"As far as I'm concerned, you've been 'immediate family' since I received your first letter. Come on, let's go see them."

A wave of relief swept through Claire. She liked Nancy Holland—really liked her.

Keenan was wolfing down pancakes when they walked in. "Grandma! They brought me pancakes!"

Nancy hugged her cheerful grandson. "Hello, my favorite person!" She turned to Jake, who looked disheveled, unshaven, and gaunt. She fought the urge to gasp. "Oh, my dear boy, look at you." She kissed his cheek. "I know it hurts, and I'm sorry. Your dad says hi, and he'll fly up if we need him."

"Thanks for coming, Mom." He struggled to say the words.

She gave Claire a side hug. "Jake, I see why it was love at first sight for you. Claire told me about saying she was Keenan's mom, and I sure hope she'll get the job one day."

"I'm calling her Mom, Grandma," Keenan said proudly.

"I know, and I like it. Jake, if the doctors come by with continued good news, I want Claire to take you home. You need to rest. I'll stay here with Keenan."

Jake shook his head. "I'll be fine staying here, Mom."

"Jacob Keenan Holland, I'm your mother, and you will do as I say."

"Mother," he said in an irritated tone, "I—"

Claire jumped in. "Jacob Keenan Holland, you will do what your dear mother says, and that's the end of it."

It startled him when she piggybacked on his mother's demand, right down to using his full name. But he quickly recovered. "I need to be here if something happens."

Before the conversation could go any further, Drs. Cassidy and Singh walked in. "Hello, Keenan," said Dr. Cassidy. "How are you doing?"

"My back hurts."

"I know. If it hurts too much, we can increase your pain medication."

"Doctors," said Claire, "This is Nancy Holland, Keenan's grandmother. She flew up from Spokane to watch Keenan so I can take Jake home to rest." Her eyes gestured for them to jump in.

"Claire, I was just about to suggest you take Jake home, as was Dr. Singh."

"Mr. Holland," said the other doctor, "you've already signed the paperwork in case something should happen, so there's nothing more you can do here. Go home and get some rest, or you'll be the one in the hospital, but this time as a patient."

"Good," said Nancy. "It's settled."

Jake was too tired and hurting to argue. "How's Keenan?" he quietly asked.

"He showed improvement this morning. We'll do another test this evening," said Dr. Cassidy. "Keenan, you'll need to stay in bed, probably for a week, but I think we'll move you to the general care unit later today. The food is better there, I hear." He turned to Jake. "If you aren't out of here within the hour, I'll have security escort you out. I mean it."

Completely outnumbered, he nodded.

"I'll ask for a wheelchair," said Claire. She left without waiting for concurrence.

The doctors were leaving his room as Claire returned. She hugged Dr. Cassidy. "Thank you for what you did. I'll take good care of him."

"You're welcome. As I said, keep reminding him to take deep breaths."

"I will." She turned to Dr. Singh. "Thank you, too."

He smiled and nodded. "Good luck getting the mother job."

In the hospital's parking garage, Claire remembered his car from when he was in Washington and found the green Honda Pilot next to the elevator, where his neighbor had left it. She let the car warm up because the frigid air wouldn't be good for Jake. At the main entrance, an orderly wheeled Jake out and helped him get into the car. Despite the fifteen-degree air, Jake sweated profusely from the pain.

Claire gave him a tender look. "Okay, my man, how do we get home?"

He couldn't answer. The cold air felt like daggers in his lungs. With his good hand, he pointed to where she should go. It took twenty minutes to get to his home in Southport, a housing community on the southwest side of Anchorage. She turned onto his driveway on Leander Circle. He pointed to the garage door's remote control. She pulled into the two-car garage and pushed the remote again. "I know this is going to be hard, Jake, but you're almost there. I'll come around and help you out."

"Wel-welcome home," he said, trying to smile.

With much effort, they entered the house. She looked around. "Jake, your house is really nice and clean. You said it was a notch above being a pigsty."

"We cleaned it before going skiing," he rasped.

"Where's your bedroom?"

He frowned and pointed upstairs.

"Uh-oh. Well, come on, let's get it over with." With his good arm around her, they took their first step up the stairs. He moaned in pain. "Oh, baby, I know. Come on, one more …" It took five minutes to ascend the steps. To the left was the master bedroom. She looked around as they entered the room. One of the walls was covered with drawings, many of which were stick figures with exaggerated smiling faces. She smiled, knowing they were Keenan's creations. "I like your art wall, Jake. Why don't you use the bathroom so you won't have to get up again for a while. Before you do, let's take off your clothes." He nodded. She helped take off his ski pants and then carefully took his arm out of the sling to remove his sweater and the T-shirt. His body was deeply bruised in several places where the moose had struck him. She decided not to put him through the agony of putting on another T-shirt. The fact that he was half-naked, wearing only boxers, didn't register with her.

In the bathroom, she averted her eyes once more, slid his underwear down, and helped him sit on the commode. Leaving the room to give him privacy, she scanned the many Keenan pictures and noted how most of them appeared to be of him and his dad together, sporting exaggerated smiles. It touched her. When Jake called for her, she helped him to the bed and tucked him in. The struggle to get settled left him exhausted. "Okay, you made it. You just rest now. I'll be back in an hour with pain meds. It's time to up your dose to two pills as your doctor prescribed." He nodded. She kissed him. "Call if you need me."

She left the room and quietly closed the door. Although feeling a bit like a voyeur, she decided to explore his home. There were two more bedrooms across from Jake's room. One was obviously Keenan's, with an assortment of stuffed animals and numerous toys in an open chest under the window. The tastefully decorated bedroom next to his room appeared to be for guests.

The upstairs also was home to a laundry room and bathroom. She smiled when looking at the washer, the one that did only one load a week with everything they owned crammed into it.

Downstairs, there was a living room, dining room, family room, and kitchen, along with a powder room. Several watercolor paintings, all abstracts, adorned the living room walls. They were stunning, alive with vibrant, flowing colors. She remembered Jake saying he was a watercolorist and looked for the artist's signature on one of them. On the bottom, in small letters, she saw his name. "Wow," she said softly. "The talented Mr. Holland."

In the family room, one of the watercolor works stopped her in her tracks. Above the fireplace was a two-foot by three-foot painting with a simple, inch-wide black matte metal frame. It was the only non-abstract painting in the house, and it was jaw-droppingly beautiful, yet haunting. A woman filled the frame from her waist up, with only half of her body and face in the picture, as if someone had taken an off-center photograph. With only half of her face and body exposed, it conveyed something disquieting, as if the person were not whole. The woman's lips, devoid of emotion, formed a straight line. Her eyes, which seemed to follow the viewer, ached with melancholy, a sadness that seemed to emanate from her soul. A tangle of twine covered her head and body. Nearly monochromatic, the top of the piece was a washed-out glaze of green that transitioned to a pinkish tinge toward the bottom. It was a painting of her. Claire moved closer to see if it had a title. *Untangling Claire,* it said. It was signed *Jacob Holland.*

Tears welled in her eyes. She remembered her letter to him: *"I wonder, sir, if I knocked on your door, would you open it and invite me in? Would you be willing to help untangle Claire?"* He must have painted it after he read the letter. She stepped back, brushed away her tears, and looked at the picture again. It was a breathtaking work of art. "I love you, Jake Holland," she whispered. She fought the urge to go up and hug him.

On the adjacent wall, two guitars were hung on mounts—one a vintage-looking six-string acoustic guitar and the other a much newer-looking twelve-string guitar. She wished he could play them for her.

After touring the kitchen, Claire smiled. Overall, she thought, the house was neat and well kept. Admittedly, it could use a woman's touch, but he and Keenan could be proud to call it home. She retrieved her pack from the car and debated whether to take it to the guest room or not. She wanted to share his bed. After several moments of deliberating, she decided to put the pack on the living room couch and take a cue from him regarding what he wanted her to do.

She opened the refrigerator and frowned. Not much there to make a meal. The freezer had a big bag of prepared meatballs, fajita chicken strips, a bulk pack of frozen veggies, and several frozen pizzas. *Ah, bachelor living,* she thought with a smile.

The pantry had an assortment of canned soups, and there were root vegetables on the floor, no doubt for his crockpot meals. She thought about what to make for him. Probably soup. She looked in the fridge again and saw some cheese slices. With the bread in the pantry, she knew what the meal would be: grilled cheese sandwiches and tomato soup. It would be easy to make and tasty.

In the living room, Claire spotted a book about Alaska on the coffee table. After reading it for a while, she called Maddy, gave her an update, and told her how much she liked Nancy.

When it was time for Jake to take his pills, she found a glass in the cupboard and filled it with water. Upstairs, she quietly opened his bedroom door. Jake was awake, and he smiled when her eyes met his. "How are you?" she asked.

"At first, the two pills work great, but when they wear off, the pain is so bad that I can't sleep." Beads of sweat laced his forehead.

Claire sighed and held up the bottle of pills. "I'm sorry, Jake. I brought your pain meds." She handed him two tablets and gave him the glass of water. "I'll let you rest." She started to leave.

"Please stay with me." He tried to lift the covers but winced in pain.

Claire smiled, kicked off her shoes, and crawled under the covers on the side opposite his damaged ribs. Careful not to jostle him, she turned on her side to face him and gently kissed his lips. "Alone at last."

"I love you, Claire. I can't believe you came." He tried to kiss her, but the movement caused him to convulse in pain.

With empathy, she spoke. "Close your eyes, my sweet man. I'll be here. Close your eyes …"

She stroked his hair and began humming Brahms' Lullaby. Her soft voice calmed him, and his panting soon subsided. He fell asleep. She studied him as he slept, noting his facial features, his mouth, his nose, how handsome he was; she moved closer and inhaled the scent of his skin. Her fingers slid delicately along the stubble on his cheeks and down his neck; she paused at his chest to feel his beating heart. With love in her heart, she kissed him softly. In that moment, she knew the rest of her days would be with him.

An hour later, the doorbell chimed, ending her reverie. She went downstairs and opened the door. A teenager greeted her with a smile and a dozen brightly colored, helium-filled balloons emblazoned with *"Get Well Soon!"* "Hello. My name is David, and I'm one of Mr. Holland's students. We all chipped in and got him these balloons and a get-well card." He handed them over. "May I see him to wish him well?"

"Thanks, David. He's sleeping now—he's in a lot of pain, so it's best not to disturb him. If your last name is Hernandez, we met your father when he came to take a statement about the accident."

"Yeah, he's my dad. He told me what happened, and I passed it on at school. How's his son doing?"

"He's better, but he's still in the hospital. Please tell everyone thanks for their kindness. This will brighten his day."

"Okay. By the way, we tease him a lot about being sweet on you."

She laughed. "He told me about you guys razzing him after I sent the email. He loves all of you; I hope you know that."

"We do. Everyone wants to be in Mr. Holland's class. Well, I better go. Goodbye."

"Goodbye, David. And thanks again to all of you for thinking about him."

She took the balloons upstairs, tied them to his desk chair, and put their card on the desk.

Later, when Jake awoke, the bright balloons and card lifted his spirits.

The day passed into the early evening. In bed together, they both slept. The change in his breathing woke her. He was panting again. "The pain is back, isn't it?" She felt silly after asking when the answer was so obvious.

"I've … never experienced anything like … this. I'm … in agony."

She looked at her watch; it was a little early for his pain pills, but she decided he couldn't wait. After helping him take it, she touched his hand. "I'm going to call your ER doctor and let him know how much you're hurting. Maybe there's something more effective he could give you."

"Could you also call my school's principal and tell him I won't be in?" Just saying the words hurt. It required inhaling.

"I already sent him an email saying you'll be out for at least a week. I'll leave you alone to rest and will come back in an hour with something to eat." She ran her fingers through his hair. "I love your home and feel comfortable here. Your paintings are beautiful, especially the one of me."

"I'm glad you liked it. I'm also glad we cleaned the house before skiing and that I put on a fresh pair of underwear."

She laughed. "I'll bet in your wildest imagination you never would've thought I'd be seeing you in that underwear when you put them on." He smiled in reply. She kissed him again; kissing him now seemed quite natural. "After I talk to your doctor, I'll ask your mom how Keenan's doing. Rest easy." With a parting kiss, she went downstairs.

She called the physician, who told her Jake was on the maximal recommended dose. Unfortunately, he said, Jake would have to tough it out. It wasn't the news she wanted to hear.

A call to Nancy brought more good news about Keenan. He needed less pain medication. She asked Claire to bring some board games, and she voiced her concern when Claire told her about Jake's continued intense pain. They agreed to talk again at noon.

Claire went upstairs to see how Jake was doing. He was awake and seemed to be in less pain. "Do you think you can eat? I can make you a grilled cheese sandwich and tomato soup," she cheerfully said.

He nodded. "I'm starved."

"I'll be back in a few minutes."

She brought the meal upstairs on a makeshift tray that normally served as a baking pan. "Are you ready for our first meal together?"

"I am."

She set the tray on the dresser. "This will hurt, but I need to prop you up so you can eat. Are you ready?"

"You can grab more pillows from Keenan's room."

After Claire returned with more pillows, they managed to elevate his torso. He took half of the sandwich from her with his good arm and began eating. "Mmm, this is good."

"I'm glad you like it. I'll help you with the soup when you're ready."

After one spoonful of soup, Jake smiled. "Can we dispense with good manners and let me drink it from the bowl?"

She smiled. "Sure." She brought the bowl to his lips, and he savored each sip.

After the meal, he touched her hand. "Thank you for comforting Keenan at the hospital. It melted my heart when he called you Mom. I love you."

Claire pecked him on the lips. "It melted my heart, too. I love that dear boy and you." She put the tray back on the dresser and sat on the edge of the bed, facing him. "I'll leave you again so you can rest."

"Please stay," he said with a smile. "I need more than a perfunctory kiss."

"Your pain pills must be working," she said with a grin. She moved to him, and this time, her kiss was full of passion and need. Jake returned her kiss with equal urgency. The air around them seemed electrified. She looked into his eyes. "I so want to make love to you."

The love they made was tender, slow, and intimate. Afterward, Claire curled into the curve of his body. A deep feeling of peace came over her. She kissed his cheek. "Jake Holland, I always hoped making love would be like this."

"I know. I've hoped for this kind of love, too." He smiled. "I think the person who coined the phrase 'it hurts so good' must've had broken ribs." He turned serious. "Claire, you're everything I've ever wanted. I knew it would be this way when I first saw you. Would it scare you away if I said I'd like you to be my wife?"

Tears filled her eyes. "Is this a proposal?"

"If you want me to get down on a knee and ask you while I'm opening a box with a ring in it, then I suppose we'll have to wait. If having me look into your eyes and saying, "I will love you for the rest of my days" is acceptable, then brace yourself, for I have something to say ..."

"Speak to me, sir." Her voice was shaky.

"Before I do, please get the envelope with your name on it out of my desk drawer."

She looked at him, baffled. "Okay." She found it and came back to bed.

"I wrote two letters the day Keenan and I got back from driving the Alaska Highway. One of them was the first letter I sent to you, and you're holding the other one. Please read it."

Claire did as he asked and read the words aloud: *"Note to self: I don't know why I feel this so strongly, but I cannot shake this overwhelming notion. A woman named Claire sent shivers through my body, and her soul touched mine. I cannot explain this, and as insane as it sounds, I'm hopelessly in love with her. I know she is God's perfect choice for me. One day, Claire, whose last name I do not know for sure, I'm going to marry you. Jake Holland"*

In tears, she looked at him. *"My God, Jake.* You knew it way back then?"

"I did." He took her hands. "Claire Lofton, I've always seen the treasure you are, and you fill my heart with joy. I want a life with you, and I promise I'll always be faithful and never tire of you. I'll earn your love every day, and you'll always know you're cherished and loved. My sweet lady, will you marry me?"

She looked at him, tears pouring down her cheeks. "I'll be honored to be your wife. I'll love and cherish you, too, every day for the rest of my life." She hugged him so hard that he gasped. "Oh my God, I'm so sorry!" She kissed him. "You saved my soul, Jacob Holland. Thank you for 'seeing' me and being so persistent in your quest for my heart. I won't let you down. I hope you know that."

"Ours ... will be a forever love." He labored to say the words. "How soon before I get more pills?"

She looked at the clock and sighed. "You've got a while to go."

He frowned. "I ... I'm very tired. Can you let me rest?"

"Sure. Call if you need me." She kissed him. "The way you made love to me was incredible. God help me when you're able to move." Her levity didn't register with him.

She carried the dishes down, cleaned them, and put them away.

Unable to contain her joy, she called home. "Hey, it's me. Guess what?"

"From the cheeriness in your voice, I'd say something's up."

"Jake just asked me to marry him, and I said yes."

Maddy let out a whoop. "Congratulations! So did you discuss where you'll live?"

The reality of the question struck her.

"N-no. We didn't get that far."

"Well, don't forget you live in different states. You both are going to have several hard choices to make."

The euphoria of his proposal ended with the thought of leaving Maddy and Roediger Orchard. Her throat tightened.

A few moments of silence passed.

"Maddy, I will never leave you."

"I'll be fine, Claire, no matter what your decision."

"Maddy, hear me. I will never leave you. It's not an option."

"Talk to him, Claire. If you genuinely love each other, you'll find a way that'll work for everyone. Helen and I are about to eat, so I need to go."

"Okay. I'll call you tomorrow with an update on Keenan. Bye."

A while later, she heard Jake moaning and went upstairs to check on him and give him his pain meds. When she saw him, she gasped. With a face twisted in agony, he clutched his ribs. Tears rolled down his cheeks as he panted. He looked at her, frightened. "Oh, Jake, my poor Jake. I brought your pain medicine. After you take it, I'm calling Dr. Cassidy."

She grabbed his cell phone and found the doctor's number. "Dr. Cassidy, this is Claire Lofton," she said in a panic. "I'm with

Jake at his home, and he's in agony. I called his ER doctor earlier today and voiced my concern about Jake's debilitating pain, and all he said was Jake had tough it out. So I'm calling you. Should I take him to the hospital?"

"Is he taking the full dose of medication that his doctor recommended?"

"Yes."

"Does he have a fever?"

She touched his forehead. "He feels warm and clammy."

"You need to take his temperature."

"Jake, where do you keep a thermometer?"

He pointed to the bathroom. "M-medicine cabinet."

She found it and placed the thermometer under his tongue. When it beeped, she looked at the reading. "It's ninety-nine point one, Dr. Cassidy."

"Okay. Is he coughing or spitting up blood or green or yellow mucous?"

"No."

"Has he been making any sudden movements, or did he try to lift something heavy?"

A wave of guilt swept through her. "Oh God. We made love. He didn't seem to be hurting then."

The doctor chuckled. "Claire, sex releases natural opiates within the brain, and an orgasm releases a surge of morphine-like endorphins that will knock out almost any pain. But after they wear off, you come crashing down. I suspect Jake was moving his torso during your, um, session, so now he's paying the price for it. Go easy with him for a few days, and then I recommend giving him all the natural pain relief that he and you can handle."

"I'm so embarrassed."

"Don't be. I'm happy for the two of you. Keep him comfortable, put an ice pack on his ribs for the next day or two, and don't apply heat to them. If he develops a fever over 101 or is suddenly short of breath, feels dizzy, becomes weak or faints, or develops a cough, or starts spitting junk up, then you need to take him to the ER immediately. In the meantime, keep him on

Percocet, and don't miss a dose. It's tough, Claire, this type of injury. Oh, starting tomorrow—and I don't care how much it hurts him—he needs to start doing breathing exercises where he takes ten slow, deep breaths every hour. If he doesn't do it, the air sacs in his lungs could collapse, and he might develop pneumonia."

"Okay. I'll keep an eye out for the things you mentioned and insist that he does the breathing exercises. Thank you, Dr. Cassidy."

"You're welcome. Tell him Keenan's latest urinalysis showed continued improvement. We removed his catheter today and moved him to the general care unit, so it's all good news."

"I'll tell him. Thank you."

She hung up and looked at Jake. The pain pills appeared to be easing his suffering.

"He said to apply ice to your ribs. Do you have an ice pack?"

"It's in the cupboard above the fridge." She nodded and left.

"Where does it hurt the most?" He pointed and winced when the cold pack touched his skin. She sighed, her eyes filled with empathy. "Dr. Cassidy said we made it worse by making love. I'm so sorry."

"Don't be. I ... was in ... heaven." He yawned.

"Dr. Cassidy said Keenan is doing so well that they moved him to the general care unit."

He nodded groggily.

"Jake, try going back to sleep. I'll join you shortly."

An hour later, she got a nightie from her pack. After brushing her teeth and washing her face, she joined him. He was sound asleep. The night passed uneventfully.

The next morning, Claire tiptoed to the bathroom, showered, and put on her last set of clean clothes. The casual outfit gave her an appealing peaches-and-cream look. Jake was still asleep, so she decided to make a quick trip to the store for groceries.

When she returned, she went upstairs with his medication and a glass of water. He was sleeping peacefully, so she put them on the desk.

Downstairs, she put the groceries away and made a quick call to Nancy, who sounded tired. Other than some dull pain where the moose had struck, Keenan was doing fine. He wasn't thrilled about using a bedpan, she said, but he was in good spirits otherwise. Nancy told her about the hospital having a cafeteria in the basement and said she had a nice breakfast there. Claire said she'd make breakfast for Jake and then would pick her up so she could get some rest in the guest bedroom. After that, Claire offered to spend the day with Keenan. Nancy agreed and reminded her to bring some board games, especially Monopoly.

Since it was almost ten, Claire made a brunch of scrambled eggs and bacon. When she brought the meal upstairs, Jake was awake. "Good morning, my dear man. How are you?"

"The pain is back. I saw the bottle of pills on the desk and considered a forced march to get it."

"I didn't want to wake you, so I set it there." She set the tray down and handed him two tablets.

"I smelled the bacon, and I'm drooling. You must've made a trip to the store."

"I did. Do you want to eat it while it's hot, or do you need to use the bathroom first?"

"I'd rather eat than go through the agony of getting up. By the way, you look beautiful today."

"Thanks. I didn't pack a lot, so, gasp, I'll need to use your manly washer."

"Be sure to kick it a few times to show it who's boss."

She playfully rolled her eyes and then helped him with the meal, which he eagerly consumed. Afterward, she kissed him. "I need to go to the hospital and pick up your mom. Then I'll run back and spend the day with Keenan. She said he'd love to play Monopoly with me, so if you tell me where it and your other board games are, we'll have something to do."

"They're in the downstairs hall closet on the top shelf. I'll get dressed and join you."

She gaped at him, shocked. "Sir, you certainly won't be joining me. I plan on being there through the evening."

"He's my son, Claire. I have to be with him."

"Jacob Holland, unless you were in a drug-induced fog and didn't remember, you proposed to me yesterday. That makes me his fiancée-mother if there's such a term. So he'll be fine with just his 'mother.' Besides, it'll give us a chance to bond."

He smiled. "Okay. Today, I won't argue with you. Tomorrow, I'm seeing him. Period."

She gave him a sly smile. "We'll see. Dr. Cassidy said you need to start doing breathing exercises. You're supposed to take in ten slow and deep breaths every hour. If you don't take deep breaths, the air sacs in your lungs could collapse, or you might develop pneumonia."

"I'll try, but it hurts like hell."

"Jake, you need to do it. I told your mom I'd be there by noon, but something's bothering me. Could we talk about it?"

"Sure. What's up?"

"Maddy asked a basic question when I told her about us getting engaged. She asked where I planned on living. That's when the reality of 'us' set in. Jake, I can't leave her, and ... and Leavenworth is my home." Her disclosure caused tears. Her tears failed to dull Jake's cheerfulness.

"Claire, Maddy will have a place with us, always. That said, when we're able, let's meet as a family—you, me, and Keenan—to discuss what would work for each of us." He saw the continued doubt in her eyes. "If you only knew how deep my love is for you, you'd know I'd do anything for you. Claire, while you're here, let's not lose the joy of the moment by getting lost in countless details. We'll have plenty of time to work out the specifics in the months ahead. If it makes you feel better, we could make love again to drive home the point of being joyful."

She laughed. "I learned my lesson yesterday on that; you were in agony after our tryst." She kissed him tenderly. "Thank you. You're right; we should relish the happiness of our union and not get buried in the details. I can't wait to be your wife and Keenan's mother. Can I adopt him?"

"No."

His abruptness startled her.

"Forgive me. That sounded harsh. Claire, because of his birth mother's profession, Keenan is considered a military dependent, so the Navy helps pay for his medical bills. The sad fact is that his condition could bankrupt me without this safety net. Plus, I'm putting half of her child support in the bank for his college education. If you adopted him, all that would go away. These financial ramifications can't be ignored. Besides, legally, as his stepmother, you can make decisions regarding him just as if you were his real mother."

Claire sighed. "I understand. It's sad how there are other aspects to consider besides love. Even if I can't adopt him, I'll love him like my own, which is all that matters."

"When I saw you lying with him in the hospital bed, you demonstrated the genuineness of your words. You'll be a great mother to him in every way, and you don't need a piece of paper to do that. Not to change the subject, but, uh, I have to use the restroom rather urgently."

"Okay. I'll help you up. Afterward, my scruffy man, I have just enough time to give you a sponge bath and a shave. It's either me doing it now or your mother doing it when I bring her here. Take your pick."

He laughed and then grimaced from the pain it induced. "The days of my mother washing me have long since passed."

Claire smiled as she drove to the hospital, thinking about how sensual it was to give her man a sponge bath and shave. As she waited at a stoplight, she admired the beautiful snow-covered Chugach Mountains bordering Anchorage. She reached for her phone and called Nancy; they agreed to meet at the main entrance.

As she pulled in front of the hospital, Nancy came out and waved. Despite her smile, she looked tired. She got in and kissed Claire's cheek. "Keenan can't wait for his 'mom' to join him. All he could talk about was spending the day with you."

Claire smiled. "I've grown pretty attached to the little guy. It'll be fun playing Monopoly again. I loved it as a kid."

"He'll like that."

"Jake had a tough evening, but he seems better today. I hope we've turned the corner with both of them. I called Keenan's doctor last night about Jake, and he said Jake must breathe in deeply several times a day to clear his lungs. So before you rest, please use your motherly influence to get him to do it. I also got some groceries for us this morning, so help yourself."

"I will, and thanks for making the store run. Claire, with all my heart, I hope Jake asks for your hand. All I've had are boys and now men in the Holland clan, except for a few brief years with Erin, Jake's former wife. She and I were never close, so with you, I'll finally have a daughter."

Tears rolled down Claire's cheeks with those words. She pulled into a store parking lot and stopped the car. "I'd like more than anything to have a mother who loved me, especially you. Nancy, Jake proposed to me last night, and I accepted. Forgive me for spoiling the surprise, but I need to tell you while we're alone that I'll love both him and Keenan for the rest of my days. Jake's heart will always be safe with me."

The news delighted Nancy. "For years, I've been praying for him to find a kind woman who would love him and Keenan. Welcome to our family, sweet girl. I couldn't be happier." She hugged her future daughter-in-law with heartwarming sincerity. "May I call Ethan and tell him the news? I know he'll be thrilled."

Claire nodded.

"Honey, I'm with Claire, and she just told me Jake proposed to her. I'm getting the daughter of my dreams. I have you on speaker, so say hello."

"Congratulations, Claire! Welcome to the Holland clan."

Jake's words about the Holland clan being a lively, barbarous bunch of ill-tempered, grog-loving pirates played in her head. She smiled. "Thank you, Mr. Holland. I'm very much looking forward to a life with your son."

"Hey, no daughter-in-law of mine will refer to me as 'Mr. Holland.' It's either Ethan or Dad." His deep, baritone voice sounded both friendly and potentially imposing if you got on his bad side. She imagined little Jake hearing that voice as he drove his father "to near distraction." She also flashed back to another Holland man not wanting to be called Mr. Holland. *It must be in the genes.*

"Yes, sir. Dad it is. Growing up, I never had a father, so I'd be honored to call you that."

"When and where is the wedding?"

"I don't know, sir. We haven't gotten that far yet."

"Understood. How are he and Keenan doing?"

Nancy jumped in. "I just left Keenan, and he's steadily improving. Jake's been having a tough time, but he's better this morning."

"Okay, keep me informed. Claire, from everything Nancy has told me about you, I think you and Jake will get along famously. Now we'll have two of you 'one-percenters' in the family. Give me strength."

She laughed. "You can count on us sending you a poetry book every Christmas."

He chuckled. "I'd prefer a hammer. I see that Jake has told you about his Neanderthal father."

"He's told me often about how much he loves his parents, and I sure see why. I look forward to meeting you, Dad." Calling him that brought a lump to her throat. These were good, warm-hearted people, so unlike her parents.

"I'll call you later tonight, hon," said Nancy. She put down the phone and looked at Claire. "I'd be honored if you call me Mom."

Claire nodded and hugged her again. "I'm so happy."

"Me, too. Come on, let's go see your fiancé."

30

JAKE'S PAIN CONTINUED throughout the day and into the night. After making him breakfast and giving him another sponge bath, Claire kissed him. "Well, I'm off to pick up your mom," she said with a cheerful smile. "I'll see you in a bit."

"I'm coming. Can you get me a shirt and a pair of jeans from the closet?"

She looked at him with alarm. "Jake, after how restlessly you slept last night, I can't imagine your wanting to go with me today. Please stay home. Keenan's fine with Mom and me watching him."

He smiled at her calling her 'Mom.' "He's my son. I can't bear not seeing him. He needs me."

"Jake, it's only five above. The cold air will be hard on your lungs. Please stay home."

He shook his head. "I'm going."

"You're as stubborn as Maddy, and maybe even more so, if that's possible. Can we reach a compromise? How about you come with me, say hello to him for a half-hour or so, and then come back with Mom and me."

He thought about it for a few moments.

"I'll agree if you take me to a store on the way."

"Jake, you're in no shape to go shopping. You can't even make it to the bathroom."

"I'll stay in the car, and you can shop for me."

"And if I say yes, will you come back with Mom?"

"Yes."

She sighed. "Honestly, I think you should stay home."

"I'll be fine."

Dressing and walking down the stairs exhausted him. Despite the pain pills, his distress was evident. Beads of sweat shimmered on his forehead.

Claire had tears in her eyes. "Jake, please don't go. I'm begging you."

"We have a deal. Please help me get in the car."

Reluctantly, she did as he asked and headed down the road.

"Let's go to the store first."

"Okay, but just remember, you promised to stay in the car while I shop. Are you buying something for Keenan?"

"No. Please turn left up ahead on Arctic Boulevard." A few minutes later, he pointed. "In about a hundred feet, make a right."

She slowed down and signaled.

"Right here. Turn here."

She pulled into the lot and saw the store's sign: *Michael's Jewelers of Alaska.* She looked at him. "Are you sure?"

"I am. Several weeks ago, I had their master jeweler start making a ring for me. I planned on giving it to you this summer, but an angry moose sped up events. They said it would be ready today, but we had to guess your size from the picture of you and Bluebell, so I have my fingers crossed on that. I hope you'll like it."

"It suddenly seems so real."

He smiled. "I know. They know I'm hurting, so they'll bring the ring out to the car."

He called them, and a minute later, a man with a goatee came out, smiling. Jake motioned for him to get in the rear seat. "Hello, David," he said after the man got in and closed the door. "This is Claire."

"Pleased to meet you, Claire. Your man commissioned us to design something striking." He handed a small box to Jake. "I'll let you do the honors."

Jake grimaced as he took the box. "Claire, you'll have to open it. Imagine me on my knee."

Her hands trembled as she opened the box. Inside was a simple gold band that was split, with the two ends overlapping each other. The gap between them created the pressure and tension needed to hold a sparkling diamond. It was elegantly simple. "Oh, Jake, it's stunning." She took it out and handed it to him. He slipped it on her finger. "It fits, and I love how the diamond appears to be floating." She kissed him and then glanced at the jeweler. "Thank you, sir. It truly is perfect."

"I'm glad you like it. In the trade, this is called a bypass, tension-set engagement ring. I love the look of the floating diamond. Bring it back any time you need an adjustment." He looked at it again. "Your man has impeccable taste."

She beamed as she eyed the sparkling gem. "I agree."

Jake thanked David and said goodbye. The friendly jeweler, who wasn't wearing a coat, bolted back to the store to escape the bitter cold.

Alone with her now-fiancé, Claire kissed him. "Jake, I never could've imagined my life changing like this when I read your first letter, but look at me. I'm so in love with you—and beyond happy. Thank you."

He smiled. "I feel the same way. I can't wait to be your husband. Hey, I have an idea. Let's get married this summer at Claire Hill. It would be the perfect place for us to say our vows to each other."

Claire sprang out of her car seat and wrapped her arms around him. "I love you so much." Instantly, she realized what she had done, and his groan confirmed it. She gasped and returned to her seat. "I'm so sorry. Jake, if you were healthy, I'd take you home and thank you properly."

"How about a rain check?"

She laughed. "Of course." She started the engine and called Nancy as they drove to the hospital. When they arrived at the main entrance, Nancy was there with a borrowed wheelchair. Claire showed her the ring. They hugged, and then Nancy kissed her son's cheek. He was noticeably tired and began coughing in the cold air, which caused spasms of pain. Nancy wheeled him inside while a worried Claire parked the car. She hurried to Keenan's room, hoping he'd be better when she got there.

Jake looked pale and listless when she entered the room. Nancy glanced at her, alarmed, and gestured to meet in the hallway. "Claire, he's hurting so badly that he didn't even notice Keenan. Was he like this all last night?"

"He had a hard night, but the coughing is new, starting when he got out of the car. Should we take him to the ER since we're here?"

His mother thought about it for a moment. "Let's give him a half-hour. If he's still coughing, then yes. If not, let's take him home. I think the cold air is the culprit."

"Mom, I tried to make him stay home. He insisted on seeing Keenan and surprised me by taking me to the jewelry store. We didn't leave the car; they came out to us with the ring."

"Staying in the car was good. Let's go back in and see what happens." She took Claire's hand and looked at the ring. "It looks gorgeous on you."

"Thanks. I love it."

They returned to the room and found Jake and Keenan conversing with each other in German. Claire went to him. "Jake, are you okay?"

"I'm better now," he said, his voice raspy.

She glanced at Nancy with eyes conveying doubt and returned her focus to him. "While we're here, I'd like to take you to the ER and have them look you over. I'm worried."

He shook his head. "I'm okay." He smiled and winked at Keenan. "Ask her."

"Can I see your ring, Mom?"

Keenan's question momentarily deflected Claire's apprehension. "Um, sure. Isn't it beautiful?"

He touched the ring and smiled. "It sure sparkles. Do you like it?"

"I do. I love it." She looked at Jake, still unconvinced that he was okay.

Dr. Cassidy walked in, and Claire fought the urge to hug him. The cavalry had arrived. She offered him her hand. "Hello, Doctor. Thank you again for taking my call."

"You're welcome." After shaking her hand, he looked at Jake. "Are you taking deep breaths as I instructed?"

"Sometimes."

"Damn it, Jake. You need to do it regularly."

He nodded.

"Dr. Cassidy, he had a hard night and began coughing as we walked from the car to the front entrance," said Claire. "Should I take him to the ER?"

The doctor felt Jake's forehead with the back of his hand. "Take in a deep breath."

Jake gingerly inhaled. He winced in pain and then exhaled without coughing. "See, no worries."

The physician frowned. "My advice is to go home and get some rest. You have no business being here."

"Okay. We were about to leave. I just wanted to say hello to Keenan."

The doc nodded and turned to Keenan. "If your tests look good tomorrow, we'll let you go home on Saturday. How's that sound?"

Keenan smiled. "It sounds good."

"When you get home, you need to be very careful not to hurt yourself. No running or jumping, and no school for another week. Can you do that?"

"Yeah."

"Good." He playfully messed up Keenan's hair and then looked at Claire. "We plan to release Keenan by noon on Saturday. Will that work?"

"It'll work fine." Suddenly, it dawned on her that she'd be leaving on Sunday to fly back home. A wave of sadness rolled through her. After days of alone time with Keenan, playing board games and talking, she had bonded with him. And with the man she loved.

The doctor saw her anguish. "Is something wrong?"

"I'm scheduled to fly out on Sunday. The thought of leaving just hit me."

"I see."

"Show him your ring, Claire," said Jake.

She held it up with a smile.

"Nice! My, oh my. Jake, you old so and so. You found yourself one pretty lady. Congrats, Claire. I'm happy for the two of you."

"Thank you. Are you sure about not taking him to the ER?"

"I don't think they'll be able to do anything, short of taking another X-ray. Just take him home and keep an eye on him. We discussed the reasons for considering a trip to the ER when we last talked."

"Okay. Thanks."

"Well, folks, I'll let you be. Congrats again, you two." He shook hands with them and left.

"Keenan," said Claire, "I need to run your dad and grandma home, and then I'll come back. If it's okay with your father, if they have a McDonald's in Anchorage, I'll stop by and get you something." She winked at Jake. "I'll bet you love Chicken McNuggets, right?" From their letters, she knew nuggets were the bane of his existence.

"I do! Can she bring me some, Papa?"

Jake rolled his eyes. "Sure. I'll tell her how to get there. Maybe next week, we can buy some frozen chicken nuggets and fries at Costco." He said it while looking at her. Already, they shared the intimacy of personal jokes.

"Yes!" his son exclaimed.

Jake rolled his eyes again. "Miss Lofton, my fast-food junkie will miss you when you leave."

Sadness filled her eyes. "I'm going to miss you both so much."

"I know," he said with a sigh. "Me, too …"

"All right, enough sad faces," said Nancy. "You all will soon be having a life together."

"Mom," said Claire, "we agreed to get married in our orchard sometime this summer. It'll be an easy drive for you and Dad to make from Spokane."

"I picked apples there, Grandma," said an excited Keenan. "It's a cool place."

"It sounds wonderful. Ethan and I passed through Leavenworth a few years back and loved its Bavarian theme. Did Jake tell you my parents were from Germany?"

"He did, and how your mom taught him German." She looked at her man. "Are you ready to go home?"

He nodded.

"Give me ten minutes to warm up the car, and I'll pick you up at the main entrance again."

The cold air once again sent Jake into spasms of coughing as he got in the car. He hacked all the way home. Going upstairs added to his pain. By the time he made it to the bedroom, he was exhausted. Claire undressed him and tucked him in. Downstairs, she sat at the table with Nancy, who had made herself a snack. "I'm still worried about him. He just doesn't look right. Will you check on him often while I'm with Keenan?"

"Sure. The warm bed should help him feel better."

"It hit me in Keenan's room that I'll be flying back on Sunday. I'll miss you all so much." Tears welled in her eyes.

"I know. We'll miss you too. Claire, being apart is only temporary. I hope you and your grandmother will come to see us in Spokane. The welcome mat is out. Ethan will love meeting you."

"Thanks. We'd love to show you our town as well. Leavenworth is my Eden."

"Have you two talked about where you'll live after getting married? I'd love to see them move back to Washington to be closer to us."

"No. Jake said we shouldn't get bogged down by details. He has a lot of confidence in our ability to work things out." She glanced at her ring. "Mom, just before he proposed, he asked me to get a letter out of his desk drawer and read it. He wrote it the day he and Keenan got home after spending the summer in Washington. In the letter, he said he was going to marry me. Can you believe it?"

Nancy chuckled. "With him, yes. Given what you just said about his intention to marry you, he's had plenty of time to work out scenarios about your life together. A lack of imagination has never been one of his shortcomings. So that's why he said you shouldn't get mired in details because he probably has several ways worked out that'll be agreeable to everyone. Anyway, you're both teachers, so you're employable anywhere. For now, focus on the joy of your lives merging."

"You're right. I'll say goodbye to him and leave. It's been wonderful having one-on-one time with Keenan. Already, I love him as if he were my own."

"The feeling is mutual. All he could talk about yesterday was you, Bluebell, and Mrs. Kerfuffle. He said Bluebell loves to eat your purses, and Mrs. Kerfuffle always gets into Maddy's yarn."

Claire sighed. "Mrs. Kerfuffle is a feral cat I adopted. Unfortunately, when she's upset, she'll either swipe you with her claws or give you a good nip with her teeth. With Keenan's bleeding disorder, I'd live in constant fear of her breaking his skin ..." She didn't have to elaborate on what that meant. "When I get back, I need to try to find her a good home."

Nancy put a hand on hers. "I see your pain; it's tough, sometimes, having a special needs child."

"I love him and would do anything for him. By the way, I hope you like grandchildren because I'd love to have a bunch of kids."

"I'll love as many as you two make. You'll be a great mother. I see it from the way you are with Keenan."

"Thanks." She stood. "I wish we had more time together. We're like two ships passing in the night. I wasn't kidding about having you visit me in Leavenworth. I'd love to spend some one-on-one time with you."

"Let's talk about it after you get back. I'm sure Ethan wouldn't mind. He'd love to host marathon poker games with his buds at our house while I'm gone. Knowing that husband of mine, when I returned, it'd take a week of hard effort to get the place looking livable again."

Claire smiled at the thought and nodded. "I'll say goodbye to Jake and head out." She ran upstairs. He didn't look good. "Hey, are you okay?"

"No. The pain is back. The focus of my life seems to be on how much time remains before I get more pain pills."

She sighed. "You've got an hour to go. I'll tell Mom to bring it to you. The good news is your body can repair itself. You have to be patient. Remember to do your deep breathing exercises. If you need anything, Mom's here. I'll be back around eight. Jake, the ring is beautiful. I'll never forget this day." She kissed him. "Oh! How do I get to McDonald's?"

Claire spent an enjoyable day with Keenan, who delighted in her bringing him a high-calorie meal of nuggets, fries, a couple of chocolate chip cookies, and a vanilla shake. She sampled his shake and ate a few fries he graciously shared. Talk centered on becoming a family and the possibility of living in Leavenworth. She shared her hope of farming their entire 160 acres again, with her children one day taking over the business. From what she could gather, he'd love life on an apple farm. On the way home, she imagined how delighted her grandpa would be if her family continued his legacy at Roediger Orchard.

Nancy met her at the door when she walked in, looking worried. "Jake's had a hard day, Claire. I think we should take him to the ER."

Her stomach tensed. "I'll run up and check on him."

She gasped when she saw him. He looked at her with a "help me" expression. His face was gaunt, and he was panting. "Oh, Jake." She touched his forehead. He was burning up. "Give me a second; I'm going to take your temperature." She grabbed the thermometer and gasped again when she read it: 103.4.

"Cl-Claire … I … can't … breathe." He touched his sternum with his good hand. "It … hurts … here."

"Mom!" Claire screamed.

Nancy ran upstairs. "Call an ambulance!" Claire said with panic in her eyes. "He may be having a heart attack. Tell them to hurry!"

"Oh God!"

Claire held him. "We're taking you to the hospital. Focus on breathing, focus on breathing …"

After making the call, Nancy ran back to them. "They'll be here in a few minutes."

"Mom, turn on the porch lights and go outside to flag them down so they won't lose any time finding our house." Fear, stark and vivid, glittered in her eyes. Nancy bolted downstairs without replying.

A few agonizingly slow minutes later, they heard a siren. "They're nearly here. Breathe, Jake. Breathe." He looked ashen and struggled to get enough air. "Oh, God, don't you die on me! Breathe, damn it, breathe!"

Nancy flagged down the paramedics and told them of Jake's broken ribs, chest pain, and inability to breathe. They charged upstairs. "We're giving you oxygen, sir. Breathe it in." Jake's eyes conveyed terror: unable to catch his breath, he felt as if he were suffocating. He began flailing his good arm, trying to show his desperation. Claire sobbed as she watched him struggle. An EMT turned to her. "What's his name?"

"Jake."

The EMT got face-to-face with him. "JAKE, LISTEN! You're making it worse! Look at me! Breathe with me!" He took in an exaggerated breath. "Breathe like this with me. You're on oxygen now. You aren't going to die. Breathe." He continued doing it, inches away from Jake's face. Jake calmed enough to get some oxygen into his system. "Good, that's good, Jake. Keep breathing with me. Focus only on your breathing."

The other paramedics came up with a stretcher. "Are we good yet?"

"Yeah," said the guy breathing with him. "Jake, we're taking you to the hospital. I know it's going to hurt, but we need to put you on the stretcher. Look at me. Keep breathing. Focus only on breathing. You're doing good."

Jake moaned in pain as they lifted him from the bed and put him on the stretcher. The EMT looked at Claire and Nancy, who were clutching each other. "He's doing better. One of you can come with us to the hospital."

Claire spoke. "Please take him to Providence because his son is a patient there. Nancy, you go with them because you might have to sign emergency care paperwork. I'll follow you in the car."

"Okay."

Outside, a few neighbors had gathered to see what was wrong. The paramedics hustled Jake out of the house and loaded him into the ambulance. One helped Nancy get in and pointed to where she should sit. In a flash, it sped down the road with sirens and emergency lights on. Claire locked the house door and jumped in the car. She drove as fast as possible on the icy streets. "Please, God, don't let him die, don't let him die ..." At the hospital, she parked the car and sprinted to the ER. Nancy was there to greet her. "They're giving him a CT scan now." She hugged Claire tightly.

An hour later, a doctor came out. "Are you two related to Mr. Holland?"

"I'm his mother, and Miss Lofton is his fiancée. Will he be okay?"

The doctor frowned. "He has pneumonia in both lungs. We believe it's bacterial rather than viral, so we're administering IV antibiotics. Because of his fractured ribs, we'll keep him on antibiotics for at least a couple of weeks. He'll need to be here for two or three days, and after that ... even healthy people can take a month or more for their lungs to clear." He looked at them intently. "Mr. Holland is not a healthy man, not with his fractured ribs. He has to do deep breathing exercises, or he'll be back in the hospital, even worse than he is now."

"I understand," said Claire. "He's on Percocet, and it doesn't seem to be enough. That's why he hasn't been breathing deeply. Isn't there something more powerful to take for the pain? What about oxycodone?"

"Miss Lofton, Percocet contains oxycodone and acetaminophen, which is the main ingredient in Tylenol. The limiting factor with Percocet is acetaminophen; too much of it can damage the liver. Although acetaminophen is a less potent pain reliever, it actually increases the effects of oxycodone. Straight oxycodone isn't recommended when you have severe breathing problems because it can impair motor skills, which can result in respiratory depression.

"We'll eventually need to shift him to either acetaminophen or ibuprofen. Oxycodone is a narcotic, so he risks becoming dependent on it. We'll keep a close eye on him and his pain, and if need be, we can try something more powerful, but these drugs come with risks, especially for those with breathing complications.

For now, I think Percocet is the best choice to manage his pain. By the way, when did he receive his last Percocet?"

"At seven tonight," said Nancy.

"Okay, I'll pass that on. We'll be moving him to the general care unit shortly. You can see him there."

"Thank you, Doctor." Nancy shook his hand.

After he left, Claire took Nancy's hand. "After what's happened, there's no way I'm leaving. Would you mind giving me a few minutes to call my school's principal to get more time off and change my airline ticket?"

"No, not at all. Instead of waiting here, I'll see Keenan for an hour or so."

"Okay."

"I'm glad you were there tonight, Claire. The last time I was this scared was when we rushed baby Keenan to the hospital with his first major nosebleed."

"Jake described what happened in a letter to me. It must've been terrifying."

"It was. I sure hope you can stay."

"Even if it means losing my job, I'm staying. I just hope Maddy will be okay."

Nancy shook her head. "Don't risk your job, Claire. If you can't work things out, I'll have Ethan fly up. We'll get through this."

Claire nodded and hugged her.

Alone in the waiting room, Claire called her principal. There was a lot to tell, beginning with Jake being taken by ambulance to the hospital, news about Keenan, and her being engaged. She got the okay for another week off, plus some heartfelt congratulations for her engagement. Next, she dialed Maddy and told her the news.

"Good Lord. You tell that man of yours he better live, or I'll kill him."

Claire sighed. "Maddy, I thought I was going to lose him; he was gasping for air when the paramedics showed up. I was beyond scared."

"He's in good hands now. I'm glad he'll be there for the next few days so they can watch him round-the-clock."

"Me, too. Are you sure you'll be okay if I stay another week?"

"Hold on." A minute later, she got back on the line. "Helen's fine with staying longer, so don't worry about me."

She looked up and mouthed "thank you" to the heavens. "Please thank Helen for me."

"I will. Give Jake my best. He's a good man, and your love for him is powerful."

"My love isn't limited to Jake. I adore Keenan. Maddy, we'll need to find a new home for Mrs. Kerfuffle. She expresses her frustrations with her teeth and claws, and with Keenan's blood disorder, even the slightest wound could send him to the hospital. I can't risk her hurting him."

"I understand. I know how much you love that cantankerous cat and how hard it'll be to say goodbye to her."

"My son comes first." She smiled. *My son comes first.* The words resonated in her heart. "I'll call you tomorrow with a progress report. Goodnight."

She put the phone in her pocket and subconsciously touched her engagement ring to emphasize her new family's importance to her.

A nurse came out. "Are you here for Mr. Holland?"

"I am."

"They're ready to move him to the general care ward. You're welcome to accompany him."

"Thank you."

She led her back to Jake, who was in a wheelchair with an IV line attached to his arm. Compared to earlier, he seemed much better. Claire smiled. "Welcome back to the living."

"Thanks. I guess I'll be here for a few days. Sorry about scaring you and Mom. Is she okay?"

"Yes. She's with Keenan and will join us in a bit."

They wheeled him to his room; he grimaced when they transferred him to the bed. A nurse came in, said hello, and asked if he needed anything. When she left, Claire tucked the covers around him and hugged him gently. "You scared me, Jake. You looked like you were dying."

"It scared me, too. It's an awful feeling when you can't catch your breath—it's like being held underwater. I'm okay now." He touched her hand. "Really, I'm okay. They'll keep a close eye on me here."

"Jake, I love you so much. The thought of not having you in my life terrified me."

"I know. If it would help calm you down, we can make love. Hang the "Do Not Disturb" sign on the door, and let's get to it."

Claire laughed. "I can't say I admire your romantic getaway choice." She turned serious. "You really scared me …"

Nancy walked in, and Claire greeted her with a smile. "Jake's okay, Mom. He wants me to hang a 'Do Not Disturb' sign on the door so he can be alone with me."

Unconvinced, with a mother's eye, she checked her son over to verify Claire's reassuring words. "Don't do that again, Jake. You scared the bejeezus out of us."

"Sorry, Mom. The perfect epitaph came to me in the ambulance: '*I told you I didn't feel good.*'"

"Are you sure you're okay?"

"Yes." He squeezed her hand to emphasize it.

"Well," said Claire, "you guys are stuck with me for another week. I got the okay from my principal for more time off, and Maddy's friend can stay with her longer."

Jake's eyes sparkled. "Would it sound self-serving to say I'm glad you're staying?"

"Not at all. I'll love having you and Keenan together at your house." She looked at Nancy, who seemed tired. "Mom, it might be good for you to go home and rest while I stay here. One of us needs to be fresh for bringing Keenan home."

"That's a good point. Tomorrow will be a busy day."

"Mom," said Jake, "I'd appreciate it if you could be the main caretaker of Keenan while I'm here."

"Of course. He's excited to be going back home."

Claire reached into her pocket. "Here are the car keys. I parked on the A level to the left of the elevators."

"Thanks," said Nancy. She looked at Jake. "Keenan's worried. I told him I'd come back right away to let him know how you're doing."

"Tell him I'm fine and will try to see him tomorrow," said Jake.

When Nancy left, Claire stroked his hair. He winked at her. "You're welcome to kick off your shoes and join me."

"Don't tempt me."

"I mean it. I'd love to feel you next to me."

"Me, too." She joined him. On her side, she looked into his eyes. "I have a family now—a son and a husband. I don't need a minister saying a few words to feel this way." She kissed him. "It's going to break my heart when I have to leave in a week."

He touched her cheek. "Welcome to my world. I've had the same intense feelings for you since the day I saw you at the orchard."

"I'm sorry I made it so hard on you, but I needed to learn my lessons to be ready for you and Keenan. I wish we could make love. I crave you physically, emotionally, and spiritually. You complete me." She kissed him again.

"I ... feel the same about you." He yawned. "It's hard to ... keep my eyes open."

"The pain medication they gave you is working. You need to rest."

"Will you sing to me again?" He struggled to say the words.

"Sure. Close your eyes."

She began singing a lullaby to the man she loved.

31

THE WEEKEND PASSED uneventfully, with Nancy caring for Keenan at home and Claire tending to Jake at the hospital. Jake's school colleagues visited him on Monday, bringing flowers and get-well wishes. He delighted in introducing his fiancée to them, and Claire proudly showed them her new ring. How genuinely they cared for him touched her.

Although the pain was still there, Jake could make it to the bathroom and back without being in intense agony. That afternoon, his doctor said he could go home the next day. The physician asked if he was doing the breathing exercises and smiled when Jake said Claire was worse than a drill sergeant, ordering him to do them every hour on the hour.

On Tuesday morning, an orderly came with a wheelchair. "Well, sir, they're giving you your freedom."

"Hallelujah. My lady should be at the main entrance by the time we get there." He thanked his nurses on the way out and looked thrilled to be going home.

Claire pulled up with a smile and hopped out. "Let's hope we don't see this place for a long time."

"Amen, sister," he said with a big grin.

On the road, she put her hand on him. "Keenan and I are going to make dinner tonight. How does broiled chicken thighs with a tangy honey glaze sound?"

"It sounds wonderful. May I have you for dessert?"

She laughed. "Easy there, Stallion. Remember that little thing you have called pneumonia?"

"Maybe we could get an oxygen tank on the way home." He touched her arm. "Thank you for all you've done. I'll never forget it."

"I'm glad to help."

"I was thinking, before you leave, let's all go cross-country skiing. I know where there's a nice lit trail."

"Har, har. The thought of you going skiing again horrifies me. As I recall, you two tangled with a moose once before. Jake, for my sanity, will you give up skiing, at least for the rest of this year?"

He nodded and smiled. "By the time my lungs heal, we'll be in breakup, which will put the kibosh on skiing. But after breakup, Keenan and I plan on taking pictures of bears coming out of their winter dens."

"Argh! I hope you're kidding. What's breakup?"

"Breakup is when everything thaws. It's a muddy mess everywhere, and potholes breed prolifically, spawning scores of little potholes. Breakup usually starts in late March and is over by mid-April. And then comes what we Alaskans all live for. There's nowhere in the world as beautiful as Alaska in the summer."

"I'll bet it's nice. After enduring the long winters, you've sure earned your summers."

"There's beauty in every season if you're willing to see it." He paused for a moment to reflect on what he had said. "Well, maybe not during breakup."

She smiled, wondering if he was lobbying for staying in Alaska. Rather than ask, she decided to deflect his possible intent. "Jake, I have to fly out at ten on Sunday morning. I'm already fretting over it."

He frowned. "I know. Maybe Keenan and I can fly down on spring break. Ours is in March—when's yours?"

She sighed. "In Washington, it's in April."

"Summer it is," he chirped, pretending not to be crushed by the mismatch of schedules.

She drove down the Seward Highway, lost in thought. "Jake, I can't take any more time off from school; my absence is hard on my kids, especially having to adjust to another teacher."

"I know. I've missed my kids, too. Do you like teaching?"

"I do. It's very rewarding, and I think third grade is the best grade to teach. And you, do you like it? Do you ever wish you could be a geologist again?"

"Teaching is rewarding, but I sometimes feel like my mind is on autopilot. I miss flexing my mental muscles. Maybe I could try teaching college geology, but I don't know ..." He paused, looking reflective. "Don't laugh, but painting ignites my soul. The hours melt away when I'm behind the easel."

"I'm not laughing. Your pictures are stunning. You're a gifted artist."

"Thanks, but the term 'starving artist' too often describes those trying to eke out a living in that profession. Unlike artists, you never hear 'starving plumber' used in a sentence. But I do love painting. My mind is always on fire, as if I have a hundred radio stations playing in my head at once. But when I'm painting, a calm comes over me. I think as a one-percenter, you probably understand what I mean."

"I do. For me, my calm comes when I'm at Claire Hill. I read there as I listen to the birds or just watch clouds drifting by. For me, it's like heaven."

"I'm looking forward to seeing your special place."

"You'll love it."

Claire turned on Leander Circle and touched the garage door remote. As she pulled in, Keenan came out, waving frantically, his face ablaze with delight. "You know," Jake chuckled as he waved back, "I was hoping he'd be a little more excited about my homecoming."

She laughed. "If he were any more excited, he'd be bouncing off the walls. Just look at him."

"I've missed him so much."

"Willkommen zu Hause, Papa!" [Welcome home, Papa!]

"Es ist gut, wieder zu Hause zu sein, Keenan." [It's good to be home, Keenan.]

"Remember, sweetie, give your dad only a tiny hug."

"Okay!" He gave his father a feather-like embrace.

"Ich habe Dich lieb, Papa."

"Ich Dich auch. Hey, let's use English around Claire and Grandma. Otherwise, they'll think we're up to something."

"Okay. Mom, I welcomed him home and said I loved him." Even though the hospital ruse was no longer needed, he continued calling her "Mom."

"Keenan, are you ready to help me make dinner?"

"Yep!"

"Okay. Let's get your dad comfortable first."

Inside, a delighted Nancy greeted her son. "We have orders from your fiancée to treat you most delicately, so a kiss will have to suffice rather than a hug." She pecked his cheek.

"Thanks, Mom. You all know how to make a guy feel welcome."

"Come on," said Claire. "You need to rest before dinner." He didn't argue. She helped him up the stairs and into bed. "We'll be ready to eat in about an hour. When is your next round of medications?"

"Percocet at six, antibiotics at eight. I'm looking forward to getting off the Percocet and switching to ibuprofen. The last thing I need is to get hooked on them." He touched her cheek. "I wasn't kidding about making love. I long for you, and knowing you're leaving soon makes it more urgent."

"I know. But for now, rest is what you need. We'll have time together later. Oh. Keenan is dying to show me his school, and he misses his classmates terribly. Would you mind if I take him there on Thursday for a few minutes? It would help me learn why Anchorage is so special to you two."

"Do you think he's up to it?"

"Jake, he's like a caged animal around here. His bruises are barely noticeable. By the way, we have a follow-up appointment with Dr. Cassidy this Friday at ten. I'll drive him there."

"How did we ever manage without you?"

"I already feel as if I'm part of your family. It's been wonderful, my time here with all of you."

"I told you you'd fit right in."

She laughed. "When your mom introduced me to your dad on the phone, all I could think about was your grog-loving pirate family. I almost burst out laughing. By the way, you were right. He also doesn't like being called Mr. Holland. He said to call him Dad. I can't wait to meet him."

"He'll love you. After we get married, they can watch Keenan during our honeymoon. I'd love to sail with you in the Puget Sound area, and I'm sure there are plenty of romantic B&Bs in the San Juan Islands."

"It sounds perfect. How I wish I could grab the hands of the great cosmic clock and advance them forward a few months. Well, I'd better head down and get dinner going." She made it to the door, turned around, and went back to him. "Welcome home, my dear Jake. I love you so much."

He smiled. "I'd settle for moving the hands of the cosmic clock up to this evening so we can be alone. I love you, pretty lady."

"Mom!"

"Coming!" She kissed Jake and went downstairs.

In the kitchen, she put on Jake's barbeque apron. It looked a bit worn, with several faint sauce stains that refused to come out in the wash. She smiled at the thought of suggesting Jake try something called bleach with his whites—his separated whites. She hugged Keenan. "Okay, let's begin. First, we need to move the oven rack to the top position and turn on the broiler. Can you do it?"

"Yep."

She lined a baking sheet with aluminum foil and got out a large bowl. "Now we have to put the ingredients in the bowl." She had him measure out several spices and honey and then let him dip the chicken thighs in the mixture. They arranged the thighs on the tray, and Keenan then put them into the oven.

Nancy came in from the family room. "Do you two need any help?"

"No, Grandma, Mom and I are fine. We put the chicken in the oven, and now we're going to cook the rice and asparagus."

She looked at Claire and winked. "Okay. I'll run up and get a load of wash together. Do you need anything washed?"

"I do. May I give them to you when I get Jake for dinner? If he's sleeping, I don't want to wake him."

"Sure. It can wait. I'll go up and call Ethan. Send Keenan up if you need anything."

A half-hour later, dinner was ready. Keenan beamed. "Cooking with you was fun, Mom."

"It was. When you and your dad visit me this summer, we can make an apple pie with apples we pick from our orchard."

"I love apple pie."

"Me, too. It's my favorite dessert. How about you get Grandma, and I'll get your dad."

"Okay. I think they're going to like this dinner."

"I hope so. Thanks for your help."

Jake was asleep when she entered the room. She kissed his cheek, which roused him. "Dinner's ready."

He sighed. "I'm hurting again. Do you mind if I eat up here?"

"Not at all. I'll be right back." She closed the door.

Keenan and Nancy were seated at the table. "Isn't Papa coming?" said Keenan, looking disappointed.

"Sweetie, his pain is back, so he needs to eat in bed. I have an idea. Let's have a picnic in his bedroom. We all can sit on the bed and eat."

Keenan's eyes grew wide in anticipation. "Can we?"

She looked at Nancy. "Will it work for you? You can use his desk if it would be easier."

"It sounds like fun. Let's bring up the food."

They dined in his room a few minutes later, with Claire and Keenan on the king-size bed and Nancy at his desk.

Jake took a bite. "Oh, my, this is good. My applause to the two gourmets."

"It's better than good, right, Papa?"

"Oh, yeah. It's spectacular." He mouthed a thank you to Claire.

Nancy sampled the rice. "I love the taste of lime and cilantro in this. You'll have to share your recipe with me."

"Grandma, you and Grandpa should cook together. It goes faster with two people."

"Grandpa in the kitchen cooking with me? Now that's a scary thought. He's a great electrician, but a cook? Maybe if he were willing to serve as an apprentice for a while."

Claire winked at Keenan. "Changing subjects, your papa said I can take you to school, but only for a little while. Will you be my interpreter there?"

"I will. I can teach you a few German words tonight if you want."

"I'd like that. How do I say I love you?"

"Ich liebe dich."

"I can remember that. "Ich liebe dich," she parroted back to him. She turned to Jake. "And Ich liebe too dich."

Keenan looked at her with empathy in his eyes. "It's not quite right, Mom, but we know what you mean."

She smiled and nodded. She loved being part of this family.

That night, they made love—tender, sweet love. He fell asleep afterward, and Claire stayed up most of the night, watching the candlelight dance on his face. *I love this man with all my heart* played over and over in her head.

Jake woke early the next morning; his pain was back in full force. He roused Claire and asked for more pain pills. After they kicked in, she helped him to the bathroom. He declined her offer of a sponge bath and shave and shuffled slowly back to bed. When she brought up a three-egg ham-and-cheese omelet, he ate only a bit of it and fell back to sleep.

A couple of hours passed. Keenan paced downstairs, worried about his father. When Jake called for him, he dashed to his room. Claire followed. "Are you okay, Papa?" he said, looking scared.

"It hurts, Keenan, but I feel better now. Son, I'd like to talk to you about Claire and me getting married."

Keenan's eyes conveyed instant delight. "Papa, since you gave her a ring, does it mean I can call her Mom for real?"

"There has to be a marriage ceremony for it to be real. We're hoping for a summer wedding in Leavenworth."

Keenan took her hand and looked at her. "I always wanted a real mom."

She hugged him. "And I always wanted a boy like you."

Jake looked at her. "Claire, will you please leave and close the door behind you?"

His request startled her. To be excluded from such an important discussion was troubling. She flashed to the letter she wrote to him: *Will I be the proverbial "odd man" out?* Her stomach knotted, and sadness filled her face.

Jake saw it. "I'm going to tell him that for a marriage to be successful, the parents must come first, and how our relationship will have to change for you."

He was right; this talk had to be between them. She smiled. "Sure. Call if you need anything." She left and closed the door behind her.

"Papa, can I marry Mom, too?"

"No, Keenan. It doesn't work that way ..." A thought flashed through his head ... "But maybe, with us, it can."

They spent the next hour talking. Keenan went downstairs and got his dad's cell phone. Before heading back up, with a serious look, he told the two ladies they weren't done talking.

An hour later, the doorbell rang. Keenan insisted on answering it, acting as if he were expecting someone. He took a bag from a teenager and thanked him. Without saying a word, he shut the door and went back upstairs.

A few minutes later, he opened the bedroom door. "Mom, please come up!" Claire looked at Nancy and cocked an eyebrow up, wondering what was going on. Nancy shrugged her shoulders. She went upstairs. A beaming Keenan was on the bed with his dad and motioned for her to join them.

"What's up?" she asked, noting how they both looked like cats who had just swallowed canaries.

Jake appeared tired, but calling her to come up seemed important. "Claire, Keenan and I talked about what it means for us to be married and how the union between a man and woman is a sacred thing. We talked about how, in a marriage, parents must come first so they can make a loving home for their children. Along with family time, he understands how important it is for us to have time alone." Keenan nodded eagerly. "I told him we want to talk while you're here about where we could potentially live.

"And this is the most important thing we discussed: Keenan asked if he could marry you, too. By that, he means if you two get mom-married, you will be his mom, his real mom, and he will be your real son. When you introduce each other, it won't be, here's my stepmom or stepson; it will be, this is my mother, and this is my son. Keenan would like to propose to you now if you're willing." Claire brought her hand up to cover her open mouth and nodded. Jake smiled. "You'll have to stand so Keenan can ask you properly."

She got off the bed and stood. Keenan reached under the pillow and pulled out a small box. He went over to her and got on a knee. "Claire Lofton, I'd like for you to be my mother. If you say yes, I promise to love and respect you, just like I do with my dad. Will you mom-marry me?" He opened the box. There was a gold band in it. "Papa said you can wear this on your other hand to show everyone you're my mom."

Claire glanced at Jake, her eyes full of tears—and love. "Keenan, I would be so honored to be your mother. I'll love you just as much as your dad, and maybe even more. I'll gladly mom-marry you." She held out her right hand.

He placed the ring on her finger. "Papa says it isn't for real until the wedding day, but you can wear it until then."

She hugged him tenderly. "Keenan, you're so special. How I've grown to love you."

"I love you, too, Mom. Can we call Grandma up and show her the ring?"

"I'd like that." She hugged him again and then went over and kissed Jake. "This is so beautiful. I'll never forget it. I love you incandescently."

He forced a smile. She knew the pain was back from the beads of sweat on his forehead. "Keenan, please tell Grandma to bring your dad a couple of pain pills."

Jake slept for the remainder of the afternoon. Claire and Keenan made a run to the store and cooked a pot roast for dinner. They had another picnic in his room. Everyone was happy.

Shortly after midnight, the peace of the night abruptly ended.

"Papa!" Keenan screamed. Claire bolted out of bed and went to him. Nancy opened her door, alarmed.

"What's wrong, sweetie," Claire asked, shocked at seeing him drenched in sweat, crying, and scared out of his wits.

"The moose attacked me and Papa again. We couldn't run away. He hurt Papa again!"

"Oh, baby, it's okay. We're all okay."

Jake managed to make it to his room. "What's wrong?"

"He had a bad dream. Keenan, do you want me to stay with you?"

"Yes, Momma."

"Mom, could you help Jake back to bed. I'll stay with Keenan."

"Okay. Come on, Jake, let me help you."

He looked at Claire, not sure what to do.

"Jake, he'll be fine with me. You need to rest." Her eyes conveyed that his little boy needed a mother's love.

He nodded. "Goodnight, son."

"Goodnight, Papa." Jake turned off the light, and soon the house was quiet again.

Under the covers, Keenan snuggled next to her. "I'm scared, Momma."

"I know, but you're safe with me." She stroked his hair. "Keenan, let's forgive the moose for hurting you and your papa. I think he was scared, too, just like you are now, and that's why he got angry. Most of the time, I'll bet he's a friendly moose."

"How do you forgive a moose, Mom?"

"Just say, Mr. Moose, I'm sorry we upset you. My dad and I didn't mean to scare you. The next time we see you, we'll wave and say, look, we're okay now, and we forgive you."

He kissed her cheek. "That sounds good." He paused a moment and then spoke. "Sorry, Mr. Moose, that Papa and I scared you. We're nice to animals, and we forgive you."

She kissed his cheek. "See. Now Mr. Moose has no reason to chase you in your dreams. He now knows you and your papa are friendly."

He hugged her. "I love you, Mom."

"I love you, too. Let's go back to sleep." She stroked his hair, and soon they drifted off, safe in each other's arms.

Keenan woke the next morning, acting as if nothing had happened. A mother's love was all he needed. Jake labored in when he heard them laughing. "What are you two up to?"

"I'm telling Mom some jokes, Papa. She likes them."

He saw how delighted Claire looked. When their eyes met, his smile conveyed gratitude and love.

She nodded and kissed his boy's cheek. "Tell your papa the joke you just told me. It's hilarious."

After breakfast, Claire and Keenan got ready to leave for his school. It surprised her to see him come out of his room wearing formal clothes. Jake said the school had a dress code.

As they entered the school's parking lot, Claire was impressed with the attractive but relatively small building. "C'mon, Mom! This will be fun."

His excitement and pride in his school made her smile. "I'll bet it will be." They checked in at the office, and a staff member summoned his teacher. When she came out, Keenan hugged her warmly. "Miss Haley, this is Claire, my mom—she's been taking care of my dad and me."

She shook Claire's hand. "Herzlich willkommen zur Rilke Schule. Ich bin froh, dass Sie kommen konnten."

"I'm sorry—I don't speak German."

Keenan touched Claire's arm to get her attention. "She said, *Welcome to Rilke School. I'm so glad you could come.*'"

Claire smiled. "Thank you. It's a beautiful school. I'm a third-grade teacher in Leavenworth, Washington."

Miss Haley nodded and shifted to English. "I love working here. Let me give you the standard description of our school. We're a kindergarten through eighth-grade charter school in the Anchorage School District. We immerse our students in German culture and language, and that learning is reinforced throughout the curriculum in non-German subjects as well. The German government has recognized us as a *German Immersion School Abroad.*

We have a little over 400 students, with about twenty students in our kindergarten and first-grade classes and twenty-five students per class in the other grade levels."

"Wow, how impressive. Keenan loves going to school here. I was so impressed when I first heard him and his father conversing in German. By the way, Keenan calling me 'Mom' is a bit premature. His father and I are engaged." She held up her hand and showed her the ring.

"Congratulations. I was wondering why he introduced you as his mom. Part of every family's commitment is to provide four hours of volunteer time to the school every month. Your talents will be appreciated here."

"I'd love to help in any way I could, but we haven't decided where we'll live."

"I understand. So, what's your class size?"

"I have seventeen students. We're a community of about two thousand people, which keeps our class sizes small."

"Leavenworth has a federal prison, right?"

Claire shook her head. "That prison is in Leavenworth, Kansas. My Leavenworth is in the heart of Washington, in the Cascades, about twenty miles from the town of Wenatchee."

"It sounds nice. Keenan, let's go to the classroom so the kids can say hello." He took Claire's hand and led the way.

"Keenan! Wie geht es dir?" several of them said, asking how he was doing.

"Mir geht es gut, danke," he replied, saying he was well.

Claire looked fascinated by the German-themed classroom. She leaned close to Miss Haley. "If I could speak the language, I'd love to teach at this school." Miss Haley smiled in reply.

Back in the car, Keenan beamed. "Did you like it, Mom?"

"I did. It's a wonderful school. All the kids really like you."

"Yep. When are we going to eat? I'm hungry."

"Well, where do you and your dad like to go?"

"We like Arby's. There's one not far away from here. I like their curly fries, and Papa always gets a roast beef sandwich with horsey sauce."

"That's a good idea. We can eat there and take some sandwiches home for your dad and grandma."

They drove to the restaurant and went inside. Keenan chattered away as they ate, and Claire listened intently, amazed at the stream-of-consciousness thoughts racing through his head. He was a very bright boy who inherited his father's wit. She liked him immensely. No, she loved him.

Before they left, Claire ordered food to go. On the way home, Keenan breathlessly told her about all his classmates and what they were learning about Germany.

To her surprise, Jake was lying on the living room couch when they walked in. Nancy was in the recliner next to him, reading. "Hey, you two, we stopped at Arby's and bought roast beef sandwiches for you. And I asked for lots of horsey sauce at Keenan's insistence."

Jake smiled. "Thanks. I'm starved. And thank you, Keenan, for remembering the sauce. Gotta have horsey sauce, or they don't taste right."

Since Jake's arm was in a sling, Keenan added the sauce to his sandwich and handed it to him.

Jake took a bite. "Man, this hits the spot." He looked at Claire and smiled. "So, what did you think of Keenan's school?"

"It's amazing. I see what you said about how learning another language makes life richer."

"I'll keep teaching you German, Mom!" He jumped up and hugged her. Their affection for each other was obvious and genuine.

She kissed his cheek. "I'd like that, sweetie. Remember, tomorrow we have an appointment with your doctor at ten."

"Okay. I'm going to change. We can play on my Xbox if you want."

"I don't know if I'd be any good at it. I've never played a computer game."

"It's fun! I'll teach you."

"I'll tell you what; give me a few minutes, and then I'll try it."

He nodded, hugged her again, and went upstairs to change.

"You two are getting along quite well," said Nancy. "It's good to see."

Claire smiled and nodded. "He introduced me as his mom at school. If I'm not careful, I'll be introducing him as my son. It already feels that way to me." She touched Jake. "You must be feeling better to be down here."

"Well, actually, I planned on being upstairs before you returned, in bed moaning, desperately in need of your attention, but you came home quicker than I expected."

She laughed. "I'll still give you some attention, but that dinner-in-bed service ... it's so over. I'm glad you're better." She looked at her watch. "It's time for your antibiotic." She went to the kitchen and came back with a pill. "I need to call Maddy to say hello before I start playing with Keenan." She got her phone and went upstairs. "Hey, Keenan, I'll be down in a few minutes, and then we'll play."

"Okay."

She closed the bedroom door and called. "Hey, it's me. How are you?"

"I'm fine. I just got back from a game of fetch with Bluebell. She'll be glad to see you. How's everyone there?"

"Tell Bluebell I'll make it up to her for being gone so long. Maddy, it's been wonderful here. Keenan showed me his school today, and you'd love it. Jake was out of his bed and in the living room when we returned, which was fabulous to see. I already feel so bonded to them, like I've been with them forever. I can't wait for you to meet his mom. She's terrific."

While they talked, Jake and his mom conversed ...

"My God, Jake, I so love her. I almost cried when Keenan snuggled up to her. They love each other; it's plain to see. Having him 'marry' her was brilliant on your part, and his ring on her finger means the world to her. She's so unlike his mother ..." Her voice trailed off as she said it. "Sorry. I can't help noticing the difference between the two of them. Claire's a treasure."

"I know. I choke up when I see them together. She'll love him with all her heart."

"Jake, she'll love you, too. I'm so happy for you."

"Dad's probably wincing at the thought of another one-percenter in the family."

"When they meet, she'll melt his heart. So, when are you two going to talk about your future? You can't live in two different places."

He sighed. "Before she leaves, I'd like to have a family meeting to discuss where we want to live."

"You tell me when, and I'll go see a movie to give you all time alone."

"Thanks. I know if you had a vote, you'd want us to move back to Washington."

"Jake, I want you to be happy. So make your choice independent of your dad and me."

He nodded.

Claire came down, looking cheerful. "Maddy's fine and is glad you're better. Bluebell says hello, but Mrs. Kerfuffle was her usual self, quite indifferent to your condition."

"Ah, that confounded Mrs. Kerfuffle." He looked at his mom. "That's her cat."

"I know. Claire told me about her."

"Mom!"

"Coming!" She kissed Jake. "I'm being summoned. Are you okay staying here?"

"Yeah. I'll hang out with my other lady and tell her again how she ruined my childhood."

"Hey, watch it!"

He laughed heartily, something he hadn't been able to do since the accident. Claire smiled. He was definitely getting better.

The evening passed agreeably. In their bedroom, after making love, Jake was quiet. She kissed his cheek. "Is everything okay?"

"I was wondering, what would you'd think about getting married before you left?"

"Jake! Really?"

"Yep. I'd like to make an honest woman out of you. You could go back as Mrs. Holland."

"I'd love to, but it would break Maddy's heart not to be at my wedding. I couldn't do that to her."

"Well, we could get married here and renew our vows there in the summer."

"Wouldn't it make getting married there seem a bit disingenuous?"

He sighed. "I suppose. Well, summer it is. Are you going to invite your parents?"

He felt her body go rigid.

After a few moments, she answered him, her voice soft as a whisper. "No. I forgave them, and that's all I'm ready to do."

"I understand. Tomorrow, after Keenan's doctor visit—which, by the way, I'm going to, so don't even attempt to argue with me about it—I'd like for us to meet as a family, so we can each talk about where we want to live. No decisions will have to be made—it'll just be us talking."

A pang of alarm went off inside Claire. The image of Maddy being "orphaned" flashed in her. Her body went tense again. Silence ensued.

"Breathe, Claire. We'll just be talking. I'm not opposed to moving down there."

"God, you read me like a book. It's that obvious how I feel?"

"Yes. But, Claire, I need to be honest and say I have concerns about moving there."

"Talk to me."

"Are you sure you want to go into this now?"

"Yes. We're just talking, as you say. It's important to me."

"Okay. Let me ramble a bit. As a man, I take pride in earning a living and owning my own home. I assume if Keenan and I move there, you'll want us to move into Maddy's house. I find the idea to be somewhat emasculating. It's not my house or even your house, so I wouldn't feel right making any changes to it or suggesting we move something here or there. I'd feel like a boarder. And you've seen the fireball that is Keenan. Older people tend to loathe high-energy kids who shatter their peace. Expecting him to suddenly turn docile is only a theoretical concept, and it would be injurious to his spirit to throttle him. I've never been in your home, so I don't know if it's large enough for us. Also, if I couldn't find a job, I'd be dependent on you and Maddy, almost as if I were back to being a kid again, living with my parents. I don't relish the thought."

"I understand. Jake, Maddy set up a trust, stipulating the house and land will pass to me when she dies, so it will be ours one day. But what you're saying is valid. I'll have to think more about how this will affect you and Keenan. I know you'd love living in Leavenworth. It's such a beautiful place. All I can think about is our children growing up with 160 acres to explore and you reading poetry to me on Claire Hill. For a one-percenter, Roediger Orchard is Eden."

He kissed her. "It sounds appealing; I can't deny it. If you sweetened the pot by saying I can have all the apples I want to eat, well, how could I say no?" She giggled and squeezed his hand.

"Claire, tomorrow, let's just talk. Again, no decisions will be made. Sometimes, in the course of conversations, a solution emerges. Let's make talking about our future together something fun."

"Okay. Jake, you know Maddy rescued me, first as a child and then after my awful college experience. I owe her so much. We can't—I can't—make decisions without her best interests in mind."

"She made you who you are, and I'll be eternally grateful to her. All of our choices will include what's best for her. Rest easy on that."

She snuggled closer to him.

"By the way, is there a lot of debt on your orchard or with your finances?"

"You can rest easy, too, Jake. The farm turns a profit each year, and I'm frugal. I have no debt and live rent-free. Most of my salary goes straight into my 401k and investments. And you? Are you financially viable?"

"I am. I'm not rich, but I'm debt-free. It sounds as if we have a similar philosophy regarding money management."

"I think so, too."

He sighed. "Let's keep focusing on the joy of now and not get buried in details. I want you to fly home full of joy and not consumed by doubt about future decisions we'll have to make."

"I love you so much. Leaving all of you this Sunday will be the hardest thing I'll ever do."

"Let's not talk of that, either. We can be sad after we're apart. Until then, let's savor our time together rather than moping around."

She kissed him. "Sounds good to me."

Keenan's medical appointment went well. Nancy decided to join them to get out of the house. The urinalysis done in the doctor's office showed no traces of blood in Keenan's urine. Dr. Cassidy cleared him to return to school the following Monday, but with no strenuous exercise for a month.

After they got in the car, Jake looked at them. "Hey, odd as it sounds, I'm dying to go to Taco Bell for lunch. How about we eat there, and after that, I'd like to show you where I work."

"Okay!" Keenan howled. "I love Taco Bell."

"Jake, are you sure you're up to it?" asked Claire, concerned.

"The Percocet is working nicely. Let's do it."

"Okay. Tell me how to get there."

At Taco Bell, the cheerful lady at the register smiled at Jake. "Sir, may I have your name so we can call you when your order is ready?"

"Sure. My name is Giuseppe Pastafasalla." The lady looked at him, bewildered. "With a 'G,'" Jake said to help clarify the spelling. The woman was at a loss.

Claire shook her head and nearly poked Jake in the ribs. "You can use my name instead of Giuseppe's. I'm Claire." The lady looked relieved.

As they walked to the soda machine, Claire grinned at him. "You're so bad."

He smiled. "I'm feeling mischievous today."

Lunch was fun, with everyone talking and laughing at Keenan's jokes.

They pulled into the parking lot at the King Career Center shortly after one o'clock. Claire noted that the building looked pleasant but smaller than she had imagined.

The office staff was delighted to see their missing-in-action teacher. Jake introduced Nancy and Keenan first, and then his fiancée. Claire smiled as she showed off her ring, drawing lots of oohs and aahs from the women. While they were chatting, Jake mentioned to the principal that he hoped to be back in a week or two. After that, Jake led the family to his classroom and surprised his students when he walked in. The substitute teacher didn't mind the interruption and let the kids gather around their teacher.

"Hey, everyone, this is my mom Nancy, and my son Keenan. And this is Claire, the beautiful lady you've been teasing me about. By the way, she's now my fiancée."

They all clapped. "Way to go, Mr. H!" Claire blushed and showed them her ring.

"I've missed you all, and I'll be off for another week or two," said Jake. "Thanks for the card and balloons. Johnny, I noted your wisecrack on my card, so prepare for some payback when I return." His remark brought an impish grin to Johnny's face, which caused everyone to laugh, including Jake. Claire smiled at the rapport he and his kids had. Jake said his goodbyes and thanked the teacher for allowing the interruption.

On the way to the car, Jake beamed. Being back with his kids energized him. "Hey, I have an idea. Let's run down to Beluga Point and show Claire a little of Alaska. It's about a half-hour from here, and we won't even have to get out of the car. After that, I promise we'll go home."

"Let's do it, Mom!" said Keenan. "You'll like it."

Claire looked at Nancy, who nodded her concurrence. "Okay, Jake, but we go right home afterward. Deal?"

"Deal."

She started the car. "Which way, sir?"

"We need to get back on the Seward Highway and head south. It's an easy drive."

Claire nodded, knowing how to get to the highway. A smile came to her as she drove. In her whole time here, not once did her agoraphobia surface. Love can fix many things, she mused.

After a bit, they were out of the city. "We're coming up on Potter Marsh," said Jake. "See the boardwalk over there? It's a great way to view all the coastal birds that migrate here in the summer. There's also plenty of local wildlife that frequent the marsh."

"We saw five moose here last fall," said Keenan excitedly. "They were friendly moose."

Claire laughed. "Do the friendly ones smile at you?"

He chuckled. "They can't smile, Mom. Moose don't have upper front teeth."

"Really?"

"Yep," said Jake. "It's true, but they sure have sharp hooves."

They drove past the marsh and began hugging the edge of the inlet. Sharply sloped mountains jutted up from the water's edge, and the road carved its way into them in many places. "Jake, it's breathtaking," said Claire as she marveled at the beauty. "It reminds me of a Norwegian fiord."

"I know. This is called the Turnagain Arm. It marks the northern end of Cook Inlet, which stretches 180 miles from the Gulf of Alaska to Anchorage. In 1778, James Cook led an expedition that sailed here in search of the Northwest Passage. One of his sailors, William Bligh, later became the captain of the HMS Bounty. Bligh was Cook's Sailing Master, and it was he who traveled up this inlet, hoping it was a huge river. He soon saw it wasn't and ordered his crew to turn again and go back. That's how this inlet got the name Turnagain Arm. If you ever come back, we could drive to the end of it, which is about 40 miles from here."

"How fascinating. Can you imagine coming here in such primitive vessels? They truly were adventurers. I didn't know Captain Bligh had a connection with Alaska."

"Yep, he did. As a geologist, I could teach Geology 101 right here. During the Ice Age, glaciers carved Turnagain Arm, and the towering volcanic mountains across Cook Inlet are being formed by the Pacific tectonic plate subducting under the North American plate. The Chugach and Kenai Mountains, on each side of Turnagain Arm, are made up of metamorphic rocks ..." He looked at her and saw her eyes glazing over. "Okay," he said with a laugh, "just take my word for it—this area is a geologist's dream."

She chuckled. "I'm thinking about what you said in a letter to me: *See that thing, right there on the ground? It's a rock. I know that because I've had college.*'"

As they headed down the road, every curve brought another scenic wonder. "I love this drive," said Nancy. "I think it's one of the prettiest stretches of road in America."

"I agree," Claire replied.

Jake pointed ahead. "We're coming up to Beluga Point. You can pull in at the turnout there, and we can park for a few minutes."

A dramatic inlet view greeted them as they parked. "Mom, look—beluga whales!"

"Where, Keenan?"

"Over there!"

She spotted them. "Oh my God, look at how white they are!"

They watched the whales from the comfort of the car and took in the beauty before them.

"Well, I guess we should head back," said Jake. "Claire, I hope this gives you a taste of what it's like to live here."

"It's beautiful. I'll never forget this. Thanks for suggesting we come here." She leaned over and kissed him. "I hate to go, but you need to rest."

Conversation on the way home came easily. Claire asked if there were any craft stores near his house, and Keenan offered to take her to where his dad bought art supplies. When they got home, she dropped Jake and Nancy off and went to the store with Keenan.

"What do you want to get, Mom?"

"I'd like to make something for your papa to remind him of me when I'm gone."

He looked at her, puzzled. "Mom, Papa won't forget you. I won't, either."

She smiled. "I know, sweetie. I just want to make him something to remind him that I love him."

"Oh."

"If I find what I'm looking for, you can help me make it. We'll need to do it in the garage."

His eyes sparkled. "Okay. I like doing things with you."

At the store, she found everything she needed. On the way home, Claire smiled at Keenan. "This shouldn't take long to make. When we get home, will you get me some newspaper so we can paint the puzzle pieces? Oh, and please tell your dad not to come into the garage."

"Okay."

She pulled into the heated garage. Keenan went into the house and came back with several newspapers. "Is this enough?"

"It is. Let's lay them on the floor." She took the puzzle box from the bag and opened it. "We need to find two puzzle pieces that fit together." It took them a while, but they found an interlocking pair. "Now we need to spray one white and the other black."

"Okay."

She handed him the white can of paint. "Hold the can up about ten inches away and go back and forth quickly so the paint won't run." He did as she asked, and she sprayed the other piece black. "Let's wait a few minutes and spray them one more time to make sure they're covered."

After the second coat, they waited for the paint to dry. "Okay," said Claire, "let's connect the puzzle pieces and spray their backs with glue." Once more, Keenan did the spraying honors. "Now I have to align them on the mat," said Claire. She centered them and pressed firmly. "One last thing to do—the mat goes in the picture frame." They slid the mat in and crimped the back tabs of the frame to hold it in place. She held up the picture and smiled, satisfied with how it turned out. "What do you think?"

Keenan looked confused as he eyed the interlocked black and white puzzle pieces. "It's an easy puzzle, Mom. Even a baby could do it."

"It's not a puzzle. Imagine I'm the white piece, and your papa is the black one. See how well the black puzzle piece fits into the white one? We had to search through all the puzzle pieces in the box to find the two that fit perfectly together—just like your dad and me."

A lightbulb went off in his head. "Oh, I get it now. Like fries go with chicken nuggets."

She laughed. "Exactly." She touched her hand to her forehead. "Darn! I forgot the gift wrap paper. Do you guys have any?"

"I don't think so."

"Do you have any newspapers with colored comics? We can use that as gift wrap."

"We have lots of old comics, and we keep scissors and tape in the kitchen drawer. I'll get them."

After they wrapped the gift, Claire put her arm around him. "Will you hide the gift under your shirt and put it in your dad's bedroom desk drawer? While you're doing that, I'll distract him."

He smiled. "Okay."

They went inside, and Keenan did a great job with the ruse, saying he had to go to the bathroom upstairs.

Jake looked quizzically at her when she kissed him. "What mischief have you two made?"

"I'll show you later."

"Claire, we ordered pizza since it's getting late," said Nancy.

"Sounds good. I'm going upstairs to freshen up. Do you need anything, Jake?" She looked at her watch. "You're past due for your next round of meds."

He rolled his eyes. "Geez, I feel like I have two mothers dogging me. Yes, I took my meds, and no, I don't need anything." He winked at her. "Thanks for asking."

After dinner, Nancy looked at the wall clock. "Well, I'm heading out to catch a movie so you can have some family time. I'll be back in a couple of hours."

"Thanks, Mom," said Jake.

She nodded, put on her coat, and left.

"Hey, everyone," Jake said with a smile, "let's have our first family meeting in the living room."

They formed a triangle, with Keenan sitting on the floor, Jake lying on the sofa to take the burden off his ribs, and Claire on the recliner.

Jake began. "Let's start with where we should live. I'd like each of us to give reasons for staying here in Anchorage and for moving to Leavenworth. Who wants to go first?"

Silence …

"Okay, then, I'll start. Here's my case for Anchorage: I like our house, and I like living here. I like my job, too. Plus, I get the summer off, so we can do fun things. Now, here's what I like about Leavenworth. It's a cool little town, and they serve German food in the restaurants. The Cascade Mountains are beautiful, and Claire's orchard would be a wonderful place to live. Okay, who's next?"

Keenan raised his hand. "I like Anchorage because of my school. And I like my doctor when I get hurt. I like hiking in the mountains in the summer, and I used to like skiing in the winter. Maybe I will again if that moose moves to Wasilla. I like Leavenworth because it's fun to pick apples if you don't fall off a ladder."

Claire covered her mouth, fighting the urge to burst out laughing. The little guy definitely had his father's sense of humor.

"Oh!" he said. "In Leavenworth, Grandma and Grandpa could see us more because they'd be closer. And Uncle Eddie could keep teaching me about women."

Jake looked shocked. "Uncle Eddie has been teaching you about women?"

"Oops. He said not to tell you."

Jake rolled his eyes, pretending to be exasperated. "Do you have anything else, son?"

"In Leavenworth, we could be with Mom."

Tears came to Claire's eyes.

"Well, pretty lady, the floor is yours."

"Um, I'd like to live in Anchorage because there are lots of things to do here, like hiking in the beautiful mountains we saw today. I like the people here and would love to teach at Keenan's school if I ever learned German. I like Leavenworth because it's a nice place to live, and we have a wonderful orchard. One day, I'd like our family to farm our orchard again. Keenan, you could take over running the orchard along with your brothers and sisters if your dad and I have children. Then, one day, you could all pass the orchard to your children. Plus, if you lived in Leavenworth, you could eat as many apples as you wanted." She gave Jake a sly look when she said it.

"I love apples!" Keenan said.

She winked at Jake.

"You know, Claire, I haven't the slightest idea about how to be an apple rancher."

She smiled. "Jake, apple trees are plants, and you grow them. So you're a farmer, not a rancher. Ranchers raise animals."

"Oh. See, that's how clueless I am. Keenan, they don't have a German immersion school there because there aren't enough kids in the community to support it. Would you be okay with attending a normal school if we moved there?"

He looked sad at the idea. Then he said something that came from the depths of his heart. "Papa, if it would make Mom happy, then let's move to Leavenworth."

Claire gasped and ran upstairs in tears.

"Is she mad at me, Papa?"

Jake shook his head. "No, son. You made her very happy. People sometimes cry when they're happy. I'm proud of you for saying you'd move there for her. She loves you, you know."

"Yep. Mom tells me all the time."

After a few minutes, Claire came down and hugged them. They talked until Nancy returned, with the conversation coming easy. Claire felt they really were a family.

That night, she snuggled next to Jake. "I like these family meetings. It reminds me of Sundays as a kid when we turned off the TV and talked. I hope we can continue this when we're married."

"I'd like that. I think Keenan showed you again how special he is."

She nodded. "Why his mother couldn't love him escapes me. He's such an incredible boy."

He sighed. "Her not loving him never ceases to confound me. Some things just can't be explained."

"Hey, Giuseppe, I made you something with Keenan's help. Do you want to see it?"

"Sure. My guess is you two didn't make fudge for me."

"You would be correct, sir. Let me get it."

She opened the desk drawer and took out the comic-wrapped package.

"Forgive the humble wrapping. I forgot to buy gift wrap at the store."

He smiled. "This is fine."

"Go ahead, open it."

Tears came to his eyes when he saw the simple piece of art. "It's beautiful. This so describes us. We're the perfect fit."

"I hope you'll look at it often when I'm gone. It's how I feel about us."

"I love you so much, Claire. This picture is a wonderful metaphor for everything we have."

She nodded, turned off the lights, and undressed. "This body of mine craves you. We're the perfect fit physically as well as emotionally and spiritually." She moved atop him and moaned as their bodies became one.

32

THE NEXT MORNING, Jake woke before Claire and took his first shower since the accident. It felt good. Dressing afterward was difficult, but he did it, and he felt proud of himself for his efforts. She was still asleep when he came out of the bathroom, so he went downstairs. Nancy and Keenan were in the kitchen. "Am I smelling pancakes?"

"Yeah, Papa. I'm pouring the mix in the skillet, and Grandma is flipping them."

"You two make a good team. How soon, Mom?"

"About five minutes. Better rouse your lady."

"I'll leave that to Keenan. Son, please encourage the fair maiden to join us."

"Okay!" He took off, running toward the stairs.

"Whoa! No running for a month, remember?"

"Sorry!"

Claire came down, looking happy and refreshed. Even without makeup, she was beautiful. "Good morning. There's nothing like having an enthusiastic boy waking you."

Jake put an arm around Keenan. "Welcome to my world."

She yawned. "Thanks for letting me sleep in." She winked at him and then turned her attention to Nancy. "It smells good, Mom. I love pancakes. Is there anything I can do to help?"

"Grab the pancakes, and I'll get the butter, syrup, and orange juice."

"Sure. Boy, you made enough to feed an army."

Jake laughed. "Keenan can eat his weight in pancakes. Once he turns on his inhaling mechanism, don't expect leftovers."

As they ate, a quiet Claire watched the family interact. There is love present at this table, she thought, and it touched her heart. Sadness swept through her; by ten o'clock the next day, she'd be on a plane, leaving them. Tears filled her eyes. Jake noticed. "We'll miss you, too, Claire."

"Forgive me for spoiling this wonderful meal." She took a deep breath. "Okay, I'll be better. Keenan, would you tell me a joke to lift my spirits?"

"Sure. Papa, you play along, okay?"

He nodded.

"Hey, Papa, my teacher hurt herself at school and now has a weak back."

Jake gasped and brought his hands to his face with exaggerated drama. "Oh, my goodness! When did it happen?"

"About a week back." He laughed. "Get it, Mom? A weak back a week back?"

His animated expression was as funny as the joke. It cracked her up. "Oh, sweetie, if I'm ever down, I'll call you for a joke. It was just what I needed. I love you."

"The joke is from The Three Stooges," he beamed. "I love watching them, but now you can't hit each other like they did."

"Claire, do you have plans for the day?" asked Nancy.

"Mom, if it's okay with everyone, after we clean the dishes and I get presentable, could we go somewhere for coffee? I'd love to spend a little time with you."

"I'd like that."

"There's a place called Kaladi Brothers, and they're not far from here," said Jake. "That's where I got the coffee for Maddy."

Claire chuckled, regaining her cheerfulness. "Mom, the coffee he bought for her is called Red Goat. Every time we had it, we wondered if there was a subliminal meaning behind Jake's choice. Maddy often said, 'Let's make some Red Goat for this old goat.' We loved the coffee, and I'd love to take some back with me."

"Tell her it was a completely innocent purchase," said Jake with a sly smile.

"I will not," Claire said with a laugh. "All the speculation regarding your motives made you an interesting person in her eyes."

An hour later, the two of them entered Kaladi Brothers café located just off the Seward Highway. It was a stylish place, and the beguiling smell of brewing coffee added to its allure. They both ordered Red Goat, which the establishment touted as their "coffee of the day, every day."

After finding a place to sit, Nancy took a tentative sip after blowing on the hot liquid. "Oh, this is good. Ethan will love it. I'm going to take some home, too."

"When do you plan on heading back to Spokane?"

"In about a week. Jake will need me to run Keenan to and from school and do the cooking and cleaning. I love being with them."

Claire took a sip of her coffee. "Mom, as bad as this sounds, their injuries advanced our relationship. I feel so close to Jake and Keenan now. I told Jake I'd like to adopt Keenan, but he told me it wouldn't be possible."

"Because Keenan needs Erin's medical insurance?"

"Yes. Plus, Jake's putting half of her child support payments toward Keenan's college education."

"I could make a case for socialized medicine, especially when it comes to special needs children. Claire, Erin never took to Keenan, ever. I had to watch him while Jake did his fieldwork in college because she wanted nothing to do with him. I can't tell you how many times it broke my heart to see Keenan go to her and get rebuffed. There wasn't an ounce of maternal instinct in her." She reached over and touched her hand. "The way you two already love each other ..." She had tears in her eyes.

"I know. I wanted to tell you today that I'll love Keenan like my own, but I think you already know it."

She nodded.

"Mom, do you, um ... do you think Jake finds me as attractive as Erin?"

"Oh, Claire, put your mind to rest on that, and don't be jealous of her. It was nothing but an extended fling for him. They had nothing in common."

"I meant physically ... in one of his letters, Jake said they had torrid sex, and I guess you confirmed it. I ... I'm not ... I'm not a wild woman in bed." It sounded like an apology.

Nancy shook her head. "Claire Lofton, I've never seen my son so happy. He told me how perfect you two are for each other and even quoted a poem from someone whose name I don't remember. *I am through you so I,* or something like that. Believe me: he's enamored with you physically—he's enamored with you in every way. And don't think I haven't noticed the smiles on both of your faces."

She blushed. "I ... so want to please him, you know, physically."

"Claire, shortly after he and Erin got married, he said, 'Mom, isn't there supposed to be more to sex than sex?' He looked so sad when he said it, and that's when I knew his marriage was destined to end. With you, I have no doubt his question has finally been answered. The answer is a resounding yes, there is more, much more, and you showed him that. Trust me on this: you have nothing to fear about any of his past loves."

Claire wiped tears from her eyes. "Thanks for telling me this. I felt the same emptiness in my relationships as Jake did."

"I'm confident you and Jake will have a happy union."

Claire nodded and took another sip of coffee. "Mom, I mean it when I said come see Maddy and me. Dad, too, is welcome, but I think he'd be bored around us girls."

"I'll be glad to come. When will you have some free time?"

"Spring Break would work. Unfortunately, Alaska and Washington break times don't coincide, so Jake and Keenan can't come down until school is over."

"I'd love to visit you then. Have you thought about when you'll get married and what kind of ceremony you want?"

"If Maddy were here, I'd gladly marry him today, but mid-June is probably best. I'd like a small wedding with only immediate family. Jake feels the same way. It's a one-percenter thing, I suppose."

"Are you going to invite your parents?"

Claire froze in mid-sip. She put the cup down and sighed. "No. They haven't communicated with me in any way since dumping me off with Maddy and Grandpa when I was six. To me, they're strangers." She paused for a moment and looked Nancy in the eye. "I abhor what they did to me and don't want them around my family."

"Can you tell me a bit about them?"

She sighed again. "There's not much to tell. They're both quite wealthy, part of the East Coast elite. With that crowd, it's all about trying to one-up your peers with ever-more spectacular displays of opulence. I find it repugnant. Mom, could we talk about something else? They abandoned me long ago, and I have no desire to re-establish relations with them. I'm a small-town girl who doesn't need much of anything to be happy. My parents are Maddy and Grandpa, not them."

"I understand. And I'm honored that you call me Mom. Now I understand the significance of it to you."

They talked for another hour before heading home with several packages of Red Goat coffee. As they entered the house, a heavenly aroma greeted them. "I wonder what they've been up to?" said Nancy.

"I'll bet my fiancé got out his crockpot."

Jake was in the kitchen, looking happy. "Good afternoon, you two. I hope you're hungry. Tonight we'll be having my famous crockpot blueberry chipotle barbeque ribs and baked beans. And for dessert, homemade chocolate chip cookies and a side of vanilla ice cream."

"That sounds yummy," said Claire. "Do you need any help?"

"No, thanks. Most of it is cooking. Keenan will help make the cookies in an hour when he returns from playing with Tommy. I wish I could take you out for your last supper here, but it is what it is."

"This will be better," said Claire. "Thanks for the effort. I know you're still hurting."

He nodded. "Mom, may I spend some time with this lovely lady?"

"Go right ahead. I'm dying to finish the book I've been reading. Where will you two be so I can be out of your way?"

"Upstairs," they both said in unison.

She laughed. "I see you're both on the same wavelength today."

Jake managed to make it up the stairs a little easier than on previous days, and Claire was right there if he needed help. She closed and locked the bedroom door. "I feel a little chilled. Do you mind getting under the covers?"

"Not at all." He started to get in with his clothes on.

"Oh no, mister. I need to feel your skin on mine."

"Yes, ma'am."

She snuggled next to him. He kissed her. "This is nice. Did you have a good time with my mother?"

"I did. We get along well."

"So, did she provide you with information to cause me eternal embarrassment, or did she wax eloquent on what a catch I am?"

"She loves you, Jake. I envy you for having a mother's love. As bad as it sounds, I told her how the accident was a good thing because I got to be with you and Keenan. I've treasured this time. Jake, the way you make love to me ..." Her voice trailed off. "I'm going to miss you so much."

"I know ..."

They lay quietly for a while.

"I suspect you wanted to be alone with my mom to ask her about things that are troubling you. Am I correct?"

"Your intuitive abilities amaze me. I asked if I'm as pretty as your former wife."

"I think there's more than her prettiness that's bothering you."

She frowned. "You said she was a beautiful wild child, and the sex was scorching. I've never considered myself to be beautiful, and I'm not a wild child. So, I wonder if you'll end up missing that kind of relationship."

"Okay, you're getting warmer, but what's the real thing troubling you?"

"Gosh, Jake, you're going to make me bare it all, aren't you?"

"Yep. So say it because I already know it."

"Then why toy with me?"

"I'm not toying with you. I want us to share our inner fears so we can shed light on them as a couple."

She sighed again. "I just don't see how I can compete with what you once had. Plus, I see how talented you are, what a great father you are, and how everyone seems to admire you. I think I'm out of my league with you on multiple fronts. I'm just a girl from Leavenworth who's always been told I'm a lousy lover. Jake, I don't even know what scorching sex means. Maybe you made love to me so tenderly because you can't move, and it will all change once your body heals."

"So you're saying you're lousy in bed and not worthy of His Excellency, the great Mr. Holland, whose current immobility makes him an extraordinary lover?"

She looked at him, her absurd analysis of his sexual prowess registering. A smile came to her. They both burst out laughing.

He kissed her. "Eventually, you'll get around to talking about Mr. Heartbreaker. Maybe we could fast-forward the conversation to it."

"Okay, fine. I'm afraid that, like him, you'll replace me with the next woman who comes along and strikes your fancy. I'm so in love with you that it's terrifying to imagine a life apart from you."

"Good. It's out now. May I respond?"

She nodded. He pointed to the two joined puzzle pieces. "That's us, Claire. Body, mind, spirit—we fit, and we fit perfectly. These two weeks with you have been the happiest of my life. You're not the only one with abandonment fears. When you sent me your farewell letter, the thought of not having you in my life was equally terrifying. I spent most of last night watching you as you slept, thinking I was with the most beautiful woman in the world. I have no doubt that I'll love you for the rest of my days."

"Jake, I feel the same way. I was up the previous night, watching you, just as you were doing with me."

He chuckled. "We're so intertwined. Surely you can see it."

"I do."

"As far as Erin goes, yes, as a young stud, I enjoyed sex with her. I enjoyed it a lot. But after a while, raw physicality, with nothing else, didn't satisfy me. I learned that I needed more. The sex between you and me is like oxygen, essential to my well-being.

Torrid, scorching sex—or whatever adjective you want to use in front of it—is not oxygen. The lovemaking we have is what I need. For Mr. Heartbreaker and the others, what you offered wasn't oxygen for them. It is to me, and I can't live without it. Claire, everything about you is soft, gentle, and tender. You touch my soul in so many ways."

"I understand now how you feel. You're my oxygen as well."

He sighed. "Since we're putting our cards on the table, with my imagination, it's easy for me to picture you with your other men, and it's unsettling."

"Jake, I didn't even like sex until you, and now I crave it—I'm desperate for it. That should tell you how I feel about you."

"We both have our insecurities. I won't 'dump' you, Claire. All I can tell you is I'll earn your love every day." He kissed her and sighed again. "My chief worry is that I might not live up to your expectations."

"Jake, you're the man I've always wanted. That's why I gave you the two puzzle pieces. I want so much to marry you. I now wish I would've said yes to our getting married here."

He squeezed her hand. "So, what now?"

"What do you mean?"

"I mean, how will we get through the next few months apart?"

She looked at him with sad eyes. "I vote for calling each other every day instead of letter writing. I need to hear your voice."

"I can do you one better. Let's Skype. Does your home laptop have a built-in camera?"

"I don't think so. It's ancient."

"C'mon, let's go to Best Buy. You need an iPad."

"Jake, I'm lying here naked, craving you, and you say you want to go shopping?"

"Odd as it sounds, yes. With Skype, we can see and talk to each other for free. I know it'll make our time apart more bearable. Besides, tonight, oh baby, brace yourself—I've been saving a Percocet for our last night together."

She laughed. "Most guys would use a different kind of pill to rise to the occasion, but not my man. He takes a pain pill. You'll have to teach me how to use the iPad."

"I will. It's easy. Let's get dressed."

She chuckled. "Jake?"

"Yes?"

"Thanks."

He smiled and kissed her.

Downstairs, they told a surprised Nancy they had an errand to run. A while later, they returned with a new iPad. Jake showed Claire how to Skype and how to use it for email and going online.

Keenan came home, and they mixed up a batch of cookies and put them in the oven.

Nancy went upstairs and came back with a camera. "Okay, everyone, sit on the couch so I can take a picture of you." Claire sat between Jake and Keenan, and the three of them smiled when Nancy said, "Say cheese!"

The kitchen timer dinged. "Mom and Claire, could you bring the crockpot and side dishes to the table while Keenan and I take the cookies out of the oven to cool? Also, Mom, if you don't mind, will you dish out the food since I'm still hurting?"

"Sure." She and Claire placed the food on the table, which Jake and Keenan had set earlier.

Nancy lifted the crockpot lid and grabbed several ribs with a pair of tongs. "Here are some for you, sweet Claire."

"I hope you like them," said Jake.

"Blueberry chipotle ribs will be a first for me. This will be interesting."

Next, Nancy served Jake, Keenan, and then herself. After that came the baked beans and corn on the cob.

"I'd like to say grace. Please join hands, everyone," said Jake. He took Claire's hand in his, along with Keenan's. "Dear God, we thank you for this food, and we thank you for each other. Keenan and I also thank you two amazing women for caring for us. We are grateful. Amen." Claire squeezed his hand as she said amen. "Okay, let's eat!"

Claire took a tentative bite from the rib, and her face lit up. "Jake, this is good! Blueberries and chipotle as a combo sounds bizarre, but this works. Please give me the recipe—Maddy will love it."

"I'm glad you like it. And to think I almost made your favorite meal—chicken nuggets and tater tots."

"Hey, if I could dip them in this blueberry chipotle sauce, I'd be in heaven." She finished her first rib and started on the second. "These *really* are good. Do you like them, Keenan?"

He looked up with a face slathered in sauce. "What?"

Jake chuckled. "He's doing his imitation of a dog chewing the meat off a bone. I forgot to caution you about disturbing him when he's eating ribs; he gets territorial."

Nancy tried the baked beans. "I love how you jazzed them up with brown sugar and bacon. Jake, you're quite the homemaker."

"Thanks, Mom. After dinner, we can head upstairs, and I'll give you and Claire a lesson on how to reduce your laundry time."

Claire choked and had to drink some water to wash her food down. "I think I know the lesson: Open washer door, use foot if necessary to cram everything you own into it, turn cycle to 'Hardcore Bachelor,' and hope for the best."

Jake had an ear-to-ear grin. "Close. But you forgot to add detergent, silly goose."

Keenan giggled. "Papa calls me 'silly goose' too, Mom." He chomped down on his ear of corn, his appetite unsated.

The rest of the meal came with easy banter and lots of laughter. After cleaning up, they set up a card table in the family room, and Jake turned on the gas fireplace. They spent the evening munching on cookies and playing the board game Risk. Keenan conquered the world and looked quite satisfied with his global domination.

Ten o'clock came, and Jake sighed. "Son, you need to get ready for bed because we have to get up early to take Claire to the airport."

"Oh, Papa, can't we play one more game of Risk?"

He shook his head. "If we did, we'd be up until two. Tell you what; if you get my six-string, I'll play two songs, and then it'll be time to say goodnight."

"Will you play Sukiyaki? It's a fun song, Mom!"

"Sure." He carefully took his arm out of the sling.

Keenan removed the guitar from the wall. "Here, Papa."

"Thanks. Can you put the strap over my shoulder and then get my picks?" He helped his dad with the strap and brought him a small box of picks sitting on the mantle. Jake smiled at Claire. "Here goes."

He started playing the lively Japanese tune, picking the strings instead of strumming. In seconds, she knew he was an accomplished guitarist. It was a fun and bouncy song, and he played it perfectly. When he finished, Jake let out an exaggerated sigh of relief, glad he made it through the song without blundering.

"Did you like it, Mom?" asked Keenan, his eyes sparkling.

"I did. Very much."

"One more is all my aching body can take. Any suggestions?"

"Oh, Jake," said Nancy, "please play Amazing Grace."

"Okay." He adjusted a couple of strings and began playing, capturing the elegance of the simple song, taking his time, shifting effortlessly through the chord sequences.

"I've never heard anything so beautiful," said Claire when he finished. "I hope one day you'll play for me at Claire Hill."

"Thanks. I'd love to." He looked at Keenan. "It's time to say goodnight."

"Sweetie," said Claire, "call me when you're ready, and I'll tuck you in."

His eyes lit up. "Okay."

By eleven, the house was quiet. Claire took a quick shower and joined Jake in bed. He had lit several candles, which bathed the room in a warm, comforting glow. She kissed him. "I loved spending the evening together as a family." Her tears started. "I love you all so much."

"No. No tears. Let's not squander the night with sadness." She smiled meekly and nodded. He kissed her, tentatively at first, and then with passion and urgency.

They spent the night making love. Not a word was spoken; their eyes, tender touches, and moans of pleasure said more than words could ever convey. In her entire life, Claire had never experienced anything so sensual, so stunningly erotic, so effortlessly intimate. This was "one-percenter" love, the love she had always hoped for.

The alarm sounded at seven. They kissed once more, and she went to the bathroom to prepare for her flight. Alone in the bed, Jake looked upward. "Dear God, thank you for Claire," he whispered. He got up and went downstairs. Nancy and Keenan were in the kitchen, discussing what to make for breakfast.

Their breakfast lacked the lively chitchat of the previous evening. Afterward, Jake excused himself and went to his bedroom. He pulled out a piece of paper from his desk, wrote a few words, and put the paper in an envelope. He addressed it "My Love" and slipped it into her pack. Downstairs, he glanced at the wall clock and frowned. "I suppose we should go …"

Claire looked at them. "I have a request: Please just drop me off and go. If you all come inside with me, I won't be able to leave you."

Jake hugged her. "I understand. Mom, would you mind driving so Keenan and I can sit in the back seat with Claire?"

"I'd be happy to."

Claire sighed. "I'll run up and get my pack. Keenan, please come with me."

On the short drive to the airport, she sat between Jake and Keenan, holding their hands. Her mind was afire with desperate thinking, wishing the airport were a million miles away, hoping for a flat tire or a flight delay—anything to postpone their parting. She kissed Keenan's cheek and did the same with Jake. The agony of saying goodbye was palpable; powerful emotions within her conveyed how precious and essential these people were to her. A tear wove its way down her cheek.

All too soon, Nancy pulled in front of the Alaska Airlines departure area. When they got out of the warm car, a frigid arctic wind greeted them, as if Mother Nature were doing her best to prevent a prolonged farewell. They gathered around Claire, and Nancy hugged her first. "Goodbye, sweet girl. I love you." Claire nodded, tears pouring down her cheeks.

She knelt and hugged Keenan. "I love you so much."

He latched on to her. "Please don't forget me, Momma."

"Keenan, I'll look at your ring often and think of you." She wiped away his tears and kissed his forehead. "We'll talk every day, I promise." She hugged him one last time and stood. It was time to say goodbye to Jake.

He tried his best to muster a smile.

"I love you, Jacob Holland. Heart, body, and soul love you."

Too emotional to speak, he nodded and tenderly kissed her.

She offered them a feeble smile, turned around, and walked into the airport without looking back. If she had, she wouldn't have left.

33

THE MOOD WAS somber in the Holland home after they returned from the airport. Keenan didn't feel like acting out the comics, which was a Sunday morning tradition. At eleven, Jake asked Nancy to take Keenan to McDonald's. He needed time to be alone. After they left, he went back to bed and brought her pillow next to him. Her scent was still there. "I love you, Claire Lofton," he whispered. The thought of months without her was unbearable.

After a few minutes, he sighed, reached for the phone, and dialed a number he knew by heart.

"Hey, it's me."

"Hello, Jake. The tone of your voice reflects how you're hurting."

"Yep. I love her so much. Maddy, I've missed our daily calls. Forgive me for not calling these past two weeks. Are you okay?"

"I'm fine. I've missed talking to you, too. I'm glad you're better. So from your proposal and her acceptance, the in-person versions of you two must've matched the magic of your word relationship."

"You were right about how special she is. I can't even begin to tell you how much I'm aching for her. She's going to need you to get through our time apart."

"I know. I asked Bluebell and Mrs. Kerfuffle to dish out some extra love to her as well."

"She wants to stay in Leavenworth. Can we talk about it?"

"Sure."

"Maddy, be honest: would you want Keenan and me invading your home? He's an energetic kid, and I'm not sure I could thrive if I had to walk around on eggshells, hoping not to get on your nerves."

"Jake, I adore you, and regarding Keenan, there's nothing like a lively boy to make you feel alive. You'll be welcome here."

"I told Claire I'd feel like a boarder in your house, afraid to put my imprint on anything because it might offend you."

"Knowing this will be the home of the Holland family when I'm gone brings me much comfort. What my husband and I started, you and yours will continue. With heartfelt joy, I'll welcome you and Keenan into my home. You're my legacy."

"I'm not sure how well I could handle your feistiness or ire. I value peace in my life."

"Claire showed me your 'conditions' letter. I have no doubt of your ability to put this old woman in her place should I get too cantankerous. Jake, I'll love you and Keenan like my own. I already do if it hasn't been obvious to you."

"I know. I love you, too. Maddy, landing a job in a small town could be difficult. The thought of being a kept man bothers me a lot. Being a freeloader doesn't sit well with me."

"Jake, you and Claire could run this orchard. It's big enough to sustain a family financially."

"I know nothing about growing apples."

"Neither did Max and I, but we learned. You're a bright man, and as a geologist, you must have a love for the earth. There's something special about seeing apple blossoms bloom and turn into fruit that you harvest and knowing you had a part in nature's cycle. I know you'd love it."

"Maybe so. I love my job here, Maddy."

"Jake, she'd move up there if that's what being with you requires. But her roots go deep here, and I'm sure you'd flourish here if you gave it a chance. Think about it."

"I will. Thanks for being so welcoming to Keenan and me. Are you sure you're okay?"

She sighed. "The pain is getting worse, but the doc is giving me something for it."

"You need to tell Claire what's going on."

"No, not yet. There's plenty of time for that. Her being apart from you two will be hard, and I don't need to add to her sadness. I'm fine."

"Keeping this secret from her is wrong, in my humble opinion, but I'll respect your wishes."

"Thank you for keeping your word. So is she coming back pregnant? I want to live long enough to see my great-grandchild."

He laughed. "You crack me up. Let's just say I did everything in my power to accommodate your desire."

"My husband is smiling in heaven, knowing his precious girl has someone to take care of her. And Jake, she'll take care of you and Keenan, too. Her agoraphobia was quite real and pronounced, yet when her little boy was hurt, she jumped on a plane without hesitation. That's how powerful her love is for you two."

"I know. I was shocked when she walked into the ICU. She fabricated a story to get in, saying she was his mother."

"Claire can be quite resourceful when she needs to be. Jake, do me a favor and don't sulk around, pining for her. Keenan needs his father to be happy, and your healing will take longer if you're depressed."

"I hear you. Claire and I plan on Skyping each other every day. That'll elevate our spirits."

"I haven't the slightest idea what you're talking about."

He laughed. "She'll explain it to you when she gets back. Maddy, I hear the garage door opening; Keenan and my mom are back. I'll call you again tomorrow."

"Okay. I love you, Jake. Thanks for making my girl happy."

"I love you, too. Bye."

Talking to her was what he needed. She was right; moping around would do no one any good.

From her window seat on the three-hour trip to Seattle, Claire pretended to be interested in the spectacular mountain scenery passing below. It didn't fool the middle-aged woman sitting next to her, who saw her tears and took her hand, a sweet act of kindness by a stranger.

After the short hop from Seattle to Wenatchee, Claire called Maddy to say she'd be home soon.

Twenty minutes later, not even Bluebell's excitement and Maddy's loving arms could lessen her sadness. Maddy let her get her tears out and then took charge. "Okay, sweet girl, you've had your cry. Now, it's time to cheer up, show me your ring, and tell me what happened over the past two weeks. Did the real-life Jake live up to the abstract, letter-writing Jake?"

Claire wiped away her tears and smiled. "He's amazing, Maddy, in every way. You wouldn't believe how talented he is and how much love there is between him and Keenan. And his mom, oh my God, she's so wonderful. I invited her and Jake's dad to visit us. You'll love her, I know it." She held up her hand. "Isn't the ring he had made for me beautiful?"

"It is. I love how the diamond seems to float."

"Here's the ring Keenan gave me to mom-marry him. It melts my heart when he calls me Mom. I love him so much."

"I cried when you shared the story about how he proposed to you."

"He's already my son, Maddy. That's how I think now."

"You'll be a great wife and mother. So, did your agoraphobia ever become an issue when you were there?"

Claire shook her head. "I felt so safe there and was so busy that I never had time to think about it."

"Has Keenan fully recovered?"

"He can't do strenuous activities for a month, but he's fine. Jake is the one I worry about. His pneumonia could return if he doesn't take care of himself."

"So tell me more about him and you."

"I love him beyond words. I can't wait to marry him."

"I'm surprised you didn't come home married."

"We talked about it, but I couldn't do it without having you there. Because Grandpa's gone, I want you to give me away. Jake said he wants to marry me at Claire Hill."

Tears filled her eyes. "It's the perfect place. Grandpa's ashes are scattered there, and I know we'll feel his presence. When I'm gone, I want you to scatter my ashes there, too."

"Please don't talk of that. I couldn't bear to lose you."

"Jake and Keenan will be your family when I join Grandpa."

Claire looked at her suspiciously. "Is anything wrong?"

Maddy laughed. "I'm as healthy as a horse. I'm just saying, knowing you'll have a family when I'm gone is comforting. So how's your man in the sack?" she said with a wink. "Is a Jakelet on the way?"

Claire rolled her eyes. "Leave it to you to ask me that. You know I'm on the pill to ease my periods, so you won't be a great-grandmother soon." She paused for a moment. "I take that back. When I get married, you'll have an instant great-grandson in Keenan."

"I'm looking forward to loving him. So, are you going to ignore my question about whether he's good in the sack?"

Claire took her hands and squeezed them. "Maddy, he's an incredible lover." She took a moment to summon the right words. "Jake Holland is so far above Colin in every way. I thank God that lightweight dumped me. I'm with the man of my dreams now and know we'll be together forever."

"I'm happy for you. So tell me more about your future son."

Her eyes got wide. "Keenan's the sweetest little boy, so bright and deep for his age, and he has his father's wit. You'll love him, Maddy. He's adorable."

"Will you be able to deal with his medical issues?"

"Easily. With Jake, it's second nature. He anticipates potential dangers and adjusts what they do accordingly. It won't be a problem; I'm quite confident saying that."

"So, what are your plans for the rest of the day? I mean, you'll be back in school tomorrow. You need to get mentally prepared."

"I know. First, I'll unpack, and then I'll Skype with Jake. I want you to meet them."

"What's Skype?"

"I got an iPad when I was there; it has a program called Skype that we can use for video chatting."

"I still don't get it."

"They can see us, and we can see them while we talk. Hey, I'll wait to unpack and call them now." She got out her iPad, opened the Skype program, and called Jake.

He answered, and his face appeared on her screen a moment later. "Hello, my love. Did you arrive home safely?"

"I did. You look so clear." She showed it to Maddy, who was stunned by the technology.

Keenan popped into view. "Hello, Mom! I miss you."

"Hey, Keenan! Say hello to Maddy."

She gave the iPad to her. "Just say hello, Maddy. He'll hear you."

Maddy looked as if she were teleported to the future from the 1800s. "Hello, Keenan. Do you remember me?"

"I do. I loved picking apples at your orchard, well, except for the part about having to go to the hospital."

Maddy laughed. "Yeah, that took the fun out of it. I look forward to seeing you again."

"My papa says you'll be my great-grandmother when he marries Mom."

"I know. You'll be my first great-grandchild. That makes you special."

Jake came into view. "You're looking gorgeous, Miss Maddy. I'd like you to meet Nancy, my mother."

He passed his iPad to her. "Hello, Mrs. Roediger. I'm pleased to meet you."

"Please call me Maddy. It's nice to meet you as well. Claire told me she invited you and your husband to visit us. You'll be most welcome here."

"Thank you, and the welcome mat is out for you two to visit us in Spokane. Maddy, Claire is something. I'm so happy for her and Jake's engagement."

"I feel the same way. You raised a fine boy."

Claire leaned in. "Mom, maybe we can Skype too when you return to Spokane. It seems to work well."

"That's a good idea. I'll talk to Jake about showing me how to use it. Well, I'll give you back to Jake. I love you, sweet girl."

"I love you, too."

Jake came back into view. "I know you have a lot to do to prepare for school tomorrow, so we'll let you go. I love you."

"Jake ... I ..."

"I know, Claire. I feel the same way. Get on with your day and be happy. That's an order."

"Amen to that," said Maddy in the background.

"Okay. I love you all. Bye."

"Bye!" they all said in unison.

After taking Bluebell out to play, Claire went upstairs and started unpacking. A letter fell out when she removed her jeans. On the envelope were the words *"My Love."*

Claire,

If you remember, I wrote you a tender love story and threw it away because my heart knew the words could only be said when I was looking into your eyes. Last night was unlike anything I have ever experienced—so intimate, so beautiful, so tender. Our hearts spoke to each other with an eloquence far beyond the reach of words. You "heard" everything I wanted to say. I love you, Claire Lofton.

> *Only you know the language of my heart.*
> *In the silence, between you and me, Spirit dances.*
>
> *Jake*

That night, Keenan surprised his father by reaching under his pillow and pulling out a letter. "Here, Papa. Mom said to give this to you when you said goodnight to me."

"Oh my gosh. Thank you." He kissed Keenan goodnight and went to his room. In bed, he began reading.

My Dear Man,

I'm in your bathroom, writing you this letter, my heart aching at the thought of leaving you in a few minutes.

I don't even know where to begin to say how much I love you. I looked in the mirror after showering and liked the reflection I saw. I said, "I love you,

Claire," and meant it. At that moment, I knew my heart had healed. Jake, you made this possible, and I love you for it. Anaïs Nin once wrote, "She bloomed in his hands." That's how I feel about you.

Last night, making love to you was the most incredible thing I've ever experienced. All that I hoped making love could be came true, and more. The poet's words "I am through you so I" genuinely describe our union.

Sir, you rescued me from my past and untangled Claire in every conceivable way. For all that you are and all that you've done, it will be an honor to be your wife. Thank you for choosing to share your life with me. What we have is beautiful, and I'll spend the rest of my days loving you.

A.A. Milne said, "How lucky I am to have something that makes saying goodbye so hard." You and Keenan are now hopelessly entwined in my being, and I so look forward to our days together.

I love you with all my heart. Claire

34

A MONTH LATER, a FedEx truck pulled into the driveway and parked. The driver removed a large rectangular package and knocked on the door. Claire greeted him, trying to constrain Bluebell, who thought someone had come to play with her. "Hello, ma'am. I have a package for Claire Lofton."

"I'm Miss Lofton."

"Please sign here to accept it."

She thanked him and brought it inside. Maddy came from the kitchen and eyed the large box. "What did you order?"

"I didn't order anything." She looked at the label. "It's from Jake."

"Maybe he's sending us more Red Goat."

"If he did, it would be a lot of coffee. I wonder what it could be?" Claire opened the box and pulled out a bubble-wrapped item that appeared to be a picture. She gasped when she removed the wrap and got a peek at it. "Oh, Maddy, look what Jake painted for us. It's beautiful."

"Jake painted this?" said a shocked Maddy as she viewed the painting of Claire with Jake and Keenan.

"Yes. Mom took a picture of the three of us, and Jake must've used it as inspiration. You should see his other paintings—he's a gifted artist. Can we hang it above the mantle?"

"We sure can. Let's do it now."

After hanging the picture, they stood back and admired it. "You know," said Maddy, "if Jake moves here and can't find a job, he could sell his artwork. Are his other ones as good as this?"

"They are. His abstracts are stunning. They're so alive and vibrant."

"He's a talented man."

"I've got to call him."

They spent the next hour talking; Jake said painting helped take his mind off missing her. Afterward, she Skyped Nancy and showed her the painting and how good it looked on their wall.

The following week, Jake and Keenan were enjoying their Spring Break. His bones had healed, and he had mostly recovered from pneumonia, although he still experienced the lingering effect of fatigue if he overdid it. They'd already seen several movies at local theaters. Today, after he made his daily call to Maddy, they were going to have lunch at the Arctic Roadrunner, a locally owned restaurant in business since 1964. No one made better onion rings.

While Keenan played on his Xbox, Jake called Maddy. She picked up the phone, but she didn't greet him with her usual "Jake!"

"Maddy, are you there?"

Silence.

"Maddy?" He thought he heard a moan. "Maddy, tap the phone if you need help and can't talk." There was a distinct thump. "Okay, I'm calling an ambulance."

He ran downstairs, got on his iPad, and looked up emergency services in Leavenworth. A woman dispatcher answered his call. "Hello, my name is Jake Holland, and I'm calling from Anchorage, Alaska. My friend in Leavenworth has a health emergency. She's been diagnosed with an abdominal aortic aneurysm, and it may have burst. Or because she can't talk, she may be having a stroke."

He gave the dispatcher Maddy's address, which he knew by heart from all his letters to Claire, and told them to break her door down if they needed to. Then he brought up Maddy's physician on his phone's speed dial and called her. Her office was adjacent to the hospital, and she said she'd meet Maddy at the ER.

Keenan came to him, concerned. "What's wrong, Papa?"

"Something's wrong with Maddy. I called for an ambulance to take her to the hospital. Keenan, please go to your room for a few minutes so I can call Claire. I'll come to you when I'm done."

"Okay." He left, looking worried.

Jake called Claire's school. "Hello, my name is Jake Holland. I'm Claire Lofton's fiancé. I need to speak to her immediately. It's a medical emergency."

A few minutes later, Claire came on the line. "Jake, is something wrong with Keenan?"

"No. Claire, it's Maddy. I called for an ambulance. You need to go to the hospital now."

"How do you know something's wrong with her?"

"I just do! Claire, go to the hospital. I called her physician, and she'll meet her in the ER."

"How do you know her doctor's number?"

"Damn it, Claire, let's not waste time talking! Go be with her now!"

"O-Okay. You're scaring me, Jake."

"I know, and I'm sorry. Claire, I think it's bad."

He hung up, not wanting her to spend another second with him.

He got back online and looked up flights to Seattle. Alaska Airlines had one leaving in three hours. "Keenan!"

Keenan opened his bedroom door and came out.

"I'm going next door to talk to Tommy's mom. I'll be back soon."

"Okay. Can I come?"

"No. You stay here."

Jake left and returned a few minutes later.

Keenan was at the door when he walked in. "Son, I might have to fly to Leavenworth, and if I do, Tommy's mom said you could stay with them. I'm waiting for Claire to call and tell me how Maddy's doing."

Twenty minutes later, she called in a panic. "Jake, they said Maddy has a ruptured aortic aneurysm, and they're taking her to emergency surgery."

"Oh my God. When will they know if she'll be okay?"

"They said she could be in the operating room for several hours. Jake, Maddy was blue when I saw her and unconscious."

"I'm flying down."

"I'm so scared."

"I'm praying for her. I'll be there as soon as I can."

He hung up and booked the flight. It would be tight to make it to the airport and get through security with enough time to catch the plane.

He raced upstairs. "Keenan, Maddy had a blood vessel in her abdomen rupture. It's like a garden hose that sprang a leak. She's in surgery now, and the doctors are trying to fix it. I need to leave right away. I'm sorry to spring this on you, but Maddy and Claire need me to help them like Claire helped us."

"Can I come, too, Papa? I can help."

"I know you could, but they won't allow kids in her hospital room. I'll be back in a few days, and I'll call you whenever I can."

"Okay."

"While I pack some clothes, please call Tommy's mom and tell her you're coming over."

At Tommy's house, he gave Keenan a quick goodbye hug and told them to go over anytime to his place to get whatever clothes Keenan needed. With that, he hopped in his car and headed for the airport.

Seven hours later, he touched down in Wenatchee and rented a car. He got directions on how to get to the hospital in Leavenworth and drove as fast as he could. He tried calling Claire, but his phone didn't work. At the hospital, he parked and hurried to the admissions desk.

"Hello, I'm here to see Maddy Roediger. She was brought here today for emergency surgery."

The lady looked up the name and frowned. "Sir, I'm sorry to tell you this, but she didn't survive."

The news hit like a blow from a sledgehammer. "Are you sure?"

She nodded. "I'm very sorry."

He put his hands on the counter to steady himself.

"Are you okay?" she asked with concern.

He swallowed hard. "Yes."

He walked to a vacant seat and sat to regain his composure. His thoughts leaped to Claire, and his heart sank. *My God, where is she?*

Finding her became imperative. He tried calling her again, but his phone still didn't work. "Oh my God!" he said aloud, remembering he turned off his phone before the flight to save the battery. That's why he couldn't make or receive calls. "Jake, you idiot!"

He turned on his phone and called her.

"Jake, where have you been?"

"I forgot to turn my phone on after landing. I'm at the hospital here in Leavenworth. They told me Maddy didn't make it. Where are you?"

"I'm at home. Oh, Jake, she died on the operating table."

"I'll be there in a few minutes. I'm so sorry."

She was in the driveway when he arrived, sobbing, tears streaming down her face. He got out and ran to her. "I'm so sorry, Claire. I'm so sorry."

They went inside. On the couch, he held her. Both were lost in tears. Later that evening, he took her hand in his. "Claire, have you made arrangements with a funeral home?"

She nodded. "Maddy had it all worked out in case this happened. She wants to be cremated and have her ashes scattered with Grandpa's ashes at Claire Hill. Thank you for coming to be with me. Where's Keenan?"

"He's staying with my neighbors. He'll be fine. I need to call him and tell him what happened if you don't mind."

"Okay, but Jake, I can't talk to him, not now."

"I understand. I'll go outside and make the call. We'll get through this." She mustered a feeble smile and a nod.

After briefly speaking to Tommy's mother, who offered her condolences, Jake told Keenan the news. He took it fairly well, and Tommy's mom ended the call by assuring Jake that Keenan would be fine.

Claire hugged him when he returned. Her eyes were puffy and bloodshot. "Jake, how did you know Maddy was in trouble? Did you feel it?"

"No. I called her. She answered, but she couldn't speak. I told her to tap the phone if something was wrong and I'd call an ambulance. She tapped, so I called for help."

"You said you called her doctor. If Maddy couldn't talk, how did you know her name and number?"

"Because I've talked to her previously."

Claire looked bewildered. "Why would you talk to Maddy's doctor?"

"Sit down, please, and I'll tell you."

"No. Tell me now."

He sighed. "After you sent me your farewell letter, I called to talk to you. Maddy answered and said you were out in the orchard. We talked for a long time, and she told me to leave you alone to let you have the time you needed to accept that you loved me. Maddy said that after reading our letters, she thought we were made for each other, and she was relieved that you'd have someone to be with when she was gone. I sensed something was wrong and asked her. She said she'd been having abdominal and back pain, and while you were at school, she had a friend take her to see her doctor, who felt a pulsating bulge in her abdomen. After getting a CT scan, she was diagnosed with an abdominal aortic aneurysm. Her doc said it developed slowly over the years."

He sighed again and continued. "The aneurysm was in a bad spot, so her doctor recommended a conservative management approach because surgery would be risky. Maddy said she'd been keeping it from you because you had enough to deal with regarding me. She was concerned that you might have another bout of depression, and because of that, she swore me to secrecy."

Claire looked at him, stunned.

After a few moments, it all began to sink in.

"You knew Maddy's life was in peril, yet you chose not to tell me."

"Claire, I begged Maddy to tell you, but she was adamant about not disclosing her condition to you."

Her face turned beet red. "I don't give a *damn* about what she told you! How dare you not tell me! I ... I could've taken her to Seattle to see specialists!"

"Claire, I so wanted to tell you."

"Damn you, Jake Holland! I think you wanted her to die because she was an encumbrance to you. You wanted her dead, and her not getting the help she needed did exactly that!"

He gasped. "That's not true! I loved her."

"Get out! Get out of my house and never come back!" she screamed.

"Claire, please."

She raced to the kitchen, opened a tablet, and scribbled something. She tore off the paper and ran back to him with it in her hand. "You said if you ever got another farewell letter, that would be the end of us." She read it to him. *"It's over between us, Jake Holland. Get out and never speak to me again."* She shoved the letter at him, tore his ring off her finger, and threw it at him. It clanged when it hit the wood floor. "You robbed me of precious days with her. I could've told her how much I loved her. I could've taken her somewhere, anywhere, to get the surgery she needed. Her death is on your hands because of your selfishness."

Her accusation dumbfounded him. "Claire, I—"

"Get out of my house and never come back! If you do, I'll call the police. You're as despicable as all the other men in my life!" She pushed him out the door with all the force she could muster. "I never want to see or hear from you again!" She slammed the door in his face.

He stood there for several moments, wondering what to do, her words ringing in his ears. *"Great, Maddy, she put your death on me,"* he muttered in shock.

He rang the doorbell. She didn't answer. He rang it several times. *"Claire, open the door!"*

He went to his car, sat in it, and debated what to do. Suddenly, a sheriff's patrol car pulled into the driveway with its red and blue lights flashing. "Oh, God, she didn't." His misery just escalated.

The officer motioned for him to get out of the car. Jake complied and explained what had happened. The deputy was polite and sympathetic but said Claire was within her rights to ask him to leave, and if he didn't or returned later, he'd be arrested.

In a convenience store parking lot, Jake sat, thinking. He was out of options. In frustration, he slammed his hands on the steering wheel. *"Think, Jake!"* he yelled. A moment later, he grabbed his iPhone, brought up Google Maps, and got directions to Spokane. Four hours later, at two in the morning, he knocked on his parents' door ...

After telling his parents what happened, Nancy made a decision. "I'm going to my room to pack. Claire needs me to be with her."

"Mom, she won't see you. She called the cops on me, for God's sake."

"I'm going, and that's the end of it. Ethan, you stay here with Jake." She stood and left.

Jake looked at his father. "Dad, go tell her it's a bad idea."

Ethan shook his head. "I will not. Claire needs a woman's love. Write down her home address so I can enter it in our car's navigation system." With a tight jaw, Jake wrote it down and gave it to him. Ethan stood. "Get some sleep. You know where the guest room is, so make yourself at home." His eyes bore into Jake. "If you try to give your mother a hard time about going, you'll be dealing with me." He said it in his father's voice. Even as an adult, that voice could still penetrate Jake's psyche. With a sigh, Jake nodded.

Nancy arrived at Claire's home a little after eight in the morning. She knocked several times, but no one answered. A dog barked inside.

She walked to the back of the house and looked around. There was a doggie door cut in the back door, allowing access to a chain-link fenced area. Suddenly, a big dog dashed out, barking excitedly. Nancy laughed at how ridiculous it looked and reached over the fence to pet the happy animal. "You must be Bluebell. You're not much of a guard dog, but you sure are friendly." She looked at the doggie door again. "You know, Bluebell, I do believe I can fit through your door." She climbed over the fence, which delighted the dog.

"C'mon, girl, let's go inside." With a little effort, she managed to wiggle through the dog door. Inside, she scanned the kitchen and living room, and when she didn't see Claire, opted to go upstairs. Bluebell ran past her and into a bedroom. She followed her. Claire was in bed, on her side, in a fetal position. She was awake, her eyes puffy, looking beyond sad. Stunned to see Nancy, she asked, "How did you get in?"

"I used Bluebell's door."

"Please leave, Nancy. It's over between Jake and me, and there's nothing you can say to change my mind." Not calling her 'Mom' emphasized the point.

Nancy kicked off her shoes. "I'm not here for my son; I'm here for you, sweet girl." She lifted the covers, got in, and hugged Claire. "I'm so sorry."

Claire put her hand on Nancy's and didn't say a word. They spent the rest of the morning cuddled together. Nancy's love was desperately needed.

At noon, Nancy kissed Claire's cheek. "I'm going to make you something to eat. I'll be back soon."

"I don't feel like eating."

"I know. But you need to."

"I'm no one's little girl anymore."

"Claire, I felt the same way when I lost my mom, but somehow life goes on." She hugged her. "You're not alone. You have me. We need to make funeral arrangements for Maddy."

"Maddy wanted her ashes scattered with Grandpa's at Claire Hill."

"They'll soon be together again."

"They want me to pick up her urn today."

"Do you want me to go with you?"

"Yes." Claire squeezed her hand. "Thank you for coming to be with me."

"I love you, Claire. No matter what happens, that will never change."

"I love you, too."

"Get dressed. We'll have lunch and then go to the funeral home."

Nancy stayed with Claire—loving her, comforting her, and listening to her reminisce about her grandmother. They never once mentioned Jake. In the early morning on her third day there, they walked to Claire Hill, and under a brilliantly blue sky, scattered Maddy's ashes. She was with her beloved husband once more.

A week after Nancy left, Claire made an appointment with Maddy's doctor. She needed to know what had transpired regarding her grandmother's health. In the doctor's office, she impatiently waited in one of the exam rooms for the doctor to come in. Her anger at the doctor for not telling her about Maddy's condition rose with each passing minute.

When the door opened, Claire stood. The doctor walked in and shook her hand.

"Miss Lofton, I'm so sorry for your loss."

Claire didn't waste time with pleasantries. "Why didn't you tell me about how ill she was?"

"I legally couldn't because Mrs. Roediger insisted I not inform you about her condition."

"I could've done more for her if only you had told me. I could've taken her to specialists. I could've—"

"Miss Lofton," the doctor interrupted, "Maddy had an excellent health care advocate. He left no stone unturned. He insisted that I send her records to specialists in Seattle and Portland, and they all concurred with a conservative management approach because her aneurysm was in a difficult location, making surgery a high-risk endeavor. I could set my watch by his predictable call to me every Friday at noon."

"Maddy didn't have a health advocate," Claire said, looking baffled.

"Yes, she did, and he was adamant that Maddy get the best of care. He scoured the internet, sending countless articles to me for my consideration. Plus, Mrs. Roediger said he called her every day, insisting she take her blood pressure while they talked. He had a list of her prescriptions and made sure she took them during his calls so she wouldn't forget. Quite frankly, it's rare for me to see this level of care and concern by a non-family member."

This news stunned Claire. "Was his name Jake Holland?"

The doctor nodded. "Miss Lofton, he pleaded with me to help convince Maddy to tell you, but she stubbornly refused." She touched Claire's hand. "Mr. Holland was in an untenable position. He desperately wanted to tell you, but he gave his word to honor Maddy's wishes, and she was steadfast in her determination that you not know. Please know this: there was no doubt in my mind that Jake loved her, and Miss Lofton, Maddy loved him, too. She was so happy when she told me of your engagement to him."

"We're not engaged anymore. I ended it when Jake told me about keeping Maddy's condition a secret."

The doctor sighed. "I hope you'll reconsider. Jake's a good man. Maddy's wishes bound us both. She was determined to keep you from sliding into a depression. I hope you're taking active measures to prevent it, especially now."

Claire ignored her concern. "In retrospect, did Maddy get the best possible medical treatment for her condition?"

"She did. I can give you copies of her records, and you'll see how the specialists agreed with the course of action we took. Miss Lofton, Maddy's aneurysm developed slowly over the years, and it was amazing that she survived for so long. She died trying to protect you."

"If I knew, I could've told her how much I loved her."

"She knew. Maddy often spoke of the love between you."

"I just wasn't ready to say goodbye to her."

"Maddy was a special lady. Again, I'm sorry for your loss."

Claire shook her hand. "Thank you for your time." She walked out and sat in her car, numb.

In tears, she drove home and told Bluebell what had happened.

The next day in class, Claire couldn't keep a coherent thought. She had the kids take turns reading, and they read three books that day.

When Nancy called, as she did every day since returning to Spokane, Claire told her about visiting Maddy's doctor and what Jake had done. "Claire, I haven't said anything to you about Jake, but I'm going to now. From when he was a little boy, we taught him that his word means everything. Maddy made him swear not to tell you about her condition, and he kept his word to her. You fell in love with him because of his honor and integrity—yet now you're faulting him for those very things. You can't have it both ways. How you treated him was unfair, but I know your emotions drove it. Jake loved her and did everything he could for her."

"I know."

"You've got some soul-searching to do."

"I know."

"Claire, there was so much love between you and Jake. Maddy saw it, and she loved him for it. She knew he was the one for her precious girl. She wanted you two to be together. It was her last wish. How do you think she'd feel knowing she drove you two apart?"

"It would break her heart."

"I agree. Claire, be honest. Do you love Jake?"

There was silence …

"Yes. I love him more than anything."

"I know, sweet girl."

"Do … do you think he would accept my apology?"

Nancy sighed. "I don't know. Keenan took the news of your breakup really hard. He's very angry with his father, and it's hurt their relationship. Jake's sadness has transformed into anger toward you. He's very bitter, and he said he's done with you."

"I see. I don't blame him. I'm so sorry for hurting Keenan. I love him so much. Nancy, you know your son. Tell me what I should do."

She sighed again. "I wouldn't call him because he'd probably respond unkindly without weighing his words. I suppose I'd write or email him. Even then, I don't know. He said he told you if there were one more farewell letter, it would be over, and his pride may win out over love. Stubbornness is one of the one-percenter traits, as I recall."

"It is. I hope we can find a way to reconcile."

"Claire, he'll protect Keenan at all costs. If he thinks for a second you'll continue to do this to him, he'll drop you in a heartbeat and never look back."

"I wouldn't blame him. I'd do the same thing. Nancy, when I threw Jake out of my house, it was the first time in my life that I screamed at someone." Since then, it's been hard for me to think that I'm a good person."

"Your grandmother died, and you were devastated. I understand why you acted the way you did."

"I wanted you to be my mom more than you could ever imagine."

"Don't give up yet. Try to work it out. Claire, I still have hopes of being your mother."

After saying goodbye, Claire sat at the dining table and turned on her iPad. The house seemed so quiet without Maddy. Mrs. Kerfuffle jumped on her lap, and Claire stroked her fur. "I really blew it, Mrs. Kerfuffle. God, did I blow it."

She began typing an email to Jake.

Dear Jake,

I spoke to Maddy's doctor today and learned about how involved you were with her care. She said she'd never seen a more devoted health advocate than you. Jake, I'm deeply sorry for all those hurtful things I said to you. I would've given anything to have had just a little more time with Maddy, and I mistakenly thought you robbed me of that. I know now there was nothing else that could've been done to prolong her life. I also know how it tore you up inside to keep her secret from me, and I can only imagine how dreadful it was for you to be in such a no-win situation. Thank you for loving Maddy so much. I will be forever grateful to you for your kindness to her.

Jake, I stand before you humbled, looking into your eyes, saying I love you, asking you for your forgiveness. I pray you'll find it in your heart to love me again. From the deepest recesses of my being, I apologize and hope we can find our way back to love.

"Forgiveness is the final form of love," wrote Reinhold Niebuhr. He was right. Please don't give up on me. More than ever, I believe my life is with you and Keenan.

I love you. Claire

She read what she wrote and hit the send button. Bluebell walked up to her, looking sad. Claire hugged her. "Hey, girl, I'm sad, too. I'm going to take a bath." She looked at her feline. "Mrs. Kerfuffle, please try to be kind to Bluebell while I'm in the bathroom."

After bathing, she went downstairs and made a tuna salad for dinner. A bit later, she checked her email and found a new message. It was from Jake. Her heart tightened in her chest. She opened it. No salutation meant his message wouldn't be good.

After I told Keenan I no longer was in a relationship with you, my sweet, innocent boy looked me in the eye and said he hated me. You're just as bad as the guy who dumped you in college. In fact, you're even worse. You did the same thing to my son, shattering his heart with your broken promises. He's in therapy now, a sad little boy who lost a second mother. For what you've done, I despise you.

Throughout my relationship with you, I have always acted with integrity, yet you eviscerated me whenever your emotions ran astray. Judge, jury, and executioner—that was you. I'm so done with your kangaroo court. What a fool I was to think you were kindhearted.

You've been blocked from sending further emails to me and from calling my home and cell phone numbers. Should you call me at school or send an email to me there, I, too, will call the police and claim harassment, just as you did to me.

Forgive you? Love you? Yeah, right, I say with dripping sarcasm.

Goodbye forever, Miss Lofton, and good riddance.

For the rest of the evening, Claire sat at the kitchen table, in tears. She deserved everything Jake had said, she thought. Their relationship was over. That she hurt him was bad; that she hurt Keenan was unforgivable.

35

IN THE DAYS following Jake's email, Claire walked around in a daze. Bluebell and Mrs. Kerfuffle did their best to comfort her, but her life would never be the same. She suffered three losses: Maddy, Jake, and Keenan. They would forever be out of her life. She also ended her relationship with Nancy because not doing so would be unfair to Jake. A month ago, her life was full of hope and joy; now, it was all gone. She made an appointment to see her therapist. Getting over this hurdle in her life would be monumental. She was thankful this was the start of Spring Break; if ever she could use a week off, this was it.

She skipped dinner again and went straight to bed. Since Maddy passed, Claire had lost five pounds, and with her already thin frame, was beginning to look gaunt.

Sleep came only after much tossing and turning. She began dreaming. Jake was holding her hand in the delivery room, encouraging her to push. She bore down, and the baby's head crowned, and soon, it entered the world. "It's a girl!" the doctor proclaimed and let Jake cut the cord. Her husband beamed with pride. A nurse brought the little girl to her chest, a perfect, beautiful baby. Claire marveled at her tiny fingers, which grasped her finger when she touched them. Keenan came in, delighted to see his baby sister. They all were so happy. Then they all disappeared. She screamed for them to come back to her ...

Claire woke up panting, her sheets soaking wet. Bluebell licked her face, trying to comfort her. It took a second for reality to set in. She hugged her dog. "Bluebell, I had a baby girl. She was so beautiful." Suddenly, she knew what she had to do—*fly to Anchorage.* Her baby girl's life depended on it.

She got up and splashed water on her face in the bathroom sink. In the dim glow of the nightlight, she dabbed her face dry with a towel and looked in the mirror. "I am a good person, Jake Holland," she whispered. "I will look into your eyes and tell you so. When you see my heart, you will know." She went to her computer and booked a flight out at noon.

In the morning, she called Helen, who said she'd look after Bluebell and Mrs. Kerfuffle for her.

Following a two-hour layover in Seattle, Claire boarded a plane to Anchorage. On the way, she tried to sleep, but the jumble of thoughts racing through her mind made the effort futile. She decided to pray.

After landing in Anchorage, Claire walked out of the terminal and waved for a taxi. As they pulled into Jake's driveway a short while later, Claire's heart pounded. She thanked the driver in a small, frightened voice and paid him. As she stood in the driveway, all alone, clutching her carry-on pack, an icy fear clutched her heart. She looked upward. "Please, God, let Jake see me again."

At the front door, she took a deep breath and rang the doorbell, knowing the course of her life was about to be determined.

Inside, Jake was cleaning up after lunch and hurried to answer the door. The initial shock of seeing her flashed quickly to anger.

"You're not welcome here, Miss Lofton," he said in a voice as cold as arctic ice. "Please leave."

She mustered a feeble smile. "I flew here to see you in person. I have many things to say to you."

"There's nothing to say. We concluded our relationship back in Washington, as was your demand."

"What I said back then was my grief talking. Jake, I meant none of it. It was the first time in my life I ever screamed at someone, and that I did it to you makes me so very sad."

"You know, Miss Lofton, if I were fool enough to say, 'Sure, come back into my life,' I wonder how long it would be until your next meltdown. Maybe if I didn't take out the trash, or if Keenan made a mess, you'd dump us again. You should change your name to YoYo Lofton so the next guy who fancies you will know what he's getting himself into."

She winced at his coldness. "Jake, the only woman who loved me died. Can you even begin to imagine that? I came here so you could look into my eyes and see me again. Please put your anger aside and talk to me."

"I'm truly sorry for your loss of Maddy, but I was clear when I told you if I got one more farewell letter from you, it would be over. You won't hurt Keenan or me ever again. We're finished."

Keenan yelled from the family room. "Wer ist an der Tür, Papa?" [Who is at the door?]

Jake stared into Claire's eyes as he answered Keenan in English. "No one important is here. You and Tommy can keep on playing."

"Okay!"

A tear rolled down her cheek. "I'm a good person, Jake Holland. You know that. Let your heart speak to you. When we made love the last night I was here, our hearts spoke to each other. You can't deny our love."

He hesitated for a moment and then looked coldly at her. "In one of your letters, you promised your love would always outshine your anger. You lied. The last time you saw Keenan, you promised you'd never forget him. Another lie. Promises don't mean much to you. You hurt my son, and I won't forgive or forget it."

"I never forgot him, and you know my love for him is genuine. I'm truly sorry for the hurt I've caused. I'm here to say I want to spend the rest of my life loving you two."

He shook his head. "No. I can't trust you. It's ... it's over between us."

"Jake, think of all the emotional and spiritual capital you've expended to help me mend my heart. It worked. I'm a whole person again. You're acting like you've run a marathon and stopped a few feet short of the finish line. You've won me, heart, body, and soul." She put her pack down and extended her hand to him. "Finish what you started; take my hand, and we'll have a lifetime of happiness together. Please don't throw it all away. Remember the quote you sent to me: 'Everything you want is on the other side of fear.' Marry me, Jake. I know you love me."

He rebuffed her handshake. "You need to go."

"I came here because I dreamed that we had a baby girl. She was so beautiful. As you have done with Keenan, I'm here now, trying to save our baby girl's life. Stay with me, Jake. Stay in this relationship. You once told me that, and now I'm saying it to you."

"We both know the folly of your dreams. Your next dream could well be of me cheating on you, and then I'd go through hell again for something I didn't do." He made no attempt to hide the contempt in his voice.

"Just *listen* to yourself. You're letting your emotions run wild, which is what you're mad at me for doing. Now I'm in *your* kangaroo court, and *you're* the judge, jury, and executioner. From this moment on, let's drop the kangaroo courts and accept that we're both good people. *Damn it, Jake, you love me! You're as stubborn as Maddy!*"

Her outburst startled him. He didn't say anything for a moment, but then he glared at her. "We have nothing more to say. Good day to you, Miss Holland, I mean, Miss Lofton." He cringed at the Freudian slip. It couldn't have come at a worse moment.

"That's your heart speaking, Jake. Your heart wants me to be a Holland."

Silence.

Absolute silence ...

She looked at him with empathy. "You know me. You *see* me. *'Between you and me, Spirit dances.'* You wrote that about God's delight in our being together, and it's true."

He stared at her with an intensity that seemed to bore straight into her soul ...

A tear rolled down his cheek. He nodded slowly in silent agreement.

She hugged him. "I love you so very much ..."

His half-hearted return of her hug troubled her. She touched his cheek. "I feel the conflict within you about whether you're doing the right thing. You are. Jake, you are. I'll earn your love every day. You'll never regret forgiving me." She held her gaze on him to emphasize her sincerity.

"I ... I just can't pretend it never happened. You hurt my son and me. I don't know if I can love you in a pure way again."

"I understand. When I threw my ring at you and ordered you to leave, at that moment, I thought I hated you. But after the doctor told me of your love for Maddy and how you cared and advocated for her, my love for you returned, and it's more powerful now than it's ever been. When you again see my love for you and Keenan, it'll be the same for you. Please give me the chance."

He sighed, unsure of what to say.

"Jake, there are no words to describe the pain I've felt since being apart from you. You feel the same pain. I *see* you."

His lips quivered as he nodded. "I've missed you," he blurted.

"Me, too. There's a beautiful life with me waiting on the other side of your fear. Have faith in me, Jake. Have faith in us."

He smiled meekly and hugged her. His tight embrace let her know her words had resonated in him.

They held each other for several moments, neither of them speaking.

"I'm not sure about what to say to Keenan," he whispered. "There's so much anger in him. I'm not sure he wants you back in our lives."

"Please let me talk to him. I need to ask Keenan for his forgiveness."

"I don't know if I want you near him for a while. Maybe he should continue meeting with his counselor before seeing you. If he no longer wants to accept you, I just don't see how things could work between us."

"Jake, you know what's best, but I believe if I can tell him what happened, he'll understand and forgive me. As we both know, he's an extraordinary boy."

He frowned. "Keenan's changed since you left us. You stripped away his innocence. The sweet boy he once was is gone."

"It's not gone. He's grieving, and anger is his way of showing it. Jake, please let me see him so I can look into his eyes and tell him I love him. He needs my love right now."

Jake hesitated, weighing her words ...

"Okay. If you wait behind the house, we'll take Tommy home, and then I'll come for you."

She nodded. "Jake, you're doing the right thing. I'll love you both more than anything."

"I hope so. I'll come for you in a few minutes."

Keenan and Tommy were surprised when Jake came into the family room and said Tommy had to leave. He was supposed to spend the night. They walked Tommy home, and Jake told his parents an unexpected matter had come up.

Back at their house, he gestured for Keenan to sit on the living room couch. "Son, someone has come to see us."

"Who, Papa?"

"Wait here. I'll be right back."

When Jake returned with Claire, Keenan's eyes went wide. He didn't get up and go to her.

"Hello, Keenan. I came here to apologize to you and your dad."

He looked at her in stone-cold silence, and then his anger flared. "You lied to me! You said you loved me and wouldn't forget me."

"Oh, sweetie, I didn't lie. I do love you, and I think about you all the time."

"That's not true!" He pointed to her right hand. "See, you aren't even wearing my ring—or Papa's ring, either."

"Will you let me tell you what happened? Then you can decide if you want me to leave or stay. Okay?"

Unsure of what to do, he looked at Jake, who nodded to let her speak.

He offered a defiant nod for her to continue.

She sat next to him.

"Keenan, I loved Maddy with all my heart, and when she suddenly died, I was so sad. Imagine how sad you would be if you lost your papa. That's how sad I was to lose Maddy. When you're sad or angry, you can say things you don't mean, like when you said you hated your papa."

His lip quivered. "I don't hate you, Papa."

"I know. And Claire didn't mean it when she said she didn't want to be with us."

"Keenan, your dad knew Maddy was ill, but he didn't tell me. I thought he kept quiet about it because he was selfish and didn't want Maddy to be in our lives after we got married. Imagine how it would be if I wanted to marry your dad, but I didn't want you. Your dad would've ended our relationship if that had happened—and that's why I ended my relationship with him. Can you understand my actions now?"

"Yes. I wouldn't want to be with someone who didn't love the same people I loved."

"I was wrong about your dad. I discovered that Maddy didn't want me to worry about her, so she made your dad and her doctor promise not to tell me about her being ill. After Maddy died, her doctor told me what had happened and everything your dad had done to help her stay well. When I learned how much he loved and cared about her, I knew I had made a terrible mistake. I came here to apologize to your father and ask for his forgiveness. I also came to say I'm sorry I hurt you and to ask for your forgiveness."

His eyes welled with tears.

"Keenan, I want so badly to marry your papa and to be your mom. I love you both more than anything. The rings are in my pack, and I'd like for you both to put them back on my fingers to symbolize your love and forgiveness." She touched his cheek. "I love you. Will you please forgive me?"

He looked at his dad, not knowing what to do.

"Son, we still love her, and she still loves us. If we stay angry, we'll lose Claire because our anger will ruin that love. Do you want to lose her?"

Keenan shook his head. "I don't want to be angry anymore, Papa."

"I don't either. So what are we going to do?"

Keenan looked at her. "Will you give me the rings, Mom?"

She reached into her pack and handed them to him.

"Papa, here's your ring. Are you going to put it on her finger again?"

"I will if you will."

"Okay. Mom, hold up your hand, please." He put his ring on her finger. "I still want to marry you and have you as my mother because I love you." He looked at Jake. "Your turn, Papa."

Jake got on a knee. "When I first proposed, my broken ribs didn't allow me to get down on a knee, but now I can. Claire Lofton, will you marry me?"

"Yes! I'd be honored to marry both of you. I can't wait for us to become a family."

36

One year later ...

CLAIRE BEAMED AS she set the serving tray loaded with prime rib on the dining room table. "Well, this is the maiden voyage of our new oven. I hope it turned out okay." She kissed her father-in-law's cheek. "Dad, this was my grandpa's favorite meal, and Jake said you love it as well, so it's our way of thanking you for all your help to remodel this old house."

"It was my pleasure. I can't believe my son is now an apple rancher."

Jake looked at Claire, and they both smiled. "Uh, Dad, it's apple *farmer.* As Claire told me, a rancher raises animals. We're still subleasing most of our acreage because I've been so busy with my art business."

Ethan nodded as he placed a generous slice of meat on his plate, already loaded with potato salad and two ears of corn. "So your paintings are selling well?"

"They paid for our house remodel," said Claire with pride. "Let's say grace. My handsome son taught me how to say our dinner prayer in German, so if you indulge me, I'll give it a go." They joined hands, and she began. "Lieber Gott, wir danken Ihnen für dieses Essen und wir danken Ihnen für einander. Amen."

Ethan looked at Keenan. "What did she say?"

He smiled at his mom approvingly. "Mom said, *Dear God, we thank you for this food, and we thank you for each other.'* She's learned a lot of German since we moved here."

Claire touched his hand. "Keenan's doing an excellent job teaching me. I'm also working at it on the computer during my lunch breaks at school." She touched her baby bump. "When our little girl arrives in October, I want to be fluent in German."

Ethan put a big dollop of horseradish on a piece of his meat and took a bite. A second later, he gasped. "Oh my God, this is the most potent horseradish I've ever had." He pinched his nostrils, trying to subdue the volatile vapors. "I think … my sinuses are about … to explode …"

"Sorry, Dad. I forgot to warn you. Claire makes it from scratch in what could only be described as nuclear strength."

He downed some water and took a deep breath. "It's … deadly." He coughed, still in distress. "Wow …"

After regaining his composure, he took another bite, this time with a smaller portion of the condiment. "Most store-bought horseradish has no kick. I love this."

Claire looked relieved that he was okay. "My grandpa firmly believed in the medicinal properties of horseradish, and the stronger, the better. So we all got used to having it curl our toes." She dipped a piece of meat in the sauce and tried it. "He'd be pleased with this batch."

Nancy tried the potato salad. "Mmm, this is good. Am I tasting rosemary?"

"You are, plus the mayonnaise-based dressing has Dijon mustard and Worcestershire sauce. Of course, bacon makes everything taste better."

"It does. So, is your morning sickness better?"

"Yes, thank God. I feel great, and I'm thrilled we got the remodel done before she arrives. We'll need the room."

"Let's see; you got the new addition, a new kitchen, bathroom redos, a gorgeous green-metal roof, and an artist's studio. Did I forget anything?"

"You forgot the man-cave for Papa and me, Grandma," said Keenan. "Even though it's for men, we'll allow Mom to come in."

"The house looks brand new. I'm envious."

Ethan took another bite of meat. "Claire, you're a wonderful cook. This meal surpasses any restaurant offering."

"Thanks, Dad."

He turned his attention to his son. "It's hard to believe you've already paid for this remodel by selling your artwork. I'll bet it was a surprise, you know, being able to sell your paintings so readily."

Jake swallowed and nodded. "I know. Can you believe it? I've sold everything, and they're clamoring for more at the gallery. When Claire said to try selling them for $3K apiece, I thought all common sense had left her, but I'm selling them as fast as I can paint them."

"It turns out Leavenworth is perfect for Jake's new career," said Claire. "As a tourist-oriented town, we draw many people from the big cities, and many of them are quite wealthy. Plus, several tech companies in the Seattle area have commissioned Jake for abstract paintings. He has enough work to last a year."

"Do you like your new career, Jake?"

"I do, Mom. It's hard to believe I'm getting paid for what I love doing." He leaned over and kissed his wife. "This year has brought many blessings."

"Have you come up with a name for the baby?" she asked.

Claire nodded. "We have, thanks to Keenan. Tell your grandma and grandpa what you suggested, sweetie."

"I like the name Rigby. She was in my class in Anchorage. Mom and Dad chose her middle name, though."

"Jake proposed Maddax after Maddy and my grandpa Max."

"It's a great way to honor them. I like Rigby," said Nancy. "It's unusual, but not too 'out there.' Keenan, what do you think about having a baby sister?"

"It'll be cool. I'll teach her German. Bluebell will love her, but I'm not so sure about Mrs. Kerfuffle."

"Claire, how's keeping your cat working out?"

"Curiously, Mom, she adores Keenan. I think she views him as her own little kitten. She's very gentle with him, and they sleep together." She glanced at Jake. "As for my hubby, well, Mrs. Kerfuffle tolerates him, at best."

Jake shook his head and looked pained. "I think she's trying to eat me one chunk at a time."

"Mom says I can have my own Labradoodle," said Keenan. "I want a boy dog."

"The breeder where Claire bought Bluebell has a six-month-old male pup they say is good-natured and available," said Jake. "As odd as these dogs look, they make excellent family pets. Plus, they don't shed. We're going to see if he'll be a good fit with us."

"Have you got a name picked out if you decide to keep him?"

"They already named him, Grandpa. His name is Bozley. I like it."

"That's a good name for a dog."

Jake took another bite of potato salad. "Mom and Dad, you're in for a treat. Claire made an apple pie for dessert, and we're going to make real ice cream."

"The ice cream maker has been in my family since before I was born," said Claire. "Keenan and Jake take turns on the crank, and it takes about thirty minutes to make a batch. We'll make vanilla, which goes perfectly with apple pie."

"I'll save some room for it," said Ethan. "In all my years, I've never had homemade ice cream. I'll take a few turns on the crank just to say I did it."

"It's wonderful here, Claire. I envy you and Jake," said Nancy.

Claire smiled. "Maybe now is a good time to bring this up. We know you're considering retirement options, so we'll add one to the mix. If we give you an acre, would you consider retiring here and building a home next to us? We'd love you both to play an active role in our children's lives."

"That's an enticing offer." Nancy looked at her husband. "Ethan, you, Keenan, and Jake could become apple farmers. It would give you something to do instead of moping around the house being bored."

Ethan looked at Claire and then back to his wife. "I think our kids are just being nice. I mean, who would want their parents so close?"

Claire smiled. "I love you and Mom. Having you near would be wonderful. I was the one who suggested it to Jake."

"Dad, our offer is genuine. I love living here, and I know you and Mom would too. To sweeten the offer, you can eat as many apples as you want. Claire made that offer to Keenan and me, and it sealed the deal for us to move here."

Ethan smiled and then turned serious. "This area is beautiful. We could build a nice house with the equity from our home."

"You could use our remodeling contractor. He has built many homes in the area and said you two are welcome to discuss ideas with him. He's great to work with, plus we could do all the electrical."

Ethan looked at Nancy and raised an eyebrow. "What do you think?"

"I'd like nothing more than being near our grandchildren and our lovely daughter."

"Hey, what about me?" said Jake, feigning hurt feelings.

"Oh, you too, my dear boy," she said with a laugh. "It goes without saying."

Ethan looked intrigued. "We'll give it serious consideration when we get back to Spokane."

The rest of the day passed agreeably. In the evening, Jake played his guitar, and Keenan entertained them with jokes. Claire noticed how easily they all interacted. She loved having her new family in her grandparents' home. She could feel their spirits in the room.

Three days after Nancy and Ethan left for Spokane, there was a knock on the door, sending Bluebell into a frenzy. Someone had come to play with her. Bozley, their gangly new puppy, took the older dog's cue and went nuts as well. Jake opened the door. It was a postman. "Hello, sir. I have a certified letter for Claire Lofton."

Claire heard him and walked to the door. "I'm Claire Lofton, but my last name is Holland now."

"Congratulations. I noticed you changed your sign to Holland & Roediger Orchard. You need to sign here, ma'am."

She signed where he asked and thanked him. She closed the door, looked at the return address, and frowned. "Jake, it says The Law Office of Kidd, Cook & Peterson, LLC, Newport, Rhode Island. What's an LLC?"

"It stands for Limited Liability Company."

"I never like hearing from attorneys. I wonder what this is about."

He put his arm around her. "It must have something to do with one of your parents."

She frowned as she opened the envelope and read the letter aloud.

Dear Ms. Lofton:

Please be advised this office represents the estate of your father, the late Preston Lee Lofton. As executor, it is incumbent on me to settle the decedent's estate in a timely and efficient manner in accordance with his wishes. As an heir, you have been listed as a beneficiary in his Last Will and Testament. We request your presence at our office on August 20th at 2:00 PM, where we will discharge the distribution of assets. To cover travel expenses, enclosed is an advance distribution check for $10,000.

Very truly yours,

Emory W. Kidd Jr., Esq.

She put the letter back in the envelope. "I'm surprised he even remembered me."

Jake looked at her, baffled. "You appear to have missed the part about him being deceased. Doesn't that mean anything to you?"

"No. He meant nothing to me, and neither does my mother."

Jake sighed. "He still was your father. Aren't you even curious about the cause of his death?"

"No. And I don't want anything from him."

"I thought you said he was wealthy."

"He is—or was. Jake, I haven't seen or heard from either of my parents since I was six years old."

She tossed the letter on the credenza with a grimace. "I don't want to talk about this anymore, if you don't mind. Can we walk to Claire Hill and have a picnic dinner there? Something simple, like chicken-salad sandwiches, would be nice."

"Yeah, sure. Are you okay?"

"They made their choice regarding me a long time ago, and I'm finally at peace with what they did." She kissed him. "I'm part of the Holland clan now, and that suits me just fine."

At Claire Hill, while Keenan tossed a ball for Bluebell and Bozley to fetch, Jake and Claire lay together on a blanket. She fixated on a puffy white cloud passing overhead. He touched her cheek. "You seem a million miles away. Do you want to talk about it?"

She sighed. "He never loved me. I can't remember him ever hugging me."

"That must've been hard for you as a child."

"I never knew what a hug was until I came here. The first time Grandpa hugged me, I freaked out, thinking he was attacking me. He and Maddy were patient, and I soon learned how wonderful it felt to be in their arms. I loved them so much." She wiped a tear from her eye. "I have everything I want right here, Jake. I have you, Keenan, and soon, our baby girl. His money could change our whole dynamic, and for that reason alone, I consider it toxic."

"He might not be worth as much as you think. You said he was a coal magnate, and let me tell you, the coal industry has fallen on hard times due to coal-burning power plants being major sources of air pollution and greenhouse gas emissions. With stringent new EPA air emission limits, utility companies are abandoning coal in favor of natural gas and renewable energy such as wind-generated power, solar-generated electricity, and hydropower.

"Because of this, coal producers are going bankrupt in droves. So he very well could have little left. As for me, I'd be thrilled if there might be enough to put our children through college. That would lift an enormous financial burden from our shoulders. You accepted his money to pay for your college, so why wouldn't you do the same for our children? Let this be his legacy to our family."

"I suppose."

"Hey, with the ten grand, we could have a fabulous time back on the east coast. I'd love to see that part of the world. We could rent a sailboat again, and I could mate with you, Captain," he said with a wink.

She laughed. "It sounds like fun. After Rigby comes, we won't be able to vacation for a while." She continued to study the clouds, and then she looked at him. "I love what we have and don't want anything to ruin it."

"I know what you mean. But a few bucks going into our coffers for our children's education is hardly something to worry about."

She sighed and nodded. "I suppose so. Jake, have I told you lately how happy I am being your wife?"

He kissed her. "Once or twice, I think."

Keenan ran up with Bluebell and Bozley. "Hey, Mom, the doggies want you guys to play with us."

"Okay, but sit down for a second. We have something to share with you."

Keenan sat between them, looking happy. Bozley jumped on his lap and licked his cheek.

"Son, your mom and I have decided we'll all go on a vacation this August to a place called Newport, Rhode Island. It's on the East Coast. We can rent a sailboat there, just like your mom and I did on our honeymoon."

His eyes lit up. "Can we take the dogs and Mrs. Kerfuffle?"

"No, sweetie," said Claire. "It's too far for them to go. I'll ask Helen to watch them. They'll have a vacation too, staying with her."

"Oh."

"It'll be a fun trip for us." She patted her belly. "When Rigby arrives, we'll all be busy with her, so this will be the last vacation for the three of us."

That night in bed, Jake kissed his lady. "I want to say something, and I don't want you to reject what I'm going to propose categorically. I ask that you think about it for a while before giving me an answer."

"I know you … you're about to say something ominous."

He sighed. "I suppose …"

"Okay, what is it?"

"I'd like for us to meet your mother. I think it's important for you to see her and introduce her to your family."

Claire turned ashen, and her stomach revolted at the thought. "You've got to be kidding. Not in a million year—"

He gently put a hand on her mouth. "I said not to reject my proposal outright."

"Jake, you're asking the impossible of me. I despise her."

"People change, and I'd like to meet the mother of the woman I love."

"You already met my mother. Her name was Maddy. If you want to meet the lady who birthed me, then meet her on your own. Leave me out of it."

"Claire, for all you know, your mother may have been living with years of regret, hoping you'd reach out to her."

"Jake, sometimes your idealism gets the best of you. She has never cared about anyone but herself."

He sighed. "Maybe so. All I'm asking is for you to give it some consideration."

"You're asking too much of me."

"No, I'm not. I'll be there to support you. I think meeting her is vital for the full mending of your heart."

Claire shook her head.

"Just think about it, okay?"

She sighed and nodded. Sleep did not come easy for her that night.

37

THE PLANE TOUCHED down at the Theodore Francis Green Memorial State Airport in Providence, Rhode Island. It was a long flight from Seattle, and in her seventh month of pregnancy, Claire was exhausted. She looked at Jake and Keenan and wished she could share their enthusiasm. Being pregnant was not her only reason for being uncomfortable. In two days, they'd be meeting with her late father's attorney. She wanted nothing to do with the inheritance. Jake saw her melancholy and took her hand. "It'll all be fine. It's a thirty-mile drive to Newport, so we'll be at our hotel within an hour. You can rest there." He kissed her. "I love you." She nodded and offered a feeble smile.

After renting a car, Jake got on the RI-4 highway and headed south. Forty minutes later, they checked in at the Hyatt Regency Newport on Goat Island. In their room, Jake and Keenan looked out the window and marveled at the superb views of the harbor. "Mom, come see all the sailboats!"

Claire walked over and looked. "It's nice." She yawned. "Sorry. I'm so tired."

"Keenan, let's find our swimsuits and go for a dip in the pool. Your mom needs to rest."

Two hours later, when they returned, Claire was sitting on a chair, looking refreshed. "I'm starved. Are you guys up for a seafood dinner? I found a place online called the Mooring Seafood Kitchen & Bar. It's not far from here."

"As long as we have extra money for expenses, why don't we all try lobster," said Jake.

Keenan looked skeptical. "Are you sure I'll like it, Papa?"

"Well, you like fish and chips, so you could order that and try some of my lobster."

"Okay."

They walked into the eatery and liked what they saw. Claire looked relieved. "I love the casual elegance of this place. Since it's nice out, let's ask to be seated on the deck so we can enjoy the harbor view."

Their server seated them at a table on an expansive mahogany deck that offered sweeping views of Narragansett Bay. "It's beautiful here," said Jake. He thanked the server after he gave them menus. "Well, let's see what they have."

Claire buried her face in the menu. "Look, Jake, here it is—Maine lobster, served with warm drawn butter and potatoes. I think I'll have that with a side of roasted asparagus."

He leaned over to see where she was pointing. "Excellent." He looked farther down the menu. "Keenan, they have fish and chips made with haddock. That should be good."

"Okay, Papa."

They placed their order and turned their attention to the harbor. "I love the smell of the air along the coast," said Jake. "Do you ever remember living here, Claire?"

She shook her head. "It was a long time ago."

"You lived here, Mom?"

"I did, but I left shortly after my sixth birthday."

"Do you remember where your house was?"

"No, but I do remember that it was so big that you could get lost inside."

"How could you get lost in your own house?"

"Some of the people here have mansions so enormous that ten of our houses could easily fit inside of them, even with our new addition."

"Wow, that's big."

"Tomorrow, we're going to try to meet my mother. She lives in one of those big houses, so you'll see how spacious they are."

"I didn't know you had a mom, Mom."

She looked at Jake, not knowing what to say.

"Keenan, remember how your first mother left us? Well, Claire's mom and dad thought it would be best for her to live with her grandparents in Leavenworth."

"I would never do that to my kid." There was bitterness in Keenan's voice, no doubt from thinking of his birth mother.

"I know, sweetie. I had a lot of anger toward her for leaving me, and I'm not looking forward to meeting her tomorrow."

"Then why are you, Mom?"

"Son, I suggested we meet her mother. Maybe she regrets how poorly she treated your mom, so we're giving her a chance to say she's sorry."

"Hey, everyone, please, let's talk about something else. Since I have to use the bathroom all the time, we can't rent a sailboat, but tomorrow after we get back from seeing my mother, you two can rent a jet ski. You'll have a blast cruising the harbor."

"I want to! Papa, can I try driving it?"

Jake laughed. "Sure. Claire, you don't mind?"

"Not at all. I'll probably take a nap." She patted her tummy. "Rigby and I will spend some time together."

Twenty minutes later, the server arrived with their meals. Jake dunked a piece of lobster in the warm butter. "Oh, God, I've just tasted heaven. Here, Keenan, try a piece."

He tentatively sampled it. "I like it, kinda, Papa, but I'm glad I got the fish and chips."

Claire took a bite of her lobster and then tried the roasted asparagus. "Mmm. I could eat this meal every day and never tire of it."

They spent the rest of the evening talking, enjoying the meal, and watching boats go by in the harbor.

That night, after Keenan fell asleep on the queen-sized bed next to theirs, Claire snuggled up to Jake. "I still have a lot of trepidation about meeting her. I don't even know what to call her. I'm certainly not going to call her 'Mother,' I can tell you that."

"I know how hard seeing her is for you. Regardless of how it turns out, you tried, and I'm proud of you for having the courage to do it. As to what to call her, you called your grandmother Maddy, so do the same with her and call her Elizabeth."

Claire nodded. "I can't imagine giving away our children. How she could do it astonishes me to this day."

"I know. Maybe tomorrow, she'll offer some insights on why she did what she did."

"I doubt it. As I said, it's always been about her. Maddy said she never had an ounce of compassion or empathy. She and Grandpa were deeply hurt by how she dropped them and never looked back. A part of me hopes she won't be home. Are you sure showing up unannounced is wise?"

"It'll be harder for her to turn you away if you're at her doorstep. All I want is for you two to see each other."

"Oh! Rigby just moved. Give me your hand." She placed his hand on her belly. A second later, he felt a thump.

"That must be so weird to have something inside you moving."

"I love it. This pregnancy has touched a deeply spiritual component within me. Jake, I've never been happier in my life. I'm so honored to have you as my husband and partner, and I know you'll be a wonderful father to her." She kissed him. "I hope with all my heart that our happiness won't be damaged by what happens here."

"It won't. Tomorrow, if it doesn't go well and you get rebuffed, focus on how much Keenan and I love you. Hold on to that."

"I will." She yawned. "We'd better get some sleep."

In the morning, they had room service deliver breakfast and then set out for her mother's home. Jake punched her Ocean Avenue address into the navigation system, and it took ten minutes to arrive at her front gate. He turned off the engine, and they all got out. "Dear God," he said, "look at this place."

"It looks like a castle," said Keenan. "Mom, is your mom a queen?"

"No, Keenan, she just thinks she is. Jake, are you sure we should do this?"

"We're here. Don't quit when you're a few feet from the finish line." He winked as he said it, reminding her of what she had said to him when she made her pitch for them to get back together after Maddy's passing.

Claire nodded. "Okay, here goes." She pushed the button at the gate.

In a speaker, an authoritative voice answered. "How may I help you?"

"Um, I'm here to see Elizabeth Winthrop."

"Who may I ask is calling?"

"I'm Claire, her daughter."

"One moment, please."

The "one moment" turned into ten minutes. By that time, Claire was ready to leave.

"Please proceed to the front entrance." The gate began to open.

They got in their car and drove down the long estate drive. The closer they got to the house, the more impressive it became. "Holy cow," said Jake, "I think we've gone through a time machine to pre-revolutionary France." The perfectly manicured grounds, expansive terraces, and walled gardens gave way to a stunning, crescent-shaped "house" constructed of polished gray stones with a dramatic slate roof. Jake parked in front of the mansion on a circular, cobblestone driveway. Their Chevy rental car looked pitifully plain; this was Bentley or Rolls country.

Keenan took Claire's hand as they walked to the door. "Mom, should I call your mom Grandma?"

"No. You can call her Mrs. Winthrop."

The door opened, and a butler looked at the casually dressed threesome with an air of annoyance. "Mrs. Winthrop will see you in the sitting room."

Jake nodded and smiled, but his friendly gesture wasn't returned. Inside, they stopped and took in the view. A grand, curved staircase with wrought-iron railings wound its way upward, leading his gaze to an exquisite ceiling mural. The marble-tiled floors and Louis XVI-inspired details broadcasted one word: opulence. The impatient butler coughed, indicating it was crass to stop and gawk. "This way, please." His tone conveyed displeasure at the lower class of people invading the manor.

As they walked past a formal dining room on par with the Château de Versailles, Jake leaned over and whispered to Claire. "You could feed half of our town at that table. I see what you mean about getting lost in one of these places."

She nodded. "All this pretentiousness is nauseating."

Upon entering an elegant sitting room, the butler gave the lady of the manor a nod and closed the double doors. "Hello, Claire. I didn't realize you brought guests."

"This is my family. My husband is Dr. Jacob Holland, and this is our son, Keenan."

That Claire introduced him as "Doctor" surprised Jake. She'd never done it before.

He extended his hand. "I'm pleased to meet you, ma'am. I see where Claire gets her beauty."

She gave a half-smile to his compliment and turned her attention to Keenan. "You look quite like your father, little boy, but you have the Lofton family nose." She looked at Claire. "I see you're in the family way again. You must like being a mother." She said it in a way that made it seem like an affliction.

Claire saw no need to correct her mother's observation of her stepson having Lofton traits and put her arm around Keenan. "I love being a mother. It's the great joy of my life."

Her mother rolled her eyes. "Please have a seat." She gestured to an immense floral-colored settee.

After they sat, the older woman looked at Jake. "Your unrefined clothing suggests you aren't a surgeon. My guess is you're a family practitioner. Had a tough time in med school, did you?"

Jake ignored her overt impertinence. "I'm not a medical doctor, ma'am. I have a doctoral degree in geology. I wanted to be a rocket scientist, but my university charged tuition by the number of letters in your major. I couldn't afford the last two letters in rocket, so I became a rock scientist."

Claire laughed. His attempt at humor didn't amuse her mother. "So you make a living playing with rocks?" Her voice was laced with disdain.

"No, ma'am. My degree turned out to be incidental. I make a living as an artist."

"Oh. Aren't most of your kind starving?"

Claire turned red. "Jake is a successful artist, Elizabeth."

The woman ignored her. "Are you related to the Newport Hollands?"

"No, ma'am. I'm from the more pedestrian Spokane clan."

"They're a ruthless bunch of grog-loving pirates, and I fit right in," said Claire, who appeared to relish saying it.

Jake touched her hand, silently saying, "Enough." Claire took his cue and changed the subject. "We live in Leavenworth at what we now call Holland & Roediger Orchard."

Her mother looked surprised. "I can't believe you stayed there."

"I'd be happy to spend the rest of my days in Leavenworth."

She winced at the notion. "Well, each to their own, I suppose. How's your grandmother?"

Claire sighed. "Maddy died unexpectedly last year from an aneurism."

The news didn't faze her mother in the slightest. "Oh, well. Those things happen."

Her casualness at the news brought instant ire to Claire. "*Oh well?* That's all you can say about your mother's passing?"

"My mother and I were never close. What am I supposed to do, put on a big show of faux tears for you?"

"No, Elizabeth. You acted just as I thought you would."

"So why did you come here? Do you need money?"

"I want nothing from you. After more than twenty years, I thought you might want to see me and meet my family, but clearly, I appear to be wasting your time."

"That's not the real reason you're here. This is a small community, and word gets around. I know you're here because of your father's will."

"We are."

"Well, don't expect much from his estate. His company went bankrupt a year ago. I laugh at the thought of that serial philanderer dying of metastatic testicular cancer. It was a fitting end for him."

"And what about you, Elizabeth? What would be a fitting end for a mother who abandoned her six-year-old child?"

She looked at her daughter coldly. "You were an awful, incorrigible child, and I tried my best with you. Mother said you wanted to stay with them, so I said fine. You and I never had anything in common, and it's obvious you fit in much better with the unwashed crowd in that dreadful town than you do with the elite society here. We both made the best of a bad situation."

"Yes, I suppose we did. My husband wanted me to see you because he thought you may have regretted how you treated me and might want to make amends."

"I have nothing to apologize for, and as for making amends, it's clear we don't like each other and never have. So, why pretend?" She looked at her watch. "I'm sorry, but I have a lunch engagement I can't miss. Had you scheduled a time to meet, as basic etiquette demands, I wouldn't be so hurried." She stood and gazed at them. "I'm guessing you got the orchard in my mother's will, so you won't be destitute, what with having an artist husband. Jennings!" The butler opened the door. "Please show our guests out."

Jake had enough of her pomposity. "Mrs. Winthrop, your daughter is a wonderful wife and mother. That you cannot see her tender heart and goodness baffles me. What a loathsome person you are. Good day to you." He grabbed Keenan's hand and stormed out of the room, brushing Jennings aside.

Claire glared at her mother. "I despise you for your treatment of me, but I want you to know I've forgiven you. Goodbye forever, Mrs. Winthrop." She didn't wait for a reply and hurried to catch up with her family.

In the car, she glanced back at Keenan. "I'm sorry you had to witness that. My mother isn't a nice person."

"It's okay, Mom. Papa and I love you even if she doesn't."

"I know, and I'm the luckiest person on the planet to have you two." She wiped a tear away. "Okay, we tried, and that is that. Let's have lunch somewhere, and then you two can go jet skiing. Oh, what the heck. I feel like jet skiing, too."

Keenan smiled. "You better not go too fast, or Rigby will get seasick."

She laughed. "Thanks for cheering me up. I'm so glad you're my son." She took one last look at the mansion. "We're the rich ones because we have an abundance of love. Can you imagine if we lived here, how long it would take us to clean it?"

"I like our house better."

"I know, sweetie. Me, too." She leaned over and kissed Jake's cheek. "Enough talk of her. Let's find a Chipotle. I'm craving a chicken burrito bowl with tomatillo red-chili salsa."

Jake chuckled. "Keenan, here's a valuable life lesson: When a pregnant woman says she has a craving, never deny her."

At the lawyer's office the next day, the stately looking attorney removed his reading glasses and peered at Jake and Claire, who were sitting on the other side of his mammoth teak desk. "Mr. and Mrs. Holland, Mr. Lofton has faced many daunting financial challenges in the last few years. He, uh, well, his marriages cost him dearly, and his company declared bankruptcy last year. As a consequence, his net worth reflects these adversities."

"It's okay," said Claire. "I never expected to inherit anything from him."

"Yes, well, I suppose we should get on with it." He put his glasses back on. "You are Mr. Lofton's sole beneficiary. We have successfully liquidated his assets, which I'll soon address. He first wanted me to read this letter that he wrote to you. May I?"

She hesitated before giving him a nod. He cleared his throat and began.

Dear Claire,

Earlier today, my radiologist advised me that it's time to put my affairs in order. The sadness in his eyes, I'm sure, comes from losing a patient with deep pockets. Now someone else will have to pay for his vacation getaway on Nantucket.

I'm at home now, drinking a $3600 bottle of Johnnie Walker, reflecting. Maybe it's Johnnie talking because I've always viewed reflection as an abysmal waste of time. When I'm gone, I'll miss my old friend Johnnie more than anything. Anyway, Johnnie says it's time to do the Lofton duty, so I won't refuse my good friend's dictate ...

As is the tradition with Lofton patriarchs, when we are about to croak, we write a letter to our heirs, uttering a bunch of insufferable words before bequeathing the fortune. It's my turn to be the windbag and bore you before the lawyer hands over the family treasures.

Fear not, for my letter will be brief. I won't be asking for your pity or empathy, nor will I offer any regrets for the life I have lived. Regrets are for those who believe in God. I learned early in life that the only real god is wealth. Dying is far easier when you don't have to ask "God" for forgiveness. I hit the jackpot being born with the proverbial silver spoon in my mouth, and I've had a grand time spending a good deal of my family's fortune. I played hard, bedded an abundance of women, and lived my life aloud. So if you think any apologies are forthcoming, disappointment is about to visit you.

Take solace in the fortunate circumstance—for you—that I'm between wives at the moment, which makes you my sole heir. I've instructed my attorney to liquidate my assets and pass the proceeds to you. Consider the inheritance, as I did with my father, to be compensation for any shortcomings you may have perceived in your upbringing. Money has a way of righting all wrongs. Now it's your turn to live the good life.

My advice is to never look back, always trust in Johnnie when you need a friend, and don't try to continue the family business because coal is dying, just like me.

I'll close by paraphrasing a line by Dorothy Parker, a lady who lived her life as irreverently as me: "Pardon my dust."

Preston Lofton

The attorney looked embarrassed as he handed the letter to Claire. She shook her head, refusing to accept it. "I'm sure you have a wastebasket in this big office. That's what I think of him and his letter."

"I understand." He put the letter down and picked up another piece of paper. "Shall I proceed?"

With her face drawn and tense, she nodded.

"Your father is leaving you the sum of thirty-nine million, three hundred and ten thousand dollars, and thirty-seven cents. If you sign these documents and give me your bank account number, my staff will immediately transfer the funds to you."

Jake and Claire both gasped. "I thought you said he'd fallen on hard times," she said, dumbfounded.

"Mrs. Holland, three years ago, his wealth exceeded a hundred million dollars."

Jake recovered his composure and looked at Claire. "Well, I don't know about you, but from now on, I'm going to have guacamole with my burrito bowl at Chipotle. We can afford it."

After having Claire sign a multitude of documents and confirming the money had been transferred to their bank account, the attorney brought them to the reception area, where Keenan patiently waited. Claire looked dazed. Jake shook the attorney's hand and thanked him, and then he looked at Keenan and smiled. "We're all done, son. Let's hit the road."

Outside, Jake held Claire's hand as they walked to the car. She looked pale. "Well," he said to her with a sheepish smile, "you walked in a pauper and left as a newly minted tycoon."

"What's a tycoon, Papa?"

"It means she's someone who can buy a lot of Cheetos."

Claire stopped and looked at Jake with troubled eyes. "Are we going to have the same argument as we did when I insisted on putting your name on the house and orchard deed? We're married, and being married means we share everything. This inheritance is our family's money, not mine." Tears plunged down her cheeks. "I don't want it. It'll make me as bad as my parents, I know it. I-I don't want to have to write a letter to Keenan and Rigby one day asking them to forgive me."

Jake wrapped his arms around her as a baffled Keenan looked on. "That will never happen. You're nothing like either of them."

"My parents are wretched people who think despicable behavior is fine if you're wealthy. I abhor them, and I'm embarrassed that you and Keenan had to endure my mother."

Keenan latched on to her. "It's okay, Mom. Papa and I love you."

She hugged him. "I will never abandon you. I love you with all my heart, and that will never change." She looked at Jake. "I'm sorry for acting this way. It's been too much. I hate it here. I want to go home."

"I know. We'll work something out."

As they drove back to the hotel, Claire calmed down. "Well, Keenan, this is what happens when you're pregnant—you get teary, emotional, and irritable."

"I don't mind, Mom. Papa, let's find a fudge store for Mom. That will cheer her up—and me too, if they have rocky road fudge. After that, we can go to a supermarket and buy some Cheetos for you. I'll help you eat them." He paused a moment. "Papa, here's a valuable life lesson: When you're on vacation, and your son suggests a way to make everyone happy, never deny him."

Claire burst out laughing. "He may have the Lofton family nose, but he has your wit, Mr. Jake."

At two in the morning that night, Claire nudged Jake, who was sound asleep. "I need to talk to you. Let's go to the bathroom so we won't wake Keenan."

"Are you in labor?"

"No," she said in a loud whisper. "I need to talk."

"Okay." He got up, went around to her side of the bed, and helped her up. "I can order a pickle from room service if you want."

She poked him playfully and then took his hand to lead him to the bathroom. Keenan didn't stir as they walked past him.

She sat on the toilet, and Jake plopped on the floor in front of her. He yawned. "So, what's up?"

"I have conditions you must agree to with the inheritance."

That got his attention. He nodded.

"It's our money, Jake, not mine."

He frowned. "Claire, I'm not a gold digger. If we ever part ways, it all should go to you. I feel strongly about it, so please put it in your name."

"Jake Holland, saying we might not work out isn't something your pregnant wife wants to hear." Her voice quivered. "Do you really have doubts about our relationship?"

"I guess not. I don't want you to think my love for you is predicated on your wealth."

"Jake, you fell in love with me before knowing I'd ever be wealthy. You have nothing to prove."

"So, what's the harm of having the money in your name? I'm fine with it."

"Because it goes back to what you said about being a kept man when we talked about having you move in with Maddy and me. I don't want you to ask permission whenever you want to buy something. I want this to be our money. If you can't agree, let's give it to charity."

He sighed. "Okay, I suppose I'll let you give me millions of dollars. As you can see, I'm a heck of a guy. By the way, donating some of it to charity isn't a bad idea."

She smiled and nodded. "Good. That's settled. Next, I want to share some of our wealth with your parents. I adore them and would love to see them be able to build a nice house next to us, but let's not put conditions on our gift to them. This will be our way of thanking them for all the medical bills they paid for Keenan while you were in college."

"You're melting my heart. What else?"

"I'd like to be a stay-at-home mom and homeschool our children. We have the means now for me to do it. Plus, I'd love being around you during the day."

"I can agree to that for Rigby, but it should be Keenan's choice on schooling."

"Agreed. Speaking of Keenan, I want to adopt him and officially be his mother. Now we can cover any medical expense." She touched his shoulder. "If something ever happened to you, his birth mother could petition the court for custody. I couldn't bear to lose him."

He appeared to regret her bringing up the subject and was silent for a long moment.

"Claire, she would never want him. She's like your mom in that regard."

"Jake, is there a reason why you wouldn't want me to adopt him?"

Silence …

"Yes." He struggled to say the word.

An awkward quiet ensued, filled with disbelief and hurt for her.

"What possible reason could you have?" Her lips quivered around the words.

He swallowed hard. "If it doesn't work out between you and me, you could rightfully ask for joint custody if you adopted Keenan. I can't risk losing him."

"Well, then, why have a child with me? The same thing could happen with her. You really think we won't last as a couple, don't you?"

"I have baggage, Claire. After you dumped me when Maddy passed … I still haven't recovered from it."

Her heart sank. "I thought we were way past that."

"I can't shake the fear that you'll say you want out again."

"Jake, I insisted the house and orchard, and now my inheritance, be ours, not mine. I'm having your baby and want to adopt your other child. I adore you and do my best to earn your love every day. This ring on my finger means everything to me. I don't know what else I can do to demonstrate my commitment to you." She paused for a moment. In a long whoosh, all the air left her lungs. Her eyes conveyed panic. "Oh my God! You've grown tired of me, haven't you? It's you who wants out, not me. That's what you're saying, isn't it?"

"No!" His voice echoed off the walls, loud enough to wake Keenan. He covered his mouth. "Sorry," he said in a whisper. "You mean everything to me. It's my enormous love for you that makes this fear within me so powerful."

The tension on her face eased.

They sat in silence for a few moments.

"I understand your fear, Jake. The fear of being abandoned has haunted me for years."

He took a deep breath. "Can we address my fear now?"

"Of course. What can I do to calm your concerns?"

"Do you love me, Claire? I mean, really love me, as in, we'll be together forever, and you won't drop me if it gets hard for whatever reason?"

"Oh, Jake, I love you so much, more than anything. I'm in this relationship until my last breath. It makes me so very sad that you doubt it."

He nodded and considered her words.

"It's time for a leap of faith on my part. I'm letting this fear go, right here, right now. I want you to legally adopt my son because there's no other person in the world I'd want to raise him if something happened to me, and more importantly, it will symbolize our love and commitment to each other. I'll contact Erin when we get back. If she gives her consent, we can make it happen quickly. If she doesn't, we have the financial means to force the issue." He closed his eyes, kneaded his temples, and sighed. "I will never leave you. Please believe me."

"Jake, look at me." She waited for his eyes to meet hers. "You said something in one of your letters that I'll never forget: *Imagine us having a beautiful life together; our hearts, bodies, and spirits blissfully entwined. Imagine years of happiness and joy together, our amazing connection radiating pure love, our home filled with children, and, one day, grandchildren.*" She touched his cheek. "My dear husband, I don't have to imagine it anymore. I'm living it. You untangled Claire, and you'll forever be the light of my life. Put your fear of me leaving to rest because ours is an eternal love."

He wiped a tear away. "We've come far, you and I."

She kissed him tenderly. "Let's go back to bed because this pregnant woman has another powerful craving. I crave you most desperately. Please make love to me."

ACKNOWLEDGMENTS

Each novel has unique challenges, and this endeavor was no different. Thank goodness for the skilled folks who've been in my corner, polishing the manuscript and providing abundant encouragement. My heartfelt thanks to Wanda Oldham for her editing talents and invaluable feedback and to Kathleen Watson, my "ruthless editor" (her words), who has the kindest of hearts. Applause also to the fine people at Damonza for the book's cover design. To my wife, Carmen, thank you for your love, patience, and support and for choosing to share your life with me. I adore you.

And lastly, a special thanks to you, the reader. May the light of God shine always on your path.

ABOUT THE AUTHOR

James Randall Miller—an INFJ—was born in Germany and has traveled and lived throughout the world. After thirty years in Alaska, he now lives near the White Tank Mountains in Arizona. Other books by James include *Julius,* an illustrated children's story, and the inspirational novels *Howling Across Bridges, After the Purple Heart, Knock on the Sky, Gus and Billy,* and *Because of You.*

Hearing from his readers always delights James. You can reach him at JamesMillerBooks@gmail.com

FINAL THOUGHTS

We are not held back by the love we didn't receive in the past, but by the love we're not extending in the present. — MARIANNE WILLIAMSON

To find peace, you have to be willing to lose your connection with the people, places, and things that create all the noise in your life. — UNKNOWN

Don't set yourself on fire trying to keep others warm. — PENNY REID

You have been criticizing yourself for years and it hasn't worked. Try approving of yourself and see what happens. — LOUISE HAY

Your relationship with yourself sets the tone for every other relationship you have. — ROBERT HOLDEN

Stop looking for happiness in the same place you lost it. — UNKNOWN

Normality is a paved road: It's comfortable to walk, but no flowers grow on it.
— VINCENT VAN GOGH

Be yourself; everyone else is already taken. — OSCAR WILDE

Maybe you have to know the darkness before you can appreciate the light.
— MADELEINE L'ENGLE

Everyone has scars. We just don't all wear them on the outside.
— NATASHA FRIEND

Maybe this whole time, I already had the things I've been asking others to give me. — RUDY FRANCISCO

Your flaws are perfect for the heart that's meant to love you.
— TRENT SHELTON

The flower doesn't dream of the bee. It blossoms and the bee comes.
— MARK NEPO

No matter how long your journey appears to be, there is never more than this: one step, one breath, one moment—now. — ECKHART TOLLE

In the end, only three things matter: how much you loved, how gently you lived, and how gracefully you let go of things not meant for you. — UNKNOWN

You, teetering on the edge, flirting with the abyss, you ask me why you are here, and I, the poet, simply reply, you are here to save the world with your smile.
— JAMES RANDALL MILLER

So, do it. Decide.
Is this the life you want to live?
Is this the person you want to love?
Is this the best you can be?
Can you be stronger? Kinder?
More compassionate? Decide.
Breathe in. Breathe out and decide. — MEREDITH GREY

Be the reason someone believes in the goodness of people.
— KAREN SALMANSOHN

And then suddenly, you meet that one person who makes you forget about yesterday and dream about tomorrow. — UNKNOWN

As soon as healing takes place, go out and heal somebody else.
— MAYA ANGELOU

Goodbye? Oh no, please. Can't we just go back to page one and start all over again? — WINNIE THE POOH